THE RISING

JAMES DOOHAN

THE RISING

S.M. STIRLING

VOLUME 1 OF THE FLIGHT ENGINEER

STARLINE

The Rising: Volume 1 of the Flight Engineer

Copyright © 1996 by Bill Fawcett and Associates

A Baen Books Original

Baen Publishing Enterprises
P.O. Box 1403
Riverdale, NY 10471

ISBN: 0-671-87758-5

Cover art by David Mattingly

First printing, November 1996

Distributed by Simon & Schuster
1230 Avenue of the Americas
New York, NY 10020

Typeset by Windhaven Press, Auburn, NH
Printed in the United States of America

CHAPTER ONE

"And what happened then?" the bartender asked eagerly, her eyes shining as she leaned close.

"Why, then I died," Commander Peter Ernst Raeder said, voice solemn and low.

"Ooooh!" She whapped him playfully on the shoulder with the towel she usually carried over hers. "Watch the vid. *I've* got a bar to clean."

He sighed and thumbed the controls:

Flick

"I want you, Vorn!"

"But, Lyrica, I have a wife, children!"

"You don't want them, Vorn . . . you want *me!*"

"I pity you, Lyrica! For not knowing that there's a world of difference between wanting and loving!"

Flick

"Genuine anthracite from Earth. Formed millions of years ago of actual living matter, this glittering stone can be yours for just . . ."

Flick

"*Ssssiiiiiinnnnn!* Oh, we tried to save them. Our fallen brothers and sisters. We sought them out and

1

reasoned and pleaded, but they wouldn't hear us. And so we turned our backs and fled them and the carnival of EVIL. They wouldn't leave. They sold to us a place they thought was a desert. But we knew that we would make it a paradise!

"And yet . . . temptation was waiting for us. Yes, even here, with only our brothers and sisters beside us. In the place we sought redemption there lay a serpent . . . whispering of wealth . . . of pow-errr. We could buy our paradise, we need not build it. There was so much we wanted and the means was right there. In an almost unlimited supply of fuel. And we fell.

"*They* wanted it! *They* would pay any price. . . . And *we* fell. *We* sold them our precious resource, *we* let them build their factory platforms, peopled with their own technicians. And *WE* helped *them* spread the black stain of sin across the stars. *WE* gave *them* the means to *rrrrraaaaappppe* . . ."

"Uh. D'ya mind if I change that? When the Mollie Interpreters start talking about rrrraapppe like that I get nervous."

Raeder chuckled and handed over the vid control to the bartender. They'd been flirting mildly since he'd sat down. She seemed to approve of his black-Irish good looks, and he didn't object to her cuddly caramel-colored prettiness. And it was a very pleasant way to pass the time as he sat waiting for transit orders.

He looked around. A big square room, the light level was just right, lightened by beveled mirrors scattered around. The booths were roomy and comfortable looking, and the tables were big enough to accommodate your elbows as well as your drink; even the bar stools made you feel welcome. Golden oak accented the bar along one side with a genuine brass foot-rail—spacers were finicky about things like that—and signed holographs on the wall. The older ones were mostly Survey Service types; the people who went out and found new systems, or died trying. Lately it was fighter pilots and gunners and Marines shipping out to fight the Mollies. The Oblaths Bar of Cape Hatteras Naval Spaceport was a gem of its kind.

Of all the gin joints in all the bases in all the world, Raeder thought in a Bogart voice, *why did I have to walk into this one?* This *is what a bar is supposed to be.* He sighed. *I've only been here once and I already know I'm really gonna miss it,* he thought wistfully. But he wasn't going to miss the hospital, with the grueling hours of physical therapy, and he was eager to get back to work.

The bartender flicked to a sports contest, which broke his reverie. The wall dissolved into a montage of shapes and thuds and groans, with the roar of a crowd in the background.

Colorfully clad behemoths charged into each other at full speed, emitting spectacular grunts and growls. It was a variation on football, played without the ball. The big men pushed each other down the field to the goal-posts, grappling and gouging. The viewpoint jiggled and blinked as it shifted from one helmet-mounted camera to another.

They watched for a moment and then turned away in mutual disinterest.

"Why did we ever get into a war with those fanatics?" she asked him in exasperation, referring to the program she'd just flicked away from. "I mean if the Mollies wanted to separate from the Commonwealth, why the hell didn't we just say, 'So long guys—good riddance' when we had the chance? I mean, really?" She rolled her eyes in disgust.

"Apparently you've never heard of antihydrogen, hon." Peter took a sip of his beer. "Be awfully hard to run the Commonwealth without it."

Though he could understand the question. *The Mollies are so obnoxious it seems insane to actually fight to keep 'em around.*

She wrinkled her pert nose at him. "Don't bother me with reality when I'm grumping about Mollies. It's not polite. And why are they Mollies, anyway? They sure don't like women, so how come they're named after my favorite aunt?"

"It means Mission of Life Lived in Ecclesia." Raeder watched her take that in; she shrugged the corners of her mouth down in disapproval.

"Ecclesia . . ." she muttered. "Sounds like a digestive disease. Something with gas."

Peter snorted, then took her hand in his left and said earnestly, "My dear, I'm sorry to tell you this . . . you have ecclesia. Could you please leave my office before you explode."

She exploded in laughter. She was pretty when she laughed. *Her eyes sparkle,* Raeder decided.

"What's it really mean?" she demanded, bringing one shoulder forward coquettishly.

"Ecclesia? It means an assembly or church."

Oddly, his knowing the answer seemed to intimidate her and she withdrew shyly. *Having the right answer too many times in a row seems to do that to people,* Peter thought in resignation as he watched her walk away. He hated it when it happened with pretty women, though. He pursed his lips. *Maybe it's for the best. Be awfully inconvenient to meet the love of my life in the Oblaths Bar at this point in my career.*

His new orders had been cut and he'd be leaving Cape Hatteras Naval Spaceport just as soon as the shuttle pilot arrived to hand them to him. And who knew when, if ever, he'd see this place again.

Peter grimaced wryly and very carefully picked up his drink with his left hand, glaring at his right. *I hate that thing.* The best prosthesis medical science could provide. It looked just like his real hand had. Which was why they took three-dimensional holographs of every soldier's body, so that if you were careless enough to lose part of yourself they could come up with a mechanical duplicate.

But it ached still, and it was virtually numb. The techs had said that once he got used to the signals from the neural interface there would be more nuance—more of a perception of heat and cold, hard and soft, though never the sensitivity of his real hand.

And he was still learning to control it. Peter could see the sparkle of tiny slivers of glass from where he'd shattered the first beer he'd been given. He'd been brooding, had a flash of temper, and *pop!* he'd been picking glass out of his palm. Raeder sighed and shook his head, remembering what his physical therapist had said.

"Whatever you do, Raeder, for the first few months, anyway, don't go into the bathroom mad."

The worst thing about the prosthesis though, the thing that made him hate it, was the fact that it couldn't properly interface with a Speed's computer.

A pilot dropped his gloved fingers into receiving cups that plugged him directly into the ship's AI. The inside of the glove was filled with sensors that registered every muscle twitch, analyzed blood pressure, and the chemical content of your sweat, to make the Speed respond like your own body. The machine aimed its weapons and took direction from the position of your eyes, but it was your hands that determined if those weapons fired and where and how fast you flew.

The prosthesis lacked the subtle control needed, and the chemical component was nonexistent, which meant that half the controls on the ship wouldn't respond as they should. Which meant he was grounded.

His dark brows came together in a frown. It still bit deep and felt like the amputation of something even more vital than his right hand.

Yeah, he thought glumly, *why couldn't we have just let the Mollies go when they told us they were leaving?* He shook his head and smiled ruefully. Even the most fervent and naïve conscientious objector knew the answer to that one. *Because without antihydrogen there's no commerce between systems, and with no commerce between systems, Commonwealth civilization would be a fond memory in less than a year.*

The Commonwealth had tried to offer a garden planet to the Mollies in exchange for the desert they'd bought way back when, but their theocratic rulers, the Interpreters of the Perfect Way, had refused. *Foaming at the mouth and denouncing humanity all the way back to Adam, I believe.*

Because, just to prove God had an ironic sense of humor, the Mollie cluster proved to be the only place in human-explored space that contained large amounts of antihydrogen, naturally suspended in a magnetic matrix material. In the century or so since then, the old synthetic plants had shut down, their dribble of expensive fuel swamped by the flood of cheap, abundant power from the mining platforms. Commerce boomed. The Commonwealth became united as never before—and very dependent on that flood continuing.

Peter imagined Star Command forcibly evicting the Mollies from their withered dustball of a planet with its too harsh sun and its half-poisoned water and transplanting them to a world of soft breezes, luxuriant plant life, and sweet water, stuffed with ores and all good things. *They'd hate us,* he thought. *We'd be right up there with the Philistines, or worse.*

Whereas, normal people, like say, the denizens of a hell-world like Wildcat, which was heaven compared to the Mollie homeworld, would sell their grannies, their virtue, and their eyeteeth for the chance to change planets. Heck, they'd sell their grannies for a decent vacation.

The fall of the Commonwealth could still happen, of course. Scuttlebutt had it that the stockpiles of antihydrogen were sufficient for only eighteen months of naval operations, a stockpile only sporadically replaced by daring raids on Mollie processing plants. The newly reopened synthetic antihydrogen plants were capable of producing virtually nothing at ten times the cost.

"The plug's out of the bathtub and there's no more than a trickle coming out of the tap," one of Peter's friends had said.

Raeder raised his glass in memory of that particular buddy, killed in the same battle that had taken Peter's hand, his Speed, and his glory. He'd made four "kills" in that action, but the recording computer had been destroyed by the heavy particle beam that tore him out of the sky. Those four victories would have brought his total to seven, making him the first and highest scoring ace of the war.

Never rains but it pours, he thought, not without humor. He'd had a dream about it when he was recovering in the hospital. A crusty old admiral was about to pin a medal on him for becoming an ace. Peter was standing there proud as a peacock, when someone came hurtling onto the stage screaming, "Stop! It's a mistake. We've checked all his recordings and they show him shooting down the same Mollie every time."

"That's ridiculous!" Raeder exclaimed.

"Gimme those," the admiral growled, and grabbed the holostills from the little man. Then he glared at Peter. "We had a cake baked for you," he said. "Decorated and everything. My wife ordered it. I had my mouth all set for that cake. Now I can't eat it."

"But he's lying," Peter insisted. "That's not proof, it's only seven identical photographs. The least you should do is review the recordings themselves," he pleaded.

"Nah! It doesn't matter now," the admiral grumped. "It's all spoiled anyway." He turned and left the stage beside the little guy who'd handed him the holos and clearly wanted them back. The admiral tossed them into the air and they fluttered stageward.

Peter turned and the band was packing up its instruments, the audience was pushing back their folding chairs, gathering their belongings and departing as though this was a perfectly normal ending to the ceremony.

"But I *did* shoot them," Raeder insisted.

"G'home," the admiral shouted. "And take yer damn cake with ya." Then the stage lights went out and after a confused moment he woke up.

Loud, exuberant voices brought Peter's head around. A gaggle of fighter jocks had just come in, laughing and joking. They looked Raeder over, noting his engineering tabs, and dismissed him, taking their seats at a table and calling out their orders to the pretty bartender.

Peter turned back to the bar feeling slighted. *Jeez! Was I that arrogant?*

Well, yes, in all probability.

Piloting a Speed was grace and glory, and massive power literally at your fingertips. To a fighter pilot life consisted of Speeds and the rest of the world. No matter how hard you fought the feeling, you couldn't help but know that everything else lacked . . . something.

Color, texture, meaning, Peter thought gloomily.

Engineers, for example, were valued and respected for their service to you and your machine, but they just weren't on the same plane as fighter jocks at all.

Raeder suddenly wondered if it should be fighter jock or fighter jerk. *Ah, you're just feeling left out,* he told himself. *Missing the excitement, the camaraderie.* When he reached his assignment and felt part of something again, he wouldn't be so inclined to take offense where none was meant. *You'll be acting like the old man, next,* he warned himself, *if you don't watch out.* His father had been good at finding reasons to get angry—*when he'd been drinking*—though he was the kindest of men when sober.

There was a sudden burst of laughter from behind him, almost certainly having nothing to do with him at all. Even so, Raeder felt heat rise up his neck as though he'd heard them mocking him and his sudden ship-bound status. He carelessly picked up his glass with his right hand and it popped like a soap bubble. Fortunately it had been almost empty.

"I'm sorry," he said to the bartender.

"Not a problem," she said, smiling. "You want another?"

"Sure," Raeder said. "You got a plastic glass?"

"Nope, something much better." And she yanked a heavy frosted mug from the freezer, filled it with good draft brew, and placed it before him with a flourish.

"Now that," he said, gratified, "is almost as pretty a sight as you are, ma'am."

She laughed. "That's the first time I've ever been compared to a beer."

"But this is more than a beer," Raeder asserted, "it's an experience to treasure." *As I'm sure you are,* the devilish glint in his green eyes said.

She read that message as easily as if it had flowed by in digital letters and gave a little toss of her head, a dimple peeping on her cheek. She opened her mouth, but before she could speak a massive crowd of pilots and mechanics burst through the doors howling for attention. She gave Raeder a regretful smile and rushed to serve the happy mob.

Peter gave an inward sigh. *Oh, well,* he thought. So much for their enjoyable, light flirtation.

Raeder looked around at the patrons of the bar and wondered how long it would be before he was once again part of such a group. The other members of his engineering class had departed two weeks ago, but he'd needed to finish up his physical therapy program. Until now he'd kept himself too busy to notice that he missed them.

Raeder speculated briefly about just where he was bound and what form his new duties would take. There was an important job waiting for him wherever it was, and Peter knew he could do it better than almost anyone in the fleet. He'd attacked his retraining as he had the Mollie rebels, and had enjoyed it, too. Learning more about the machines he loved was no great hardship. *It's watching them fly without me on board that hurts.* He'd graduated at the top of his class; those he couldn't best were the men and women who'd taught him to be a flight engineer. *And once I get a little more experience under my belt, watch out folks.*

So he'd still be around Speeds, and he'd be part of the war effort. After all, it wasn't just a matter of fighting a bunch of religious fanatics anymore. Raeder's eyes strayed to a holographic poster on the wall behind the bar.

KNOW YOUR ENEMY! it demanded, and it showed a Fibian soldier in an aggressive pose. The Mollies had found themselves an alien ally lurking at the far edges of their space. Rather like a long ago Irish king who'd sought aid from the English in fighting his battles. The Mollie Interpreters were discovering that their allies had no more intention of peacefully going home again than Strongbow's Norman knights.

In my humble opinion, the Fibs've decided to grab all the fuel in the universe just for themselves, Peter thought. *Which somehow makes me feel like an endangered species.*

To human eyes, Fibians were . . . well, if some propagandist had set out to design a species which pushed all humanity's "horror" buttons, this would be it. They bore a strong resemblance to spiders, with a scorpion's pedi-palps evolved into an armored three-fingered hand. Their bodies were a dull red, covered with leathery scales and sparse, coarse hair. They had eight beady, black eyes, two of which were able to see into the ultraviolet. Fibs had eight legs, as well, each tipped with a three-fingered claw. Their mouthparts were sharp, horny cutting implements accompanied by a formidable pair of pincers used for holding prey while it was being cut up and stuffed into a translucent digestive sack in the abdomen.

Raeder shuddered. *Messy eaters,* he thought.

Fibians spoke through a flexible tube, like an elephant's trunk, located in the general area that a nose would occupy in a human. At the end of their abdomen was a long, slender tail, tipped with an acid stinger.

Only a lunatic bunch of misanthropes like the Mollies would ever turn to these aliens for help in fighting their own kind, Peter thought. *I wonder if the general population of Mollies even realizes that their Interpreters have lost control of the Fibs. Come to think of it, I wonder if the Interpreters realize it.*

Raeder found it ironic in the extreme that the Commonwealth was now shedding its blood to free the rebels from their allies, while the Mollies killed their Welter saviors in the idiotic belief that by doing so they were saving themselves.

But then, to be a Mollie in the first place you're required to have the IQ of a glass of water.

"Commander Raeder?"

Peter turned to find himself confronting the radiant grin of a *very* young shuttle pilot. She was about five feet four, with a cap of curly blond hair and a face made pretty by youth and enthusiasm.

"I have your orders, sir." She presented the disk briskly and saluted with traditional pilot sloppiness.

Raeder gave her a better one in return. "Thanks," he said with a smile. *I can't believe this infant can fly and I'm grounded,* he thought. She looked young enough to be playing hooky from school. He slid the disk into his wrist reader. Yup. Report to CSF *Invincible* via blah blah, and so on and so forth. He didn't recognize the name, which was odd—even now, fleet carriers weren't all that numerous. The numerical code was definitely for a carrier, though.

Oh, please, please, not an escort *carrier. Not a converted merchantman shepherding transports and supply ships . . .*

"We're scheduled for seventeen hundred hours, sir."

Three hours, he thought. And not much to do with them. The shuttle pilot still stood before him. Smiling expectantly. *I feel like I ought to tip her.* Except that you didn't do things like that. Not outright, anyway.

"Ah, if you have time, would you like a drink?" *What am I saying?* "Coffee, juice or something?" *You're not sucking down any ethanol just before flying my fanny to the moon, kid.* Some regulations had good solid sense behind them.

She giggled. "I am over twenty-one, sir. But I would love some coffee. Thank you." She hopped onto a stool beside him. "My name's Gardner. I had a brother in your squadron."

"You're Bo Gardner's sister?" She didn't look anything like him. "How is he?"

"Much better," Gardner said, her young face suddenly solemn. "They say he'll be walking by the end of the year."

"If anybody can do it Bo can," Raeder assured her. "Your brother's one of the best."

"He said the same thing about you." Her grin faded and she looked at him seriously, an expression that didn't suit her. "Why do you think it happened like that? Why were the Mollies at Riga Five in such numbers?"

Peter grimaced. His remaining palm turned slightly damp. "Good question. I wonder myself," he said. *As a matter of fact, kid, I dream about it, far too often.*

By rights it should have been just another raid on the Mollie processing plants. Load up the antihydrogen and get out with minimal losses to both sides. "What did Bo say?"

"He said it looked like they were expecting us."

"It did." Peter nodded. "And they couldn't have dug in and gotten ready for business that quickly if their first warning came when we crossed the line."

Raeder could see it in his mind's eye. The processing plant was a big, gray-blue island floating above the orange-brown disk of Riga Five. There'd been a couple of freighters nuzzled up against the plant's docking tubes and nothing else was visible except the planet's two moons.

"They must have been there for a while," he continued softly. "There was nothing for the sensors to report. No Transit signatures less than a week old." Peter shook his head. "The place was as quiet and cold as it should have been. The captain sent us on a quick reconnoiter and we were well on our way when the Mollies struck. Two Space Command ships gone, just like that." He took a sip of his beer, his eyes far away, the screams of spacers months dead still ripped through his mind whenever he let himself remember.

"Bo thinks the service is riddled with Mollie traitors," Gardner whispered. "He says you weren't spotted early, you weren't unlucky, you were set up."

Peter glanced at her; she was fairly twanging with outrage at what had happened to her brother. *Hell, I'm pretty outraged at what happened to* me, he thought. And she could be right. There'd be no easy way to tell a Mollie from a Welter.

Of course the Mollies might have calculated that Riga Five was the most likely of their processors to get hit and set up an ambush. *Though I hate to think of them being that smart.* Of course he hated to think of them being comfortably ensconced in the Commonwealth High Command, too. *Although at the level of the Echelons Beyond Reality, lack of brains might not be obvious.* Which was an outright slander and he knew it, but that kind of thought was almost a tradition.

In reality, since the start of the war, accelerated promotion had brought many fine and competent officers into the upper ranks and the gold far outweighed the dross these days. It had become exceedingly rare to meet an officer who'd been promoted merely because there was nothing especially wrong with him.

"Gardner," Peter said kindly, "Bo might be right. So it's probably a good idea to be cautious and close-mouthed. But we're neither of us in Intelligence, so I don't see any advantage to getting paranoid about it. That's got to be more aggravation than it's worth."

She frowned as she thought it over. "Yeah. I suppose you're right." Then she shrugged herself into a better mood. Smiling, Gardner asked, "Tell me about my brother? And give me your news so I can tell him what you're up to."

"Tell you about your brother?" Peter Raeder smiled a long slow smile.

Here's where I get even. Bo had been one of his best friends, but there was an old service axiom that you could trust someone with your life but not a bottle or your date. He'd gone to the washroom during a dance and come back to find that Bo had told the girl he was taken sick, and *Bo* was off escorting that little beauty home. . . .

"Let me tell you about the time Bo decided to release these lab rats in the air ducts of the *Defiance*. He—"

The three hours to their flight window passed very agreeably as Raeder loaded up Bo Gardner's little sister with enough juicy stories to allow her to blackmail her big brother for years to come. And if she was a real Gardner, she'd use them with relish.

CHAPTER TWO

Cape Hatteras had been a Commonwealth Space Command launchpoint for a long time, well over a century; besides that, wartime expansion had building going on in a round-the-clock frenzy. There were launch pits for everything from heavy beam-boosted cargo lifters to the smallest personnel shuttles, repair docks, giant reaction-mass tanks to hold the distilled water, barracks, warehousing, and a sprawling civilian settlement around it. All Peter saw of it was the processing facility where they checked his ID.

There was a bittersweet relief to being back in a working Space Command facility after the hospitals and physical therapy centers. Gunmetal-gray corridors of synthetic that looked soft somehow but was harder than steel; functional extruded shapes everywhere, color-coding on pipes and equipment and branch-of-service badges on the ubiquitous overall uniforms, and an equally ubiquitous faint smell of ozone. Security had been tightened up, he noticed; there were Marine guards in battledress at the entrance to the docking bays and a retinal scan before Lieutenant Gardner boarded the little bullet-shaped shuttle in its deep synthcrete pit.

"Want to ride up front?" the shuttle pilot said.

"Sure." *Twist the knife.* On the other hand, that was being ridiculous. *And I wish I could stop using expressions like "on the other hand." Talk about twisting the knife.*

There were still two seats, although copilots had gone the way of many other peacetime luxuries, at least on routine flights like this. Peter laid back in the recliner and let the holohelmet slide over his eyes.

Snap. The little ship's systems came alive, and vision opened out before Peter's eyes. It was as if the front of the shuttle had vanished, giving him an all-around view, crystal clear. Status bars across the top and bottom of his vision listed fuel (reaction tanks full), reactor (fusion systems nominal), and a half-dozen other essentials; the pilot could call up any other data as she wished.

Coupling hoses fell away from the matte-blue sides of the shuttle, trailing droplets into the water at the bottom of the launch pit.

" . . . one. Lift."

Beneath him the little ship quivered and tensed as water was bled into the plasma torch from the fusion reactor and flashed into an ionized gas. Coils directed it toward the rear. The trembling grew, and then there was a long moment when the ship felt a queasy, oil-on-water lightness. Light flashed upwards around him. An observer outside would see a huge belch of incandescence reaching into the sky above the pit, like a lance of fire spearing out of the ground. The shuttle rose smoothly, only the building g-force of inertial gravity to mark the ascent. The walls of the pit moved by him slowly at first, then with building speed; the shuttle broke the sound barrier before its nose was in the open air and leaped skyward. Suddenly sunlight broke around them, the Atlantic stretching like a vast plain of hammered silver to the east, land dark green to the west, rising to the rippled highlands of the Appalachians.

Peter sighed inwardly as the air above turned from deep blue to indigo and then to the hard blackness of space. *Home,* he thought.

Earth turned beneath them, a blue-and-white shield. Gardner drew a line across a panel before them.

"Earth-Luna Control, shuttle *Ariadne XX* bound for Lunabase Main, following trajectory—mark—boost at one gee."

Peter frowned. "I lost my hand, not my gee-tolerance," he said dryly. Shuttles didn't rate inertial compensators.

Gardner flushed slightly. "Correction, boost at one-point-seven-five gee. Transit forty-five minutes."

Gardner brought him down at Lunabase as neat as you please, and well inside the usual flight time. The holohelmet gave a ringside view as the shuttle slid backward on a far less dramatic lance of flame. Fire splashed around the claw-shape of the landing grapple, then died as they made contact with the pad. The metal fingers closed with enormous, delicate force on the hull of the little craft, and they felt a lurch as the pad beneath them came active and began to trundle away, bearing the *Ariadne* with it.

"You're good," Peter complimented her as they waited for the automatics to shunt the *Ariadne* into a docking bay. "I'm surprised they don't have you in a Speed."

"Thank you, sir," she said, blushing with pleasure. Things went *clunk* and *chank* in the background, and the ship quivered slightly. "But I live to fly, not to fight. Bo said he'd loan me some aggression, but he hasn't sent it along just yet."

"You give him my best," Raeder said, and shook her hand.

"I will, Commander." She snapped off a salute as he hefted his dufflebag and stepped out into the flat, filtered air of a closed-environment base.

Ships smelled like this, too. He took a deep breath and plunged into the crowd. Lunabase was even more crowded than Cape Hatteras had been; Peter supposed it was because of the naval shipyards here. The walls of the corridors were vitrified lunar regolith, sort of a blotchy cream color, like marble to the touch. He adjusted to the one-sixteenth gravity with remembered ease—it was like riding a bicycle, you never really lost the knack. There was a cart waiting in the row beside the tunnelway; it projected a hologram of his name and face, strobing at a slightly different frequency from the others in the row. He blinked at the sight, squinting and focusing on his own vehicle.

"Commander Peter Raeder," he said, and slipped his order chip into the cart's reader.

He stowed his duffle in the back compartment and hopped onto the padded front seat. Peter pressed first his right, and then, with an annoyed hiss, his left forefinger against the ID plate, which recognized the pattern of capillaries below the skin.

"Welcome aboard, Commander Raeder," the cart said as it trundled off. "I am programmed to take you to the freighter *Africa* in Section Four, Level Three. As departure for this freighter is scheduled in fifteen minutes, we will have a priority run through the station. Please fasten your seat belt."

The screen on the cart tempted Peter into a full readout of his movement orders. "Fast Carrier *Invincible?*" he read.

That must be a new one; as far as he knew, there were only Fleet and Escort categories in the Carrier class. Nothing in *Jane's*, which meant either the class was too new to have hit the databases, or was classified, or both. This was looking better and better.

"Ontario Base, Antares System."

His lips shaped a silent whistle. Right out near the frontier, then; the last major Commonwealth Space Command base before you hit Mollie territory.

The wind of their passage lifted the dark hair from Raeder's broad, hospital-pale forehead. Clusters of pedestrians were warned away with a highly motivating *BLAAAT!* from the cart's sound system. Peter felt like visiting royalty, grinning and waving at the startled and highly annoyed personnel left in his wake.

He turned forward to find himself on a collision course with a Marine colonel. The colonel looked straight ahead as if Peter's cart and Peter himself didn't exist; he had that look Marine combat officers often did, of being the sort who'd butt his way through walls rather than bother with civilian luxuries like doors. Even so, the closer they got the wider the colonel's eyes became and his hands gripped his cart's seat with noticeably white knuckles when impact seemed unavoidable.

"What the hell are you doing, playing chicken?" Peter demanded frantically of the cart. "Get out of the way!"

"Processing," the cart remarked enigmatically.

Just when it seemed that he and the colonel were about to become a four-legged individual, the colonel's cart swerved out of Raeder's path and they continued on their way.

"It took time to establish that my priority was superior," the cart explained.

Was that a trace of smugness in that mechanical voice? Peter could almost feel the heat of the officer's glare, but he didn't turn around to check. If he did, the colonel would see the pleased grin that Raeder couldn't suppress.

He *did* murmur, "Hey diddle diddle, straight up the middle, eh?"

A throttled roar sounded behind him. "Sir?" the cart inquired.

It was a pity humor was wasted on machinery. On the other hand, perhaps neural-net programmed machinery . . . The Marine colonel had been a beetle-browed specimen with no neck, just slabs of deltoid muscle sloping up to his ears.

"The hell with it," he said. "Do you know why Marines have sloping foreheads and no necks?"

"Sir? Is that an inquiry?"

"Well, you show them a spaceship, and ask 'What's that?' and they do this—" he shrugged elaborately. "And then you tell them it's a spaceship, and they do *this*." He mimed slapping his forehead.

The cart was silent for a moment. Then: "I have entered this remark in my files under 'Witticisms, attempted.'"

Everyone's a critic, Raeder thought, and settled back. It was still a beautiful day, he was assigned to a real fighting ship and headed to where there was real fighting to be done.

The *Africa* was a boxy, utilitarian metal giant shaped like an old-fashioned manual hammer, hanging in polar orbit over Luna. Its plating was pitted and scored from the friction of outsystem dust; even single hydrogen molecules could be dangerous at the speeds ships attained just before Transit. Peter eyed it carefully as the Luna-to-orbit jumper came in to dock with it. Halfway up the handle of the "hammer" were a ring of new-looking boxes mounted on pivots. *Antiship missiles*, he thought. Ground-defense types, from the look of it. Marginally more useful than throwing things by hand, but not much more, in deep space.

"I just hope we have a peaceful voyage," he muttered to himself. *Especially if I have to trust the shooting skills of a cargo handler to protect my own precious pink personal buttocks.*

The crew was busy enough that the executive officer, a tiny Oriental woman with a harried expression, was meeting passengers at the airlock.

"You're the last," she said to Peter. "Commander," she added; there were Naval Reserve patches next to her merchant-marine insignia. "Glad you could make it."

"Last-minute orders," he said, touching the clip pad she held to establish his identity. It beeped contentedly at them.

"Good. Getting into convoy order is a stone bitch *without* delays at dock."

Peter's brows rose as he ducked through the narrow airlock door and stood aside in the corridor within for two crew with a repair floater. "Convoy?" he asked. "From Lunabase?" *If we need to convoy ships out of Sol System, we're in worse trouble than I thought.*

Although . . . most of the escort ships were far out on the fringes, where the routes got long and Mollie Q-ships and commerce raiders were raising Cain. Not many left for the interior runs.

The merchanter exec shrugged, as if to confirm his thought. "Lot of losses recently. Not enemy action, just scavengers. They've gotten a lot more active— or hungry. We're bunking you with two of our ratings. Sorry, but everything's a bit cramped."

"There's a war on," Peter said.

He had a couple of datachips in his duffle, too, if all else failed. It never hurt to study . . . and there certainly wasn't much else to do. The *Africa* was a big ship, easily a hundred and eighty thousand tons, but most of that was cargo hold, full of everything from reactor components to bags of "real Terran anthracite." The crew quarters were cramped even by Space Command standards; he squeezed through a couple where he had to walk bending over and pushing his duffel before him before he reached the tiny living space. Everything was extruded metal, cheaper than synthetics and good enough for low-stress merchanter spacing. It was also a little chilly and dim, and the pulsing vibration of the life-support system was a continual warbling throb on the edge of audibility.

Three weeks normal-space travel before they reached the Transit jump point, and then three days in Transit space to reach Antares. It could get very boring; mind you, being jumped by raiders was worse than boredom. They used "Stealths" mostly, small, slow, but very inconspicuous ships with one short-range plasma cannon, carried in piggyback on fast, converted freighters. Not much armament, but if your engine was down—the usual reason for falling victim to them—one little plasma cannon was all it took. A few shots in the right places and you wouldn't be collecting your insurance.

Then the raiders slipped in a skeleton crew and the ship disappeared—to some breaker's yard with few scruples, way out there somewhere.

Oh, your heirs would collect the insurance, but that would be cold comfort.

Peter tossed his duffle onto the lower bunk and considered the men who'd be sharing the living space with him for nearly a month. They'd lifted the curtains on their bunks to look him over, nodded and then dropped them back into place.

One was in late middle-age, heavyset, with the faint lines of a hearing implant around one ear. *That explains why he's not in the service,* Raeder thought. The other was a younger man who looked at Peter's commander's pips with a mixture of embarrassment and envy, a flush on his freckled redhead's skin. No doubt he had a merchant seaman's exemption, whether he wanted it or not.

Damned poor excuse for privacy, Peter thought as he looked at their curtained bunks, though the cloth shut him out almost as effectively as walls would. He gave a mental shrug. *Well, close quarters, you need someplace to go that's just yours.*

"Hey," he said. "Peter Raeder here. What do you guys on *Africa* do for fun?"

"Fun?" the youngster answered sourly. "It's wartime and we're hauling Space Command cargo. No leave. Multiple Transits. We don't have fun."

"Aw, c'mon, Vic. Yer just mad 'cause you couldn't see that little barmaid at the Lunatic Cafe one last time."

The youngster pouted. "She'll be gone by the time we get back," he groused. "The pretty ones always are. Vic Skinner, by the way," he said to Raeder. "Communications tech on this bucket of bolts."

Peter shook their hands. "Jack Ayers," the older man said, grinning. "Drive Systems chief. How much fun you can have depends on how much disposable income you've got."

Peter smiled slowly, a definite spark of interest lightening his eyes.

"I've got some," he offered cautiously.

"Don't try it, Commander," Vic, the youngster warned, shoving the curtain on his bunk aside and cracking his fingers with a smile that belied his words. "We'll shear you smooth. We get a *lot* of practice."

The older man eyed Vic in silent warning.

"Sounds interesting," Peter prompted.

The Drive Systems chief swung his legs down from his bunk with the stealthy menace of the wolf in "Little Red Riding Hood."

"You come along with us," Jack said, beckoning.

"You're gonna love this," Vic assured him.

Africa had a small crew, twenty-seven people, nine on, eighteen off at any one time. The small, out-of-the-way storage locker Ayers and Skinner led Peter to was crowded with six of those off-duty personnel; they had to climb down a maintenance access tunnel to reach it. Those already there went silent, flashing to their feet as the hatch opened and the three entered, closing it behind them.

I guess gambling is as frowned upon in the Merchant Marines as it is in Space Command, Peter thought. *And just as successfully repressed.*

"Fresh meat," Jack Ayers said suggestively, waggling his eyebrows. "This is Commander Raeder and he's looking for some action."

Africa's crew looked at Raeder like he was a big shiny box and it was coming on Christmas morning.

"The game is Dynamics," said a whey-faced fellow with jug ears. "Opening stake's twenty."

Peter tried not to blink. Twenty was pretty rich for a backroom Dynamics game on a tub like this. He could almost hear Vic saying, "*Baaaa.*" Raeder pulled out a money chit and handed it over. Jug-ears snapped it into a reader and when he handed it back one of the black strips was twenty percent white.

The atmosphere turned warmer still. Someone offered him a flask, and he took a sip. Then he struggled not to wheeze; it was illicit slash if he'd ever tasted the like, and even worse than what circulated under the table on transports or at bases.

"Thanks," he husked. "I'm glad to see you can still clean the scale off transformer junctions." That brought a chuckle around the packing crate they were using as a table.

"Welcome to our little casino," Jug-ears said with a grin and a sweep of his arm. "Take your slice with the dice."

Peter accepted the dice with a grin and bounced them experimentally as he waited for the betting to subside. They weren't actually dice; they were triangular and there were six of them. The players alternated between tossing the dice and playing a hand of cards. The lowest number on the toss became the dealer, the highest won back his stake and fifty percent of whatever had been bet. Then in the card round the players usually bet a small amount, since it came only from their pockets, while the observers placed side bets. The loser got first crack at the dice, the winner took the pot on the table.

Peter's family were Space Command for generations back, or merchanters, and Dynamics was practically the official game of those services. Raeder had learned the game from his dad, who'd been a chief in Space Command and his Uncle Dennis, who was an engineer in the Merchant Marine. Both had maintained the superior skill of their services with blind stubbornness. And both had known and used every rule-shaving trick in the book.

Well, he thought as he turned the dice over in his hands, *they're honest as far as I can tell.* Peter felt at a slight disadvantage due to the fact that one of his hands was artificial and the other was his weak hand. *Which should just about even the odds.* He'd been taught by eager teachers how to control the spin on the dice so that they almost always came up the way he wanted—which, given the minute variations in synthetic gravity and Coriolis force, wasn't easy. Now he'd lost a great part of that delicate control. But not all of it. And he had a great poker face.

But judging from the wolfish grins that surrounded him, if desire had any effect on the outcome, he'd be lucky to leave this game with his shorts. It was times like these that the Merchant Marine spacer's feelings of superiority over Space Command became obvious. *And damned uncomfortable.*

Peter took his position and in a deadly silence rattled the dice in his hand, trying to make friends with them. *C'mon,* he thought, *don't let me down. Do it for the Service.* He felt a heat rise in his face and he grinned. He was going to win.

He flung them hard against the bulkhead and they bounced back rattling onto the plastic surface of the crate, giving him a score of twenty-one, a "natural." Peter barely restrained an exultant "Yes!" and with an effort of will held back the wattage on his smile as he looked around at the stunned and silent faces. *Hey, guys,* he thought, *it's a game of chance. Sorta. I'll probably lose the next one.*

Jack Ayers licked his lips slowly, and said with a forced cheerfulness, "That's what I like to see, beginner's luck. The kind that doesn't last."

Vic's thin face looked woebegone as he nodded and muttered, "Yeah."

Peter raised one dark brow.

"Boy, you guys sure know how to take the pleasure out of winning. Look," he stood up and brushed off his knees, "I'm just looking for a way to break the monotony. I don't want to push myself in where I'm not wanted. So just say the word and I'll take back my stake and we'll pretend that I've never been here." He shrugged. "It's up to you."

He'd briefly considered saying, "I'll take my winnings and go." But deemed it not worth the aggravation of dark looks and hostile mutterings for the next three weeks. Life was too short to make a battle out of everything. *That's one thing I've learned anyway.*

Silence greeted his suggestion, you could almost hear the rumble of thoughts being mulled over. Finally a woman who looked like an Indian temple statue—or would have without the jowls and the bandanna knotted around her hair—muttered: "Play."

Raeder squatted and flung the dice without preamble. They came up nineteen. A gaunt-faced woman gathered them up and passed them back to him. He rattled them briefly, felt the blush rise in his face, and tossed. They came up nineteen again, making his point and winning him a cool hundred and twenty at least.

Every eye was on him; no one was smiling.

Well, I've sure taken the joy out of this gathering, Peter thought, chuckling to give the lie to the thought. *I've been in accidents that were more fun.*

Aloud he said: "Wow."

For a moment the mood in the room balanced on a knife edge between hostility and the excitement of gambler's fever. Greed won as the crewmen calculated what they might win if Peter lost the next toss.

"Play!" the Indian temple statue demanded again. She was breathing heavily with excitement, which did interesting things to her coveralls, especially the worn spots.

Raeder tossed and got a five, tossed again and made his point. Five times he threw and felt the flush that told him he would win.

"Hey, that hand's prosthetic," someone said. "Use the other."

Peter grinned and complied. The dice flew out of his left . . . and he won again.

"Hey, switch back!" the voice complained.

"My pleasure, sports," Peter said, and did so.

Finally he said: "This is spooky," and handed the dice to the woman beside him. He bet on her and won. By the end of the shift he'd cleaned them out and had gained four completely filled money chits as well as his original twenty.

As they were filing out Jug-ears glowered at him and said, "You gonna give us a chance to get even?"

"Anytime," Raeder told him. "Anyplace." *After all, the honor of Space Command is at stake, as my father used to say to Uncle Den.*

Jug-ears nodded. "Alec'll bring yuh."

As they climbed back to their bunks, Peter confirmed this with Alec.

"Oh, yeah," the older man said. "It'll be in a different place."

"Nobody seemed too happy with me," Raeder observed.

Alec grinned, but then he was always grinning.

"Don't worry about it," Vic told him. "That was just beginner's luck. Tomorrow we'll skin ya proper." His dour face brightened almost to melancholy at the thought.

Trouble is, Raeder thought, *if I win again tomorrow, I think they'll do it literally.*

And they'd be more cautious next time, now that they knew he wasn't a novice. *Consider it their just reward for all the wet-behind-the-ears Space Command lieutenants they've no doubt fleeced of everything but their eyelashes.*

And, after all, he was giving them a chance to get even. Even so, it was a good thing that Ontario Base was only a Transit jump away. . . .

Fifteen ship-days later Raeder lay contentedly on his bunk avoiding the gloomy stares of *Africa's* crewmen, a stack of their money chits stretching his back pocket to the ripping point. Being a cool sixteen hundred richer made their obvious misery and silent accusations quite bearable, though he was glad his Uncle Dennis couldn't see him. *What can I say, Unc? Like Dad, I'm Space Command to the core.* And with everyone flat broke, he could hardly offer them the chance to get square. So despite the hangdog looks, he was quite comfortable. Even the hum of the inadequately shielded life-support system wasn't bothering him much anymore, except when it warbled up into the fingernails-on-slate range.

"You know, Raeder . . ." Vic began.

You know, it doesn't seem fair, Peter filled in. Well, it wasn't . . . but he'd been using their cards and dice.

"All hands. All hands." Everyone looked up as the ship's PA system carried the captain's singsong Parsi accent, this time with an underlying crackle to it. "Duty stations."

People began moving quickly—into their pressure suits, in case of a hull breach, and to the places they could do most good if the ship came under attack. Not that the *Africa* had much in the way of armament, just an antimeteor laser and a few short-range missile pods hastily mounted on her exterior, more as a gesture than anything else. Peter decided to take advantage of his Space Command rank and the more informal atmosphere aboard a freighter and headed for the bridge.

It was the standard arrangement, three-quarters of a circle with a liftshaft in the center and display screens at the stations around the rim. He stepped out and noticed that there was an empty crash couch beside Vic, slid into it, and secured the restraints. Nobody seemed to notice; Captain Behtab's slim brown fingers were drumming on the side of her couch as she spoke tersely into the intership communicator.

"We're decelerating," Peter said, surprised. Bad practice; it made a raider's vector-matching job easier. "What's the story?"

"The *Province of Quebec* is breaking away," Vic said without looking up.

Again? Raeder thought. "Why?" he asked.

"Engine trouble," Vic said shortly.

Oohhhh, the ship.

"The whole convoy is slowing down," the captain said. "I am not crazy about the idea, but we can not simply allow *Quebec* to go down the tubes."

No, that's what everybody says, Raeder thought. "Any Transit—" he stopped, embarrassed. Of *course* there were Transit signatures, here on one of the major jump points out of Sol System. That was the problem; there were so many and they overlapped so much that you couldn't tell anything specific from them. A raider could have slipped through a week ago and be waiting, powered-down. Space was so damned *big*.

"You could tow her," he suggested. "*Africa* has enough delta-v to get both ships to critical velocity."

The captain frowned, narrowing her eyes. She was a short slim woman, with a gray streak in her dark hair, black eyes, and skin the color of old ivory.

"I hate the thought of leaving someone out there if pirates strike," she said. "And I can almost feel them getting ready to pounce." She looked at Raeder from the corner of her eyes. "But you know the rules, our escort ship would never allow it."

"Not if we were under attack," Peter agreed. The Space Command corvette accompanying the convoy would definitely want them out of the way in that case. "But I haven't noticed that we are. We aren't, are we?"

Behtab stabbed him with a glare. "Not at the moment," she said icily. "In any case I cannot tow her into Transit."

Peter shook his head. "Different engines, Captain. No reason for their transit capacity to be down."

Behtab frowned. "Drive systems," she said. A new face appeared on the board before her. "What about a tow?"

Ayers' craggy features turned sorrowful, making him look a little like a basset hound in a spacesuit. "Not at these velocities, Captain," he said. "Any mismatch, and we'd rip the grapple field mounts right out through the hull—and I'm not joking. Too many energetic particles out there to do it with sensors, anyway; we need a precision match."

"And that would mean an EVA," Behtab said. She sighed and shook her head. "No," she said at last. "There's no one that I can spare, not in a situation like this when we might be attacked at any moment." Raeder saw her swallow hard. Doubtless she had friends on the *Quebec*. "I hope Space Command can send that corvette in time," she said. "A tug would be most welcome, too."

Peter took a deep breath. *C'mon,* he thought impatiently, *this is doable, let's not make a big production out of it.* Even if the Space Command corvette shepherding this convoy got back to the end of the line in time, it couldn't just hang around waiting for a damn tug. And there were thirty people back there who sure as hell didn't deserve to die so that some murdering thief could have a flashy suit and a hot night on the town. Especially when this was such an easy fix.

"I'll do it," he said. *I just heard myself say that and I can't believe I said it,* he thought.

He'd *already* won the Stellar Cross. *Never volunteer, never volunteer,* echoed through his mind, as if some internal censor had come belatedly online, trying to make up in frantic repetition for its tardy appearance.

On the other hand, for nearly a year he'd been the passive object of other people's poking and prodding and fixing. Fighter pilots liked to *do* things, to be the actor rather than the acted upon. It was part of the psychological profile that the assignment officers looked for.

That didn't make what he was doing any less insane, but it was some consolation to know that it was in accordance with his own inner nature. He supposed. *Besides, dammit, it's the right thing to do.* If his uncle were in that ship back there he'd sure as hell want someone to go after him.

The captain was shaking her head. "No, that is impossible. You are a priority package, Commander. I do not want to have to explain to Captain Knott why I let you leave the ship between here and Antares. *You* may have a death-wish, but I do not."

"What's the big deal?" Raeder pleaded. "All I have to do is steer the cable out to where the sensors aren't interfered with by the ship's realspace exhaust, aim, shoot out the grapple, and ride the cart back into *Africa*. A monkey could do it if you had one."

"If I had a monkey on board it would already be working at an assignment and be unavailable for this foolishness," Behtab said irritably. "Besides, you can hardly expect me to send anyone out, virtually naked, into raider-infested space. It is too dangerous!"

"Do you *see* anybody out there?" he challenged.

She looked at him from under her brows. "They are out there, Commander. They have always been there. And until Space Command does something about them, they always will be."

"Then this is the least that I can do, given I'm Space Command." Somehow, Behtab's resistance was making him ever more determined to do this.

The captain stuck her tongue in her cheek and studied him.

"I heard that you were a fighter jock. I see you are determined to prove it. Grapefruit and peas, as they say."

"Yes, ma'am," Raeder said with a winning grin. "Call sign Bad Boy."

"I can well believe it," Behtab murmured sardonically. "So if anything happens to you, I am supposed to tell Captain Knott that I got you killed for the honor of Space Command. That is what you are suggesting?"

"I guarantee that Captain Knott will be able to get behind that concept one hundred percent." Peter half raised himself from his couch and leaned toward her. "But I'm not going to get killed, ma'am. It's a simple mission and there's no reason why it shouldn't go down as smooth as a politician's lies."

The captain chewed her lip, then nodded once, sharply. "Well, Commander, since you are so determined to see if you can break that famous winning streak you have been enjoying—of course I knew of the Dynamics games, it is my ship, is it not?—I will give you the opportunity. Leighton, escort the commander and help him suit up." She turned to Raeder and stuck out her hand. "Good luck," she said, shaking his.

Peter was proud of the fact that he hadn't broken her fingers in the flush of his adrenaline-rush enthusiasm.

The pure gleeful exhilaration of knowing you were

going to be up against it, *that* was something he'd missed nearly as much as his hand, pushing himself to ten-tenths of capacity. *Whoa, boy,* he thought with amusement. *It's a repair cart, not a Speed.* Okay, so maybe three-tenths capacity, it was a start.

Behind his back Behtab shot out her lips in a soundless whistle and shook her bruised hand.

The grapple cart was stored in a corner of the echoing, cavernous launch bay. The bay was huge, built to accommodate surface-to-orbit shuttles when the *Africa* was delivering cargo to worlds without the usual orbital facilities. The harsh floodlighting made it into a blazing cave of light, the white walls streaked by color-coded docking waldos and delivery pipes. The cart itself was a simple all-purpose affair, unenclosed, with handlebars that embraced its control board; he'd seen photographs of ancient motorcycles that resembled it. It had a tiny grapple all its own set like a belly button on the outside of the control column. Behind the column was a seat which bore on its square side a rack of tools and concealed a laser welding unit. Underneath there was a set of six wide magnetic wheels made of a soft plastic for driving across the broad surface of a freighter. A pair of small rockets underneath, aided by tiny attitude adjustment jets in six strategic locations, allowed it to move up, down, or sideways in space.

Along with its other abilities, it was designed to drag a grapple and cable out beyond the fug of energetic particles from the engines to where it could be aimed with an accuracy impossible from the bridge while the ship was still under power. The cable itself was superconductor inside a tough synthetic-matrix sheath, looking like a giant pebble-surfaced garden hose. It didn't hold the tow with its own tensile strength; it was a field guide for the invisible forces that did.

Probably was created for a situation just like this one, Peter thought, pulling his shirt up over his head. *The trick now will be to match speed with the* Quebec. One of those split-second operations where you wished that, like the navigators, you could plug yourself in and interact directly with the machine. *Not that I'll ever be ready for that particular operation,* he thought queasily. *I love Speeds, but I don't want to think I am one.*

"Could you switch that for left-handed control while I get changed?" he asked Leighton.

"Sure," the crewman said. "I'll get a kit."

Peter slipped out of his pants and felt the material sag from the weight of the money chits in the back pocket. He paused and thought about that. Suddenly it seemed that leaving his winnings behind would be like leaving his luck behind as well. *Pure superstition,* he chided himself.

He began opening storage lockers at random. "Yeah!" he whispered, and snatched a roll of tape from one of them. He cut off two strips with his pocket knife and made a cross, hoping the stuff wouldn't be affected by the cold. Then he pried at the stack of money chits jammed into his back pocket, jigging them up and down to loosen the firmly packed plastic. *C'mon,* Peter begged, *Leighton's gonna come back any second and I'm gonna look like a jerk. Get outta there, dammit!* They gave suddenly and sprayed all over the place. "Oh, thank you," he muttered. "That's much better. Couldn't just give them to Leighton to hold, could ya?" he asked himself in exasperation as he scrambled to pick them up. Finally he got them together and taped them to the steering cart, a little above where his feet would go.

There, Peter thought as he gave the stack a few experimental tugs, *that oughta do it. Hope he doesn't notice.* Raeder looked dubiously at the rather obvious little package.

He's bound to misunderstand. Hmm. On the one hand, I don't want him to go away imagining that I expected him to steal them, but on the other I don't want him to think I believe in voodoo. He waffled back and forth for a few seconds. *Tough. I'll feel better if they're with me. Sort of an eight hundred and fifty credit security blanket.* The rest of his winnings were tucked into the locker under his bunk. *So you figure one half will call to the other, is that it?* he asked himself sarcastically. And a defiantly sullen, little kid part of him answered, *Maybe. Wanna make something of it?*

When Leighton returned Peter had just slipped into his skinsuit and was nowhere near finished getting ready.

The crewman blinked, but didn't comment on Peter's tardiness. "Sorry it took so long," Leighton apologized. "We rarely need these left-hander kits and nobody could remember where they were stored."

Leighton started to work on adjusting the control board, and if he saw the big silver X on the control column, he didn't mention it.

Raeder suppressed a grin as he hopped into the lower half of the bulky hardsuit he'd be wearing for the EVA. He'd had a thought.

"Could I borrow your notepad?" he asked.

"Sure," the crewman said, pulling it and a stylus from a pocket.

"I'd like you to give this to the captain," Raeder said, after writing a short note, "if I don't make it back." It authorized Behtab to give his winnings back to the crew. *More good luck hoodoo, Raeder?* he asked himself, amused by his own actions. *Could it hurt?* another part of his mind responded. Besides, it was winning that was fun. Keeping all their money would spoil the fun of it.

He handed it back to Leighton, who closed it and nodded.

"You'll be okay, sir," the young crewman said. The words were intended to reassure, but his voice sounded nervous.

Peter held his arms up and Leighton lowered the massive upper half of the hardsuit over his head. Then the crewman triggered the automatic seals that joined the two halves of the suit together. Peter initiated a series of diagnostic tests and a green light flashed in the upper quadrant of his faceplate, where the multifunction display was located. He gave a thumbs-up. Leighton activated the hoist still attached to the hardsuit's upper half, and it aided Peter as he dragged himself and the weighty bulk of it over to the cart.

I hate hardsuits, Peter thought dolefully. Even in zero g they were awkward, but where he was going, right down past the engines, the energy released would eat its way through anything softer.

It was essential, but he still hated the sense of weight and confinement. Besides that, whoever had used this one last ate a lot of garlic.

The crewman helped Raeder settle his fibrosynthetic-clad butt on the cart's tiny seat and clamped him to it. Then they ran a check on the cart's systems, getting greens up and down the line.

Raeder drove it into the airlock, as outsized as the rest of the docking bay, and clamped the cart onto the cable it would tow. Leighton leaned down to check that the connection was solid, knocked on Peter's helmet to let him know it was okay, and left, sealing the hatch behind him. Peter patiently waited for the lock to cycle, watching the lights above the outer hatch change slowly to green. It was silent inside his helmet, but he knew that outside there would be hissing and pinging as the air was pumped out of the chamber. The ambient light faded from white-green to red as the pressure dropped.

His heart was beating a little faster in anticipation. No EVA was ever completely routine, and if there were raiders and they noticed *Africa*'s attempt to aid her sister ship, things could deviate substantially from the norm.

Deviate from the norm. Peter snorted softly. *My God, you're a wild man, Raeder,* he told himself as the outer hatch opened. *Where do you get the guts to make these crazy, baseless prognostications?*

He trundled the little cart out and over the airlock's edge, where it floated free, attached to the ship by the relatively slender but massively strong cable it towed.

When he dropped away from the freighter's synthetic gravity into space, blood flowed to his head as his blood pressure equalized throughout his body; it was a little like being upside down. At first his face felt unpleasantly tight and there was the usual momentary dizziness and fleeting nausea that accompanied the shift to weightlessness. Fortunately another green light flashed on the cart's control board, authorizing him to fire his rockets. Steering gave him something to concentrate on while he adjusted to the moderately disagreeable sensations that came with switching over to zero g.

He also felt a completely delusional sense of cold. *The black kiss of space*, he called it in the privacy of his own mind. He'd never mentioned it to anyone, because he felt it was appropriate to sense *something* when you floated free of the safety of your ship into the great void.

Besides, Raeder thought as he steered down *Africa's* vast, space-scoured side, *it isn't smart to have too many personal . . . um, quirks,* was the right term, he decided, *listed on your record.* The brass were known to cut fighter jocks a lot of slack in the eccentricity department, and Peter was aware that there must be an interesting list of them in his psych evaluations. *But now I'm a flight engineer,* he thought grimly, *so I'd better keep that list as short as I can.* Keep the "black kiss" stuff to himself.

He took a fractional second to admire the chilly, multicolored grandeur of the stars. Even the very best screen reproduction was not quite like seeing them directly.

It was starkly unusual to eyeball another ship in space; the distances were just too great. There were a few exceptions; taking another ship under tow was one of them. The *Province of Quebec* was just coming into view as Peter approached *Africa's* tail. She was a great, black blot against the speckled mass of stars behind her. After a moment, the eye was fooled into seeing her as a hole in the shape of a ship. Then *Quebec's* amber-and-red running lights slowly became visible and occasional glints of starlight reflected from her surface.

It seemed to Peter that she loomed larger as she drifted; *Africa* was still decelerating.

Then he was beyond *Africa*, moving on his own toward the distressed *Quebec*. The rad counters on his hardsuit's display began to chatter and hiccup as he drifted through the fog of energetic particles kicked out by the lead ship's drive. He listened through the static for the word from Captain Behtab, telling him that *Africa* and *Quebec*'s speeds were matched. He already had the following ship targeted, making continual instinctive attitude adjustments to keep the grapple aimed at the spot he'd chosen.

So far, so good, he thought. *But if this were a vid, someone would be muttering, "It's too quiet," about now.* And Peter could feel a growing uneasiness creeping up his spine to boost his brain into hyperawareness. He looked sharply around. Nothing.

Then he saw it.

There was another rare instance when you could expect to see ships in space with the naked eye. When they were coming in for a boarding pass, to lock on to a victim and blow an access through her hull for a strike team to enter and take over. That was virtually impossible in regular warfare—even a crippled warship was too deadly, they either surrendered, or you sank a nuke into them and blew them into dust and gas. But you *could* punch out the crew compartments on a freighter and then grapple; that was why space hijacking was possible.

The shape he saw was too small to be anything but trouble, too far away to precisely identify. Not that he needed to; it would be as flat as possible, probably wedge-shaped and as black as space. The promised raiders.

Or raider, in this case. There seemed to be only one. Of course, there might be more up front; his POV was limited. The lead ships in the convoy weren't even points of light through his faceplate. *But there sure as hell can't be just one.*

"The lone raider," he whispered, amused in spite of himself.

The captain doesn't see him yet, he knew. The ships were designed to avoid detection. That there just happened to be an Eyeball Mark I in the right place at the right time was a wild coincidence. And he didn't want to tell *Africa* just now, though he should, because he knew they'd be ordered to bolt and leave *Quebec* to her fate. Merchantmen were *supposed* to run at the first sign of danger, rather than risk their expensive and hard-to-replace selves. Space Command personnel were paid and tasked to be heroes; the merchanters weren't. And Space Command enforced that opinion with killer fines when they deemed it necessary.

It was a very unpopular policy, hated by both Space Command and the Merchant Marine. But draconian as it was, it was also recognized as necessary. The natural impulse to aid their fellow merchants had caused whole clusters of freighters to enter the raider's maws, never to be heard from again. That was why Space Command had started escorting the convoys, Al had told Raeder. But they could usually only send one escort.

There were two very popular places to jump a freighter. One was at the other end of a Transit point, when the crews were exhausted and edgy from Transit. The other, like now, was when the convoy was entering Transit and someone was lagging behind. Obviously

this left the accompanying corvette with the impossible necessity of being in two places at once. And
there weren't enough corvettes to give every convoy
two, particularly not in a "safe" area like the Sol System
Transit points. The problem was that every Transit
point was accessible from too many other Transit
points; these raiders had probably come in via an
uncharted one in an unsettled system.

Even so, the law was clear: the legal duty of every
freighter was to deliver its essential supplies. The duty
of the Space Command ship accompanying them was
to defend them from raiders. And no matter how
impossible it seemed for the escort to accomplish this,
or how grossly irresponsible it seemed for a freighter
to leave a sister ship to the jackals, giving aid, particularly against the direct orders of the escort, could
result in a prison term for the captain of the offending ship and a fine so heavy it would financially ruin
the entire crew.

So the order to cut the cord, so to speak, didn't
reflect the true feelings of Behtab or her crew.

*Of course, by keeping quiet I'm risking Africa. And,
incidentally, Mrs. Raeder's little boy, sitting out here
on my tricyle, just waiting to get fried.*

It seemed to Peter in his anxiety that the *Quebec* was
close enough to hook, and a quick glance at the readings on his console confirmed it. The other ship was
within grappling range, barely. Now it was a matter of
matching speeds, a finicky operation in untroubled
times. But with everyone waiting to get jumped on,
which should happen any minute now, it became . . .
a little difficult.

"There," he muttered to himself. "I've finally
achieved British understatement."

Peter could see the raider more clearly now, and was convinced that the *Province of Quebec* was its target. Clearly out of power as she was, and at the end of the line, she made the perfect victim. *Be just like a civilian to spot that sucker and blurt it out ship to ship.* Which would pretty much seal their fate.

If everybody would just keep quiet and concentrate on the rescue, everything should be all right. The captain couldn't agree with him, of course, but in his opinion the two freighters linked together would probably be too big a bite for the raiders, who were, after all, looking for loot, not trouble.

Of course, Peter realized with resignation, *it's not just a matter of getting these guys linked, it's keeping them that way that's going to be the tricky part.* And the grapple could be released from the bridge. He was only out here to aim it. *Hmm.*

Peter hit the release on the bindings that held him to his seat and did a slow somersault over the handlebars of the cart, putting him in front of the grappling mechanism.

Right now it resembled the tightly furled fronds of a dried flowerhead of gigantic proportions. When it was launched it would spread out, extending its superconducting thread in all directions until it could encompass even the massive front end of a starfaring freighter. Just behind the "petals" was the control pod, which directed the mechanism's spread, when to grapple and, more importantly at this moment, when to release.

Peter clipped himself to a ring on the front of the cart, pulled a tool from its housing on the arm of his suit, and opened the casing protecting the pod's delicate inner workings from mishap.

"There," he muttered to himself. "I've now disobeyed orders and violated procedure and the Holy Regulations. If this doesn't work, I'm the goat they'll blame. The dead, roasted goat."

He just couldn't face the prospect of the *Province of Quebec* being cut loose and left for the raiders, though. *We're too close to the Transit point to just sacrifice these people. Besides, it's bad policy. Leaving somebody behind every other time only encourages them.* Not that it was a commander's place to buck policy. *But hey, a man's gotta do what a man's gotta do.* Which, he'd noticed, *was* Space Command policy as often as not.

The helmet of his hardsuit throbbed slightly for a second, sucking sweat from his brow to prevent it fogging his vision. After a moment's examination he used the tiny end of the tool to scrape off a minuscule section of the larger control board—an extremely difficult maneuver, considering that he was wearing thick gloves and was using his left hand. Now, if he was right, it would deploy, it would grapple, but it wouldn't release. Peter considered the casing and wondered if he should just let it float free. Then he jammed it back on in such a way that it was slightly ajar.

This way it could have been an accident, he thought. *Something we didn't notice while we were checking it out.* It never hurt to cover the old butt.

More awkwardly than he'd left it, Raeder struggled back to his seat and clamped himself onto it.

He carefully realigned himself with his target, noting that the raider was quite visible by now. At least to him. It was a matte-black triangle, shaped a lot like the paper airplanes he'd made as a kid. From the smooth, almost melted look of it, it was designed to transit atmosphere like a shuttle. At a guess the raiders had a mother ship hanging out there, one that carried them to groundside targets, as well. The pirate fighter's sides had opened out to display a formidable bristle of sensor arrays and antennae, but there was only one visible offensive weapon. To him, the guide coils showing around the lattice at the enemy craft's nose looked like those for a phased plasma cannon in the seven gigawatt range—an escort destroyer's weapon, usually. More than enough to savage a resisting freighter into submission. There was a light defense battery, as well, guided canisters of steel tetrahedrons to be launched in the path of oncoming missiles, and the usual lasers.

"Captain," he said into his suit mike, his voice quite casual. "I'm in position. Shall I fire?"

"We are almost there, Commander," she answered.

Quebec's bulk nearly blotted out the stars now and completely hid the raider stealth that crept up on her. It was, no doubt, taking advantage of the energized particles left in the convoy's wake to hide itself for as long as possible.

As long as his tactics are playing into my hands, Peter thought, *more power to him.*

"Fire on my mark, Commander. Mark."

Peter triggered the grapple and it shot off with enough power to shake the cart. He watched it spread impossibly wide, then drop toward *Quebec's* hull, sensed a jerk as the mechanism took hold, and grinned.

And then he saw the raider, a huge black arrowhead, lift over the back of the *Province of Quebec* and shoot forward, toward the peopled section of the ship.

Peter watched the stealth hovering above *Quebec* like a mailed fist. It matched the larger ship's speed with ease, but did nothing else.

By now they're making their demands, Raeder thought. He looked around; this was still the only raider he could see. Contrary to what he'd hoped, *Africa's* presence wasn't scaring them off at all.

The bulk of them must be up front, he figured. It made sense, cut off the last two ships in line while the front of the line was busy worrying about making the transit to hyperspace. And who knew how far the line was stretched, trying to give *Quebec* even the semblance of protection.

Peter tried to believe that his actions hadn't influenced this situation at all. *It just kinda changed its shape.* Which meant he had to do something to tilt the odds in the freighter's favor. *Because, as it stands, I've just made things easier for the bastards.*

Raeder started the cart toward *Quebec,* running down the cable at a nice, slow, unthreatening speed. When he bumped into the cargo ship's blunt nose he killed the rockets, leaned forward, and unclamped the cart from the cable. Then, employing the broad magnetic wheels on its bottom, he guided it up the face of the ship until he was under the wings of the stealth.

Now comes the tricky part, Peter thought, looking up. The raider's broad flat belly blotted out the stars; it looked close enough to touch with his hand. An illusion, unfortunately. It was both bigger and farther away than it looked, hovering there like a carrion bird waiting for its prey to lie down and die.

Raeder aimed the cart's own grapple at it. *If I can damage his sensors, then he's out of the fight,* he reasoned. He tried to remember if anyone had ever attacked an interstellar warship on the wing, even one this tiny, with hand tools.

He fired and the grapple shot out, hitting its target dead center. Peter started the magwinch and took a tighter grip on the handlebars, trying not to think of what would happen if for any reason the grapple failed. And failing, he'd be thrown off on an unpredictable trajectory, a small blip on screens concerned with more important matters. Would his air give out first, or was the recycler so efficient he'd starve, instead?

Suddenly the stealth's pilot apparently decided that a little fancy flying would be so mind-breakingly intimidating that *Quebec* would surrender without firing a shot. The raider flung his ship into action, plucking Raeder's cart off the freighter to swing free at the end of his tether. *I must look like the universe's most ambitious frog trying to subdue the Mother of All Flies.*

Unfortunately, grapple carts didn't extend to inertial compensation fields; neither did hardsuits. Savage acceleration and Coriolis force twisted at Peter's inner ear, and he concentrated fiercely on not letting the nausea overcome him. The consequences of tossing your cookies in a hardsuit helmet didn't even bear thinking about. Hard, bright stars pinwheeled in crazy arcs across his vision, and he held onto the handlebars for dear life. Hard edges gouged at his flesh.

The raider was a good pilot with an impressive array of dangerous moves. Peter was glad more than once that he was securely attached to the cart's seat. Twice he completely lost his grip on the handlebars and was flung backwards, legs flailing, helpless to heave himself upright until the stealth did something that inadvertently aided him.

If that winch were working any slower, he thought, gritting his teeth, *it'd be going backwards.* And speaking of going backwards, he wished he were safely back on the surface of *Quebec's* nose. *My whole life depends, literally, on that measly cable and a powerful, but awfully small, magnet.* Sweat slicked his face and his breath came fast; the suit adjusted its internal temperature until it was damned cold and still he perspired.

At last the winch rang the cable against its stops. Peter used the attitude adjustment jets to bring the cart's magnetic wheels into contact with the stealth's black surface. He experienced a strong but fleeting desire to get down on his knees and kiss it.

Then, with a last elegant fillip, the stealth returned to its station over *The Province of Quebec.*

Peter slumped forward, wheezing in relief. Time to give himself a way back home if this stunt worked. He aimed the grapple at *Quebec* and fired. Raeder didn't even check to see if he'd hit his target. *If I can't hit something the size of New York, I'd better just go home and sell lemonade for a living.* He knew that leaving the contact disk powered would drain the cart's batteries. He checked the gauge and found that he'd already expended more than half their available energy. But it was his safety line; even if everything went well, the last thing he'd want to do is go home with these pirates.

Wish I knew what was happening up front, he thought. He knew that by now, if *Africa* was going to try to cut *Quebec* loose they would have. For good or ill, that option was out. If he'd failed to eliminate that possibility, she'd already be falling behind, left like someone thrown out of a sled to satiate a pack of wolves. And the stealths up forward would be winging their way toward her.

He was tempted to call the captain, but then the raider would know he had a rider. *A rider named Raeder. Better do what I came here for.*

Now, how could an unarmed utility cart harm an armed, stealthed raiding ship? Peter grinned like a wolf and yanked a hammer from the tool rack on the side of the cart. Some inventions were made only once and never needed to be improved upon: chairs in ancient Egypt, and hammers in the Stone Age. He drove toward a sensor array. It was an intimidating complex of hair-fine antennae and multiphased flat-panel sensors. *Now, how to put this out of action?* No doubt there was some subtle adjustment. On the other hand, subtlety bought no yams, and he was in a hurry. He whacked at the array in passing, like some mechanized polo player.

To hit something in zero gravity, you had to be securely fastened. Peter was; his first blow jerked him back against the restraints of the cart and sent delicate components pinwheeling away into space, glittering like fragments of mirror as they flew. It was soundless in the vacuum, but he could feel the vibrations through his arm and shoulder and the seat of his pants. It also nearly tore the handle from his hand. He shifted it to his right, working the left to get the stinging numbness out of it. The second try jarred up his elbow into his shoulder, but the array crunched and shattered beautifully.

Whacking the hell out of it may not be subtle, but

there's a certain primitive satisfaction to it. Most of it crumbled easily, but the antenna was stubborn and merely bent. He looked to his tool rack. *Ah! Metal shears.* Peter reached out and snipped it off. "And how did you defeat this raider, Commander?" he muttered. "Well, sir, I pruned it," Raeder said with a wild grin.

Inside the stealth, the alarmed raider pilot watched his sensor screens go dark, one by one. *Attack virus!* he thought, and imagined himself out here in the middle of nowhere, blind and helpless. He ran a diagnostic check. Five of his arrays were down now. *Severe external damage,* the computer said. *A new weapon,* he thought. A sixth screen went dark and he licked his lips. Whatever it was, he wasn't sitting here like a fool while it finished its work. There were easier pickings out there somewhere. You didn't become a pirate to be a hero; fools with those inclinations were in the Space Command.

"I'm pulling out," he said to his fellow raiders, covering himself. "They've got some kinda weapon down here that's wrecking my sensors."

The raider's sudden acceleration tore the magnetic wheels loose with a wrench that battered Peter against the restraints and the padded inner surface of his hardsuit. *Ouch!* he thought. *Bruises upon bruises.* The hammer he'd been using tumbled free on a trajectory that would leave it in interstellar space for the next few billion years, joining the battered remnants of the pirate's exterior sensor systems. As the grapple slowly reeled him in to the welcoming surface of *Quebec,* four more stealths came arrowing toward him, close enough for visual contact. For a heart-stopping moment, Peter was sure the leader was going to catch him right in the chest. But they swept by, well overhead.

He turned to watch them go. Pinpoint flashes of light marked their departure; the Space Command corvette that was the convoy's only escort had finally caught up and was letting them have it with particle beams and . . .

Something blew up with a white flash that triggered the protective layers in his faceplate. They went dark, leaving only a ghostly image of an expanding globe of light. One of the pirate craft had had its fuel core containment vessel destabilized . . . which meant that it was now a cloud of subatomic particles expanding slightly slower than light.

Peter let out an exuberant cheer and waved a fist in triumph. "Ee equals em cee squared!" he shouted. "Take that, you murdering bastards!" You could feel an occasional stab of professional sympathy for a Mollie—hell, they were brainwashed from birth—but not for these jackals hanging around the edges of the war and snapping up defenseless scraps. This time the meal had bitten back.

He was still chuckling when the cart touched down on *Africa's* surface. The gentle bump sobered him, reminding him that there might very well be music to face for what he had done. *And I'll have to make sure that Behtab and her people don't have to pay the piper.*

He wondered how he'd be received back on *Africa*. *That Captain Behtab looked like a tough lady. And smart, too.* He had no doubt she knew in her bones that he was responsible for the equipment failure that had kept them linked to the *Province of Quebec. But I suspect, since everything turned out okay, that she'll be pleased.* Not that the captain could ever say so.

He figured that, like Space Command, the Merchant Marine had two categories: if you violated orders and lost, you were an insubordinate goat and you got canned. If you violated orders and won, you were a hero who'd displayed the initiative that was expected of all personnel. He shrugged. *Well, done is done; better get it over with.*

Peter started the cart wheeling over the scored hull plates of the huge freighter, swerving around surface attachments and the unfired missile pods still clamped to the hull. Perhaps he could convince everyone that it was a series of highly improbable accidents. . . .

Behtab was waiting for him, arms crossed, one hand thoughtfully stroking her chin.

"It's a little odd that we couldn't disengage the grapple," she said in a dangerously quiet voice.

"Well, ah, there must have been a malfunction," Peter said. "Wartime . . . everyone overworked . . . drop-off in maintenance standards, it's unavoidable, really—everything worked out for the best —"

The captain stood there, her eyes glittering strangely, while with one hand she seemed, literally, to be pulling down the corners of her mouth.

"We were ordered to release the grapple by Commander Hall," she said. "He was not pleased that we did not comply." She pursed her lips and slowly lowered her hand. "You know the penalties we might face, Commander?"

"But it was an equipment malfunction," Raeder insisted. "As I'm sure your investigation will show. Even

Space Command at its worst would never penalize you for an acciden—"

"Not another word, Raeder," she said. "And you—" she snapped at the crew "—take that thing apart and inspect every piece of it."

You missed your calling, ma'am, Peter thought. *You'd have made a brilliant actor.*

The cart was coming apart as he watched, that was when he saw that the X of tape was gone, and with it the eight hundred and fifty in money cards. *Floating out there in space,* he realized mournfully. *Not even doing the damned raiders any good.* More money than he'd ever had in his life and he hadn't gotten to buy so much as a pack of gum with it. *I wonder,* he thought dazedly, *if the crew would be happier knowing that.* Nah. They'd probably want to throw him out after them.

Oh, well. It was fun being rich, even temporarily. And what am I complaining about? I've still got half left. Glee bubbled up in him again. Dammit, that stunt was *worth* eight hundred. *And fifty.*

The disassembly of the cart continued. Captain Behtab waited with her arms crossed and her face like something carved out of smooth, hard olive wood, but her dark eyes were dancing.

"I'll, ah, get out of your way—" Peter said, sidling away.

Damn, he thought. Behtab had been getting friendly before this happened. Now everything would have to be Extremely Official.

Nobody spoke as Raeder slipped into his bunk and closed the curtains, wincing at the touch of cloth on fresh bruises and scrapes, only now fully aware of them. Someone had left a jar of topical-anesthetic contusion ointment on the covers, though, which was a nice gesture. The hammering he'd taken was getting more and more painful, stiffening him into one giant ache. You didn't notice things like that while they were happening, only afterward. He'd been concentrating, his mind full of the job—apart from that, only a certain . . . exhilaration. Now his stomach clenched and went sour, making him glad that ulcers were a thing of the past, certain that he was about to be brought up on charges despite the way things had turned out.

It's hard to have done something heroic and not be able to point it out for fear that by doing so you'll clue everybody else that your heroism put them in danger of total financial ruin.

The problem was that he was still a fighter pilot down deep, where it counted. Show him an opponent and the reaction was hard-wired, like a tortoise and a piece of lettuce. "Go for it," he muttered, and sighed. Well, no sense lying here tense and lonely.

"Hey," he said, knocking on the bunk above him, "wanna play cards or something?"

"I don't have any money," Vic snarled

"You don't need money to play cards," Peter said. Silence. *Ah, a thought!* "I don't have any money, either."

More silence. A very pregnant silence, building toward a threatening crescendo. Two pairs of feet hit the deck and Peter yanked his curtain aside.

"I taped the cards onto the cart and when I got back they were gone."

Jack Ayers' face was puzzled, as though Peter were speaking a language he barely understood. Vic's face was horrified, building to outrage.

"You took all that money *outside*?" he asked incredulously. "You took it with you? How could you do something that stupid?"

Jack started to chuckle, then to laugh. Pretty soon he had to stagger to the empty lower bunk and sit down. Tears ran down his red face and he couldn't seem to stop. He pointed at Peter and tried to speak, only to flop onto his back, feet kicking the air. Peter and Vic had looked at each other, completely in tune for the first time in their acquaintance.

"It's not funny," they barked in unison, and then glared at each other.

Jack had been slowing down for want of breath, but that set him off again. Finally he slowed down, with little hoots and chuckles and groans. He sat up and wiped his eyes.

Shaking his head he said, "Y'know, if I were a superstitious man, I'd say that's what saved us."

"What?" Vic demanded with a scowl.

Peter just shook his head and smiled.

"Like a sacrifice," Jack explained. "You know, propitiating the gods?"

"What gods?" Vic shouted. "You're weird, Jack! Gods! Jeez, sometimes you scare the *hell* out of me. Oh, Jeez, you know how much beer sixteen hundred could buy? Ahhhrg!" he began to thump his head gently against the side of the compartment wall.

Peter started to chuckle.

"Don't start me up again," Jack begged.

But Peter couldn't help himself and when he started to laugh, the Drive Systems chief held out as long as he could and then joined in. Vic looked from one to the other in disgust.

"I'm outta here," he snarled. "You guys are weird."

Peter just waved at his stiff back, too choked with laughter to speak. *I guess I saved this ship one way or another,* he thought. *But I could've saved myself a world of trouble if I'd realized all it took was a pagan sacrifice.*

They'd entered Transit space by the time the cart had been thoroughly inspected and the report on the engineer's findings had been equally thoroughly scrutinized by the captain, and, no doubt, by Commander Hall.

"Raeder, report to the day watch cubby."

The announcement was less formal than it would have been on a Space Command ship, but just as abrupt. He wormed his way through the cramped corridors and accessways of *Africa*, a utilitarian maze of narrow metal passageways half-filled with cable housings and pipes. The cubby was the office used by the officer of the day; this morning, ship's time, it was the captain. She was sitting behind the battered desk that three-quarters filled the narrow room, and like just about everyone else looked green around the gills. Transit made most people nauseated, and she and the rest of the crew were involuntarily fasting. An exploded hologram of the cart was revolving slowly above the desk, and she glared at it as if it were the source of her queasy stomach.

No wonder they're all so thin, Peter thought. The captain and crew of *Africa* had been through Transit after Transit without a break. Probably laws were being broken and safety regulations ignored entirely to keep supplies moving. *And for me, the downside of this is that I don't think she's in a good mood.* Her mood would be worse, Raeder knew, if she was aware that he could settle his stomach during Transit by eating. Sometimes he even gained weight.

"The inspection proved inconclusive," Behtab said, her black eyes boring into his hazel ones. "And Commander Hall wanted to speak to you about it." She tapped a key and the holograph of the cart was replaced by one of the escort ship's commander.

Peter put on his best innocent expression and saluted gravely. He didn't quite stand at attention—they *were* equal in rank, after all—but he did stand at parade rest.

"Commander Raeder," Hall said gravely. "I have some questions for you. You were outside of *Africa* for quite some time, I understand. Would you care to tell me if anything unusual occurred?"

"Unusual, Commander?" Raeder asked, looking puzzled.

"Anything unusual about the cart, for example?"

"What exactly are you looking for, Commander? The cart performed up to spec. Even above that at times." *Especially that tiny magnet when I was swinging around on the end of my tether. I'm buying stock in the company that makes those babies.*

Hall's mouth worked as if he'd bitten into a lemon.

"I was told, Commander, that Captain Behtab could not disengage the grapple once it had deployed," he said sharply.

"But *why* would you order them to disengage it?" Peter asked, horrified. "That would have left *Quebec* at the raider's mercy." Behtab covered her mouth quickly and lowered her brows, but Raeder could see a dimple on her cheek. "Surely you don't expect me to believe that you would leave those people to die?"

Peter stared him down, look for look, and the commander, biting his lip, lowered his eyes first.

"There was never a question of that," Hall said glumly. He looked up again. "We were on our way back to the *Quebec*, and we'd have stayed with her until her engines were up. Nobody asks us to like our orders, Commander Raeder. They only ask us to follow them."

Peter wondered. Too many people had been left behind in similar situations for him not to be suspicious. *I think we've all gotten into some bad habits here,* he thought. *One ship lost and it's, gee, too bad, but it happens. But two ships, Commander Hall . . . Tsk, tsk. That wouldn't look too good on the old record, now would it?*

"If you freighter captains would take a little more of the responsibility for defending yourselves," Hall lashed out, "these situations wouldn't arise."

"We are barely armed," the captain said carefully. "And a freighter is not as maneuverable as a corvette." Behtab glared at Hall's image. "We were lucky this time."

Peter nodded. "Yes," he agreed. "You were."

Hall tapped his fingers on his desk, tightened his mouth and glared. But only for a moment, then he let out his breath in a rush.

"Yes," he said. "You were lucky. I'm inclined to agree that this was just a fortuitous chain of events leading to a satisfactory conclusion." He smiled, very briefly. "Would that accidents always ended so happily. Good day to you, Captain, Commander." And he was gone.

"You are dismissed," Behtab informed him. "With my thanks." The dimple in her pale cheeks the only clue to her feelings; it looked very much as if she

was trying to suppress a grin and not entirely succeeding. "Try to stay out of trouble."

Peter stood and saluted her, trying to convey the
respect he felt for Behtab and her crew. The captain was tired; they were all tired, with no end to
their labor in sight. One day she might be at the end
of the line and her luck might run out.

"I'll write a report on this, Captain," he promised.
"It may not do anything by itself, but if the brass hear
about this from enough sources it might wake them
up."

She smiled slightly at that and extended her left
hand. He took it and was surprised by the strength
of her grip and pleased that she'd remembered which
hand to use.

"I'd appreciate it, Commander. I'm inclined to think
that every little bit of goodwill helps."

CHAPTER THREE

Ontario Base hovered over Antares Prime like a dangling spider. A spider with far too many legs and brightly gleaming eyes, granted, but still, from this distance the comparison was apt. The body of the station was circular and ships nuzzled the docking tubes only on the port and starboard sides of the station. The fore and aft compartments had been closed due to reduced traffic, because of the fuel shortage. Most of the ships in dock were military: warships, fast transports, or fleet replenishment vessels. Probably most of the remainder were under Space Command requisition for the convoys that kept essential materials flowing. They came in an assortment of shapes; the double hammerhead most common for warships intended for vacuum work, a weird assortment of globes, boxes and jointed arrangement for the merchantmen, and a few sleek knife blade types meant to land on planetary surfaces.

What was really alarming were the number of mothballed freighters drifting in parking orbits around Antares Prime, from ones close enough to the base to see—down to more distant ones that were merely drifting points of light. The fuel situation was getting *bad,* even as the Commonwealth's military remained successful. It was essentially a race now, to subdue the Mollies before the storage tanks ran dry, or they might win every battle and still lose the war. Despite that, the naval dockyard had several skeletal shapes in it—warships under construction.

Dear God, I'll be glad to get off of this ship, Peter thought as he watched Ontario Base grow larger on the screen in the crew's mess. Not that *Africa* wasn't a nice enough ship, for a merchantman—and the crew were friendly enough now. It still wasn't Space Command. He wanted to be back on a warship so bad he could *taste* it. A worn pack of cards riffled through his hands as he shuffled and dealt endless games of solitaire. It was good occupational therapy for his prosthetic hand, at least. He'd gained a good deal more dexterity with it. *It seems I've been crawling to nowhere for three years instead of three weeks.*

The news that he'd lost every one of the money chits had made him popular for a few hours. Or at any rate, a popular target for what passed for wit among *Africa's* crew.

"Aw, I bet those raiders are buying beers with your money right now, man."

"Nah. It's still out there. We'll pick it up on the way back and you can buy us a beer."

"Beer, hell! Champagne and a good steak." And they began adding things to the wishlist—foot powder, kimchi, oysters, on and on—until you could have filled the freighter twice over.

Then word began going round that the captain suspected sabotage and was having the grapple mechanism checked. After that he got a lot of sly smiles, slaps on the back, and winks. One or two still glared, possibly because he'd risked their butts without consulting them, more probably because of the possibility their ship might be fined for breaking orders. Unfortunately one of the still-hostile ones was the crewwoman with the Indian temple figure and the bandanna; he'd had hopes . . . *Then again, eager as I am to get to the* Invincible, *some dockside liberty might be a good idea, too.*

Peter gazed unblinking at the screen. He yearned toward the station and his new assignment with an ardor he'd never expected to feel. Frowning, Raeder forced himself to look down at his coffee cup. He swirled the coffee and then took a gulp. *Be good just to be doing something,* he thought glumly.

Peter had two Irish grandparents and one Scot. So he tended to blame an occasional urge to brood on his Celtic heritage, even while allowing that the Germans were certainly no slouches in the gloom department.

The only sure cure he'd ever found for brooding was hard work. *Which I'm sure to find on the* Invincible, he thought with satisfaction. *Brand-new ship, brand-new crew, brand-new responsibilities. That ought to keep me from thinking dark and dolorous thoughts.*

As flight engineer he'd be responsible for keeping the thirty-six Speeds and seven stealths on the *Invincible* operating. He'd be in overall command of forty-three flight crews, as well as the fuel, repair, and armament sections, five hundred people in all.

Peter allowed himself an imaginary whistle. *Hell, even I'm impressed.* Frankly, he was also surprised. He'd commanded a squadron before, and he'd done a creditable job if he did say so himself. But this . . . to be frank, the gold plate on his flight engineer's tabs was still wet.

He'd been well trained and had put in a lot of virtual overtime learning his new trade. His teachers had been impressed by his dedication and sent him off with a sheaf of highly enthusiastic endorsements. Even so he'd expected more of an apprentice's berth.

Maybe Captain Knott likes to break in his officers himself, Peter speculated. *Or maybe knott. . . .* In that case, he may have bitten off more than he can chew. An inexperienced crew led by inexperienced officers on an experimental ship. "Brrrrgghh!" he said aloud, with an accompanying shudder.

Best not to dwell on that. He looked up and saw that *Africa* was already positioning herself for her approach to the station. Ontario Base had gone from a toy turning in blackness to an immense acreage of modules and enclosures, like an enormous metallic plant sprawling across the stars. The organic metaphor was appropriate, he knew; it had grown by accretion ever since the Space Command put in a forward base here two generations ago.

He thought he could even see the beckoning lights of *Africa*'s docking position. *Wishful thinking, probably.* Still, he might as well get his gear together and hie himself down to his disembarkation station. Peter had a new ambition: to be the first man out of *Africa*.

To his surprise, Captain Behtab was waiting for him at the docking tube.

"I suspected that you would bolt at the first opportunity," she said, one eyebrow raised in mild reproof.

"I'm, uh, eager to begin my duties," he confessed,

slightly wistful. *I think she likes me.* And, of course, a captain was always lonely. . . .

"And eager to cease being the most popular man aboard," Behtab said blandly. "Or the most unpopular, with the holdouts."

Peter just grinned, one of those cheese-eating get-me-out-of-this grins he hoped she wouldn't notice was false.

Captain Behtab laughed out loud and extended her small hand.

"Thank you, Commander, for what you did." She gave his hand a single firm shake and released it. "In a week all my people will be feeling the same way that I do and regretting the way they have treated you. They are very good people, Commander, just terribly tired and worried about the possibility of a fine. The examples that have been set for us are terrifying."

"I know," Raeder agreed with a grimace. He shook his head. "Punishing people for not being inhumanly callous just doesn't seem right."

"No," Behtab agreed. "You are welcome aboard my ship anytime." She pursed her lips and gave him an arch look. "Provided you can keep yourself from doctoring my equipment."

It was a genuine grin this time.

"Yes, ma'am. Next time I'll just let you carry me where I'm bound. That is, if you can manage to keep me inside."

"Short of chaining you to your bunk," she said dryly, "I do not see how I can guarantee that, Commander."

He laughed, then stuck his tongue into his cheek. "Um," he began, his eyes narrowed, "after all that's happened this cruise, don't you think the crew deserves a small bonus?"

The captain blinked. "Ye-es," she said cautiously. "But it will depend on what is in the budget."

Raeder dug into his back pocket and handed her the stack of money chits that he withdrew. "This is actually theirs," he said. "Tell 'em to blow it in port, or to have a party or something. But *don't* tell them where it came from."

Behtab gave him a wondering smile. "These are your winnings from Dynamics!"

"Yeah, but I wouldn't feel right about taking it— or not all of it, at least. I *am* keeping half. Specially since I gave them so much to worry about."

"You are sure that you do not want me to tell them?"

Peter shook his head. "I'm just sorry I lost half of it."

"Well," the captain said with a lift of her eyebrows, "your loss may have been what made everything turn out so well."

God, Raeder thought in mild surprise, *it's amazing how superstitious we spacers are.* "Who can say?" he asked politely.

Raeder gave her a nod and made to leave, but she said quickly, "You won't forget that report you were going to make?"

"No, Captain." He turned a little awkwardly in the narrow hatchway, burdened as he was with his personal gear. "It's the first thing I intend to do." He looked her directly in the eyes. "No promises, though."

Behtab nodded thoughtfully, unconsciously shuffling the money chits in her hands. "Understood," she said calmly. But she was counting on him, he could tell.

"Perhaps," she went on, "we will run into each other

stationside someday. The war will last a long time, I think."

Peter nodded gravely. "That would be pleasant." His smile turned slightly smug as he walked away down the access bay. *Glad to see the old Raeder charm is still working,* he thought.

Even though the damned war was making it impossible to stay in one place long enough to get any practical results out of it.

Ontario Base wasn't quite up to Lunabase standards, but then, you wouldn't expect it to be, out here on the frontier as it was. Everything looked functional enough, and everything that could be done by the crews of downlined ships put to busywork to keep them from going slack had been done, too. There were even murals, and pretty good ones for amateurs killing time. Blank spaces along the walls and corridors had been turned into scenes of forest, rock, lake, pine, and muskeg; someone was taking the base's name quite seriously. Occasionally there were subliminal odors of pine needles in the recirculated air, or the very faint twittering cry of a loon on a distant lake.

Pass me my mackinaw and my toque, Peter thought. *I need to get into the spirit of things.*

Once again, and somewhat to his surprise, there was a cart waiting for him. Raeder stowed his gear and hopped aboard, entered his orders, confirmed his identity with a capillary scan, and leaned back to relax as the cart started off. He gazed around curiously, noticing that in this sector, at least, merchant mariners predominated. Ontario Base had never been a luxurious station, but now it had a stripped-down look. Fewer kiosks than he was used to seeing and more people than it was designed to serve, all of them looking hurried and overworked.

The war, he thought with an underlying bitterness. *It's set us back.* Then he shook his head. *Temporary setback, my man. Nothing will keep the Commonwealth penned for long.*

The cart brought him to a checkpoint at the center of the station. Warning bars of glowing light extended from the roof of the corridor to the floor, like the bars of a castle's portcullis, visible light marking the perimeter of the shockback field. The lasers that would slice any unauthorized entry who made it past into thin charred slices were invisible within the glowing pillars, but anyone would be extremely conscious of them even without the DANGER LETHAL BARRIER AUTHORIZED PERSONNEL ONLY BEYOND THIS POINT which blinked in the air in front of them. He presented his documents for inspection and pressed his left index finger on a handheld identification module.

"Thank you, Commander," the MP said. She turned off the barrier and the solid-seeming white bars disappeared.

Raeder disliked this kind of fence and never passed though one without at least a touch of suspicion. Once, when he was about fifteen, from sheer, idle curiosity, he'd touched one of those beams—just a shockback barrier there, without the lethal laser reinforcement. When he woke up he was lying on his back, staring at feet. As the ringing in his ears faded, he could hear the owner of those feet demanding to know what had possessed him to do something so infernally stupid. Twelve years later, he still didn't have an answer, and he still shuddered as he passed through.

The cart trundled off again. Instead of heading for

the docking tubes, it wended its way toward the office complex. Industrial metal gave way to soft synthetic floors, and the amateur murals run up by spacers with too much time on their hands yielded to professional holographs. He found those rather less interesting.

"Where are we going?" Peter demanded.

"Space Command Sector Intelligence HQ," the cart answered.

Ah, yes. Where mountains of supposition are constructed from molehills of information and presented as incontrovertible fact. He sighed. They were probably going to debrief him about the raider attack. Peter wondered how long they'd keep him. *Futile to speculate, since it depends on their workload. About which I know nothing.* He shook his head; this was like one of those dreams where you tried desperately to get somewhere, and the harder you struggled, the further the goal receded.

Oh well, he thought, looking at the bright side, *at least I'll be able to make my report to a human face.* It might not mean any more than just writing it out and submitting it, but he would *feel* better about it. *And hey, that counts. At least to me.* The cart dropped him at the entrance to a corridor that looked more like a hallway in a building than a street.

He reported to the receptionist, who confirmed his ID and asked him to wait until someone could escort him. Peter sat on the stiff, ultramodern couch and slowly scrolled through a magazine until he finally came to an interesting article. At which point a young MP showed up.

"Commander Raeder? Follow me, please."

He left Peter, sans reading matter, in a white cube of a room with two chairs, cousins to the B&D couch in the lobby and an immovable coffee table that bumped against his shins.

He waited for a half an hour, until a pleasant-faced young woman opened the door and gravely asked him to follow. She led him to an empty conference room with what appeared to be a football play drawn on the wall-screen. Other than that there was no reading matter here, either, although there was a portrait of the prime minister on the wall. Peter looked at the jowly face and stern blue eyes for a while, then away. They seemed to be accusing him of voting for someone else in the last election.

He had; he'd voted for the Rhinoceros Party, one of whose pledges was to make all roads run downhill.

Peter sat with a sigh in the nearest chair and looked around the room idly. There was a carafe and six glasses on a tray at the head of the table. He reached out hopefully and hefted the carafe. Empty. He sighed again.

There's something about being left by yourself in a conference room that makes you feel truly alone, Raeder thought. *Probably the sound-proofing,* he reasoned. *For all you can hear the whole human race may have snuck off somewhere fun and left you behind.* Time passed and he began to tap his fingers impatiently. *If it was this low priority, why didn't they let me go directly to my assignment and call me later?*

Finally a lieutenant came bustling in, a nondescript youngster with hard eyes and a take-charge manner.

Perfect for Intelligence, Raeder thought.

"I'm sorry to have kept you, sir," the lieutenant said in a clipped voice. "Something came up."

Yeah, sure. Why not just admit that you were going

over Hall's report and my testimony? Does Intelligence have actual rules against being straightforward? Peter wondered sourly.

"Shall we get to it, then?" Raeder said, stealing the lieutenant's next line.

"If you would please face the recording module in the center of the table, sir," the lieutenant requested, still clipped. "This is Lieutenant A.T.C. Clark," he announced, and gave the time and date.

Both of which would automatically be imprinted on the recording and were therefore unnecessary to mention. *Heaven spare me from the detail-obsessed,* Peter groaned inwardly. There was something about the service's desk jobs that seemed to attract those with a permanent metaphorical pickle up the butt. *And I find it's good policy to beware of people who identify themselves with no less than three initials instead of a name. Of course, the poor guys initials could stand for Aloycius Thaddeus Cuthbert. Which wouldn't leave him much room to maneuver, now would it?* Academy ring, too.

"Now, Commander, you were aboard the *Africa* when she was attacked by raiders, were you not?"

No, I was square-dancing on a Martian beach with Letta D'Amour.

"Yes," he said aloud. *Pity.* D'Amour was his favorite holovid actress. He'd always wanted to meet her, although there was a rumor she was a virtual-reality AI in real life . . . if you could call that real. Or life for that matter.

"How many of them were there?"

"I saw five," Peter said.

"Um-hm. Now, this is very important, sir. We intercepted a remark made by one of the raiders to the effect that a new weapon was being used. Do you have any knowledge of such?"

Peter grinned; he couldn't help it.

"A new weapon?" he asked.

"Yes, sir. He said it was, I quote, 'wrecking his sensors.'"

Peter started to chuckle. *I suppose it was a new weapon in this context.* About thirty thousand years old in another.

"It's not funny, sir." The youngster's face was stern. "If the Merchant Marine companies have some unknown weapon at their disposal, and they aren't willing to contribute it to the war effort, it's a serious matter."

"Are you suggesting they'd use it against Space Command?" Raeder asked incredulously.

"No, sir, of course not. But they may be withholding it from us, and it certainly sounds like something Space Command could use. There's a lot of bitterness against us from that quarter," Clark said confidentially. "And if they're withholding vital information like this . . ." he leaned forward, "at the very least it's inappropriate. At worst . . . treason."

Oh, come on! I know paranoia is an occupational requirement for spooks, Peter thought, *but this is ridiculous.*

"It was me," Raeder said. "And I used a hammer. Not the most high-tech equipment you'll run across, I grant you, but effective nonetheless."

"You?" Clark said. He looked at Raeder as though he'd suddenly started speaking in tongues.

Peter nodded.

"Would you mind telling me how you accomplished that, sir?"

So Raeder did.

"I see," Clark said when Peter finished. He gave the commander a measuring look. "You drove around on the surface of the raider's ship beating on its sensor pickups with a hammer." The Intelligence Officer's lips pursed.

"Yes."

Peter could imagine Clark wondering what he was hiding, why he was sympathetic to the Merchant Marine. What vile plots were being hatched, what faithless alliances made. Because it was as plain as the snub nose on his bland face that the lieutenant hadn't believed a word of Peter's story.

"Thank you, sir," Clark said suddenly. Standing, he gathered the notebook he'd brought with him. "Someone will be along shortly to show you back to the lobby."

"We're not quite finished, Lieutenant," Raeder said in a soft, even tone that implied *sit down* quite loudly. "I have something to say, for the record." *Though you can bet I'll back it up with a written report.* "The Merchant Marines have good reason to be bitter toward Space Command. They're virtually unarmed out there. To the raiders it's like some kind of game where there's no penalty, just prizes. How many ships have we lost in the last month to these pirates?" he demanded.

"That's classified." Clark snapped, his expression puzzled. It was plain he couldn't understand why Peter was stating the obvious.

"Without commerce the Commonwealth will evaporate," Raeder said. "If we're not going to defend what we're fighting for, why bother to have the war?" A stupid question, of course, but he also had a point.

And if you're talking to the dense or distracted, some-times a stupid question will get their attention.

"We don't have enough ships, or fuel," Clark said slowly and carefully, "to provide heavier escort for the convoys. We are literally doing all we can."

"I disagree," Peter said. "We can't send more ships, there you're right. But we have unused weapons in storage, we have trained gun crews waiting for assign-ment. How much antihydrogen would it expend to put those resources together with the freighters them-selves?" he asked. "If you send them out heavily armed and in convoy you may not even need the escorts."

Clark looked like he'd been hit by a two-by-four. He nodded slowly.

"You may have a point," he conceded.

Of course I have a point, you donkey.

"Do you really think so?" Raeder asked, as though genuinely surprised.

"Yes. It could work."

"I'll leave it in your hands, then." *Like hell.* Peter rose and offered his hand. *The more directions the idea is heard from, the more likely it is to be heard at all.* Glory won behind the controls of a Speed was one thing, a victory a man could be proud of. Vic-tory in some bureaucratic bun-fight, however, had no glory in it at all. *Of course, the bureaucrats might get together once a year and hand out the golden spleen award. But not to me, thanks.*

"Yes, sir," Clark said, steely-eyed, jaw set. "I'll do my best."

Peter nodded, smiling. *I have a feeling,* he thought, *that your best might well turn out to be quite a bit.* He allowed himself a satisfied little smirk behind the lieutenant's back and sat down to wait for his escort.

As he approached the *Invincible*'s docking tube, Peter's heart began to beat faster. He smoothed back the stubborn wing of hair that insisted on dropping over his forehead and took a quick check of his uniform to assure himself that it had maintained its pristine condition.

He was frustrated that he hadn't gotten a good look at his new ship as *Africa* approached the station. *But getting packed and ready to go seemed more important at the time.*

Now he longed to know what she looked like. He pictured her sleek and rakish, as though designed for atmospheric work. Raeder was already half in love with her and meeting her this way, at what was essentially a hole in the station's wall with her name spelled out in digital letters above it, was anticlimatic and deeply unsatisfying. And yet . . . his heart beat faster. Just at the sight of her name.

Peter fairly sprang from the cart when it stopped, grabbed his gear, and approached the petty officer on duty at the security desk beside the docking tube.

The young petty officer noted the commander's tabs on Raeder's shoulders and gave him a brisk salute, which Peter returned with pleasure, taking it as a sign of a well-run, mannerly ship. He offered his orders and the lieutenant fed the chit into a reader.

"Welcome aboard, sir. The captain is expecting you." He tapped a series of symbols on his console and in a moment a rating first class arrived who automatically hoisted Raeder's duffel.

"Kamel will escort you, sir," the petty officer said, with one more salute in farewell.

Raeder returned it, then followed the rating into

the tube and onto the *Invincible*. A sort of energy blazed through his blood as his foot fell on her deck, a crackling aliveness. He was *back*. Back where things were happening, if not in the cockpit of a Speed. He paused and took a deep breath. Inhaling the scent of her newness, a raw, clean smell that pleased him and somehow hinted at her power.

The walls gleamed, the corridors were bright and surprisingly spacious, the color-coded sheathing of pipes and cables and conduits crisp with newness. Each of the compartments he glanced into as they passed was neat and well planned. Members of the crew they encountered were busy and had an air of competence, appearing as pleased as Raeder felt about being aboard the *Invincible*. After the raw metal and cramped spaces of the *Africa* it was an inexpressible relief.

This was put together with love and a lot of work, Peter thought. *Everything and everybody, handpicked by someone who knew just what they wanted and exactly what they were doing.* Possibly too good to be true. He pushed the thought aside, refusing to spoil his pleasure in his good fortune until he had to. If there was a catch it'd reveal itself soon enough. *Besides, maybe my luck is due to change.*

They took an elevator up several levels and walked; it seemed like a couple of klicks before the young rating stopped before a door that bore a modest brass plate bearing a name: *Captain Roger Knott.*

"Not quite as big as a fleet carrier," Peter said, "but she's spacious enough inside. Isn't there a connecting elevator?"

Carriers had to have big hulls, to handle the smaller craft that nestled inside them like a swarm of lethal wasps. That usually meant bigger crew quarters, as

well; in a destroyer, say, the captain would be lucky
to have enough room to turn around between his bunk
and the far wall. Hence they usually had interior
people-movers, tubes running lengthwise down the hull
and carrying pods for crewfolk in a hurry.

"There are a number of them, Commander," Kamel
confided. "But Captain Knott insists that same-deck
people-movers only be used if time is a vital factor.
He says it reduces congestion and helps keep people
in shape."

Raeder nodded amiably at the information and the
young rating knocked.

The captain sounds like a disciplinarian, Peter
thought, and mentally girded himself for battle. He
tended to have problems with disciplinarians.

"Enter," a muffled voice commanded.

Kamel opened the door and stood aside for Raeder
to enter.

"Take the Commander's gear to his quarters," the
captain said to him.

Kamel murmured, "Yes, sir," and withdrew.

Raeder saluted, standing stiffly at attention as he
studied his new commander, liking what he saw. *So
far.* Knott was close to his own height, about six feet
tall, had bold aquiline features and a cap of close-
cut white hair. He had a spaceman's tan, the sort you
got from a lot of EVA or hot-sun planets and that
could stay with you for life. The sleeve of his uniform carried the small gray-blue pip of a former Survey
Service officer.

He examined Peter with the directness of the bird
of prey he resembled, the gray eyes disconcertingly
keen.

"At ease, Commander," he said in a gravelly voice

that held a twang Raeder placed as North American, somewhere western. "Please be seated."

As Raeder complied he realized that this was the captain's private office, attached to his personal suite. There were ship holos on the walls: a destroyer of obsolete type, a Survey Service deep-space explorer, chunky and functional, a heavy cruiser. *Models of his previous commands,* he thought; not an uncommon affectation for a commander. Then he froze and half rose in his chair as he noticed the holo hanging behind Knott's head. He stopped himself and sank down again.

"Is, is that the *Invincible,* sir?" he asked, unable to take his eyes off the holo. She was everything he'd wanted her to be, only more beautiful than she'd been in his imagination.

Roger Knott smiled, a subtle, almost hidden expression that appeared as a slight lightening of his stern features. *You'll do, boy,* he thought. He'd been worried; fighter pilots were clannish and tended to be loyal to their squadrons first, everything else second. But Raeder had obviously made the transition; the love in the young engineer's eyes was unmistakable. He belonged to the *Invincible. You'll do very well.*

"Security held onto you for quite a while," the captain observed.

"Yes, sir," Raeder agreed.

"Their interest was, no doubt, sparked by the incident with the raiders."

Knott watched with interest as the commander's face became as mild and innocent as a choirboy's.

"Yes, sir." Raeder agreed again. "They were under

the impression that the Merchant Marines had a new weapon they weren't sharing with Space Command."

"Really? Tell me more."

Suddenly Peter felt as though he'd stepped into a minefield. His instincts told him that Knott knew everything; he'd better tell him everything. Everything? Hmmm. Now there was a knotty problem. "Well, sir, as I reported to the debriefer . . ."

He began to sweat slightly halfway through the interview. It was frustrating talking to an unvarying expression of polite interest.

Knott gave him no clues and speculated with amusement how frustrated the commander must be growing. Not that it showed; he still looked like butter wouldn't melt in his mouth.

"What about the grapple?" Knott asked after a moment's silence.

"The grapple on the cart, sir?"

"The grapple used to tow the *Province of Quebec*. Tell me about that. Usual merchanter practice in a situation like that would be to cut the grapple loose and run like hell. No sense in risking another ship for one that can't be saved . . . can't be saved those times there's no maniac with a hammer around."

Suddenly the archaic word rogering, to roger, to be rogered, popped into Peter's head. As in, he was screwed. Clearly, Captain Behtab and Captain Roger Knott were on fairly good terms. If he gave Peter a direct order . . . then he'd have to own up. Even if it meant the stockade. But until he did, they'd have to dance.

"Uh, the housing on the mechanism was apparently not fully closed and some micrometeor damage was incurred. Or, at any rate, that was *Africa's* engineer's estimation of the damage. So I was told." Raeder struggled to look uninvolved, professional, and innocent, all at the same time.

He's good, Knott thought. The captain considered ordering the young commander to tell him the truth. *But I'm pretty sure I already know what it is. And then I'd have to deal with it and I don't see the advantage to the* Invincible *in that.* And the *Invincible* came first. After all, he'd asked for someone smart, independent, courageous, and principled. *How can I complain if that's what I've got?* Even if those principles were a little elastic when it came to achieving what Raeder saw as the greater good. Maybe he should have left out "independent."

The captain studied his new flight engineer, resting his chin on his fist, thumb and forefinger pulling at his upper lip. *No, it was the right thing. This isn't a battlewagon.* The *Invincible* wouldn't be operating as part of a fleet, or even an attack flotilla. They'd be out on their own.

"Would you care for some refreshment, Commander?" he asked at last.

"Yes, sir," Peter said, somewhat surprised. Obviously the captain had come to a decision about him. *In spite of what he knows about my little adventure with the raiders.* Interesting. Why would Knott ignore Raeder's sabotage?

The captain pressed a button on his desk and his aide entered from an inner door.

"What will you have, Commander?" Knott asked. "Coffee? Tea?"

"Coffee would be great, sir. Thank you."

The captain nodded dismissal and then began going over Raeder's record with him. Asking questions, commenting, inquiring about officers he and Peter knew in common.

The coffee came and when the aide had left, Knott leaned back in his chair, quietly sipping the rich brew, studying Raeder over his cup.

Finally he asked, "Have you been wondering why you were selected for this particular assignment, Commander?"

Roger that! Peter thought. *Stop it!* he warned himself. If he kept thinking funny stuff like—"Roger" that and "Knotty" problem—it was only a matter of time before it slipped out. *Which I don't think the good captain would appreciate.*

"Yes, sir," he said, after he'd swallowed. "I'm sure there must have been other candidates."

"Oh, there were," Knott agreed. "People with more seniority and much more experience." And major problems in their folders that would keep them off of any deck the captain happened to be on. He was convinced in his soul that it wasn't just short notice that had caused him to be offered such a list of losers. But then there was little old, inexperienced Raeder. With his sterling character references and excellent performance record. A calculated risk that was, quite frankly, looking good at this point. "But you see," he said as he leaned forward, "this is a very special situation. And required a very special candidate."

Why do I suddenly wish I'd flunked? Raeder asked himself.

"Your predecessor," *God, what a miserably appropriate term*, the captain thought, "had ten years of experience as a flight engineer. He came to us from the *Merlin*."

"A tight ship, sir," Raeder said wisely, since something seemed to be expected of him.

"A very tight ship. Commander Okakura was a first rate officer. Knowledgeable, cautious where appropriate, and truly gifted at his profession. Which is why I find his death so inexplicable. He wasn't the sort of man who makes elementary mistakes."

Raeder felt the back of his neck clench, and for a moment his throat refused to swallow the last mouthful of coffee. *He died? The guy died?* How did you manage to *die* on a ship just out of the dockyard, with the contractor's technicians barely a day or two off the deck?

"How exactly did he die, sir?"

"From the appearance of things, he'd apparently crawled into the exhaust cone of a Speed." The captain paused to take a deep breath. "And, I'm told, a glitch in the AI caused it to start the engines."

Peter felt himself blanch. "With the commander . . . ?" he began.

"With the commander in the exhaust cone. Yes." Knott tightened his lips at the memory. So did Peter. They would have had had to scrape him off the metal with sonic cleansers, the carbon atoms of his body bonded to the material.

"Okakura was a good man," Knott said grimly.

Raeder didn't say anything for a moment. His mind raced. *Okay, so the captain's about to tell me that he wants me to get to the bottom of this thing.* It was the only place this buildup could be leading. *He thinks the commander was murdered.* Peter's insides curdled at the thought. *If so, whoever did it should get to share the experience.*

"Captain," he said cautiously, "I'm getting the

impression that you think there's something more to this than just an accident." At Knott's sharp glance, he leaned back and said, "Or perhaps the commander's death was so horrible, it seems to me that there should be something more behind it than just . . . happenstance."

"Well," the captain said, and paused. Then he caught Raeder's eye again. "We've had an unusually high rate of parts failures and AI glitches since we came online here. People have been hurt, even killed." He watched the commander take that in without flinching. "I think we've got a saboteur—a murderer aboard this ship. Aboard *my* ship," he snarled. "It was suggested that you might be the man to help me find out who."

Suggested by whom? Raeder wondered.

"Sir, I have no training in Intelligence or police work—" he began.

"I'm aware of that. I don't want to call them in until I have some evidence to show them. Right now I've got some parts failures and a few accidents, one of them fatal. But we're a new ship, new crew, we haven't even gone on our first operational cruise yet. They'll tell me it's to be expected."

Peter nodded. They would.

"But I've been in Space Command a long, long time, and *I* know something's rotten on my ship." His eyes bored into Raeder's. "You're new, you have no ties or loyalties or conflicts to trip you up. And I've been told that you've got guts and good instincts. I don't think I'm wrong about this, Commander, though I wish I were. But if I am, I think you can find that out for me. And if I'm not, I think you can help me deal with it."

Raeder squared his shoulders. With a vote of

confidence like that, how could he possibly say no? *But I'd sure love to know who else is in my fan club.*

"I'll do my best, sir," he said.

"I know you will, Commander," the captain agreed. He signaled for his aide again. "We'll be having a 'dining in' this evening to welcome you aboard. I'll send a petty officer to escort you to the officers' mess at nineteen thirty." The captain stood just as his aide entered.

Peter rose with him and saluted. The captain returned it, a look of approval warming his gray eyes.

"Escort the commander to his quarters," he instructed his aide. "I'll see you this evening," Knott said to Raeder, and then he took his seat behind his desk, eyes on some report, the commander apparently forgotten.

Gee, Raeder thought as he followed the captain's aide, *remember when you wondered if this terrific assignment had a catch? Wasn't that a great time? A time of innocence, full of bright hopes for the future. When was that golden age? Forty minutes ago? Yes, yes. Of course that was before I knew my predecessor had been murdered*—God! What an eerily appropriate term that was. *And that I'm supposed to be the one to bring his killer to justice.*

He was both honored and exasperated. *I thought being a flight engineer was going to be tough. Now I'm a private eye. Had I but known, I would have spent my time studying detective stories instead of engine specs.*

Which was unfair, and he knew he was overreacting, but he'd always felt that, if there was time, getting the grousing over with and out of his head tended to clear his mind for more constructive thoughts. *Like who recommended me?*

Someday, maybe he'd ask.

The aide stopped in front of a door and keyed in a master code. The hatch slid aside.

"It's a standard lock, sir," the man said.

Which meant that it would take voice code, capillary scan, or a code tapped out on the keypad. Or all three if you were paranoid and security obsessed.

Peter stepped into his new quarters and the aide followed.

"This is great," Peter told him as he paused just inside the hatchway.

"Yes, sir. I'll return for you at nineteen thirty hours."

Raeder nodded his thanks and keyed the hatch shut. Then he turned to take in his surroundings.

This was the first time in his military career that he hadn't had to share his quarters, and he couldn't help but gloat. The truth was that, thanks to humane societies across the Commonwealth, prison cells afforded more space, but still . . . *Utter privacy,* Peter thought greedily, looking at the single bunk.

The cabin was laid out for maximum efficiency in use of space. The desk folded flat against the wall; let down it revealed a keypad built into its inner surface and a flat multipurpose wall-screen. He reached down under the bunk, folded down a flap, and withdrew the desk chair from where it lay collapsed in its compartment, tapped it once on the floor, and it blossomed into the latest ergonomic unit.

Wow, he thought in awe, *untouched by human tush.* Then he remembered Okakura, his predecessor, and grimaced. *Virtually untouched,* he amended.

Raeder slid a plastic strip on the desktop toward

himself and behind it a row of datachips flipped up. No doubt the personnel records on his staff, as well as reports on the functioning of his department. He started to draw the chair up, then stopped and looked at his duffle.

I ought to at least unpack my dress uniform so that the wrinkles will smooth out. What the heck. He'd unpack the whole thing. It would only take a few minutes, then he could dive into the chips guilt free.

After an apparently short stint of working on those files, Peter checked the time and was surprised to see that it was seventeen hundred. He'd been hard at work for three hours. Raeder stretched and rotated his shoulders, deciding to take a quick jog before showering and changing for dinner.

It would take him hours yet to even give a brief scan to the five hundred people who would be under his command, but the few he had studied in depth had certainly given him food for thought.

Particularly his second-in-command, Second Lieutenant Cynthia Robbins. She was a first-rate technician; in fact, some of her ratings were off the scale. But, reading between the carefully written lines her other commanders had laid down, she lacked people skills. Big time.

Peter had checked the map of the ship on his data terminal and then directed his jog to the Speed hangar. He hadn't even been near one of the sleek, deadly birds in weeks and had felt a sudden impatience to wallow in the sight, sound, smell of them. The fact that it came out to a run of almost four klicks was a bonus.

Just enough to get the blood flowing, Raeder

thought. *Not enough to wear me out.* He felt he ought to be on his toes for the captain's dinner. Especially if he was supposed to find a saboteur. The problem was that it had been a long time since the Commonwealth fought a human opponent with any sort of real espionage capability. Things with tentacles and scales had trouble infiltrating; Space Command had plenty of firepower, but counterespionage capacity had gone to hell. Plus the Mollies were extremely good at infiltration. Their faith allowed any amount of duplicity in a good cause.

He could smell the Speeds now, and it drove mysteries and frustrations from his mind. Water and lubricant and burned metal, the scents came from the hangar door up ahead. Peter speeded up a bit and then stopped in the doorway, a slow, delighted smile spreading over his face like the breaking dawn. There were so many of them crammed into the colossal hangar, lined up nose to tail. They nuzzled together like battle-horses drowsing in a pasture, peacefully waiting for the trumpets to summon them awake.

Peter stepped into the giant room and gloried in the sight. The sleek black shapes towered over him, their heads tilted upwards haughtily. He could *feel* their weight, their leashed power. Something in these magnificent machines called to him, as though they were organic or he were part machine. There was an undeniable connection, a sense that each was a missing part of the other, each incomplete by themselves.

Raeder reached up to wipe the sweat from his brow and struck himself harder than intended with his numb machine-hand. It brought him back to reality, literally with a thump. Peter grimaced and pushed the feelings away, continuing his run, continuing his covert inspection.

He began to hear a woman's voice, sharp with irritation, but as yet the words were inaudible. Ahead a group of people in stained coveralls stood grouped around the exhaust tube of a Speed. He quietly moved closer in order to hear what was being snarled.

"If you're that worried about the AI, take the damn thing offline. This isn't science fiction, y'know, where the things turn themselves on and run amok. And we sure as *hell* can't just ignore this part of the machine."

Raeder stood with his arms folded over his chest and watched the small crowd of techs shift uncomfortably. He agreed that they couldn't just pretend that Speeds didn't have a backend, but he sure couldn't blame them for feeling that way after what happened to poor Okakura.

"*Look* at this!" the unseen woman shouted, and a blackened bit of metal came flying out of the exhaust cone. Peter placed it automatically: part of the waveguide apparatus, the field extension that vectored the exhaust.

The startled young tech who'd almost dropped the thing glared at it sullenly.

"You were actually going to send this bird out with that crack in it? What's the *matter* with you?"

Peter shifted closer, until he could look over the tech's shoulder to see what she was holding. It was one of the mechanical parts of the exhaust system. He watched the tech turn it in her hands, and at first glance he couldn't see anything wrong with it, either. Then the light caught it at just the right angle and he saw it. A hairline fracture right across the disk. The tech saw it, too, and turned it over; it was invisible from that side, but when she flexed it in her hands it snapped like a saltine being crumbled into soup.

There was a profound silence for a moment, then the whole crowd of techs shifted and murmured uncomfortably.

"You have to get beyond your emotions, here," the woman in the exhaust cone continued. "You can't just let your feelings interfere with your duties. If this Speed had gone out, someone would have died. And it would have been *your* fault. Because you were so wrapped up in how *you* felt about the commander's death, how afraid you were . . ." The bitter voice trailed off.

"Maybe I'm giving you too much credit, Elisa," she said acidly. "I've never actually noticed that you were intelligent enough to have such sensitive feelings."

"Hey," Peter said mildly. That was going a little far, particularly under the circumstances. Yes, the tech who'd screwed up should have gotten reamed, but not in public, especially not with such nasty, irrelevant remarks.

"Who said that?" The woman in the exhaust cone came forward and Peter recognized Second Lieutenant Cynthia Robbins. She cast a contemptuous glare over his sweaty jogging clothes. "Whoever you are, you don't belong on *my* deck in *that* outfit, mister. Get yourself gone, before I put you on report."

Your deck? Peter thought, blinking. Everything but operational deployment was *his* command, here on the hangar deck of *Invincible*. On the other hand, he'd be a bit ticked if someone broke in on him in a similar situation. It wasn't surprising that she didn't know him, of course—there must be a lot of unfamiliar faces on a new ship with a crew of thousands.

And wasn't she going to be surprised when he told her who he was and who this deck really belonged to . . .

Well, I guess it might be hers until I take command officially. Still she was coming at it a bit strong. *Tomorrow's time enough,* he warned himself. It would hardly be fair to embarrass her in front of the techs. *But lady, you and I are going to talk,* he promised himself. He gave her a significant look, then turned and after a few steps began jogging again.

Saying that woman is somewhat lacking in people skills, Raeder reflected, *is as great an understatement as saying that eating nuclear waste might give you indigestion.*

CHAPTER FOUR

There were times when Raeder was grateful for the insubstantial armor of his dress uniform. This was one of them. He glanced around the room filled with other officers, equally resplendent in their official evening-wear, and enjoyed the ineffable sense of passing muster. In civilian life he disliked both formal occasions and formal wear, they'd always felt phony to him, and anachronistic. But he'd never felt that way about his uniforms, work or dress.

I suppose it's because they're elements of an ongoing tradition, he thought as he studied the people around him. *And it binds us together, takes us beyond the personalities and the individual preferences to enable us to work together for the greater purpose we all serve.* Peter took a sip of his drink and grimaced. *I wonder why I always end up thinking garbage like this at parties.*

He supposed it was leftovers from the Academy; he'd loved those pep talks when he was eighteen. *Still do, for that matter,* he thought, a little embarrassed. *Hey, those talks did me good.*

They had. They'd inspired him, given him direction and a sense of belonging. So, at the sight of dress uniforms, the words of his instructors, neatly stored in his subconscious, were brought out by the occasion. *I guess I'm just a sentimental fool,* he mused fondly. *To the Academy,* Raeder thought, raising his glass slightly and then taking a sip.

The captain had allotted twenty minutes for cocktails and mingling, but thus far no one had shown any particular desire to mingle with him. Without the solace of his uniform he would have been wondering if the trouble was something he was wearing. *I showered after my run, so I know* that's *not the problem.* He studied a painting on the wall: some obscure moon or planetoid with a gas giant rising in the background.

Odd, that everyone felt so tight after such a short time together. *Probably it's Okakura's death.* It wasn't unknown for something so harrowing to bring people who hardly knew each other much closer. *And there had to have been an official investigation,* Raeder thought. That, too, would cause people to close ranks.

There were only two women on the senior staff: Mai Ling Ju, the executive officer, and Ashly Luhrman, the astrogator. The XO was tall for a Chinese woman, standing approximately a hundred seventy centimeters, give or take a few. She was about forty, with a calm, efficient air about her, and Raeder had liked her instantly. He'd left her and the captain in private conversation with the surgeon, Dr. Ira Goldberg, a wiry, energetic man with the most soothing voice Peter had ever heard. Luhrman was a small blond in her mid-twenties and full of nervous energy. She was huddled with the communications officer, Havash

Hartkopf, who was younger than she was and still had the drooping face of a basset hound. Tactical Officer Truon Le was in animated conversation with the tall, dark, mustachioed squadron leader, "Rotten" Ronnie Sutton, under the watchful eye of Chief Engineer Augie Skinner.

That left the dark-haired, sallow-faced security chief, William Booth, talking to Lieutenant John Larkin, the quartermaster. Raeder didn't envy the friendly quartermaster his task, since Booth was looking around like he thought everyone in the room wanted to pick his pocket.

Well, he is the security chief. I suppose it's in his job description that he has to be suspicious. But Raeder secretly thought he would turn out to be one of those officious, obnoxious, oversensitive jerks who delighted in offending everyone they met. And the jealous way he looked at the XO made Peter suspect that he suffered from a classic case of "short man syndrome," overcompensating like mad for those missing centimeters.

Larkin, on the other hand, had a face as wholesome as fresh bread, topped with angelically fair blond hair. He seemed prepared to like all of his brother officers, even the grimly muttering Booth.

One of the captain's aides struck a small gong to announce that dinner was served and the whole crowd of them moved to the table.

Peter found himself placed at Knott's left hand, in a welcoming place of honor. *I wonder if this is going to be my usual spot, or if the captain seats his officers in rotation.* With the probable exception of the XO.

The table was very elegant, with damask linen cloth

and napkins, hand-cut crystal, and porcelain plates with a heavy gold rim. There was an attractive silk flower arrangement in the center of the large, round table.

Knott saw him studying it and said, "A gift from my wife, for those too frequent times when we can't get fresh flowers." He smiled. "She assured me it would add a civilized touch."

"It does," Raeder assured him. "It's lovely."

The captain nodded his thanks and then leaned slightly to the side as the wardroom attendants began serving.

Conversation was pleasant and inconsequential, and after awhile Raeder was wishing impatiently that he'd been seated next to the squadron leader. There were any number of things they should be discussing.

"But if I'd done that," Captain Knott said to him, "you wouldn't have met anyone else. Which is the purpose of this gathering."

Peter stared at him in surprise and then laughed.

"Was I being that obvious?" he asked.

"You were yearning over the table," Knott said out of the side of his mouth. Then he quirked his brows. "Don't get me wrong, Commander, I'm glad you're so enthusiastic about your duties. But there's a time for everything. And right now," he said with heavy meaning, "it's time to get acquainted."

Meaning? Raeder wondered. *Does the captain suspect someone on his command staff?* He suppressed a grimace. If that were so, he'd have to walk awfully softly. *If the Old Man does have some ideas, I wish he'd share them.* Peter's exasperation melted quickly. *No, he was looking for someone who didn't know these people. Someone who wouldn't pick out Booth because he's a jerk, or Sutton because he's obvious.* So it was reasonable to suppose that Knott wouldn't want to contaminate his investigator's thought process at the outset. Peter suppressed a sigh. *Why me? I have no idea how to even begin looking into something like this.* Which was not a feeling he enjoyed. *But then, Booth is supposed to be an expert and I wouldn't trust him to find his own butt with both hands, a mirror, a map, and a flashlight. Come to that, I imagine the old man shares that opinion.* Booth seemed to be the one officer who hadn't been picked with care. Considering the delicate touch that security work often required, it was a glaring oversight.

"Commander," Dr. Goldberg said from Peter's left.

Raeder looked inquiringly at him.

"Would you mind dropping into sick bay tomorrow before you go on duty?" he asked. "I'd like to go over your records with you and introduce you to my physical therapist."

Peter blinked. "I was told that I wouldn't need PT anymore," he protested.

"Not actively, no," the doctor assured him. "But it's best to check in periodically to make sure you're doing the exercises correctly. And yours is the latest model. I'd really appreciate an opportunity to examine it and to hear how you're progressing."

"Sure," Raeder said quickly to shut him up. *Before you ask me if I'd mind disrobing. Sheesh!* At the same time, Peter was annoyed with himself for not being as matter of fact about his prosthesis as the doctor was. *But how can I be?* he asked himself. *It's my hand!* And its loss was altogether too recent.

Goldberg opened his mouth to speak when the quartermaster broke in.

"You're certainly going to have a full plate for the

next few days," Larkin observed. His cherubic face wore an expression that told Raeder he was well aware he was interrupting the doctor. "You'll have almost four weeks of reports to get through."

"Lieutenant Robbins has been doing a good job," the captain said quietly.

Sutton's eyes flickered over the captain to Raeder and Peter felt his heart sink.

"She's a good engineer from her file," Peter offered diplomatically.

"She is," the chief engineer agreed judiciously. "But she's not a people person."

Strictly speaking, it wasn't the chief engineer's business. He was in charge of the ship's drive systems and powerplant, not the Speeds. However . . .

The squadron leader passed that look again and Peter could practically hear him thinking: *Neither was Attila the Hun a people person.*

"All in all," Commander Ju observed as she lifted her wine glass, "we have an exceptional crew. I consider myself fortunate to be serving with everyone here."

Raeder impulsively lifted his glass. "To the *Invincible!*" he said.

"*Invincible!*" they responded enthusiastically, and drank.

They dispersed shortly after dinner. There was too much work waiting before they turned in, with too few hours of sleep afterward to linger.

Peter found himself walking with Lieutenant Larkin down the echoing corridor, still smelling faintly of the solvents used in the shipyard's final cleaning.

"I'm in the cabin next to yours," Larkin said cheerfully. "Hope my snoring doesn't keep you awake."

"I doubt I'll hear it over mine," Raeder boasted. "They were thinking of using me as a sonic weapon for awhile there."

"Hah!" Larkin gave him a playful punch on the arm. "The man's full of himself!" He shook his head as Raeder chuckled. "Have you had a chance to look around yet?"

"I gave myself the opportunity to get down to the main deck," Peter said. "Got a look at my second; didn't speak to her, though."

Larkin said nothing. They walked a few steps.

"Isn't this what's known as a 'speaking silence'?" Raeder asked.

Larkin nodded. "It is that."

"C'mon, give," Raeder prompted. "I'm a brother officer."

"Well . . . you've heard . . ."

"That she's not a people person, yeah." *Seen it, too.* Not that he would say so.

"She is, however, a Michelangelo of mechanics, an artist, a perfect poem of an engineer." Larkin looked rapturous, his hands raised like a conductor's as he almost sang Cynthia Robbins' praises. He looked at Raeder out of the corner of his eye and laughed. "Thus sayeth Augie Skinner, one of her fans."

"Well," Peter said wryly, "they're both engineers. Same song, different tempo."

"She tends to treat the rest of us like we're in the way," the lieutenant said with a sigh. "I think the only reason she's been promoted so far is because she's so technically brilliant. And she's young; she might outgrow those rough edges. But to be honest, I'm glad I won't have to deal directly with her anymore. The woman's got a tongue like a flaying knife."

"Well, I'll find out for myself tomorrow," Raeder said cheerfully. *And I thought you liked everybody,* he thought. *I guess it's true what Gramma said. Still waters run deep, but not necessarily pure.* Of course, to be fair, Lieutenant Robbins did appear to be hard to warm up to. *And based on observation, she actually* does *have a tongue like a flaying knife.*

In any case, he ought to take advantage of Larkin's confidential mood.

"What's the deal with Booth?" he asked. "He looks like a starling at a parrot convention."

The lieutenant laughed. "He does, doesn't he? Will was an extreme last-minute replacement," Larkin said solemnly. "The original security person was Margaret Lester, a very good woman."

Raeder blinked. "You sound like she's dead."

Larkin grimaced. "No, but she'd be better off that way. She was seriously hurt in a freak airlock accident. There was considerable brain damage."

"And Booth was the best they could get on short notice."

"Mmmm. My mother used to say that the bird that flies in on the winds of expediency is seldom a swan," Larkin observed.

"Umm. John, I believe I cruised in on those very winds," Raeder said with a smile.

"She said seldom," Larkin protested, hands raised defensively, "not never. Personally, I think we lucked out this time, roomie."

Peter chuckled. "I refuse to believe the walls are that thin."

"You'll hear me turning over," Larkin promised. "Goodnight," he said as he walked on to his hatch.

"'Night," Raeder said.

Raeder wasn't in his best mood ever as he hastened to the meeting he'd arranged between himself, Cynthia Robbins, and the CPO who'd been supporting her. The previous night he'd stayed up much later than was wise as he studied his most recent set of reports and was feeling frazzled as a result.

His meeting with the doctor had gone better than he'd anticipated. But then, he'd anticipated decking the guy. Fortunately, perhaps because Goldberg's intrusive questions weren't so out of place in sick bay, it wasn't the ordeal Raeder had expected.

He'd liked Sergeant Kedski, the physical therapist, too. She obviously knew her job. And noting Raeder's discomfort over Goldberg's drooling fascination with his prosthetic hand, she'd somehow managed to hustle the commander out of the sick bay long before the surgeon would have released him otherwise.

Still, Peter was running later than he liked and was close to a jog as he neared his ready room.

What he'd discovered with his late-night reading was that the captain had, if anything, downplayed the parts failure problem. Commander Robbins had provided ample documentation of vital components that fell well below standard, and that she considered too fallible to be used.

On the other hand, there were protests filed by the quartermaster citing Lieutenant Robbins' "obsessive perfectionism" as the problem. *These parts have been inspected and passed,* he'd written. *Both by the manufacturer and by my people, who are all qualified technicians. Minor surface blemishes do not necessarily indicate defective equipment. They may not be beautiful, but they're passing their tests. I request that*

Second Lieutenant Cynthia Robbins be restrained from this gratuitous waste of our time and valuable Commonwealth equipment.

People often come across differently in writing, but Raeder had been surprised by the tone of rancor in Larkin's letter. *He seems like the kind of guy you have to push to the wall to get a protest out of.* But then, Robbins didn't have a soothing reputation.

He sighed. He'd worked with one or two geniuses in his time, and they were seldom team players. *Well, I'll soon be finding out what kind of animal she is,* he thought.

He saw as he rounded a corner that someone was already waiting for him: a solidly built man with grizzled hair and dark brown skin. Doubtless this was Chief Petty Officer Jomo arap Moi. Twenty years in Commonwealth service, with a solid reputation and an excellent record; one commendation for some very cool-headed work during a containment-vessel breakdown on an assault transport. Raeder was glad to have him and looked forward to working with him.

There was no sign, however, of Lieutenant Robbins.

Damn, this is just what I wanted to avoid, he thought. *She's going to find us talking together and it's going to look like the boys against the girls.* It was inevitable. And frankly he wasn't too happy that Robbins had chosen not to be punctual.

"Chief Petty Officer arap Moi?" he asked, smiling. The CPO snapped off a salute and Raeder returned it.

"Yes, sir. Commander Raeder?"

"Yes, Chief. Has Lieutenant Robbins been delayed?" he asked quietly.

"Yes, sir. It's always something these days," the noncom said lugubriously.

"So I gathered from the reports I've been reading. Well," Raeder said, smiling again, "perhaps we should go and find her so we can be of some help."

"Yes, sir."

They started off for the elevator that would bring them to Main Deck, arap Moi casting an occasional glance at Raeder from the corner of his eye.

"You have something you want to say, Chief?" Raeder kept his eyes ahead as he spoke.

The chief cleared his throat and frowned. "Ah, Lieutenant Robbins is one hell of an engineer," he said, and paused as though waiting to see how his comment was taken.

"But she's not a people person," Raeder finished for him. "I've heard that."

The chief bit his lower lip to hide his smile, but his attitude brightened considerably.

"Personally, sir, I think she's got the instincts of a good officer. But the lieutenant's picked up some bad habits somewhere. If we can coax her over those rough spots, she'll turn out all right someday."

"I sure hope someday is today, Chief. Because as of now Lieutenant Robbins will have to start doing things my way." He suppressed a grin at the CPO's frown. "Tell you what," Raeder said, "you coax, I'll bully, and between us we may get where we want to go." He turned to look at arap Moi, who regarded him with calm brown eyes.

"Yes, sir. That might work," he agreed.

"Unacceptable!" The angry voice belled out in the cavernous hangar, then flattened rapidly and faded.

"Sir. I will not release a Speed that is not testing right. It is my job—"

"It's your job to fix them and then give them back, Lieutenant. Except that you seem to be having this little problem with letting the pilots use them. But that's what they're *for*, don't you know."

"Yes, sir. I do know. But this Speed—"

"Yes, this Speed. It's always *this* Speed, Lieutenant, and I'm tired of it. D'you understand me, Lieutenant?"

Looks like the Rotten Ronnie portion of Squadron Leader Sutton's personality is uppermost this morning, Raeder thought with resignation. Sutton's sangfroid had completely vanished as he virtually pushed his red face into Lieutenant Robbins' pale one the better to shout at her. *Good thing I got here when I did, or we'd be having another funeral on the* Invincible. *For Sutton's career. I think he's on the verge of decking her.*

"Morning, Sutton," he said casually. "Lieutenant Robbins." He nodded to each of them, then glanced at the equally angry young pilot who stood at Sutton's elbow with an inquiring expression.

"Thank God, you're here!" Sutton exclaimed. "The lieutenant here," he began, placing a distinctly uncomplimentary emphasis on "lieutenant," "has apparently decided to persecute Lieutenant Givens by never letting him fly again." The squadron leader's eyes were almost bugging out as he glared at Robbins. "Four times, Commander, *four times*, she's pulled his Speed apart at the last minute. I'm beginning to think that all I need do to ruin an exercise is to file a flight plan!"

Raeder grinned at that. "No, I think we can do better for you than that, Ron. What *do* we have that's cleared to fly?" he asked Robbins.

"Two-seven-seven-six CBF, sir," Robbins answered immediately, her face sullen.

"She's all yours, Lieutenant Givens." Raeder made a general sweeping gesture, since he didn't know the exact location of two-seven-seven-six CBF.

"But it's not *my* Speed," Givens protested.

"Exactly!" Sutton agreed, only slightly mollified.

"Understood," Raeder assured them. "But," he gestured at the Speed's engine where it lay on the deck, "for today, it's the best we can do. At least you'll be able to fly the whole squadron. And you know . . . I was under this curious impression that these spacecraft belonged to the Commonwealth and Space Command, somehow."

The lieutenant commander sighed in mournful resignation. "Yes, I suppose." He sighed again. "But, really, Peter, can't you do *something?*"

"We'll do our best, Ron. Have a good flight."

"Thank you." Sutton shook his head in disgust and slapped his lieutenant on the shoulder before walking away.

Givens cast one last contemptuous glare at Cynthia Robbins and jogged off to find his Speed.

"If you're free now, Lieutenant, perhaps we could have that meeting we scheduled," Raeder suggested mildly.

Robbins glanced at the engine her people were working on. Her obvious desire to pitch in was plain on her face.

"Lieutenant," Peter prompted.

"Yes, sir. Of course."

Raeder, Robbins, and arap Moi headed off for Peter's office. Peter studied Robbins surreptitiously as they walked along.

Her dark hair was cut no-nonsense short and the habitual glower she wore did nothing for her, either.

But she was, on second glance, rather pretty. She had a nice clear profile, a neat little pointed chin, and large, lustrous brown eyes that would have made up for a slew of other defects, but didn't have to.

It was immediately apparent, though, that Robbins was not a woman who projected self-confidence. Her movements were awkward, almost gawky, and though her posture was upright enough—the military had no doubt seen to that—her head drooped on her neck like a flower dying of thirst.

They didn't speak until Raeder, pulling his chair up to his desk, said, "Why don't we spend a few minutes on this kerfuffle with the squadron leader."

"We are not deliberately singling Givens out, sir," arap Moi said immediately.

"I would like to hear from the lieutenant first, Chief," Raeder said quietly.

Robbins bit her lip and her frown grew more thunderous, while her hands, which she held clasped in her lap, grew white at the knuckles.

Peter glanced at the chief, then shifted in his chair.

As though the movement had prompted her, she said, "Like the chief says, we're not picking on him. The problems are there."

"Usually," arap Moi said.

Robbins threw him a look of shocked betrayal. She paused, biting her lower lip, still not meeting Raeder's eyes, and with a shrug, continued. "One time it was a crack in a feed tube, and not really a hairline fracture, either, but a damn big one. Last time it was disequilibrium in one of the magnetic containment bottles of the fusion generator."

Peter leaned forward. "But that's not a part failure," he said quietly.

"No, sir." She shifted nervously. "The problems we've been having aren't always."

How did this woman ever get to be a lieutenant? Raeder asked himself. She might be a talented technician, but based on this interview so far, she had no business being in charge of people.

Aloud he said: "Feel free to volunteer information, Lieutenant. If I have to ask for everything we'll be here all day. And none of us has time for that. What other kinds of problems have you been having?"

"What I've mentioned, and scrambled electronics. We've had some very strange AI failures. All without warning. I realize that battle stress, heck, even just flying will cause some of these problems. But the sheer volume of them is extraordinary." For the first time she looked up at Raeder, then quickly looked away, her cheeks flaming.

"Is Givens' craft more likely than most to have problems?" he asked.

"I'd have to check my books to be sure, sir. But I'd say yes. Marginally."

"So you check him out more carefully than you might otherwise?"

She looked confused for a moment, then the frown came down again. Still she appeared to give it a moment's thought.

"Perhaps," she conceded.

"Then maybe you're being overly cautious," he suggested.

Robbins started shaking her head before he'd finished speaking. "No, sir. The problems were there. Check my reports, ask the techs, they'll confirm what I'm telling you. I did not shut down Lieutenant Givens for a whim. The problems were real." She glared across the desk at Peter, real anger blazing in her brown eyes. "I don't play games," she proclaimed.

I wonder, Raeder thought. She was coming across as exactly the kind of person who played games. Games like deliberately damaging parts and then claiming they were defective, or claiming someone's Speed needed repair and then making damn sure it did. His predecessor hadn't said much about Robbins beyond the universal observation that she was a genius at engineering and a flop with people. Of course, they'd only worked together for about a month before he died.

Would Okakura have been writing something a lot more critical about her if he'd lived?

Something wasn't right here. Larkin claimed his parts were good; Givens said his bird could fly. Things passed through the lieutenant's hands and suddenly everything was garbage. *If she's a genius at fixing,* Peter thought, *maybe she's a genius at breaking things, too.*

Heck, his little adventure on *Africa* told him how easy it was to fake damage. *And how easy it is to get away with it.* Of course he had a little range when it came to facial expressions and was convinced that his "choirboy" look had helped carry him through.

Angry and resentful seem to be little Cynthia's entire repertoire. No, I lie, he thought as her expression changed slightly, *she could be the demo model for sullen.* Raeder felt an almost irresistible urge to pin the blame on the unpleasant young woman before him. He suppressed it as unworthy and also because she had arap Moi's support. *And I was prepared to respect his judgment before I ever laid eyes on him.*

"Well," he said aloud, "we've got too much to cover

in this meeting to dwell on the lieutenant's misfortunes. But in the future, if his Speed is going to be down, I want another up and ready for him. Understood?"

"Yes, sir," both Robbins and the chief answered.

They bent to their work with a will, but in the back of Raeder's mind a small voice insisted that the lieutenant and the chief might well be allies.

Oh, hell, he answered it, *I can't suspect everybody, or I'll never get to the bottom of this. Next thing you know the only two people I'll be able to trust are me and the captain.* And of course, how could he be sure of the captain? *Better stick to the evidence,* he advised himself. *If I only had some.*

Wait a minute! He did have some. The records of defective parts received. *Of course, Larkin's records will show them to be good.* Which meant that one of the quartermaster's people, or maybe one of Raeder's, or John himself, or someone, somewhere . . . or maybe everybody, everywhere was guilty. *Well, that was a short trip through futility,* Peter thought in disgust. *Clearly I have a gift for narrowing things down. I must thank Captain Knott for giving me the opportunity to discover it.*

"Sir?" arap Moi asked uncertainly.

"Sorry, Chief, I was in a brown study." He tapped a finger against his mouth. "From what Lieutenant Larkin tells us, the parts he receives are good. But from the time they leave his hands to the time we receive them they somehow become defective. Any thoughts on that?" Raeder looked from arap Moi to Robbins.

"I thought at first," the CPO said, "that maybe they were getting rough handling from some inexperienced people. So I thought things would get better after awhile." He shook his head. "But they've gotten steadily worse. And I now know that there are no inexperienced people on this ship."

Raeder nodded. "I've noticed that, too." He allowed himself a mental sigh as he looked at Robbins, who was sitting stiffly in her chair, apparently miles away. *And having a good sulk wherever she is,* he thought. *Well, that answers my question. She's definitely not a team player.*

"Lieutenant," he prompted. She looked up. "Do you have any thoughts on the matter that you'd like to contribute?"

She paused for a moment, apparently holding her breath. Then she took the plunge, her words coming out in a rush. "Other than observing that Lieutenant Larkin would like to blame me for the problem, no, sir. I have no idea where or when our parts are becoming defective."

"Denying that he is responsible is not the same as saying that you are, Lieutenant. But I've taken note of your point." *Paranoid as it is.* She'd lowered her eyes again and he studied her for a moment. She was about twenty-one standard years old, a mere baby seen from his mountain of twenty-seven years. She also seemed rather beaten. *And everyone's been yelling at her and blaming her for what's going wrong. Then they yelled at her for trying to fix it.* And of course, she'd never expected to be in charge of five hundred people as well as the technical side of things. *So all in all, the poor kid's had a very tough row to hoe.*

Of course as an officer in the Commonwealth Space Command, she should be able to do a lot of hoeing before she got this downtrodden. Still, people joined the force for all sorts of reasons. *And I doubt hers was to look for the fast track to power and glory.*

In spite of everything she was doing to prevent it, somehow Raeder found himself liking her. She seemed to be *trying* to live up to the position she'd found herself in. *The only thing is there's this nagging thought she could have created the situation that put her in that position.*

"Well," he said, rising, "I think I should take a tour of Main Deck and start meeting the people."

Robbins and arap Moi rose also.

"Would you mind if the chief escorted—" Robbins began.

"Yes," Raeder said, cutting her off. "You're going to be my second, Lieutenant Robbins. We're going to have to learn to work together. Besides, I want a technical rundown on our facilities, and I think that you're the right person to give it to me."

"Yes, sir."

"Don't worry, Lieutenant, it's not going to be that bad. I just got out of school and I had really good marks."

He thought she almost smiled, and glanced at arap Moi.

The chief's eyes twinkled and he mouthed the word, *"Bully."*

That's "Bully, sir," to you, Chief, Raeder thought.

CHAPTER FIVE

Raeder had grown used to eating in solitary splendor in the officers' mess while the *Invincible* was in Transit. Peacetime luxuries like steward service were left to admirals and other Echelons Beyond Reality these days, but the mess was really quite nice—someone had already put in a series of murals, pleasantly old-fashioned stuff, lunar landscapes and views of Saturn's rings. On a new ship the smells of food and coffee were just beginning to overpower those of drying sealant and synthetics, both enjoyable to a spacer. He was used to tucking away more than his share of the better-than-average chow. He smiled, remembering yesterday, nodding benevolently at a neighbor as he loaded his plate with sausage, ham, eggs, shiny fried potatoes . . .

The neighbor shut her eyes and tried to stop breathing, a piece of dry toast halfway to her lips.

It must be awful, he'd thought at the time, *to have to cook for hundreds when the very thought of food makes you ill.* Especially since all anyone else wanted was maybe some dry toast.

Not *this* morning though. They'd come out of Transit last night and today everyone was making up for lost meals. Almost the only thing *left* was dry toast, and the tables were packed elbow to elbow. The dispensing line was empty because everyone had already been through.

Peter sighed and took some toast—not even whole wheat—as well as a desiccated sausage patty and the teaspoonful of scrambled eggs he'd managed to scrape out of the warming pan. *I should have come earlier,* he thought sadly. It stood to reason that everyone would be hungry. *And I don't think I'll get much sympathy if I complain.*

He sat down beside the quartermaster, who looked at his plate and smirked. "I was going to take that, but thought I ought to leave you something."

"Y'know, John," Peter said, looking at the three juicy patties on Larkin's plate, "it's not a good idea to eat such rich food after a fast."

"Get your eyes off my plate, Raeder," Larkin growled, moving his tray a little further from Peter's. "You've had first, second, and third pick for the last two days. Now it's back to every man for himself."

Peter glanced across the table at Ashly Luhrman, who looked up from her cloud of scrambled eggs with the eyes of a tigress defending her young.

"The same goes with me," the young astrogator said, "only double."

"Good morning, Lieutenant," Raeder said mildly.

She returned her attention to her plate with a soft, feline warning sound.

"Jeeez, guys, I'm not going to try to take the food off your plates," Peter said, wide-eyed. *But I* am *gonna be here first for lunch.* Which shouldn't be hard since

the rest of *Invincible*'s officers had a strenuous day
ahead of them, while all he had to do was monitor
everyone else and keep his Speeds in a state of perfect readiness.

Their two-day Transit had brought them to the
Commonwealth's main firing range. Today *Invincible*'s
weapons would be live-fired for the first time, and
given the extraordinary failure rate of much of their
equipment, the tension in the mess was thick enough
to chew.

In fact, Raeder thought, forlornly watching the
champing jaws of his fellow officers, *it's about all there
is to chew.*

"So," he said cheerfully, "everybody ready?"

"Ready as we'll ever be," Augie Skinner said laconi-
cally, not even interrupting the rhythm of his eating.

"Easy for you to say," Truon Le commented with
a grin. "The hardest part's over for you," he said, referring to their high-speed cruise through the Antares
System and their Transit jump to the firing range. "It's
tactical that'll be getting a workout today."

Augie pointed his fork at the tactical officer. "An
engineer's work is never over. Right, Raeder?"

"Absolutely, Skinner."

"Anytime I tell you my work's finished," the chief
engineer went on to Truon Le, "it means I'm retiring."

"Gotcha," Truon Le said, smiling.

"Sometimes I think that guy's from another dimen-
sion," Larkin whispered to Raeder. He shook his blond
head. "I mean, I like to think I'm dedicated, but I
can get up from my desk and say, that's it, day's over."

"Yeah," Raeder said softly. "But the crew's not
endangered if you forget to order fava beans."

"Well, I'd like to agree with you, but unless you've

ever faced a frustrated fava bean aficionado, well," Larkin shrugged his shoulders eloquently, "there's just no way to describe the carnage."

"I'm off," Truon Le said, rising. "Good luck, everybody."

"Luck," they all said. One by one they finished their massive breakfasts and left to prepare for the day, until only Raeder and Larkin were left.

"I feel guilty," Larkin said. "The hardest part of my job *is* done."

He was referring to the massive job of ordering and storing the thousands of items needed to run a ship the size of *Invincible*. Outside of a combat situation, dispensing them was nearly automatic.

"While mine probably won't really begin until tomorrow," Raeder agreed. "But we both have to be on standby."

The quartermaster snorted derisively. "Yeah, you never know what the Old Man will do. I just don't see him calling for an emergency inventory in the heat of battle."

"We also serve who only stand and wait," Raeder quoted. He gave the quartermaster a sideways look. "You *do* have fava beans, I trust."

"Not only do we have fava beans," Larkin said rising, "we have the new, improved, laser-guided, homing fava beans. A bean so explosive it will bring the Mollies to their knees!"

"I take it these are a weapon of last resort?" Peter asked in mock awe, pressing his napkin to his chest.

Larkin looked him in the eye with holovid seriousness. "Who knows what the Old Man might call for."

"Gosh," Raeder said, and gulped the last of his coffee, "I'm sure glad I'm on our side."

Down on Main Deck, Lieutenant Robbins was having a coot; dancing around and swearing, tugging at something on her overall. Raeder called up a closer view on his office monitor and grinned. *Well, that's a classic.* Someone had put a dab of hull sealant in the bottom of one of the tool pouches clipped to her working uniform and wrapped it in thinplas. Standard procedure—for which Robbins was a known stickler— was to slide every tool in and out of its holder at the beginning of a watch. The point of a multitool had punched the thinplas, and now it was indissolubly bound to the fabric . . .

And Robbins would have to run back to her quarters and change. No real damage, of course. He had to back her up, of course. Peter touched a relay on the control surface in front of him.

"Arap Moi! I want the name of the person responsible for this and put them on report. No skylarking in wartime!"

Actually it was a welcome sign of good morale.

The office above Main Deck had a feed slaved to the bridge; he keyed it back and sat, his eyes glued to the monitor showing the bridge's activities, while his own people worked without his supervision. He watched and listened tensely as the *Invincible* came up on her first target, an irregularly shaped asteroid a good twelve hundred meters long. *It's almost ship-shaped,* Raeder thought. He wondered just how they were going to attack it. They were a little too close to use missiles without risking at least some damage to the ship's sensors. *Though it would make a beautiful explosion,* he thought.

"Target acquired," Truon Le intoned.

"Fire on my mark," the captain said. "Mark."

Suddenly the ship's forward laser stabbed at the target. The beam was invisible in vacuum, but as nickel-iron sublimed away into space, it glared red through the scattering mist; even reduced by filters it was still hard to look at as it neatly sliced its way down the center of the asteroid. The two halves drifted slowly apart, the molten rock down their lengths cooling to gray almost instantly.

"Following vector, Mr. Goldberg," the captain ordered.

"Vector entered, aye," the helmsman answered.

"Targets acquired," Truon Le said again.

"Fire on my mark," Captain Knott said quietly.

The two sides of the asteroid were already a hundred kilometers apart by now, though on the screen they appeared to be separated by only a few yards. The captain held his peace, doubtless waiting for a more significant separation to see if his people could hold their targets.

Finally, Knott said, "Fire." And all twelve of the starboard antiship lasers fired simultaneously, hitting the two long pieces of asteroid crosswise. Twelve red lances struck cold rock and sliced through it like butter, and the pieces tumbled apart as spurting gas gave them unpredictable trajectories along the asteroid's former orbit.

"Stand by to reverse vectors," the captain ordered.

"Aye, sir," Helm answered.

Raeder watched the corner of the screen showing the target, anticipating a change of viewpoint as the *Invincible* swung around to bring her larboard laser cannon to bear.

"Reverse vectors," Knott said.

"Reversing vectors, aye," Goldberg announced.

Raeder noticed a brief lull in the background noise that the ship's engines provided as they cut power to everything but the thrusters which would turn her as she coasted. On the screen he saw a constantly shifting perspective of the massive, broken asteroid as external cameras compensated for the ship's change of position relative to its target. Finally the angle stabilized, but they continued to drift away from the asteroid and it grew steadily smaller. Then a surge of the engines stopped *Invincible*'s backward motion and with the briefest of pauses pushed her forward again.

I always think I should feel something when we do that, Peter thought. In a Speed, which lacked the *Invincible*'s gravitational compensators, he would have. *Something annoyingly lacking in the tactile department here,* Raeder mused, and he shook himself hard to make up for it. On the other hand, nothing big enough to mount compensators could rival a Speed's power-to-weight ratio.

As they approached the target, Knott calmly said, "Larboard laser cannon, prepare to fire. Fire," he said immediately.

Raeder chuckled. He was willing to bet there was at least one gunner who'd been expecting a long pause. In fact, one of the shots was so wild you'd have thought whoever manned it was out of their chair.

"We appear to have a misfire," the captain drawled.

We do, indeed, Raeder agreed.

"Sir," said a woman's voice, which, though calm, fairly bled with embarrassment. No doubt she was one of the gun maintenance crew. "We've found the problem in laser placement eighteen. A part of the targeting sensor was put in backwards. It passed the sims, and didn't show in the diagnostics because it wasn't interfering with the gun's function. We've replaced the board."

"Why don't we test it one more time," the captain said after a pregnant pause. "Choose your target."

"Yessir." There was the briefest of pauses, then, "Target acquired, sir."

"Fire," Knott barked.

Red light flashed out and sliced a chunk of asteroid in half.

"Fire," the captain said again. And again the laser cannon hit its target squarely. "Fire," Knott snapped. Another chunk of asteroid was reduced. "Looks like you've got that puppy under control," the captain drawled, the barest trace of satisfaction in his voice. "Now let's give our missile batteries a workout."

They kept at it until that asteroid was sand.

Whew! Raeder thought. *Show no mer-say.*

He grinned in appreciation. Through the whole, long afternoon they'd maneuvered and attacked, firing until Raeder could have sworn the whole ship felt hotter. *Well, we are hot. Hottest shots this side of the galaxy.* He slapped his desk, still smiling. *Damn if we're not.* At least when it came to defenseless asteroids, he had to admit. The only glitch in the whole exercise had been that one laser miss. He shook his head. *This is one hell of a fine crew,* he thought, eyes shining. Then he pulled a wry expression. *And tomorrow will bring me the opportunity to show what my people are made of.* This was a carrier, after all. The beam weapons and missiles were backup; the main striking force was the Speeds.

Okakura's death and Cindy's harangues had brought

his bunch to the verge of a collective nervous break-down. They were jumpy and grim when she was around, and jumpy and given to the blackest of humor when she wasn't.

To her credit, the lieutenant seemed obsessed with solving the many problems the unit was facing, rather than simply throwing her weight around. But good intentions didn't go far in mitigating the effects of her constant criticism. Morale was in the cellar in Flight Engineering Section, and that was a tenth of *Invincible's* crew; pilots aside, perhaps the most impor-tant tenth.

Raeder had made a point in his first week of memo-rizing the names, faces, and functions of his people to the confusion and amazement of his second.

"Did you serve with all of these people?" Robbins had asked, after he'd greeted the fourth person she hadn't yet introduced him to by name.

"No," he'd said with a deprecating laugh. "I got it from the personnel files."

"You memorized their names?" she'd exclaimed, as astonished as if he'd told her he'd read their minds.

Raeder shook his head at the memory. *Here's a woman who can name every part of a Speed off the top of her head. And she doesn't know the names of more than four of the people she works with.* In fact, as far as he could tell, to Cynthia Robbins the entire crew were interchangeable parts, as individual as a pound of penny nails. *And about as human.*

He sighed. There'd been definite progress, he allowed. Morale had improved perceptibly since his arrival and Cindy herself had become marginally less grumpy and reclusive. Raeder had also made his people go through the mountain of discarded parts that had accumulated and repair those they could. A depressingly small number, given the state of his department's budget. Fractures and curiously mangled components had been the main problems, most of them near invisible to the naked eye.

Another reason to respect the lieutenant's skill, he reflected. *Or to doubt her integrity, if that's your pleasure.* And truth to tell, he honestly couldn't decide.

Anyway, he thought shutting down his terminal, *the squadron is as ready as she'll ever be.* Every Speed checked and rechecked, his people drilled to a fare-thee-well. *There's always the unexpected to watch out for,* he thought, knocking on the little piece of wood he kept on his desk for luck, *but we've covered all the bases we can.*

Today was going to be a hard act to follow, though, particularly coming from behind as they were. *But, y'know, I think we're gonna surprise everybody,* Raeder thought confidently. *We're gonna blow 'em away.*

The *Invincible*'s first operational cruise had been easy street for Raeder and his people until now. The captain's anxiously awaited order to fly the squadron had finally been given, and the flight deck was so palpably relieved you could practically see a giant happy face manifesting. Men and women scrambled to and fro at top speed, creating a scene of polished efficiency combined with total chaos, each of them behaving as though they were alone on the deck. Yet by some miracle, no collisions took place, no one tripped and fell, everyone reached their preordained place and performed their task, moving on to the next as though they were more than human. Carts and overhead cranes rumbled, and there was a faint scent of ozone and sealant in the air.

Even so, Speeds were fueled in less than record time, Raeder noted with displeasure as he watched a crew leaping balletically as they attached the restraints and hoses. But the work was competently done, and while not as fast as he would have liked, it certainly wasn't a disgrace to the outfit. Not that he'd tell the petty officer in charge that. After all, this is why they had drills—to put the crew through their paces to measure performance against expectations.

Truth is, Raeder thought happily, *my expectations were too low. I have got some* top *people here.* And they could and would be better next time.

Raeder was in his cubby overlooking the flight deck, watching his monitors and listening to and advising various sections as they went about their business, growing more smug by the minute. Until the squadron leader patched himself through with the solemn announcement, "She's doing it again, Raeder."

"On my way," Raeder replied.

No need to identify who "she" was.

A few minutes later he approached the eye of this minor tempest to hear Robbins bellow, "My machinery *is* calibrated!"

Robbins, shouting at an officer? Peter thought in disbelief. "What's going on?" Raeder asked calmly.

Three red faces and arap Moi's black one turned to him with varying expressions of appeal.

"Your second is refusing to let Givens fly," Squadron Leader Sutton growled. "Not that there's anything specifically wrong, mind you. It seems there's a mysterious 'spike' on her monitor."

"Y'ask me, the only spike around here's the one in her head, Commander. She just doesn't like me for some reason." Givens looked from Robbins to Raeder with a glowering sneer.

What a weird expression, Raeder thought. *Doubles the offense without actually looking demented.* He gave Sutton a meaningful look, one that demanded he rein in his boy.

Sutton, with rather ill grace, muttered, "Mind your manners, Givens. We're all Space Command here."

"Sorry, sir," Givens said politely, simultaneously directing a sneer at Lieutenant Robbins. "But the two times there has been something wrong with my Speed it showed clearly on the diagnostics. Every time I was grounded for some mystery reason nothing was ever wrong, even after they tore my machine apart. So if I'm a little unimpressed by the lieutenant's instincts and diagnostic flukes, I don't think you can really blame me."

Then both pilots turned accusing eyes on Raeder, while Robbins simply looked at the deck, obviously expecting to be overridden.

Oh, great, Peter thought. *I feel like a single father whose two sons are mad at their sister. Of course, Robbins* does *keep taking their toys apart, so it could be a male psychology thing. Hmmm.*

"The lieutenant raises a good point, Commander," Sutton said. "Six out of eight times that Givens has been denied the use of his Speed, tearing it apart down to the shell revealed no hardware or software problems at all. And to make it even more peculiar, these mystery problems only indicate themselves in the half hour before we're to fly a mission. Now," Sutton adjusted his stance, his eyes never leaving

Raeder's, "I'll just say that something isn't right here, and that I don't think it's mechanical."

Raeder was taken aback. Givens was obviously a jackass, but Sutton had impressed him as being rather a stable type. Certainly not the kind who made rash statements in front of witnesses.

"We obviously have things to discuss," Peter conceded, "but I don't think this is the appropriate time."

The squadron leader closed his eyes slowly, as though hanging on to his temper by a thread.

"You're absolutely right, Commander Raeder, this is a poor time for a debate. So I won't give you one. But if Givens doesn't fly with us today, I don't see how we can fly at all."

"*What?*" Raeder couldn't believe his ears. Sutton was carrying this thing much too far; he couldn't not fly the squadron because one Speed was down. That was like volunteering to be court-martialed. *What is this, some kind of test?* This was another thing he hadn't expected from Sutton, the kind of macho brinksmanship stupidity that forced a bad choice on someone.

"I mean what I say," Sutton said quietly. He looked like he meant it, too. In the background, Givens looked like a gaffed fish.

"Well, Squadron Leader," Raeder said, leaning in close, "what I'm going to do is check out this craft. And if there's anything wrong with it, this bird will not fly. What you choose to do about that is up to you. But my conscience will be clear." Sutton thinned his lips, but said nothing. "Show me what the problem is, would you, Lieutenant?" he asked Robbins.

She immediately scrambled up the steep, narrow ramp that led inside the Speed. Looking at their smooth, melted shapes maneuvering in space you forgot the hulking, massive menace they had at close range. This one was still factory-burnished, the cermet synthetic of the skin without the minuscule pitmarks that came from high-speed maneuvers through the "dirty" vacuum near large ships with their inescapable, multitudinous microleaks.

"It's in the cockpit," she said over her slender shoulder.

He followed her up and crouched beside her where she sat in the pilot's seat, stifling a touch of envy over her easy assumption of that chair. The little pang of grief never seemed to go away.

"It appears to be in the master AI," she was saying. The lieutenant pulled out her diagnostic unit. "When I set up a combat simulation situation, such as Givens will be flying—" she showed him the simulation program she'd chosen, and when he nodded she started it running "—I get this."

Raeder took the unit she offered, and on one of its screens there was a sudden spike in an area that should have been dormant. There was a flat line across the screen and the spike had been a bright spark gone almost before he could register what it was. Had not Robbins pointed it out to him, Raeder knew he probably would have missed it.

"What does the AI say about it?" he asked.

"That it's unaware of any problem," she said. "But you know what they're like—they're intelligent only in the narrowest possible definition of the word."

Like some . . . like a lot of people I've known, Raeder thought gloomily.

"Frankly," she continued, "I think it's a software problem that's going to take a specific set of circumstances to bring to light. Since I don't know what that spike represents, my inclination is to treat it as dangerous." And she looked at him expectantly.

Almost as though she's forgotten to be wary, Raeder thought. That had been the most she'd said to him in the time he'd known her. *Or maybe she's trying to make me forget to be wary. Though she always seems to feel a lot more in control when she's discussing Speeds.* Well, he could understand that. Still. *This isn't the Cindy I've come to know and wonder about.*

"Have you checked your instrument?" he asked.

"That's the CPO's unit," she said, a stiff defensiveness creeping back into her voice. "The first thing I did was cross-check with someone else."

Raeder grimaced. There'd been so much to do this week. He'd wanted to have the machines that calibrated the diagnostic units checked, but there'd been no time.

"I've been wondering about these," he told her. "If the main unit we check them against is flawed, then they're all skewed the same way. It's possible that what we're seeing here is a fluke in our units instead of in the Speeds or their parts."

Robbins shook her head a couple of times, then stopped and looked at him, started to say something, then shut her mouth and looked away.

"If you send Givens out in this Speed, sir, I want it on record that it was done over my protest."

Raeder blinked at that. *That's coming at it a little strong,* he thought. *What is it with everybody today? Is this lay your career on the line day and nobody told me?* Then he felt a brief chill at the back of his neck. Did she know something? Did she *do* something? *Now I'm worried.* If he had another Speed to send Givens out in he'd do it in a flash, but there wasn't one. This was a full scramble and every Speed had a pilot. *Although at the moment, thanks to this, it's a scramble going forward in slow motion. In fact, I think it's going backwards.*

"Noted," he said sharply. "But based on a single spike that doesn't seem to lead anywhere I can't justify grounding this Speed. Get me arap Moi, please, I want to check this out myself and I want to check it with your unit." With that he turned awkwardly in the small space and duck-walked to where he could stand. Robbins brushed past him and left the Speed, and Peter instantly hustled himself into the pilot's chair.

He ran through the Speed's internal diagnostics while he waited for the CPO, even his right hand flashed through the familiar motions without mishap.

"Sir," arap Moi said as he fitted himself into the small cockpit to kneel at Raeder's side.

"Have you seen this spike the lieutenant found?" Raeder asked.

"Yes, sir."

"What do you make of it?"

The CPO chewed on his lower lip for a moment, then shook his head. "I honestly don't know, sir. As the lieutenant says, it's probably a software problem, but whether it's dangerous or not . . ." He shrugged, his expression perplexed. "Until we've tested it, we can't know for sure."

Raeder rested his chin on his left hand and thought. Was this extreme caution just the same paranoia he'd been getting since he arrived, particularly in relation to the comps? Considering the previous commander's crispy end as a result of a faulty AI, it was understandable, but dammit it was getting in the way.

"Have you ever seen anything like this before, Chief?"

"Uh . . . yes, sir, I have."

Raeder just looked at him expectantly. "And?" he prompted after a moment.

"And it was just a little glitch that made a jig in the diagnostic," arap Moi admitted. "It happened every time we booted a combat sim." He grinned. "I sorta thought it was like an adrenaline spike," he said.

"Chief, you're—"

"Anthropomorphizing, I know. But that Speed had a very excitable pilot. I sort of thought the AI was imitating her."

"You think Givens is that excitable?" Raeder raised a dubious brow.

The chief rubbed his chin briskly and shook his head. "Well, he's no bandicoot, but he ain't no nun, either. And, anyway, that doesn't mean—"

"That this spike means the same thing," Peter finished for him. "Still, we've checked it out on two diagnostic units, we checked the AI, we've run the ships internal diagnostics, and all we've got is a little hop in a sine wave." He tapped his fingers on his armrest impatiently. "Is there anything else you can think of short of a major overhaul?"

"No, sir," the CPO said.

"Neither can I." Raeder firmed his lips. Decision time. There really didn't appear to be anything significant wrong with this machine. *Significant, hell. There doesn't seem to be anything wrong with it at all.* On the other hand, Cindy was acting all spooky. And on the third hand, it looked like the whole fighter squadron would rebel if he grounded the lieutenant for this reason. And he was pretty sure that further tests would show nothing wrong. *Just like Lieutenant Givens says they always do.* Maybe this was Robbins' way of showing she liked the guy. Raeder suppressed a snort. He gave the girl credit for better taste. Her interest was in his Speed, not the lieutenant.

"Let Givens have it," he decided, and slid out of the pilot's seat.

Sutton and Givens were crowded around the base of the ramp wearing the grim, defiant expressions of men determined to have their own way. Raeder paused. *Sort of makes me want to disappoint them,* he thought.

"Well?" Sutton said icily.

"There's definitely something there," Raeder told them. Givens rolled not only his eyes, but rotated his whole head in silent exasperation. "It appears to be a glitch in the AI programming." Peter watched Givens with a gimlet eye. "But we won't be able to tell what it means without extensive tests."

"Aw! Maaaann!" Givens exclaimed. "She set it up, man!"

"Don't whine at me, Lieutenant!" Raeder snapped. "And in case no one has ever informed you, there is no branch of the service where a lieutenant may address a superior officer as 'man.'"

Givens' head snapped back as if he'd been slapped.

"Heat of the moment," the squadron leader murmured.

"Lack of discipline," Raeder countered precisely. "Just because I've been a pilot doesn't mean I'm going to forget my rank. And I'll tell you both something right here, right now. If I had a thread to hang it on I wouldn't let this Speed out of here. But I don't. Even so, it's going out under protest. I strongly advise you to let us hold this Speed back," he said to the squadron leader.

"Ridiculous!" Sutton exclaimed. "Three of you experts have looked it over and you can't find anything actually wrong, can you?"

Raeder shook his head reluctantly.

"Well, then, very likely, as in all the other cases of phantom problems with this particular Speed, closer examination will reveal nothing wrong. I say she flies," Sutton said, and set his jaw in a stubborn line.

"It's on your head, Sutton, and yours," Raeder said turning to Givens, "if something goes wrong."

Sutton simply gazed back at him, tight-lipped.

"Except nothing is going to go wrong, sir," Givens said in a carefully modulated voice. He brushed around Raeder and sneered down at Robbins, who stood at the commander's shoulder.

"There *is* something wrong with this Speed," she said impulsively, and her brown eyes pleaded for him to believe her.

"The only thing *wrong* with this Speed, Lieutenant, is that it's going out when you don't want it to." Givens awarded her a disgusted look, then climbed into the belly of his Speed.

"Not good form," Sutton muttered to Raeder, his eyes bright with anger, "to castigate a brother officer in front of one of his men."

True, Raeder thought, *not that I'm prepared to admit it.*

"We should discuss this later," he said coldly. *Like the day donkeys fly out of your butt.* "When we have less to do," he added significantly.

Sutton nodded, spared a glare for Robbins, and trotted off to his own Speed.

"Thank you for backing me up, sir," Robbins said shyly.

Raeder froze the expression on his face before his shock could show.

"I'd have grounded him if we'd had more evidence, Lieutenant," he said, and was a little surprised to find he meant it. "But Givens was right. All but two of the times you've held him back based on something this slight nothing was ever found to be wrong. And given his insistence that you were only doing it to persecute him . . ." He shrugged. "Those are conditions that are ripe for a board of inquiry."

He looked around at the bustle in the cavernous launching hangar and shook his head. "We've lost this one, but it's sure not your fault."

"I hope I'm wrong," she said, looking sorrowful. "But I don't think I am, sir."

The way she said it gave Raeder the willies.

"In any case," he said briskly, "we have a lot to do right now. But as soon as possible we're going over the diagnostic machines."

"Yes, sir."

The klaxon rang to clear the deck for launch and everyone swept into motion, diving for the crash doors, hauling their portable equipment with them.

Then they were gone and the giant room seemed to hold its breath, the huge machines the men and women of Space Command had labored over stood poised for action. Another klaxon sounded and the great doors in *Invincible*'s side slowly lifted, opening Main Deck to the cosmos. The Speeds in their rows began to tremble as their pilots powered up, almost expectantly, like thoroughbreds at a starting gate.

Paths of lights rippled across the decking. Magfields

gripped and thrust, and the first wave of three Speeds were hurled forward with shocking force, dwindling from full size to dots in less time than it took to draw a full breath, then vanishing. Another wave and another, soundless and all the more intimidating for that. Raeder felt his eyes prickle at the glory of it, at the memory of acceleration crushing him back and the universe opening before him in a cold splendor of multicolored stars.

CHAPTER SIX

Peter watched his Speeds go. Simulated Attack Mode, launching at crash-emergency rates, and everything had to be *perfect*. The results of a screw-up in a crash launch sequence just didn't bear thinking about. At the velocities involved, even the AI's couldn't possibly react in time to prevent a disaster.

"Smooth," he said aloud, letting his crews hear it. "Pretty damned smooth . . . for a trial run. We'll need to do better in combat, of course."

Jeez, the last time I was this nervous was the day I walked my kid sister down the aisle. He'd been filling in for his father, to whom Debbie refused even to speak. There wasn't a person in the room he hadn't known all his life; even so, he'd been shaking. *Of course that might have been due to the fact that my aunts were visibly cranking up for the dreaded, "Well, you're next" speech.*

He walked into the Flight Engineering briefing room. His department heads were already there, riveted by the events on the screen. All you could hear in a room filled by thirty people was the voice of flight control and breathing.

When the last Speed exited the flight deck and the space doors began to close, they all burst out with a spontaneous cheer.

"As if you didn't know it," Raeder said with a grin, "well done, people. And pass my congratulations on to the troops; they've done a great job."

There was a short burst of applause and Raeder was slightly taken aback. He wasn't used to having his remarks received with such an outpouring of enthusiasm. *Well, I doubt they'll appreciate my next comments as much.*

"We *were* a little slow out there today, and we're definitely going to have to work on that." Heads nodded gravely and Peter was pleased to see it. *Hey, suddenly I feel like applauding.* There was nothing worse than having to first convince people that they could be better, before you could begin actually making them do better.

They settled down for a quick debriefing before everyone returned to the work of preparing for the squadron's return. The Speeds' exercise would take approximately four hours. An hour of that was allowed for transit time, and Peter wanted to go over the morning's work while the details were still fresh in everyone's minds. So they spent the first hour of their downtime vigorously evaluating performance.

When they broke off their meeting, Raeder was feeling pleasantly smug and ready for anything.

Peter hurried into his office cubby and set his audio and one of his monitors for the Squadron's mock dogfight. He hadn't been going to do this. He'd told himself it would be masochistic, because he knew himself well enough to realize it would hurt, at some level, not to be out there and part of the action.

But I just have *to know what kind of leader Sutton is.* He thought the squadron leader would be one of the best, based on his staunch support of Givens. And Raeder knew that if he were assigned to a Leader who backed him that way, he'd have followed the man anywhere. *But is that feeling justified? Is he as good in a Speed as he is on the ground?* There was a universe of difference between the two.

The squadron was too far away and too dispersed to actually be shown on the ship's monitors. The computers had created a simulation map which indicated their speed, direction, and distance from the ship along the margins of the screen. On the bridge it was an enormous holo-map, which showed their motion in three dimensions, with twisting cones showing possible vectors. In the confines of Raeder's office cubby that complex display was squashed under the flat screen of his monitor, giving him a confusing mass of blips and their ID numbers.

The screen was almost unreadable, but Peter was an old hand at untangling the mess before him and making sense of it. The squadron had broken into two parts for the exercise, blue and green, and the dots on the screen were displayed in those colors.

Raeder grinned at that. In his time everyone had wanted to be in Red Squadron. It had created such bad feelings that finally the powers that be decided to eliminate Red from games like these. *An unusually sage idea,* Raeder thought approvingly. But then, he'd always been picked for Red, so he could afford to be generous.

He watched the screen intently and listened to the

crisp command and response of the pilots. Raeder's mind created the three-dimensional image the screen only hinted at. His mind's eye saw the fuzz of stars burning in the distance, sensed the presence of his fellow pilots around him, just as Sutton and the others must.

Peter shook his head. *Whoa, boy! Let's not get too into it,* and he forced his mind to simply evaluate the marks crawling across the monitor. And he was riveted. They were good! Sutton was an excellent leader and his people were terrific fliers. Even Givens, whom Raeder had secretly hoped would be cockier than was called for, proved to be a superb pilot. *No wonder Sutton wanted him along.*

He settled down to enjoy the exercise with a connoisseur's appreciation. In a Speed you were the fastest thing in space, or at least the most maneuverable . . . except for a seeker missile, or a laser, or a plasma burst. Seekers you could detect coming at you, but the load from an energy weapon arrived faster than any possible sensor reading. You had to have a *feel* for what was going to happen, something no AI did; that was why pilots were worth the extra weight of life-support systems, despite the fact that they couldn't take as many gravities as a computer.

Givens settled himself a little deeper in his seat, a hidden sign of his deep satisfaction with the way things were going. His handsome face was almost serene in its concentration as he smoothly made his turn on his teammate's wing. *And they wanted to ground me,* he thought sarcastically.

He looked less handsome with a sneer. Not that anyone could have seen it; the suit reduced him to a smooth-edged outline, like a clay model of a human being, and most of that was hidden by the petal-like restraints that held and cushioned him.

For just a moment he allowed his thoughts to dwell on the rather weird Lieutenant Robbins. She was kinda cute in an intense sort of way. *Maybe this is her way of getting my attention,* he thought and smirked. *She sure isn't the type I usually go for.* He wondered idly if he was disposed to give the little geek a chance. *Or should I report her for sexual harassment?* He chuckled. *Tough call.*

"Hey, buddy," his teammate, Apache, called. "What's so funny over there?"

"I was just thinking of Lieutenant Robbins and her incredible glitch machine."

Apache laughed. "Yeah, that little honey's got it in for you, bud. Go to silent running on my mark. Mark."

Givens and Apache cut their engines simultaneously and allowed their craft to drift. The plan was to allow Blue Squadron to overfly them and then to catch Blue in the rear; without the drive pumping out ionized particles, a Speed had a surprisingly small sensor signature. A classic move, and they'd be watching out for it. Which was why the two Speeds lay so close together, hoping to fool the "enemy's" sensors into wasting time looking for the "other" Speed until it was too late. He lay in eerie silence, nothing but the stars around him and the glowing graph-and-schematic projections of the passive sensor array, filtered through the AI.

And here they come, Givens thought with satisfaction. *Come on fellas, step up for an early retirement.* He enjoyed a moment of pure, boyish glee as his prey swept toward him all unaware of their danger.

Then his engines fired.

"What the hell are you doing, Givens?" Apache bellowed as Blue Squad swept toward them with cries of victory.

"It isn't me!" Givens shouted. His disbelieving eyes swept the control board, watching things happen that shouldn't, couldn't happen like this. He yanked his fingers out of the control cups and began hitting auxiliary keys, but the computer was there before him, locking him out of the manual controls. Suddenly it hit him, squeezing at his gut.

"My, God! It's gone into automatic combat mode! I'm locked out, Apache, this Speed's gone rogue!"

Givens watched the monitor that showed the AI's *thoughts* as they scrolled across the screen in the control panel before him, and what he read dried his mouth with sheer horror.

"Blue Squadron, Blue Squadron," he shouted desperately, "my Speed is malfunctioning. I repeat, this Speed is malfunctioning. It is identifying you as Mollie fighters. Break off your attack pattern, repeat, break off your attack."

His fingers flew over the controls, trying again and again to disarm his weapons, only to have his authorization codes repeatedly rejected.

"Nice try, Givens," Blue Leader said. "But today you get *your* ass kicked for a change." Her smiled died an instant death as her computer informed her that Givens' weapons were hot and locked onto her Speed. "Givens," she growled and sent out her IFF beacon.

Givens watched in horror as his insane computer swept aside Blue Leader's Identification Friend-Foe beacon without so much as a second's pause. "It doesn't recognize you," he screamed. "Eject! Eject! Eject!"

It was amazing how fast a seeker missile could travel when two ships were less than four kilometers apart. He felt the Speed rumble slightly as the fusion-powered magnetic rail slammed the weapon out at literally astronomical velocities. Blue Leader knew she had no time to maneuver, so she followed Givens' frantic advice. She was well away from her Speed when the missile found it, grimly enduring the fierce ride the ejection seat provided.

Givens watched in numb horror as his energy cannon lazily tracked her arc. Sighting pips strobed on the curving holoscreen before him.

"No," he begged the monster in whose belly he rode. "Please, don't."

The traitor Speed jolted under him; all it was firing was a handful of copper atoms, but they were accelerated to lightspeed. Blue Leader *flared* as the plasma struck, subliming into a cloud of monatomic hydrogen and oxygen and carbon, with trace elements from the ejector pod. And both squadrons cried out in the horror Blue Leader had no time to express.

Raeder sat stunned, his mouth and eyes wide open in shock. Alarms were ringing through the *Invincible*, voices were shouting . . . and there was nothing anyone could do. If the Speed wasn't responding to Givens' override codes from inside, it certainly wouldn't to a broadcast. The cramped office cubicle was rank with the smell of his sweat.

This isn't happening, he kept thinking, *it can't be*. There were fail-safes for this kind of thing. Over a dozen of them. *Givens should have been able to do something*, he thought. *At least one of his options should have worked*. And in the back of his mind

Robbins' phantom spike sparked over and over again. Such a tiny warning for such a major malfunction.

Givens was cursing with raw inventiveness as he strove to take control of the Speed. As though he could verbally abuse it into submission.

"Shall we break off, sir?" one of the pilots asked.

"No," Sutton said grimly. "I'll remind you, Conan, since you've forgotten, that the next item on the preprogrammed Battle Options Menu that damned AI has loaded is to turn on the nearest enemy capital ship. And since Givens' computer thinks we're all Mollies, I imagine that would be the *Invincible* herself. However, there's no reason for all of us to be out here." He rattled off a list of names, sending twenty-seven of his squadron home.

Raeder knew that Sutton was keeping the best fliers in his squadron, the ones who could do witchcraft with their Speeds, who never got caught flatfooted.

Unfortunately the AIs were programmed to learn from their pilots. They added their human factors' moves to their own preprogrammed set, the better to take over should the pilot be killed or injured during combat. *And Givens is one of the best I've ever seen,* Peter thought. *Almost as good as me.*

He reached for the comm to call the captain, but Knott's voice found him first.

"Commander," the captain said in a voice like frozen steel, "are you aware of the situation?"

"Yes, sir. I was just going to call the bridge to ask if I may be patched through to Lieutenant Givens. There may be something I can suggest to him."

"Commander!" A dark haired whirlwind swept into Raeder's office and then stopped short in confusion as Raeder held up a hand. Cynthia blushed as she realized she'd breached protocol again.

"That sounds like Lieutenant Robbins," Knott said dryly.

"Yes, sir, it is," Raeder said.

"Well, listen up, both of you. Fix this if you can. For obvious reasons I want to save that Speed. But I'm not going to keep those people out there dodging fire forever. You have ten minutes, then we'll have to destroy it."

"Understood, sir," Raeder answered seriously.

"Good, we're patching you through now. Don't disappoint me, Raeder."

"I'll try not to, sir."

"See to it."

"Sir!" Givens said to Sutton. "It's issuing itself a mission." He read the AI's thoughts as they scrolled across the screen. He'd been doing this right along, to the considerable benefit of his squadron-mates. "It's going to break off and head for *Invincible*. It's going to ram the bridge! You were right, sir, it thinks *Invincible*'s the enemy mother ship!"

"Then we'll just have to keep it too busy to leave us. Won't we?" Sutton said calmly. "Just keep working on it, Givens," he said. "Something's bound to give."

"Yes, sir."

Frankly the lieutenant was surprised that he could still communicate. The AI had to know he was doing it. "What if the computer cuts off my radio?" he asked nervously, addressing no one in particular.

"Don't worry, Givens," Raeder said, "that system's triple protected and the AI has given itself more important things to do."

"Where the hell have you been, man, do you know what's happening out here?" Givens' voice was so tight from tension it almost squeaked.

"That's why I'm here," Raeder said, ignoring Givens' plaintive "man" where there should have been a "sir." "Tell me what you've done."

And the lieutenant did. Most of it was stuff Raeder had been going to suggest, but there were one or two options left.

"I want you to break out your toolkit," Raeder said. "Where is it?"

"Put your right arm out, straight from the shoulder. Your hand should be touching what looks like a small drawer," Robbins said, a trace of exasperation in her voice.

"Got it," Givens said. He pulled it out and it dropped open, revealing a few tools and a lot of empty spaces. "What can I do with this garbage?" he demanded.

"Take out the laser cutter," Raeder instructed.

"Haven't got one," Givens said.

Raeder looked at Robbins, who was hovering over his shoulder. She shrugged, with a bitter twist to her mouth. "Diagnostics said the toolkit was full." She pulled her belt recorder and made a note. "Physical checks from now on."

"Then take out your wire cutters," he went on.

"Haven't got one," Givens said, a tone of rising impatience clear in his voice.

"Well, what have you got?" Raeder asked. *By now you may have gathered that we need a cutting instrument.*

"I've got a set of jewelers' screwdrivers and what looks like a miniature crowbar."

"That's it?" Raeder and Robbins cried as one.

"What did you do with your tools?" Robbins demanded. Her eyes were narrowed suspiciously, as if she thought he'd sold them for beer money.

"Nothin', I didn't even know where they were! What did *you* do with 'em, Lieutenant? What did you do to my Speed, for that matter?"

"Calm down, Givens," Raeder snapped. "That isn't gong to get us anywhere. I want you to take that little crowbar and use it to pry open the panel that covers your electronics. Don't argue, do it now."

"Those tools are supposed to be there," Robbins muttered angrily.

"Lieutenant, could you put a sock in it, please?" Raeder said.

Givens wasn't one hundred percent sure just which of them Raeder was addressing, so he shut up and stuck the flattened end of the tool into a slot and pried. There were four other slots and the panel gave a little at each until it floated free and he thrust it behind him impatiently.

"Oh, my God," Givens groaned.

"What is it?" Raeder asked urgently.

"That's what I was going to ask you." Before him was a dizzyingly complex array of lights, connections, and brilliantly colored, closely patterned boards. They'd all been there in the familiarization lectures, but he hadn't looked at them since—it was specialists' work, and doing his own job was hard enough. He hadn't the rudest idea what any of it was and panic tightened around his chest like a vise. How was he supposed to do *anything* with this mess?

"Don't let what you're seeing get to you, Lieutenant," Raeder said reassuringly.

"Easy for you to say," the pilot replied with a hint of desperation. "I've never seen anything like this mess!"

"Neanderthal," Robbins muttered.

Raeder shot her a poisonous look and she crossed her arms and looked away.

"Ignore the complexity of it," Peter advised. "What I want you to do is very simple. Counting from right to left, I want you to stop when you reach the fourth board. It should be red."

"Got it."

"That board controls your weapons. Yank it out."

"Yes, sir!" Givens' heart leapt as he reached out. He'd thought this was going to be hard.

SSSSSNNNAAAPPP!

"*AAAhhh!*" he snatched his hand away and held it by the wrist. "Son of a *bitch!*"

"What is it?" Raeder shouted. "What's happening? Answer me, Lieutenant! Givens!"

Givens wondered if there was fire inside his glove; it sure as hell felt like it.

"Force field," he gasped. "There's a goddamn force field protecting that goddamn board!"

Raeder and Robbins looked at each other.

She looks as astounded as I feel, Peter thought. Robbins' hand was clutching her chest as if her heart were trying to claw its way out, and and her eyes fairly bulged.

"You might have warned me," Givens snarled.

"That's not standard issue, Lieutenant," Raeder told him. *This is out and out sabotage.* "No way that field should be there." *And probably the generator is deeper inside and therefore out of reach.* "If you can't touch the electronics, there's nothing we can do."

"In that case, Givens," the captain broke in, his voice painfully matter-of-fact, "much as I hate to give this order, eject. Squadron Commander, as soon as the lieutenant is clear I want you to kill that Speed."

"Yes, sir," Sutton answered.

Givens pressed the firing stud that would blast away the canopy over his head and rocket him into space. Nothing happened. He pressed again and again with no result.

"Goddammit, Raeder! What the hell is this, a placebo button? It's not working!"

Christ! Peter thought. *This can't be happening.* Then: *That thought is getting monotonous.* "Okay," he said aloud. "There's an auxiliary system. Reach down with your right hand. You should find a handle."

"Of course," Givens muttered, sounding embarrassed. "Got it."

"Give it a yank," Raeder instructed.

Givens bit his lip and did as ordered. He felt a metallic *chunk . . . click!* The handle came off in his hand.

"Dammit! Dammit! Dammmit! Damn, damn, *damn!*" He flung the handle at the bulkhead in frustration, realizing as it left his injured hand that he'd made a mistake. It came right back at him. "Shit!" he yelped and ducked.

"It didn't work," Raeder said softly. *Ye gods, whoever set this up really wanted Givens outta the gene pool.*

"What happened?" Robbins shouted. "Stop swearing and tell us what's going on."

"I threw the damn handle and it's ricocheting all over the cockpit."

"Well, get it back," Robbins exclaimed. "You've got to reattach it."

Givens laughed bitterly. "It won't work," he said scornfully. "Even if I reattached it perfectly, it wouldn't work. Don't you get that yet?"

"Yes, it will," she snapped.

"Lieutenant," Raeder said quietly. "Have you noticed that all of our fail-safes are failing?"

She looked a little sick for a moment, but then she nodded. "What do we do?" she asked in a small voice.

"What do you mean *we*?" Givens bellowed.

"All right, Lieutenant," Raeder broke in, "you have one option left. What I want you to do is get out of your chair, crawl to the hatch, and manually release it."

"Are you crazy? You want me to jump out of a Speed in a combat situation?"

"Givens," Raeder said patiently, "the only Speed firing out there is yours."

"And did you see what it did to Blue Leader?" Givens demanded, his voice harsh and ugly.

"So don't turn on your homing beacon until the squadron takes care of your Speed."

At the rate they'd be traveling Givens would be left hundreds of kilometers behind in seconds. His throat closed. He tried to speak, to answer the commander, but all that came out were choking noises. Until he faced the prospect, he'd never realized just how the idea of being lost in space terrified him.

"The commander is right, Lieutenant," the captain said. "It's your only chance. Your other choice is to stay where you are and die. Because I'm not going to let that Speed ram this ship. I've lost one pilot today, Lieutenant Givens. Don't make me lose another."

Givens took a ragged breath and unhooked his

harness. "Yes, sir," he managed to say, and began crawling toward the hatch. He was terrified that the manual release lever would come off in his hand. The lieutenant could feel it happening, his palm antici- pating the weight of the broken handle, even though he had three meters yet to crawl. He was deeply shaken, not only by the horrible events of the last hour, but by the knowledge that someone he knew loathed him and wanted him to die. He'd always sort of blithely assumed that he was a great guy and that everyone he'd ever met wanted to be his friend. Those he rejected were naturally angry and jealous of those in his inner circle. But he'd never imagined that anyone actually hated him.

He couldn't help but think of Robbins. She not only had the knowledge and the opportunity, but she'd never made any secret of her dislike for him. He'd always assumed she was frustrated. But she'd had nothing against Blue Leader. In fact, the two women had seemed to get along, which, with Robbins, meant she ignored you. And to go to such elaborate lengths to kill him, it was insane! But then, the lieutenant had always been strange. Maybe strange was thin veneer over crazy as a bandicoot.

Givens reached the hatch and, yanking open the cover over the manual release, he muttered a short, urgent prayer that it would work. He grasped the handle and turned. He felt it release, and if he'd been in gravity he'd have dropped to his knees in relief. He moved to the second of them and it too released. But his success made him wary and he moved to the third and final lever with an almost unbearable ten- sion leaving a taste of sour bile at the back of his throat. If the third latch failed to open, he was dead.

He turned the handle and it stuck halfway. In spite of the fact that he'd half expected it, Givens still felt a surge of absurd indignation.

"Shit," he said simply.

"What is it?" Raeder asked. *Don't tell me they've rigged the hatch, too.*

"They've rigged the hatch, too," Givens said.

This is too much! Peter covered his eyes with his hand.

"The third latch is jammed," Givens said, grunting with effort. He couldn't even get it back into position.

Oh, great, Raeder thought. *You can't get to those things without dismantling the whole hatch.*

"Go back and get the crowbar," Robbins suggested. "When you've got it you can try prying the—"

"Hold it," Peter said.

"The crowbar? You want me to get the crowbar?" Givens screamed. "How the hell do I know where the damn thing is?"

I can tell by the way he's talking that if he and Robbins and a crowbar were in proximity it would be a bad thing for Cynthia, Raeder thought.

"Didn't you put it back where it belonged?" There was a touch of horror in Robbins's voice.

"No, I didn't put it back! I'm trapped in a rogue Speed that's going to be shot to hell in four minutes and you want me to go looking for some damn tool?" Givens screamed. You could practically hear him foaming at the mouth.

"I said hold it!" Peter barked. "Givens, get a grip, and kick that sucker till it breaks open." *C'mon boy, give it a go. Imagine it's Robbins' butt.*

"Kick?" The pilot said it in a strange voice, as though

he didn't know what the word meant. "Yeah!" he snarled.

Givens grabbed the handles extruded from the wall on either side of the hatch and slammed both feet into it just below the jammed latch. His body bucked backward, though his grip remained firm, and it took a moment to bring his feet up again, and again and again. He could see a thin slice of space all around the edges, but that was all.

"It's—not—working," he panted.

"Well, of course not!" Cynthia snapped in exasperation. "Those latches are made of tempered—"

"We know what they're made of, Lieutenant," Raeder said through his clenched teeth. "Didn't I just ask you to—"

"Put a sock in it? Yes, sir." Robbins assumed a sort of seated parade rest stance, her eyes fixed on a point straight ahead.

Boy, you don't do anything by halves do you, Cindy? When you're annoying, you're as annoying as hell; when you're being a jerk, you're the mold they make them from.

"I can't do it," Givens said, his voice plainly despairing. "It won't give."

"It will," Raeder insisted. "It's got to," he grimly reminded the young pilot.

"Oh, yeah. That's right," Givens said, and brought his feet back up.

He was almost shocked when the pounding finally broke the recalcitrant latch. He stared out at the stars in astonishment.

"Hoo-ah!" he cried, and dove. He tumbled, stars whirling by his faceplate; the Speed whirled by as well, maintaining its relative position, then disappeared in a flare of drive gasses as the rogue AI made a vector change to dodge its opponents.

"I'm out!" he shouted.

"Understood," Sutton's voice said in his ear.

And far off, a sudden brightness blossomed and died. He put on his homing beacon, and while he waited he had time to feel regret, sorrow, and fear, as well as a growing anger.

A tiny red dot sparked on Raeder's monitor and Robbins leapt happily out of her chair.

"He's safe!" the young engineer cried.

Peter was astonished by the genuine delight in her smile.

"I thought you didn't like him," he said.

Cynthia stopped her little victory hop and stared at him with her mouth open.

"Well, we're not friends," she said, "but I wouldn't want him to die or anything."

Raeder just stared at her. *Not friends. I see understatement is one of your many gifts,* he thought. He couldn't help but feel that she made a good suspect in what was obviously sabotage. *And when Givens gets back, I think you'd better be somewhere he can't find you.*

"What I want you to do, Lieutenant Robbins, is go to your office and write up a report on this incident. Then I want you to finish writing your report on this morning's activities. Then I want you to diligently clear your desk of any paperwork you may have outstanding. I want you to lock your office door and to not come out until I come for you. Do you understand?"

Her face had screwed itself in to a puzzled, narrow-eyed, frown.

"Nnno, sir. I don't. We're going to have wounded Speeds coming in here in the next twelve minutes. I'm needed on Main Deck, not in my cubby," she objected.

"Well, I think that when Lieutenant Givens gets back he's going to be looking for someone to blame. And since you don't seem to like him, he's very likely to focus on you."

Cynthia stiffened and slowly brought herself to attention.

"Is that what you think, sir? That *I* did this?" Her brown eyes were wide with disbelief.

Raeder thought that, for just a moment, real pain had flickered across her face. *But then, if she's guilty she'd want me to think she's innocent. Maybe she's a really good actress.*

"Lieutenant, it isn't what *I* believe, it's what Givens and the others will believe," he said. "There's going to be an investigation of this incident. And they will find that you had access, knowledge, opportunity, and possibly a motive to—"

"Motive! What possible motive could I have for wanting to murder Givens? You don't murder people just because they're macho jerks! You avoid them." She looked at the commander for a moment, breathing hard. "You heard me, sir. I begged him not to take that Speed. I've nursed that craft like an ailing child and everyone in the squadron knows it. How could you possibly turn my concern into guilt?"

"Good question," he admitted. "I don't know, but—" He paused. "I think it would be best if the whole crew for that Speed were spoken to and cleared by Security before we do anything else."

If possible Cynthia stiffened even more. "Am I being accused, sir?"

"No," Raeder said patiently. "But you and the flight crew are going to have to be questioned. Given what happened, that's both necessary and inevitable. Bear in mind, Lieutenant, that I cleared that Speed, and therefore I'm going to have to answer some hard questions, too. The sooner we get them asked, the sooner we can get back to work." He looked her in the eye as she, apparently, fought her way through a conflicting morass of emotions.

"Yes, sir," she said finally, through her teeth. Then she pivoted and marched out, her stiff shoulders looking as though they expected a blow from behind.

CHAPTER SEVEN

You can feel *the difference already,* Raeder thought as he moved around the cavernous brightness of Main Deck, talking to the flight crews, making his presence felt.

"My confident attitude isn't making much headway against the failing morale of my people, though," he muttered to himself.

"How long to fix this?" Raeder asked arap Moi.

"This Speed, sir?" Arap Moi was studying a section of wing as he spoke. "Twenty minutes, maybe half an hour." The CPO shrugged. "If you're asking about the way everybody's feeling, sir," he glanced at the commander, "I have no idea when, or how, or even if it can be fixed."

"Don't hold back, Chief," Raeder said dryly. "Tell me how you really feel."

"Mad as hell, sir. Betrayed, beaten up," he looked at Raeder seriously, "and damned sad. You didn't have a chance to get to know Pilot Officer Longo, but she was a nice woman and a good pilot." Arap Moi shook his head. "This really hit me hard. Things were going so well since you got here, I guess we all thought maybe we weren't going to have any more 'accidents.'" He put a bitter spin on the word.

Raeder thinned his lips. He'd known that Captain Knott thought he was supposed to save them all from whatever was going on. But he somehow never imagined that everybody else expected him to be the knight-hero of the *Invincible,* too. He shuddered to think what the Old Man was going to say to him.

He won't have to say anything. All he'll need to do is look at me with those cold gray eyes of his and I'll feel like a three-year-old who's lost his toilet training.

"Commander Raeder," William Booth said. The head of Security was looking formidably official as he approached.

"Would you mind leaving us alone, Chief?" Booth's eyes studied arap Moi with suspicion and dislike. "I have something confidential to discuss with the commander."

"If you could hang on just a minute, Mr. Booth," Raeder asked, smiling insincerely. "I have something to finish up with the chief. Why don't I meet you in my cubby?"

"Certainly, Commander," the Security chief said, stiff-faced. "I was going to suggest that." Booth saluted, and when Raeder returned it, he spun on his heel and strode off toward the office area.

That fool has a serious pickle up the butt, Raeder thought. His eyes met the chief's, and Raeder couldn't help but grin, because he could see that arap Moi had thought much the same thing.

"You and the Security chief don't seem to be on good terms," Raeder remarked casually.

The chief pursed his lips thoughtfully. "It's more like, Mr. Booth sees it as part of his responsibilities to regard everyone below a certain rank as innately suspicious."

"So he's a bully," Raeder said.

"Now, I didn't say that, sir. I tend to think of Mr. Booth as just being . . . overwhelmingly conscientious." Arap Moi looked at the commander blandly.

Raeder's lips twitched, but he suppressed his smile. *Booth's not awfully bright, or very good at his job, but he is overwhelmingly conscientious. That's kinda scary.*

"If there is any history between the two of you, Chief, even if it was an argument over someone else, I'd like to be informed."

The CPO nodded. "I wouldn't exactly call it a history, sir. He threw a couple of our people in the brig for a fistfight and I thought he was being a little hard on 'em."

"And," Raeder prompted.

"And I told him so and he told me to mind my own business. As it happens, the captain agreed with me and ordered the men released. And no," he said quickly, anticipating Raeder's next question, "I didn't speak to the Old Man about it."

"But Booth doesn't know that," Peter said thoughtfully.

"Well, he should," arap Moi sounded disgusted. "It's not like the captain and I are tight. *Or* like either of us would violate the chain of command."

Raeder did laugh at that. To a career NCO like arap Moi, the chain of command was sacred . . . but, well, adjustable.

"Well, I'd better go see what he wants. Carry on Chief."

"Yes, sir."

The chief turned back to his inspection and Raeder headed for his cubby.

Booth paced back and forth in front of Commander Raeder's locked office, a luxury possible only on a capital ship, and still involving an occasional unconscious duck-and-dodge as someone else used the corridor. He was annoyed to be kept waiting and equally annoyed at how it put him at a disadvantage. It was important to maintain a certain status, a certain balance. Particularly while conducting an investigation.

If, as now, someone succeeded at putting you in a subordinate position, undermined your dignity, then you had a responsibility to do the same to them. "Get your own back," he muttered to himself, wondering just how much longer he would wait. It would serve the commander right if when he finally showed up it was only to find him gone.

He was just turning to leave when Raeder turned the corner.

"I'm sorry Mr. Booth," he said, holding his hands out and shaking his head. "Every time I turned to go someone else stopped me. As you can imagine, things are chaotic down there." *Actually I did intend to make you wait, but not this long.* He'd resented the way Booth had treated the CPO and wanted to take him down a peg or two. But this *was* stretching things; it had been almost thirty minutes.

"As you can imagine," Booth said coldly, "it's pretty chaotic in my department, too." He watched Raeder thumbprint his lock open and then preceded the commander through the door, stopping in the doorway to look around, then stepping forward so that Raeder could enter as well.

"Please, have a seat Mr. Booth," Raeder said mildly, as though he hadn't almost walked right into the jerk when he'd stopped short in the doorway. "What do you have for me?"

"I have questions," Booth said, looking at Raeder from under his eyebrows.

Well, damn, so do I. Good comeback, though. "So you haven't really learned anything?" Raeder said.

"I didn't say that," the Security chief protested mildly. "I said 'I have questions.'"

Suddenly Raeder understood that the Security chief thought he was living a crime novel and, big surprise, Booth was the beleaguered hero. *Great, just what we need. The kind of die-hard cynicism that insists everybody's guilty of something. That oughta move things along nicely.* It was also the kind of attitude that would dismiss out of hand anything that didn't fit into the ongoing storyline. *This guy doesn't have conversations, he recites dialogue.* Peter allowed himself an imaginary sigh. *Maybe we'll get further if I get into character.* Raeder leaned back in his chair.

"Shoot," he said.

Booth narrowed his eyes and casually crossed his legs. "Tell me what you know about Lieutenant Robbins," he invited.

"What I know is pretty much what's in her personnel folder and that is that she's good at her job and not a people person." Raeder shrugged. "I've only been here for a short time, I've had a lot to catch up on and the lieutenant isn't what you'd call a forthcoming person. My overall impression of her is positive, though. She's just not someone who handles people well." *Which is what even her most ardent partisans, all two of them, will tell you. So it's not like I'm betraying one of my own.*

It just felt that way.

Booth tapped his right forefinger on Raeder's desk as he studied the commander. "What about the rest of the flight crew?" he asked.

Raeder shrugged. "I'm in the same position with them. There just hasn't been time to really get to know anybody. Heck, I've been wanting to talk to you practically since I came here and I haven't had the chance to do more than say hello at the captain's dinner."

Booth's eyes glittered and he sat forward eagerly. "You wanted to see me?" He looked at Raeder from the corners of his eyes. "Why?"

"I had questions about Commander Okakura's death. Like, what exactly did the investigation turn up. I've heard it was a defective AI that caused the accident." Peter leaned forward, elbows on the desk, his hands folded before him. "Considering this latest incident, I'd really appreciate your sharing whatever information you might have. I need to know what to be on the lookout for." *Boy, do I need to know!*

Booth leaned to one side, his eyes narrowed, his lips pursed. "The bare facts you've laid out are all the facts," he said, and shrugged. "The AI malfunctioned. It wasn't as big a deal as today's, of course."

I imagine Okakura would dispute that, Raeder thought.

"So was it a hardware or a software failure?" he asked aloud.

"I was told it was software," Booth said, looking uncomfortable. "But of course I was obliged to take the lieutenant's word for it, she being the primary expert on the scene. We were sort of forced to bring in a verdict of accident. You know what I mean?"

"Mmm," Raeder said noncommittally. *No wonder the captain wanted me to investigate. This bozo sure didn't.* "So, when can I have my people back? We could use the extra hands."

"We're still interviewing them. I'll probably be releasing the flight crew by tomorrow sometime. But I'm going to keep the lieutenant in custody."

"Do you really suspect anyone in the flight crew?" Raeder asked, wrinkling his forehead. *I mean, even I can see the lieutenant makes a good suspect, but that doesn't carry over to everyone who touched that Speed.*

"Not really," Booth said, the faintest of condescending smiles pulling up the corners of his mouth, "but they may know something. If we keep them isolated and question them thoroughly, we might just help them remember a minor detail that could be the key to the big picture."

"And Lieutenant Robbins?" Raeder asked.

"Well," Booth leaned forward confidentially, "this can't become common knowledge, Commander." He waited for Raeder's slow nod. "She was seen late last night entering Lieutenant Givens' Speed." The Security chief pursed his lips and shrugged his brows suggestively. "Y'ask me, that doesn't look too good. Y'know what I mean?"

"I'm told that she always does a last check on all the Speeds the night before they fly," Raeder said. "Who saw her?"

"That would be telling," Booth said coyly.

"Yes. It would be telling me. Which I insist that you do, Chief. Those are my people you're holding

and this fiasco happened on my watch. I want, no, I
need to know everything about this incident and the
last one so that I can help you get to the bottom of
this." *Because I can see that you couldn't investigate
your way out of a revolving door.*

The Security chief shifted uncomfortably in his chair.
"I shouldn't," he muttered. "It's an ongoing investigation."

"Are you saying that I'm a suspect?" Raeder asked
in disbelief. "Even though this stuff started long before
I got here and I hardly even know my own staff."

"No, no of course not, Commander."

"Then tell me what I need to know so that I can
help you." Raeder was barely holding on to his temper now. *I can just imagine how Robbins must feel.
Matter of fact, I think I can feel a super-nova heat-
ing up down brig-ward.*

"The quartermaster was down on Main Deck, looking for you, he said.

"For me?" Raeder asked in surprise. "What time
was this?"

"Twenty-four hundred," Booth said, looking a little
petulant.

"Kind of late, wasn't it?" Raeder asked. *And what did
he want with me? He never mentioned it at breakfast.*

"Not for the lieutenant," Booth snapped back.

"Mmm. Well, as I've said, she's unusually dedicated."
Raeder wanted only two things from the Security chief.
One was for him to go, the other was to get his people
back.

"Look, Chief," he said, rising, "I'm afraid I'm going
to have to insist that you either charge my people or
let them go. We can order them not to discuss
anything with each other or anybody else, but if you

hold them overnight it's going to look like you think they're guilty of something. Given the emotional temperature out on Main Deck, I'd rather not subject them to that kind of suspicion. For one thing it's not fair. For another I'm pretty sure it's not legal, even under the wartime sections of the Space Command Justice Code. And last but not least, it'll play hell with performance. This ship *is* supposed to be working up to combat readiness, you know."

The chief, who'd been about to protest, shut his mouth with a clop.

"You may be right," he said darkly.

"And the captain probably wouldn't like it."

"No," Booth said, more darkly still.

"So when can I expect them?" Raeder pressed, walking around his desk.

The Security chief rose with a heavy sigh. "Now, I guess. If I can't hold 'em I might as well let them go. But," he raised a cautionary finger at Raeder, "don't let them discuss this with anybody but me."

"Or me, naturally," Raeder said with a smile.

"Yeah," Booth said grimly, "or you."

"And Lieutenant Robbins," Raeder persisted. *Although the brig might be the safest place for her until Givens cools off.*

But Booth was shaking his head. "No," he declared firmly and turned to the door, "sir," he said, just as he left.

Is everyone on this ship an eccentric? Peter wondered. *Don't we have any normal people?*

Suddenly, Lieutenant Givens, followed by the squadron leader, appeared in the door, righteous anger blazing in their eyes.

Oh, oh. It's the attack of the normal people.

Cynthia Robbins' fine brown eyes were practically shooting sparks as she sat stiffly, hands folded on the tabletop before her and answered the Security chief's questions *again.*

"As I said, I do a last check on every Speed that's scheduled to fly. I've always done so." She shut her mouth and stared mulishly at the chief.

"And what do you—"

"I run a brief diagnostic," she said anticipating Booth's question. "Look for tools that may have been left behind, make sure that everything that should be sealed is, that kind of thing. Maybe if you wrote this down, Chief, or recorded it, you wouldn't have so much trouble remembering it."

"Except for Lieutenant Givens' craft," Booth said, ignoring her sarcasm and giving her a look of oily suspicion. "You took your time with his."

"Yes, sir, I did. We've had a lot of funny little problems with his Speed, so I felt the extra attention was justified."

"And that's how you just happened to find that insignificant little glitch in the diagnostic," Booth jeered.

"Found it, logged it, and recommended that Lieutenant Givens' Speed be withheld from the exercise," she said with deceptive calm. "But I was overruled."

"But isn't that what you expected, Lieutenant?" Booth goaded. "Isn't that what you planned?"

"*What?*" Robbins leaned forward as though to hear better, her elfin face screwed up into a perplexed expression.

"All those times that Speed was held back and taken apart, only to find that nothing was wrong. All those false alarms adding up to today." Booth was really hitting his stride now, the accusations coming faster and faster. "Cry wolf often enough and nobody believes you. Isn't that right, Lieutenant? You don't like Lieutenant Givens do you, Lieutenant?"

"About as much as he likes me, Chief. Perhaps he sabotaged his Speed to make me look bad. Did you ever think of that?" *Do you ever think at all?* she wondered.

"Lieutenant Givens was almost killed today. He was trapped in a rogue Speed, hell, he only barely made it out!" Booth's face reddened slightly in annoyance. He didn't appreciate being force-fed new ideas when he'd made up his mind.

"So he says, Chief, but we only have his word for it. The evidence has been reduced to drifting atoms." Robbins gave the Security chief a straight on look that demanded he listen to her.

"Are you suggesting that he deliberately killed Longo?" Booth's eyes went wide as the implications hit him. "Why would he do that?"

"I have no idea what his relationship with the pilot officer was like," the lieutenant said primly. *And I'll bet you don't, either,* she sneered mentally. "All I know is that my vigorous protest of releasing that Speed for duty is a matter of record. As are Lieutenant Givens and the squadron leader's equally vigorous insistence that I be overruled."

"Are you accusing the squadron leader now?"

Booth was aware that he'd lost control of this interview, but he didn't care. These were such intriguing ideas. And, hell, he wouldn't object to bagging bigger game. For a few seconds he imagined the sheen it would put on his reputation. But then, Robbins was disliked and alone, whereas the squadron leader and Givens were charismatic and well liked.

"I'm not accusing anybody, Chief, I'm merely pointing out that there are other people you might be suspicious of." *And would be if you weren't so lazy.*

"Ah, but you, of all people on the ship, have both the specialized knowledge and the widely known dislike of the lieutenant. And you were seen lurking on Main Deck last night. And those three things make you the ideal suspect, Lieutenant, and that's why I'm arresting you." The urge to shout "*Book 'er!*" made Booth's lips twitch.

Robbins leaned forward and snapped, "The only thing I'm guilty of is doing my job! And I do not lurk," she said through her teeth.

Booth rose and slowly walked to the door. "That's not how I see it," he said grimly. Then he whisked himself out of the room before she could utter another word.

The Mollie laid the steel rod on the floor and, arms in a position of crucifixion, knelt upon it.

"Forgive me, O Mighty One, for my failure. I had thought to put that swaggering fornicator before you for judgment. Forgive me my pride, O Mighty One, that let me imagine myself your tool in bringing sinners to justice. If it were so, then that disgusting pig would be wallowing before your throne begging for mercy, ready for the everlasting flames. Forgive me, O Mighty One, for my self-serving anger that blinded me to my duty. Instead of being motivated by their neglect and scorn for You, O Mighty One, I was angry over their indifference and disdain for me. Forgive me, O Mighty One, I offer my pain in reparation of

my selfish lapse in my duty. This moment, I rededi-
cate myself to Your service. I pray that You will hear
my plea and accept my unworthy offering. Amen."

The Mollie infiltrator would remain in this painful
position for four hours. Far too little time in the eyes
of the Interpreters of the Perfect Way. But it was
imperative the agent appear unimpaired. Therefore
the punishment would be repeated every other night
for four nights.

"I am a weak and feeble vessel," the Mollie whispered, arms already beginning to shake with weari-
ness, "yet I will succeed, for my cause is just, and
the Mighty One will protect and guide me."

The agent tried to take comfort in the fact that the
sabotage had effected some successes. One of the
Godless pilots was dead, two Speeds were totally
destroyed and would not trouble the Ecclesia again,
and many other Speeds were severely damaged. Addi-
tionally, the pathetic weaklings, unsustained by the Perfect Way, suffered a severe drop in morale.

The agent shyly laid these accomplishments on the
altar of atonement, in hopes of making the offering
more sweet.

"May their hearts break within them," the Mollie
intoned, "may they die of despair, may they drown
in bitterness." Hatred spurted through the wall of
shame, as boiling lava springs from the planet's broken crust. And the Mollie knew forgiveness, knew the
offering of pain had been accepted.

"Oh, thank you, Mighty One," the agent prayed,
while tears as hot as the anger burning within fell,
unchecked, to the floor. "Thank you!"

CHAPTER EIGHT

A week later the *Invincible* had returned to Ontario Base for resupply and the inevitable Court of Inquiry. Peter Raeder stood watching the huge construct grow slowly in the wardroom holoview, glumly noting the swarming dots of light that surrounded it, markers of growth and new building. New ships and new personnel, the Commonwealth girding itself for war . . . and the *Invincible* wasn't nearly as much a part of it as it should be.

The reception at the docking bays didn't help. Whenever he left the ship, as now, everyone around took note of his passage, staring until he'd passed by. It wasn't just him, either. The entire crew was going twitchy from the awed silence that followed them wherever they went. And the officers discovered that good company was hard to find as their brother officers from other ships or from the station kept them at arms length or worse, pestered them with obnoxious questions.

Peter's mind was racing and so was his pulse as the hour approached when the Court of Inquiry would convene. He wasn't looking forward to testifying. The thought of sitting up before his fellow officers as well as the members of the committee to tell them all in public and for the record just how badly he'd screwed up was like a vise around his heart.

In addition, there was so much to do on the *Invincible* and there were so many places he had to be. He had an appointment with the quartermaster of the Forward Supply Depot this very afternoon to plead that *Invincible's* needs rated a priority status.

Raeder knew he had a good case. He also knew that had little to do with whether he would actually receive the necessary replacement parts and Speeds he'd requisitioned. *Politics,* he thought bitterly. And if the court's session should run over and he had to cancel the appointment, the Virgin Mary and all the saints wouldn't be able to shake more than the bare TOE minimum from FSC's grasping hands. *Or so my instincts tell me.*

Then later in the afternoon Pilot Officer Longo's funeral was scheduled. An event he dreaded. He wasn't looking forward to offering condolences to her husband and ten-year-old daughter. Facing their pain seemed impossibly difficult and he would rather do anything else. *Especially since they're bound to blame me for her death.* With considerable justification.

Peter couldn't get out of his mind the look in the captain's eyes as he'd listened to just how the defective Speed was released for duty. Knott had accepted Raeder's report without any other comment than, "There'll be a board of inquiry, of course, Commander Raeder. Hold yourself in readiness to testify." Peter squirmed inside at the memory. It was obvious that he hadn't lived up to Knott's expectations, either as an investigator or as a flight engineer.

Besides that, he was easily as depressed as the rest of the crew over Longo's untimely and unnecessary death, but his position forbade him to show it. And for someone with Raeder's emotional Celtic blood, not to show his feelings was stretching his acting abilities to the limit.

But who could possibly have imagined— Raeder stopped that train of thought cold. He knew from frustrating experience that it only went round and round. *And beating myself up will solve nothing.* Just as he'd solved none of the mysteries surrounding the two murders on the *Invincible.* But he would, by God. For now, it was time to think of the matter at hand.

He took his seat and looked around the courtroom, thinking with mild surprise, *It looks just like I expected.*

The walls were paneled, or very good virtual paneling, possibly a holo-generated image of richly veined and carved mahogany. There was a long table of solid oak at the head of the room with six chairs upholstered in green leather behind it.

On the wall in back of them hung a magnificent painting of the battle of Chung Quo, when a group of excessively ambitious mining consortiums had hired mercenaries and rebelled against the Commonwealth. Space Command had defeated them utterly, freeing the miners and their families from the virtual slavery the consortiums had imposed on them and giving both the mercenaries and their employers considerable cause for regret.

The star-spangled flag of the Commonwealth was displayed to the right of the painting, the blue-and-black flag of Space Command on the left. Facing the committee's table was a smaller one with a single chair in front of it for the witnesses. The small room was elegant, well proportioned, official. And it smelled of beeswax polish; that probably was real mahogany, then.

It's so rare that things live up to expectation. Why did it have to be a courtroom? Raeder looked down at his folded hands, feeling depressed and put upon. *All right,* he told himself sternly, *that's enough of that "poor little me" stuff.*

Peter straightened in his seat. *Think of Cynthia. The poor kid is the only one of us who wanted to keep that damn Speed in the hangar and she's in jail for it. Besides, I just can't see her as a murderer. I can see her getting murdered, she's that aggravating. But frankly, people just aren't that important to her. What they say, what they think . . . it's simply of no consequence.*

In the very first row Captain Knott and the XO, Mai Ling Ju, sat in solitary splendor, glimmering with medals and braid. Raeder was in the row behind them. Beside Peter sat a silent and grim-faced arap Moi; two vacant seats down from him was the *Invincible's* quartermaster, John Larkin, looking unusually solemn. Behind them sat Squadron Leader Sutton, Lieutenant Givens, and the rest of the squadron. Raeder thought he could feel their accusing eyes on him, but resisted the urge to look.

There was a stir at the rear of the hearing room and the sound of quite a lot of people moving forward. Raeder looked up and saw William Booth, Lieutenant Robbins in handcuffs, and two security guards.

"Would you excuse us," Booth said harshly, indicating

that he wanted them to move down so that he and his prisoner could have the first two seats.

The captain turned around, glanced over the Security chief's party, and motioned Booth over to him. The chief leaned down and the captain spoke softly in his ear. Raeder watched Booth's neck slowly turn pink, then crimson, then as close to true red as he'd ever seen a human being go.

"Yes, sir," Booth said. When he straightened up his face was dewed with sweat. The Security chief saluted and after a beat the captain acknowledged it.

"Carry on," Knott growled.

Booth turned to Robbins, fumbling with the cuffs until he could find the thumbprint scanner that would unlock them. Then he handed the cuffs to his minions and dismissed them gruffly.

Arap Moi moved one seat over and Raeder tugged Cynthia down into the vacated seat, leaving Booth to glower briefly and then clamber over an unmoving arap Moi to the vacant seat beyond.

The sergeant-at-arms entered from a door at the front of the room and barked, "Ten hup!"

All those present stood to attention as one, a legacy of academy days. At the front of the room, six men and women quietly filed in and took their places at the table. Three of the members were flight engineers like Raeder and Robbins, one was a squadron leader, one was in administration, and one was a quartermaster: the chair would be the highest-ranking officer.

"Please be seated, ladies and gentlemen," an attractive woman with wavy, silver-gray hair invited in a delicate Danish accent. "I am Vice Admiral Paula Anderson, chair of this committee. We are met today to determine if there is sufficient evidence of criminal negligence or sabotage to hold Commander Peter Raeder and Second Lieutenant Cynthia Robbins for court-martial." She looked out over the courtroom, her ice-gray eyes pausing briefly at Knott, Raeder, and Robbins. "These are serious charges and I assure you that this board will explore this incident zealously and with all due dispatch." She struck the gavel once on its board and said, "This committee is now in session."

"Lieutenant Oswald Givens, please come forward," the sergeant-at-arms commanded.

"*Oswald?*" Cynthia murmured in pained disbelief.

Raeder glanced at her. *Maybe I've been wrong about you, Lieutenant,* he thought, admiring her sympathetic reaction.

Givens approached the table and chair before the committee awkwardly, as though physically he'd regressed to sixteen. He hesitated so long with his hand on the chair that the vice admiral said, "Please be seated Lieutenant Givens," with just the faintest touch of asperity.

"Yes, sir," he said and dropped into it like a sack of potatoes.

"Originally, Lieutenant, your Speed had been pulled from the roster on the day of the incident. Would you please tell us about that?"

He did, and went on to describe the incident in full: the Speed going rogue, its unbelievable murder of Pilot Officer Longo, his rescue, and relief on his return to the *Invincible* that Lieutenant Robbins was in custody.

"But by your own admission, Lieutenant, she alone was adamant that you should not take that Speed out," one of the flight engineers, an older man with smooth dark hair and a formidable jaw, remarked.

Givens seemed nonplussed. "But don't you find that suspicious, sir? Two other qualified experts didn't think that little glitch was anything significant. Yet Lieutenant Robbins insisted on having her objections made a matter of record." He made a small nervous gesture. "To me that just smacks of trying to cover herself." He shrugged. "It's just suspicious, that's all. To me."

"Thank you, Lieutenant, but we are more interested in your direct observations than your opinions. Next witness."

"Like Lieutenant Givens," Squadron Leader Sutton said after he'd been examined, "I find Lieutenant Robbins' prescience entirely too coincidental to be believable." He shook his head dubiously. "No, it's just too pat. Who knows but if Givens had flown that Speed one of the previous times she wanted it held back, it might have gone rogue the sooner. And with no superior officer to look over her shoulder we might have lost Givens, as well."

"But why would she do that, sir?" the board's quartermaster member asked. "What could she possibly gain?"

Sutton gave a little laugh, "As to that, sir, I've no idea, the human mind is not my forte. Some bizarre variety of Munchausen by Proxy disease, perhaps?" He lifted his fingers from the table before him in a kind of shrug. "Our Speeds are like surrogate children for the lieutenant; perhaps she makes them 'sick' to get attention and sympathy. Though she's not really a very sympathetic character."

"Good grief!" Robbins muttered to Raeder. "Thank God he's not a Freudian. If he was he'd be talking about how penile Speeds are and how I equated Givens' with an unfaithful lover that was having an affair with the lieutenant. So I decided to kill them both in a jealous rage. Tsk!" She glanced at Peter from the corner of her eye, then did a double-take at his astonished expression.

Thanks a lot, Cindy. It's sure going to be easy testifying with that thought in my mind. "Some choice," Raeder said aloud, "Medea or Clytemnestra."

She gave him an odd look, and so did Vice Admiral Anderson, so Peter shut up, turned forward, and tried not to slouch down in his chair.

"What is your reaction to these accusations that Lieutenant Givens and the squadron leader have made against you?" the vice admiral asked Cynthia before she asked Lieutenant Sutton anything else.

Robbins looked thoughtfully down at the table before her and spoke without looking up, as though reading from a text.

"I suppose they're regretting the force of their arguments which resulted in reversing my decision to withhold Lieutenant Givens' Speed from the exercise. They want this to be anyone's fault, anyone's mistake but their own."

Raeder heard a sibilant hiss as the entire squadron sucked in its breath, whether in fury or astonishment he couldn't tell. *But personally, I think it's a pretty perceptive answer.*

When Raeder's turn came, he sat and replied crisply, answering the board's questions as best he could, all the while trying to fight off the recurring feelings of guilt that had assailed him since the incident.

"Why didn't you back up your second?" Anderson asked him.

"Because, sir, we had run every diagnostic we could think of, and none of them provoked any sort of negative response. The AI handled everything we threw at it with ease. Certainly there was no sign of a complete breakdown."

"So there was no warning whatsoever?" one of the flight engineers asked him.

Raeder shook his head, his gaze steady. "Just a slight peculiarity on one diagnostic screen and the preternaturally sharp instincts of Lieutenant Robbins, sir."

Vice Admiral Anderson raised a brow at that. "You praise the lieutenant's instincts, Commander Raeder, yet you overruled her on the day."

"I am now painfully aware of how mistaken I was," Raeder said. "I had read in her personnel file of how uncanny she could be in diagnosing problems. But it seemed to me at the time I read it to be merely hyperbole."

There was no need to ask if the error disturbed him; it was obvious to all present that it did.

It was a long and arduous day, with all of them being questioned closely by the committee. The questions were probing, intelligent and, much to Raeder's relief, completely unbiased, so far as he could tell.

As Vice Admiral Anderson had promised they were working with dispatch, as well. By 1400, they had only John Larkin left to examine.

Although why they want to question the quartermaster is beyond me, Raeder thought. *He doesn't deal with software, except to hand over the sealed package, and that's almost certainly where the problem was.*

The panel didn't have much to ask him, either. They managed a few polite questions for form's sake, learning about all the perfect parts that left his hands and became dreck in Lieutenant Robbins', and that he had felt driven to protest this anomaly in writing.

"Thank you for appearing, Quartermaster," the vice admiral said. "You may step down."

"Vice Admiral," Larkin said, his face a study in anxiety, "I'd like to make a statement for the record."

Anderson's eyebrows went up, but she nodded.

"I regret the necessity for saying this," Larkin went on, "but I feel an obligation not to waste this opportunity to speak out." He paused and chewed his lower lip, his eyes fixed on the floor at his feet. "It is my considered opinion, after working with her for approximately two months, that Lieutenant Robbins is a dangerously unstable personality. She takes umbrage at the most commonplace remarks, she holds grudges, she's resentful and sullen and as obstructive, when anyone's opinion clashes with hers, as she can possibly be. I honestly feel that she is quite capable of rigging someone's Speed to teach them a lesson."

He gave Raeder a quick glance, then coloring slightly, he looked away. "I therefore urge this board to find that Second Lieutenant Cynthia Robbins be held for court-martial. I suspect that this young woman is in dire need of counseling and therefore to be pitied. Nevertheless, her general behavior hints that she is potentially extremely dangerous and capable of anything. It is my fervent belief that she should be removed from her duties as soon as possible for the safety of all aboard the *Invincible*."

Anderson gave him a quizzical look, then nodded. "Thank you, Quartermaster, for your *opinion*. It will be given all the attention it deserves, I assure you."

Raeder stood. "Vice Admiral, may I also make a statement for the record?"

The vice admiral's lips puckered as though she were tasting something sour. "Very well, Commander," she said evenly, "you may proceed."

"I have only worked with Lieutenant Robbins for a short while, sir. But in that time I have found her to be an unusually competent flight engineer, passionately devoted to her work. Frankly, sir, I believe that if the lieutenant wanted to attack someone, she would never damage a Speed to do it."

Anderson's brows rose once again, and her eyes widened. "Thank you, Commander. And we shall certainly take your opinion into consideration as well." She looked left and right at her fellow board members, each of whom shook their heads, and then announced, "As there are no more witnesses to examine, this board will retire for its deliberations. We will convene again in this chamber at the same time tomorrow." With that she struck the board with her gavel and rose, the rest of the committee, the spectators and witnesses rising just a beat behind her. Then the board filed out and the sergeant-at-arms closed the door behind them.

Raeder turned to Robbins to reassure her and met an expression that was half stunned, half glare.

"Thank you, sir, for your defense of me. It made me sound . . . *so* much more sane."

"C'mon, Robbins," Booth said, taking her arm. "You better come with me."

Raeder opened his mouth and then closed it. *The woman has a point,* he told himself. *But, hey, I was caught completely off guard here.* He'd never have expected the cheerful, pleasant quartermaster to be

capable of that kind of unwarranted attack. *Although,
if it's his honest opinion* . . . Still, he hadn't liked it.
Raeder looked around, but Larkin was gone.

"That was an unpleasant surprise, sir, wasn't it?" arap
Moi asked, his face a stiff mask that ill-concealed his
anger. "He has so little to do with the lieutenant, I
wonder how he came to form such strong opinions."

"So do I," Raeder answered. *And come to that, I
wonder how he just happened to be on Main Deck
the night before the exercise.*

"Peter!"

Raeder's hesitation was more mental than physical.
He kept on walking, pushing past a group of off-duty
Marines with the look of people getting their first
liberty after some hard action. One of them was trying to balance a glass of beer on her shaven head
while juggling what looked like eggs . . .

"Yup, eggs," he muttered as one landed on the
corridor deck near his foot with a crackling splat.

"Hey, Raeder, wait up!"

A hand grasped at Peter's elbow; he froze and looked
down at it, a slight frown marring his otherwise bland
expression.

"Hey, man, don't be like this. Just let me explain.
Okay?" Larkin's earnest face looked more choir-boyish
than usual.

Raeder tightened his lips and just stared into the
quartermaster's blue eyes, looking for he knew not
what.

"You have something to say to me?" he asked evenly.

"Look," John said holding up his hands, "I couldn't
warn you because I didn't even know myself that I
was going to say it."

"That's very perceptive of you, John," Peter said, cocking his head to one side. "You've put your finger on one of the reasons why I'm thoroughly disgusted with you."

"You haven't worked with her as long as I have," Larkin snapped defensively. "When the parts kept coming back defective, you think I just boxed 'em up and put 'em away? I have a budget too, y'know. I went to Okakura and said, 'What should we do about this?' And he suggested that I get together with his second to see what we could find out. I tried, man! I arranged meetings, I double-checked my stuff, I questioned my people." Larkin was taking on a sort of belligerent pout now. "You know what she did? She was late or missed meetings, she kept things from me, she complained I was harassing her, and on and on. Hell, Okakura tore a strip off me, off *me*, like I wasn't even a brother officer for some stupid complaint she made about how aggressive I was. She'd missed four meetings, Raeder! No explanation, no apology, nothing. I outrank the buffoon and she's treating me like some little nuisance! Wouldn't you get aggressive eventually?" He stood with his hands on his hips, breathing slightly faster. "It needed to be said," Larkin insisted, looking away. "And no one else was going to do it. It wasn't easy, and I'm not proud of it, but it had to be done."

Raeder switched his case from one hand to the other.

"So, is this an apology, or what?" he asked.

"It's not an apology for saying what I thought needed to be said," Larkin said calmly, looking directly into Peter's eyes. "But it is an apology for not being able to give you fair warning." He hesitated and then held out his hand.

Raeder looked at it, considering, then took it. *What the hell. I'm not happy, but if it's his honest opinion, based on previous experiences that I don't happen to share,* he allowed himself an inner sigh, *then I don't feel comfortable holding it against him. After all, it's so rare you meet an honest quartermaster. I feel we should encourage the breed.*

Larkin grinned like a kid getting a bike for his birthday. "I've come down to add my voice to yours, here," he said, gesturing down the corridor to FSC. "I'm also going to hand in a report on our damaged parts problem."

"Great!" Peter said, and meant it. *Just don't make any unexpected denunciations of my character. Okay? I can't afford it.* His own reception, as he'd foreseen, had been chilly in the extreme. Being on the verge of a court-martial hadn't won any hearts in Forward Supply. *Assuming they have hearts to be won in the first place.* "Go get 'em with my blessing," Raeder said. "I didn't get the impression they liked me."

"That's 'cause you don't know the secret handshake," Larkin said with a grin. "I'll catch you later."

Well, that's a load off my mind, Peter thought as he walked on. *Though I don't think it would cut any ice with Lieutenant Robbins.*

CHAPTER NINE

Raeder entered Patton's Bar and Grill with his head slightly bowed. He took no notice of the brass planters filled with softly glowing flowers that tumbled down their sides like living fire, or of the faux wood and plaster that gave the place its Olde Pub look. He merely slouched up to the maître d'. The dining room was full, so he left his name and went into the less crowded, and poshly archaic bar. It was full of uniforms, and the people in them were mostly talking in cheerful, brightly optimistic tones. The Commonwealth would win the war—few doubted that—and in the meantime promotions were coming thick and fast, between casualties and the buildup.

Peter settled into his seat with a long sigh. *I hate funerals,* he thought, signaling the bartender. *Even when they're for people I know. But when they're not . . .* The grief of other people was sharper when you had none of your own to distract you. He always felt so helpless and ashamed before the pain of bereaved strangers.

And there's not a single platitude you can murmur

comfortingly about the death of a perfectly healthy young woman with everything to live for who has died for no reason.

"*Ich hatt ein kamerad,*" he murmured to himself. A service saying older than spaceflight: I *had* a comrade.

You felt bad when one of your buddies bought it, but that went with the territory. There was a rationale to it, a structure.

He could hardly say, "Well, she didn't suffer," or worse yet, "Don't worry, she never knew what hit her." It wasn't even loss in combat, just a stupid accident— or a sneaking murder.

Longo's daughter had placed her small hand in his and said, "I'm going to be a pilot. Like my mother," somewhat defiantly.

"Allie!" her father said warningly. He looked at Raeder with eyes dead from exhaustion and loss. "We're not encouraging her in that," he said firmly.

Well, okay, Peter thought. *I can understand that.* He glanced back and found himself looking into Allie's solemn, determined eyes. *But I think you may have better luck keeping sunshine in a can.* Because if ever there was a girl destined to achieve their childhood ambition, that child was Allie Longo.

Then the widower seemed to realize just who stood before him and, deliberately ignoring Raeder's outstretched hand, took the hand of the person behind the commander instead.

Raeder lingered just long enough to be thoroughly frozen out by the entire squadron. Then he left. *Okay,* he thought, *I can see that, too.* But he wasn't happy about it. In fact, he was beginning to become just a little angry.

Hell, he thought, *I know I'm not guilty. I'm pretty sure Robbins isn't and I'm positive arap Moi is clean. Which leaves me with a nice wide field to choose from.* So, was it, as Cynthia had suggested, a ménage à trois, or some simpler form of rivalry between Givens and Sutton?

He wrinkled his nose in disgust. *Suddenly, the inside of my head feels dirty.* He didn't like Givens, but the guy just didn't seem like a casual murderer. And he was certain that Sutton wouldn't be. *I'm also pretty unhappy about sliming up Longo's reputation. Even if it's only taking place inside my mind.* So clear away those three and that left . . . Larkin. Larkin?

Raeder sat up straighter. *That's right. His name does keep cropping up. He's always on the fringe of things, never doing anything overt, but still, he's always there. Like on the flight deck at midnight. . . .* Peter ran the idea around a few times, finding it had definite possibilities. *I'm going to have to do a little research on the quartermaster,* he thought. He liked John, but . . . *Well, frankly he's the only one left to investigate. Which makes him as good a place to start as any.*

"God!" a woman said to the bartender as she took a seat. "It's crowded tonight."

"Yep, it's a busy one," the man said as he set a coaster before her and waited for her order. "Just got two assault transports in." There *were* a lot of people in Marine green around.

"Gin and tonic with a lemon twist," she said. "I'm starving. I hope I don't have to wait long," she grumbled.

Raeder glanced at her. She was tall, and slim, with a lean intelligent face and curling, auburn hair, cut short. *I've seen her someplace,* he thought. It must have been on the *Invincible*, since, though he couldn't place her, Ontario Base didn't feel like her element. On the other hand, there were over six thousand people on the carrier.

Well, obviously, he thought mildly disgusted with himself looking at her insignia for the first time. She was a lieutenant commander, a pilot, and she wore a reconnaissance badge. *Very likely she's in command of our WACCIs. Warning, Assessment, Control, Command, Information,* Raeder recited to himself. As clumsy an acronym as you can find. But everybody liked saying it. Maybe because WACCI pilots are anything but. In fact, usually they were excruciatingly stable people, which drove Speed pilots wild. And there hadn't been nearly as many problems with their space-craft. For one thing, they generally pulled a lot more of their own maintenance.

"I put my name in with the maître d' awhile ago," he said to her. "So I should be getting a table pretty soon. You're welcome to join me, if you like."

The lieutenant commander looked him over with nononsense hazel eyes, one eyebrow lifted. "My parents always warned me against accepting invitations from strangers," she said dryly.

Peter laughed. "I'm not offering to pay," he said, "I'm just offering to share the table. I'd hate to think of you starving in here while I stuff my face. Especially when the solution . . ." he gestured vaguely.

"Sharing a table," she suggested.

"Sharing a table," he agreed, "is so simple." He turned his deep blue eyes on her and smiled.

The lieutenant commander just looked at him for a moment, then suddenly grinned.

She has a killer smile, Raeder thought, enchanted.

"Does that little boy lost look usually work?" she asked.

Raeder blinked and imagined he could feel a blush stealing into his cheeks. *Ouch!* he thought. *She's one sharp lady.* And her tongue not the least sharp part of her. He placed his artificial hand over his heart.

"But I *am* a little lost choirboy," Peter said plaintively. "All alone out here among the stars. I've grown taller, but, y'know, I've never really lost my innocence." Then he gave her a look that his mother had called "puppy eyes."

She chuckled and then waved a hand in his face. "Don't! Don't look at me like that! I can't stand it." And, laughing, she turned her face away.

"Will you share my table if I don't look at you like this?" he asked wearing an almost idiot look of appeal.

Closing her eyes, she cried, "Sure, yes, all right! Just stop it. Okay?"

"Absolutely," he said, sitting up straight and grinning at her.

She opened one eye and, reassured, opened the other, relaxing with a sigh. The lieutenant commander took a sip of her drink, and when she turned back to him, Raeder was wearing the expression of a lost and heartsick hound. In the rain. At midnight. On its birthday.

"Nnnnnnnoooo!" she wailed, turning away again, laughing helplessly.

"Okay," he said, laughing too. "I'll stop. Promise."

"Commander Raeder," a haughty voice announced. "Your table is ready." The tuxedoed maître d' waited by the door that led to the dining room.

"Shall we?" Raeder said, slipping off his stool.

But she was looking at him differently now, suddenly wary and almost a little shocked.

"C'mon," he said quietly. "I won't bite, and I promise, no more puppy eyes."

She smiled slightly at that. "Is that what it's called? If the Mollies knew about it they could roll right over us in a week."

"True, but it would require them to have a sense of humor, and that they'll never have." He held out his hand to her.

The lieutenant commander pursed her lips, unsuccessfully trying to hide a smile, and hopped off the stool to join him in following the, visibly impatient, maître d' into the restaurant.

When they'd been left alone, the lieutenant commander leaned across the table and said softly, "Uh, Commander, there's something you ought to know."

"That you're serving on the *Invincible*?" Raeder asked. Then he nodded. "I thought I recognized you. But I don't know your name, I'm afraid."

She raised her brows and cocked her head. "I'm Sarah James," she said. "I command the seven WACCIs we've got on board."

"I'm embarrassed," he said. "I should have known that." Raeder sighed and shook his head. "You weren't at the captain's party."

"No," Sarah said, shaking her head. "I wasn't aboard that evening. I was finishing up a crash course on a new imaging infrared." She leaned forward excitedly, "You'd have to see this thing to believe it. The range! And it's so sensitive." Sarah shook her head in wonder. "It's infinitely better than anything I've ever worked with before." Then she sighed. "But I've no idea when we'll be installing them in my little wing."

Raeder grinned at her enthusiasm. "You look hungry," he said. "And I don't mean for dinner."

She bared her teeth and growled, then laughed. "I'd sell my firstborn to get those systems."

"Y'never know," Raeder said. "Though I don't think they'll take firstborns until they're at least out of diapers, say around nineteen or so." She chuckled and the sound pleased Peter. "Anyway, we're out here on the frontier; the top brass might actually have designed this thing just for us."

"Aw, c'mon," Sarah countered. "When the brass get a toy this special, they like to play with it themselves for awhile." She shrugged good-naturedly. "I just hope I haven't forgotten everything I've learned by the time I get my hands on one again."

Peter's engineering education and Sarah's machine-dependant branch of the service gave them a common ground and they enjoyed talking shop throughout dinner. By tacit agreement they avoided discussing the unpleasant current events that had brought them back early to Ontario Base.

When dinner was over and the bill paid, Raeder asked, "May I see you back to the *Invincible,* ma'am?"

Sarah blinked. "Well, it's been a long time since anyone offered to take me home," she said with a grin.

"Well, as a little lost choirboy, I'm actually clinging to you for protection. So I hope you won't let me down," he said, and offered his arm.

"Um," she said, looking a little worried, "I don't know how the captain would feel about us walking arm in arm."

Oops, Raeder thought. "Sorry," he said aloud. "For a moment there I thought I was a civilian. Happens every time I eat chocolate mousse. I oughta stay away from that stuff."

"At least until you retire," she agreed. Then she jerked her head in a come-along gesture and led him out to the "street."

Patton's was in the civilian section of the station, in a corridor that had seen better times and hadn't yet been recolonized by the wartime boom. Its exceptional food and service still attracted clientele, mostly military, but Patton's bright lights stood as a lonely beacon in the station's night. Most of the formerly chic and prosperous shops were closed, or converted to storage spaces. Even when the station was in its day phase the area was mostly deserted.

Raeder suppressed a belch. Every individual part of the meal had been justified, from soup to dessert, but taken together . . . perhaps he should have gone for the seven-ounce prime rib instead of the twelve. On the other hand, he'd be back to shipside meals tomorrow.

"Let's walk it off," he said.

"Amen," Sarah agreed.

This late in the station's "night" even their whispers echoed as they walked along, and their footfalls sounded like the advance of a small army. Once in a while a maglev floater went by, some piloted, most on automatic. The little craft swerved around them noiselessly and vanished into the echoing distance. The further they went toward the military side, the darker the corridors became.

"There sure are a lot of lights out around here," Sarah commented, gazing at the ceiling. "We probably should have called for a floater cab."

"Yeah," Raeder agreed, feeling very uneasy. "I don't remember it being this dark earlier."

"Mmm," she murmured, a slight frown marking her

high forehead. Her foot crunched in shattered glas-plas. From the spacing it was clear that this was from a now nonfunctioning overhead lamp. "Mmm?" emerged on a distinctly different note, almost a growl.

There was a scuff in one of the side corridors, sounding like a stealthy footstep.

"How are your self-defense skills?" Raeder asked as they instinctively stood back to back. They kept moving toward the check-point, eyes straining into the darkness that seemed deeper the closer they came to their goal.

"Pretty good," Sarah said off-handedly.

Meaning, I suspect, very good, Raeder thought. *As for myself, I don't know.* He had been very good at one time; balance and reflexes were the core of it, and he'd enjoyed the training. But that was before he'd lost his hand. He honestly didn't know whether it would be a help or a hindrance in a fight. *Somehow it was something I forgot to ask about.* They'd just said the hand was "robust enough for normal usage." Peter imagined himself hitting a guy and having his hand explode in sparks and flame. *Sometimes I really hate my imagination,* he thought mournfully.

There was a low chuckle off to the left that seemed to come from a height of two meters and the sound of a pipe being slapped into a horny fist, while off to the right came a flurry of soft scufflings.

"You aren't armed, are you?" he asked.

"That's right," she agreed. "How about you?"

"Only in the sense that I probably have a bigger vocabulary than these guys."

Their attackers had advanced out of darkness into dim light of the main corridor. There were four of them, of average height, all males, all bulging with the kind of muscle that makes even a tall man look squat. They didn't seem to have any energy weapons either. *Or necks,* Peter thought. They did have half-meter long sections of pipe, and one man was lazily twirling a hefty length of chain as if he knew how to use it.

Jeez, Raeder thought, *where do thugs find that stuff? Is there a shop or what? I can never lay my hands on a nice piece of pipe when I want to. Like now.*

"Not good," Sarah murmured.

"Not as bad as I thought, though," Raeder said. "Two for you and two for me."

"You really are into sharing, aren't you, Commander?" she snarled.

"It's something my mom always insisted on," he said.

The group was moving in on them quietly. No threats, no taunts, no requests for money. They came on cautiously, but with none of the gloating criminal foreplay the vids led you to expect.

For a single second the unworthy thought that Givens or Sutton might have hired these men crossed Raeder's mind. But he immediately knew better. Both men were too direct, too honest to hire muscle like this. If they wanted Raeder beaten up, they'd give themselves the privilege.

So maybe this isn't directed at me, he thought. *Maybe it's just . . . random.*

The advancing men had made their decision. Two circled over to Raeder, the chain and one of the clubs; the other two stalked Sarah, though one of them hung slightly back, keeping an eye on Raeder.

That was his mistake. Sarah feinted toward the man facing her, and then took a skipping step to the side. One long leg snapped out and caught the thug hovering in reserve in the throat. Not full force, because the neck didn't snap or the larynx shatter, but he went down gagging and spluttering.

"Bitch!" the other club man snarled, and swung the pipe above his head.

"Bad tactics," Sarah said mildly, and lashed out with her leg. The heel of her boot met the soft flesh of his groin with a meaty *thud!* The man crashed to his knees, too stunned with pain to scream.

Raeder watched his pair as they advanced. The man with the chain spun it in lazy loops, passing it from hand to hand expertly. *Damn,* Peter thought. *Chain can make even a geek with no forehead dangerous. It also makes a nasty wound. I need a weapon.*

"Hello, weapon," he said, spinning toward the man with the club. A clumsy overarm slash with the pipe gave him a wrist, and the artificial hand gripped it just fine. Better than fine, in fact; the same surge of strength that shattered glasses crushed the small bones into pulp. The thug's face went purple, contorting with a pain too great for a scream. In the same motion Raeder leaned over, got the sole of his boot in the armpit of the wounded attacker, and heaved—releasing the wrist at the same time.

The ex-club wielder catapulted through the air. The man with the chain saw him coming, tried to dodge . . . and they crashed together, ending up in a writhing heap around which the chain clattered and whipped, driven by its own momentum.

Raeder stepped up to the chain-wrapped bundle, grabbed both by the hair, and bashed their heads together as hard as he could.

It always works on vid, he thought, curious to see what effect it would have in real life. *Just as advertised,* he thought happily as the two men hit the floor and stayed down.

He turned to see how Sarah was doing just in time to watch her toe daintily connect with a kneeling man's chin. The man's eyes glazed and he fell over backward in impressively slow motion.

"Well done, ma'am," Raeder said, meaning it.

"Thank you, kind sir," she replied.

Sarah glanced at the man before her, then moved to the other one she'd taken out. She leaned over him, then snapped upright with a gasp. "My God! He's *dead!*" she said in horror.

Raeder kneeled down and checked the man's pulse at his throat. "Yes," he said, standing. "And we will be, too, if we don't get out of here." Their attackers were beginning to stir.

She took a deep breath and tore her eyes away from the man she'd killed.

"Yeah," she said grimly.

He took her arm and urged her to come with him. Frowning, Sarah took one last look around, shook her head, and allowed him to lead her away.

She was quiet for a time, then she said, "I've been mugged a couple of times."

"Sorry to hear it," Raeder said, looking at her thoughtful face.

"This was different. Usually there's a lot of 'Hey, girlie,' and stuff like that. Like they're trying to buck each other up. You hurt them a little, and they go away." She shook her head. "But they didn't do that. It was like a job! Just like they'd been assigned a task and were out to perform it." Sarah looked up at Raeder to see what he thought.

"That was my impression, too," he agreed. "Except

I can't think of anybody who would do such a thing."

"Well, they were after you," she said, giving him a poke. "You're the bad boy of the hour."

"My call sign," Raeder said, sounding pleased. "How did you know?"

"You're a pilot?" She looked surprised.

Obviously the lieutenant commander was as aware of me as I was of her until tonight. He'd have to see what could be done to rectify that. "Yeah," he said. "I flew a Speed till about a year ago. Then I got injured." He held up his artificial hand. "And had to reeducate myself."

Her face took on the expression of a polite person who's just been introduced to someone's pet slug.

"What?" Raeder asked, feeling defensive.

"Oh, nothing," Sarah said quickly. "I just . . . usually don't get along with Speed pilots."

"Oh, really?" he said quickly.

"Well," she said, still struggling to be polite, "they're different from us WACCIs. A breed apart," she offered.

The whole time she'd been speaking, Peter had felt her withdrawing and he was embarrassed and annoyed. "But Lieutenant Commander," he said carefully, "I've been thoroughly humbled. I'm physically incapable of flying a Speed. What more could you possibly want?"

"Hey!" she snapped. "Don't put words in my mouth or attribute thoughts to me that I'm not having. If you want to feel sorry for yourself, you're on your own."

Congratulations, Raeder, he thought, watching her departing back. *That boyish charm works another miracle.*

He started after her and in a few moments caught up. But Sarah was looking straight ahead, anger sparking in her eyes and he was suddenly too tired to speak. *It's been a long, emotional day,* he warned himself. *You'd probably only say the wrong thing.*

Although, a deep instinct informed him, *silence can be misinterpreted, too.*

Oh, God, Raeder thought, *this is too complicated. I just want to go to bed.* And let the world and all its troubles roll on without him.

Raeder dropped his other boot and sat on the edge of his bunk for a moment, too weary to even pull off his socks. They'd reported the attack to the civilian side of the checkpoint, and had, most sympathetically, been sucked into one of those form-filling nightmares that are so often included in art films about the dehumanization of the common man.

Civil Security had seemed genuinely distressed about the incident and kept apologizing and exclaiming until Raeder actually believed them when they said, "This sort of thing doesn't happen here. I mean, where would they escape to?"

Which is a very good point, Peter thought wearily.

They accepted the offer of an escort back to the ship and parted company with an exhausted "Good night," accompanied by wry smiles and shrugs. There wasn't much time for sleep before they were both back on duty.

Hey, she's a big girl, he thought. *She certainly doesn't need my help to find her bunk.* But he had enjoyed her company. And he minded very much that she'd just shut down on him like that. *Oh, well. It's not like I don't have other things to think about.* He rubbed his head. *If only I could think.*

His comm chimed and he let down his desk and

pressed receive. The thin screen on the wall lit up to show one of the station's security people, and Peter suppressed a groan.

"I'm sorry to call so late," the sergeant said. "But I thought you'd like to know. The man killed was a freelancer working here as a cargo handler. His documents were very good forgeries, or I assure you he never would have made it onto the station. I wish I could tell you more." The woman shrugged her brawny shoulders. "But he doesn't seem to be affiliated with anyone. He was even scheduled to be laid off by the company he works for. Which would have meant that he would automatically be sent home. Home in this case being Wildcat." A frigid little outpost known primarily for being left behind.

"When was he scheduled to leave?" Raeder asked.

"Tomorrow," she told him, looking grim.

"You might—"

"Want to check to see if any of his companions are aboard? Yes, sir, we'd thought of that," she said primly.

"Sorry," he said. "I'm too tired to be giving anybody advice."

"Good night, sir. I hope we'll have something more to tell you tomorrow."

He just waved and hit the cutoff. Then he flopped sideways onto his bed, asleep before his head hit the pillow.

"Imbeciles!" the masked one shouted. "Fools, Morons! Apostates! What was in your feeble brains?"

"We meant well, Acolyte," Fly-from-Sin Stoops said placatingly. He was angry with himself for groveling, but he was more afraid than angry. The Acolyte could order him to kill himself and he would have to do it or suffer the torments of hell forever. "It seemed that the death of this officer would be devastatingly demoralizing."

"Yes, it would," the masked Acolyte agreed. "But it would also be devastatingly suspicious!" The last words were bellowed. "Our enemies are not brainless!" Implying that Fly-from-Sin was. "When they see that two different officers from the same ship, employed in the same position have met their death in a very short time, they're going to wonder about it. Aren't they, Stoops?"

The masked and hooded figure on the screen paused and Fly-from-Sin murmured a resentful "Yes, Acolyte."

"Oh, thank you for agreeing," the Acolyte sneered. "I feel sooo much better now." The dark figure paused, then hissed, "He is *my* prey, just as the *Invincible* is *my* task, not yours, to execute as *I* see fit. Do you understand?"

"Yes, Acolyte."

"Gooood. This incident will, of course, have to be reported to the Interpreters."

"Oh . . ." Fly-from-Sin said, one hand raised in supplication.

"It is results, and not intentions, that bring us to paradise," the Acolyte said silkily. "You must pray, Fly-from-Sin. And if your supplications are heard, your penance will no doubt be light. But for now, and forever, Stoops, stay out of my way."

The screen went dark and Fly-from-Sin stood shaking, his lower lip trembling uncontrollably. Finally he broke and, dropping to his knees, wept bitterly for the punishment he would receive. Whatever it was, it would be horrible. And no more than he deserved.

"Scourge me, Mighty One," he muttered, licking

his lips with a complexity of emotions that his mind refused to analyze. "Make me worthy. Scourge me!"

Raeder felt as though he were trembling, yet there was no sign of it when he glanced surreptitiously at his left hand. Still, there was an unpleasant quavering feeling beneath the skin. He glanced around the hearing room. Everything was so exactly the same that last night might have been a dream.

Except that he now recognized Lieutenant Commander Sarah James, who met his gaze with cool professionalism, broken only by a fleeting smile before she looked away. He turned back to the front of the room with an inward sigh. *Well, there was a brief idyll.*

"Ten hup!" the sergeant-at-arms barked. His order was instantly followed by the sound of human bodies springing to their feet and to attention, nervous systems responding even before their minds interpreted the command.

The committee filed in and solemnly took their seats. There was a brief pause after they were seated, almost as though no one wanted to speak. Then the vice admiral turned her cold eyes upon them.

"Due to the lack of hard evidence of any malfeasance," she said carefully, "this board is forced to submit a finding of causes unknown in relation to the incident under examination. The prisoner, Second Lieutenant Cynthia Robbins, is ordered released from custody. She may return to her duties. Thank you all for your testimony." She banged the gavel on its board. "This committee is adjourned." The board rose as one, looking as though they had just ordered an execution, and filed out silently.

Raeder had risen with the board, as had everyone

else, but he was light years distant from his surroundings. He'd had an almost perfect record until this
moment. A finding of "causes unknown" was tanta-
mount to saying, "We know you're guilty, but we can't
prove it." It was the black mark that essentially ended
his career.

*Unless I can find out who, if anyone, sabotaged
Givens' Speed, this is it. Game over.* He could feel
Robbins' eyes on him, but at the moment he hadn't
a thought to spare for her. From behind him he could
feel the weight of the squadron's hostile stare. *Not
guilty, your honors,* his mind shouted. *And I'll prove
it to you or die trying.*

The *Invincible* had completed her shakedown cruise
under circumstances that would have sent her back
to the dockyard in peacetime. This wasn't peacetime,
and nobody was going to let a worked-up capital ship
sit idle. He might very well die trying, and was even
more likely to die if he didn't succeed in finding the
person or persons who had constituted themselves the
Invincible's own private hoodoo.

CHAPTER TEN

"Our mission, ladies and gentlemen, is taking us to the XHO-67 System," Captain Knott said, looking around the conference table at his heads of staff. "Which means the whole system is an uncolonizable nightmare."

Places the Grand Survey team left nameless generally were. Even the totality of Earth's mythology and history didn't provide enough names for every star.

He touched a few keys and the holographic display in the center of the table came to life. Before them spun a planet with eight moons and a thin equatorial ring composed of chunks of rocks or ice, some of which were as large as the independent moons.

The planet was a gas giant, larger by far than Jupiter. Actually, it was a borderline protostar, awash with lurid scarlet and orange clouds with an occasional cobalt blue storm center fading to electric blue at its outer edges.

The pizza that time forgot, Raeder thought.

"This system is located between Commonwealth and

Mollie space. It's a little closer to us, actually. We've known for some time that it's an advanced listening post, and frankly we've fed them some ripe pieces of misinformation through it."

The captain's voice showed a deep and amused appreciation of Commonwealth Intelligence's successes in this. Space Command had been winning the outright battles so far in this war, but in the shadow war of the spooks honors were more nearly even.

"But, as ever, all good things must come to an end. They've been sneaking agents into our space on the damned blockade runners. Worse yet, there's strong evidence that the independent raiders harrying our supply convoys are based there." He looked around the table. "You can imagine how happy that arrangement makes the blockade runners."

Yeah, Raeder thought, *it must save them a huge number of Transit jumps*. And each jump avoided represented a commerce-protection cruiser avoided. *Not that there are that many out there anymore*. Just enough to keep the enemy guessing. Customs had never had a huge budget, and the Commonwealth Congress had cut deeply what they did have at the start of the war. The idea being that short-term austerity would bring long-term peace all the quicker.

"This is the moon we're interested in," Knott said and one of the giant's moons was picked out by the computer and expanded in size while the rest of the display shrank. A short paragraph of information about it appeared below, stating its size, gravity, and rough composition, indicating a thin nitrogen and hydrogen cyanide atmosphere.

Frozen piece of dirt about the size of Mars, Raeder thought.

"Naturally, all of our information is extreme long distance," he explained. "Basically we've been able to pinpoint the location of the Mollie base." A light flashed on the dun-colored surface of the moon. "But that's about it. We've documented her traffic, which has become considerable over the last few months. But since we haven't interfered with it in any way we don't know what's going in, or out, or what's staying put."

He folded his hands and looked around the table again, his eyes skipping over Raeder.

"We're assigned to escort the troop carrier *Indefatigable*, captained by Marion Neal, whose Marines are going to take that base. We'll be accompanied by two destroyers, the *Aubrey* and the *Maturin*." He grinned as he watched his people smile at the mention of those beloved names from classic literature. "Commanded by Captains Igor Kaminsky and Terry Hughes, respectively. Our minimum aim is the neutralization of the enemy base and the collection of intelligence. Our maximum is to take the base and secure it for future Space Command use.

"I want to emphasize that this mission will be a proof-of-concept raid for the new light carriers like the *Invincible*. The Commonwealth *needs* for these ships and the experiment they represent to succeed. We're faster than the fleet carriers, we represent less of a capital risk, and perhaps most important at this time, we use less fuel. Therefore, this raid must come off perfectly."

This time his eyes found Raeder and locked on. "No accidents, no mishaps. Or this program will be finished before it's really had a chance."

Well, Peter thought, *now I know what's at stake. And that a huge aspect of our success rests on my shoulders. Thank you, Captain.* It also indicated that the black mark received at Ontario Base wasn't resting beside his name alone. *I've got to find that saboteur.*

But *how* did you find that one person out of easily five hundred suspects? Or was it a team? *Stop it, Raeder, that way lies madness.*

"Any questions?" Knott growled.

Heads were shaken around the table.

"Then go prepare your people. There'll be another briefing when we reach the Transit point. Dismissed," the captain said.

On the surface, everything on Main Deck clicked along just as it should. Work got done, people got along, even though it was with a certain strained formality. In the following days the two new Speeds they'd acquired at Ontario Base were thoroughly inspected by every single flight crew, including the ones that serviced the WACCIs. Then they were reinspected by crews who'd heard that other crews had checked them out. And, of course, Raeder personally examined them after each and every unauthorized inspection. Until he hit upon the bright idea of putting a security seal, very reluctantly provided by William Booth, over the hatch, electronically stating that *only* the commander, Lieutenant Robbins, or the pilot were allowed access.

This actually seemed to settle people down a bit, because no one, according to the seal's recorders, had made any further attempt to fool with those Speeds.

But I hate the idea that none of the crews trust each other, Raeder mused. *The paranoia around here is incredible. Papers could be written on it.*

Cynthia remained brilliant and inscrutable, arap Moi calm and capable, and Larkin as good-humored and friendly as he'd ever been.

When Peter had asked, "What *were* you doing on Main Deck that night?" Larkin had answered, "I was looking for you. I figured you'd be working late and I was going to invite you for a beer."

"The night before we flew the squadron on maneuvers for the first time?" Peter had asked incredulously.

"Coffee, then. The idea was to get you to quit knocking yourself out so you could get some rest." He'd shaken his blond head, smiling ingenuously. "I figured you'd say no to whatever I offered, but that it would help you get away from the desk. You'd struck me as a nose to the grindstone type."

Meaning? Raeder thought in retrospect. *Perhaps that, in light of the disaster that followed, I was in fact fairly derelict in my duty?* Or maybe it was just a zing to shake my self-confidence. *Which is not at an all-time high just now,* he thought bitterly, and sighed. *Either way, there are no cracks in the quartermaster's surface: friendly, good-natured, a nice guy.*

At least, for the time being, the spoiled-parts problem seemed to have disappeared. Oh, there were still broken or substandard parts, but well within expected ranges. *And that we can live with,* Raeder thought.

What they couldn't continue to work with was the fact that every order Lieutenant Robbins gave was double-checked with arap Moi. The chief had complained to Raeder about it and he'd started going round to the crews to quietly point out that this was against regs, procedure, and common sense.

Those he'd spoken to no longer went to the chief

for confirmation. They consulted with each other, or with other crews, or simply deliberated over them until the last possible moment before carrying them out. With the predictable result that things were falling farther and farther behind.

It's only a matter of time before Cindy pops her cork over this, Raeder mused, wondering what he'd left out of his lectures to cause this mess. *Don't be an idiot,* he scolded himself. *What you did was, you didn't get acquitted. And neither did Robbins.* He pursed his lips. *Okay, no more Mr. Nice Guy.*

Before he could talk himself out of it, Raeder stabbed the intercom key and his voice filled the massive area of Main Deck.

"Now hear this! This is Commander Raeder speaking. I'd like to address a little complication I've been noticing that just won't go away. We've got an attitude problem on Main Deck. And I am informing you that as of now it is over. Some of you have been questioning your orders."

Raeder paused for a long moment. "Who do you people think you are? *Where* do you think you are, for that matter? Lieutenant Robbins is your commanding officer. She is Chief arap Moi's commanding officer. *You* are enlisted personnel in Space Command. And *this* is a time of war. I shouldn't have to point these things out to you. This is very basic stuff, people. What's more, questioning the orders of a duly authorized officer in the performance of his or her duty is a serious offense in peace time. In time of war it's treason and mutiny!

"Now, because we've had some tragic and terrible things happen I've cut you people quite a lot of slack. That is over. I will not tolerate insubordination and

I will not tolerate slackers. I advise you not to test me on this."

Another pause. "Lieutenant Robbins is one of the finest engineering officers in the fleet. She demands the best of you, but she gives twice that and you know it. You also know that she would no more sabotage a Speed than she would pull the captain's nose. You *know* these things. I demand that you remember that you know them and stop this malingering. Anyone who has a problem with this and wants to discuss it, make an appointment with me through the chief. That is all. Get back to work."

He leaned back in his chair feeling drained. *I have got to get over this thing I have about public speaking.* He was going to be doing a lot of it from now on and he could feel that it was aging him fast.

He turned back to his screen and resumed scrolling through his messages. *I wonder what Cindy will think of all this.*

There came a tapping at his door, and he said, somewhat impatiently, "Come in."

Cynthia Robbins slid sideways through the door, as though it wouldn't open any further.

"Thank you, sir, for dealing with that. I've tried to find out what the problem is," she shrugged, "but it was so elusive that I couldn't quite catch anyone in the act. When the chief told me what was happening I spoke to the individuals involved and explained that they were being insubordinate. They said they were sorry, and that they hadn't meant to be, and that they had simply misunderstood the order and were merely clarifying things." She stood there diffidently, looking vaguely worried. "Clearly they were lying, sir. But I knew that my bluntness in the past had caused problems and bad feelings, so I was trying a . . . softer approach." Cynthia frowned. "Which didn't work, either."

Raeder sat with his chin on his fist and finally said, "Sit down, Robbins." She sat and the vague worry became vague anxiety. "You look a little anxious," he observed.

Robbins sat straighter in her chair and her face became an absolute mask, though a faint trace of color darkened her cheek. "I'm sorry, sir," she said crisply.

Jeez, Raeder thought, *I'm sorry I pointed it out. For a moment there I thought you were human.*

"Look, Lieutenant," he said, folding his hands on the desk before him, "in my opinion, the fact that you've reached your present rank is a tribute to your talent and your hard work. But as far as I can see you have no command skills at all. If you did, you probably wouldn't find yourself in this position. I don't know what circumstances shaped your behavior, Robbins, but starting now you're going to have to learn a different style. Being in charge isn't just a matter of snapping out orders. You have to understand the people you're leading, you have to know how to motivate them. A lot of that is experience, a degree of which you should have by now. I blame your previous commanders for letting this situation drag on. But it stops now. You and I are going to be working together on this, because you are not leaving *my* command until you have at least a crude idea of how to work with others." He turned to the shelf behind his desk and pulled out a small leather-bound case.

"This is an excellent primer," he said, handing it to the lieutenant. "We'll discuss what you've read next week." He checked his calendar. "Same day and time,"

Raeder murmured, tapping in the appointment. "Unless, of course, something unforeseen comes up." He gave her a brief, encouraging smile. *The poor kid looks shell-shocked.* "Now we should both get back to work."

"Yes, sir," she said, her face unreadable, her voice dazed. "Thank you again, sir," Robbins said, and standing to attention, snapped him a salute.

Raeder rose to the occasion, literally, and returned it. Then she spun neatly around and left the office.

Maybe she's just shy, Peter thought. He'd noticed that sometimes people who were terribly inarticulate about their feelings resorted to these extravagant and clumsy gestures to show what they meant. Or at least that they meant something. He shook his head. *I really hope she doesn't turn out to be the saboteur. I'll feel awfully bad about smoothing off her rough edges if she is.* On the other hand, it was those very rough edges that had convinced him of her innocence. *I mean, the girl stands out like a sore thumb.* Not one of the attributes of a successful spy. *Then again, there was Mata Hari . . . Not that she was what you'd call successful. . . . Work, Raeder!* he commanded himself, and sat down again to lose himself in his mail.

After a week of travel the small convoy was approaching the Transit point, with the *Aubrey* poised to lead them through.

Petty Officer Donna Jamarillo sat at her comm, monitoring the signals in their vicinity of space, lost in the multiple datastreams the holo fed her in text and flashing color. A peculiar echo caught her attention, a sort of here and there effect that resembled the sending of a message pod through a Transit point.

Damn, she thought, fingers dancing on the flat surface of the control panel, calling the data up again.

"Sir," she said urgently to her immediate supervisor.

Lieutenant Barry Slade moved over to stand beside her.

"What is it, Jamarillo?" he asked.

She replayed the signal for him. "I don't know, sir. It *looks* like a message pod. But with this many ships, it could be a Transit Drive warm-up echo . . . here it is."

He nodded. "It does look like a pod, at that. Can you tell where it came from?"

She shook her head apologetically. "No, sir, only that it came from behind us."

"All right," he said. "I'll tell the captain. Carry on." He smiled. "Good work."

Jamarillo took four paces across the narrow circle of the destroyer's command bridge and bent to murmur in his commander's ear. Captain Kaminsky rubbed his broad chin without taking his eyes from his own displays; being able to focus on several things at once was an essential command skill.

"Send a recording of the echo to Captain Knott, coded, eyes only, with my compliments," he said. Then he shrugged. "There's nothing else we can do now." By the time they got through to the XHO-67 System, assuming it *was* a message torpedo and that it *was* headed for the same place, it would be long gone. And whatever damage it represented would be well on its way to being done.

Knott entered the briefing room silently and quietly moved to a seat in the back. Lieutenant Commander Sarah James did not acknowledge his entrance by so much as the flicker of a slender eyebrow, but Knott was sure she was completely aware of him. It pleased him that she was also alert enough to realize he didn't want to interrupt the flow of her briefing.

" . . . particular attention, on our return to the *Invincible*, to the ring around the gas giant," she said, indicating it on the holo-map with her laser pointer. "There's every likelihood that the blockade runners, at least, and certainly some of the raiders will try to hide there, taking advantage of the way these fragments of rocks, ice, whatever can foul up detection beams." She checked her watch. "We will be exiting Transit at eleven forty hours. We depart at twelve hundred. Are there any questions?"

No one responded. Knott rose from his seat and started forward.

"The captain will be addressing us," James said. Her small wing of twenty-one rose from their seats and stood to attention. She saluted the captain when he joined her at the front of the room and he returned it briskly.

"Thank you Lieutenant Commander," he said, then, turning to the room at large, "as you were."

They sat, readying their notepads in the event the captain had new data for them.

"I have just received some new information from Captain Kaminsky of the *Aubrey* that I thought you should be aware of. *Aubrey's* comm detected the type of echo commensurate with the signature of a message torpedo being skipped into Transit."

Knott looked out over the grim faces of his people. "All they know about it, is that it came from behind them. Which means it came from the *Maturin*, the *Indefatigable*," he paused, and anger sparked in his ice gray eyes, "or from us. Leading me to believe that there is a strong possibility that the enemy has been warned of our coming. Therefore, you must go with extreme caution. Assume that we are not only approaching a dangerous enemy, but one that has been alerted."

He looked out over the men and women before him and took a deep breath. The WACCIs were so vulnerable. They were virtually unarmed, relying on stealth and ability to keep them safe. Sending them out naked to meet the enemy never made him feel good. Today it almost made him feel like an executioner.

"Keep your heads up out there," he commanded. Then he grinned. "Or should I say down. Come back safe."

Knott stood to attention and saluted them, they rose in a body to return it. It was one of those rare moments when Knott and James and every man and woman in that room knew, to the bottom of their souls, that they were part of something greater than themselves. Knott's arm snapped down.

"Dismissed!" James barked, breaking the spell. As the crewmen began to move about she shouted out, "Be on Main Deck to check out your craft no later than eleven hundred."

"Yes, sir!" they shouted in response.

Knott raised his brows. "A little early, isn't it, Lieutenant?"

"I figure it's better to put yourself through the tedium of checking things out thoroughly, sir, than to worry about whether you should have when you ought be thinking of something else," she said, smiling.

He nodded sadly, thinking of poor Raeder trying to build up morale in a hopeless situation like this.

"I suppose you're right," he agreed. He offered his hand and she took it. "Good luck, Commander. Bring 'em home safe."

"Yes, sir," she said.

"Hi," a quiet voice said from behind her as Sarah signed off on a release pad. She turned to find Commander Raeder smiling at her. Somewhat shyly, she thought.

"Just came down to wish you luck," he said, holding out his hand.

For a second she wondered if the scuttlebutt was true. If Raeder really was some kind of spy-master come to aid Cynthia Robbins in her efforts at sabotage. She shook his hand briefly.

"Thank you, Commander," she said.

He blinked and looked at his hand. "I washed it," he said. "Really I did."

Sarah smiled, she couldn't help it. The man played a very convincing wounded innocent.

The mechanic said, "I have another, Lieutenant Commander," holding out the notepad and stylus.

"I'll take care of that, Huff," Raeder said, taking them out of her hands.

I still don't like Speed jocks, Sarah grumbled mentally as he held the notepad and she signed with the stylus. He didn't say a word, but she could feel him looking at her.

"Wish you were coming with us, Commander?" she asked flippantly.

"Nooo, ma'am," he said fervently. "If I have to face the Mollies I want a weapon between us, not just a sensor array. What I *do* wish is that they could send some Speeds with you to cover your a—uh, butts."

"Oh-ho, no," she said. "Speeds are very high-profile craft. I'll stick with our WACCIs stealth ability, thank you." Sarah glanced at him as she handed back the stylus. "We'll get home all right," she assured him.

"Good," Raeder said, and nodded firmly.

She looked down at her watch to hide her smile. "Well, I've got to go get suited up." Sarah looked up at him. "Thank you for your good wishes, Commander." She turned and walked off toward the pilots ready room, sensing that he was watching her and itching to look back at him to verify her instinct. *Serve my vanity right if I did and he was gone already,* she thought with an inner chuckle.

But Sarah kept her eyes almost defiantly front and never knew that Raeder had watched her all the way.

Raeder watched the WACCIs hurled through the carrier's launch port with the oddest feeling in his chest, as though his heart were definitely beating faster than was called for.

I have such a bad *feeling about this,* he thought unhappily. *It's just too much to hope, after everything that's happened, this mission should go off without a hitch.* Somewhere, somehow, Murphy's Law was winding up to a painful slap. *But not to anything that's been on my deck,* Raeder thought fiercely.

He'd been knocking himself out the last several days, double-checking everything he could think of. And he'd put a security seal on the hatch of every Speed or WACCI on Main Deck, not removing them until it was absolutely essential. And boy, did Booth howl— about needless expense, about stupid ideas, about, "We all know who the culprit is, Commander."

Until Raeder had said, "Well, I can always make

this request through the captain. It just seemed like this would be easier." Those seals had practically flown to Main Deck under their own power.

Come back safe, Sarah James, Peter thought one last time before he turned his mind to preparing his Speeds for launch.

You could lose yourself in work. And at last, at last, he was about to strike back at the enemy again. He looked down at his artificial hand and smiled grimly.

Sarah was able to report a clear corridor to the Mollie base. *No sign of hostility, no sign of traffic. . . . This isn't right,* she thought nervously. *It's too quiet.* She smiled at the cliché.

Her hands worked in the control cups. Lights and images ran through the holos that rose before her crash couch: neutrino signatures, thermal signatures, everything down to and including optics and radar.

"This isn't right," Yee, her gunner said, echoing her thoughts from behind her and to the left.

A WACCI's control compartment was two narrow rectangles for sensor operator and gunner, opening into an even narrower wedge for the pilot. The three of them lay encased in the petals of their couches, pivoting and swinging on magnetic gimbals to face one item of equipment or another. It was very quiet, only the subliminal hum of the power systems and the sough of the ventilators; they all had their helmets unlatched for the present.

"No," she agreed. "There doesn't seem to be anything at that base but a few freighters and a handful of Mollie Speeds." *'Course, they might have the ground defenses to end all ground defenses.* But if they did, then they were under impenetrable cover.

She shook her head. "Time to head back," she said to Davis, the pilot. Then she leaned over her boards, frowning as though she could will them to give her the information she needed.

Peter Raeder sat in darkness, watching the command deck relay of the *Indefatigable*'s Marines making their assault on the Mollie base . . . and splitscreen views from their helmet cameras. This was against regs, strictly speaking, but he'd made a few modifications. His eyes flickered back and forth. Alarms would summon him the instant Flight Engineering had anything to *do*, but this waiting was harder than he'd believed it could be. For now he could only watch. That was all Captain Knott could do, too—watch and wait and silently pray as the Space Command's men and women met the enemy. Images . . .

. . . A Mollie Speed caught jiggling in the weapons-sensor pod of one of the *Invincible*'s squadron, the one that had hit it. The image was radiation-degraded, but clear enough to see bits and pieces flickering off into vacuum . . . and then burning in the thin bitter atmosphere of the gas giant's moon. *Pilot dead or disabled,* Peter thought. His hands clenched on the rests of his chair in unconscious urging, as if they commanded a Speed's controls even now. *AI's out. Override blocks down . . . Jesus!* The plunge turned into a lance of fire; the fusion engines were firing at maximum, past redline. They must be eating the throat out of the nozzles. Either the containment vessel would go, or the nozzles would flare, or it would hit at one almighty accumulation of delta-v.

All three happened at once. The lance of fire through the moon's atmosphere ended in a titanic fireball swelling up from the off-white surface as the Speed impacted at about .01 percent of C. That put the kinetic yield of the strike well into the multimegatonne range, and rock and water ice and frozen methane vomited toward the heavens. The image of the moon pinwheeled as the Space Command pilot went through a victory roll, then slipped out of the viewer as they pulled their Speeds back toward the darkness.

. . . Gunboats and assault transports were swarming down from *Indefatigable*. Beams flickered at them, pale rose-violet and red through the thin atmosphere. Robot bombs raced downward along the ionized trails, and bright intolerable winks of fire marked where defense batteries died. Then a gush of heavy antiship missiles came up over the horizon, reaching for the Marine landing craft and the mother ship with paths marked with vector-trails by the AIs. They corkscrewed and dodged as heavy plasma guns and lasers hammered at them, then died one by one. Something wobbled into Peter's view, heading from the *Indefatigable* toward the site of the missile launchers. Something big, big enough to have its own automatic defenses flickering beam-fire as it headed toward the Mollie strong point far to the notional west.

"I didn't know they had one of those—" Peter began, then winced as the sun seemed to rise beyond that horizon.

It *was* sunlight; a Solar Phoenix bomb, a self-sustaining thermonuclear reaction that would last for whole minutes, a miniature star rather than an explosion. He hoped nothing valuable was within a couple of thousand kilometers of it.

The *Indefatigable* and her swarm of landing craft beat

down the base's defenses, assisted by Speeds with no more targets in space freed to make strafing runs. Peter switched viewpoints to the prow of an assault boat, its gun-tubs spraying fire as it came in on spikes of fusion flame. The sleek teardrop shape grounded, then opened up like a flower in stop-motion film. Its weapons kept firing as humans and machines spilled out. Beyond its landing point was an enigmatic complex of pipes and skeletal towers. Return fire lanced out from it, and the Marines went to ground. Metal sublimed into vapor, and the towers fell. Sapper teams slammed forward, faceless in their suits of cermet combat armor.

Peter's hand moved, and he was looking out through the helmet camera of a Marine sapper. The view jiggled and bounced as the trooper trotted forward; he could see the muzzle of a heavy slug-gun moving with trained wariness ahead, past half-melted shapes, harsh black shadows, and roadways with giant-wheeled haulers abandoned when the attack began. Then a looming building, a simple blank cube of cast rock with big doors for the cargo rollers, tightly shut now; undoubtedly an access point to the underground base. A figure in a ripped suit of Mollie combat armor dangled off the edge of the blockhouse, near where something had taken a bite out of the stone that still glowed red-black. The audio channel buzzed with orders and downloads, full of Marine argot and code words and call signs.

The Marines wrestled parcels off their liftsled and slapped them on the surface of the doors.

"Fire in the hole!" a tension-shrill soprano called.

The camera view swung and twisted as the Marine leapt aside into cover. It went dark as the trooper wrapped his arms around helmet and hugged knees to chest, then shook in a long rumble. The Marines following the sapper team plunged through the twisted metal that had been the doors. Beams and hyper-velocity darts swarmed to meet them.

"We're winning," Peter Raeder muttered. "Why don't I feel better about it?"

"Phase One secured, I repeat, Phase One secured," a voice calm except for the panting of exertion said. *"Proceeding."*

Autosleds whipped by, bringing back wounded. Others shuttled forward, loaded with ammunition, air, powerpacks. Peter switched the feed to a robot spyeye. It floated through the interior of the blockhouse, past wrecked airsleds and orbital shuttles, then past thick blast doors peeled inward like grapes punched by ice picks. Down a sloping corridor into the crust of the moon, past a dogleg. One last glimpse, of something long and slender turning and tracking, and that part of the screen went dead.

The same calm voice cut in: *"Request update on layout."*

"That's negative," someone answered. *"Still shielded. Will return AI extrapolation feed as you give us data."*

"Thank you." The calm was tinged with sarcasm. *"All right, boys and girls—let's go earn our princely pay."*

Peter sighed. "Yup, we're winning," he muttered to himself. "We'll have the base in a couple of hours."

He felt a fierce, melancholy pride. Point Space Command at an objective, and by God they *took* the objective.

The arm of the chair broke with a sharp snap under the ferocious grip of his artificial hand. He hardly noticed.

CHAPTER ELEVEN

Sarah James looked at the readings scrolling before her eyes, ignoring the occasional push of pseudogravity as the WACCI's engines fired course-correction bursts. The holohelmet was mostly readings. Graph bars, status lines, columns of figures; the icy splendor of the nameless gas giant's rings was lost behind them. She frowned in puzzlement.

"You won't believe this," she said to her controller on the *Invincible*, "but a lot of the ice chunks in this ring are made up almost entirely of deuterium and tritium inside a shell of water ice. It's like a heavy hydrogen slush. A fusion-fuel bonbon."

"I see what you mean," the comm answered. "I'm getting your readings now." There was a low whistle. "You don't see this very often."

"You don't see it anywhere," she said. "I can't imagine what sort of natural sorting process came up with *this*."

"Survey Service will get around to it someday," the voice on the *Invincible* said. The universe was full of puzzles, more puzzles than scientists with the time to study them. "Anything else?"

"I'm also getting neutrino signatures," Sarah said. *And something about them makes me think they're not naturally occurring.*

"Are they background?" the *Invincible* asked. "That protosun beside you has been known to burp on occasion."

Sarah was shaking her head as she listened. "Uh-uh," she said. "They look like power plant signatures to me." *But they're weak. Shut down power plants, maybe?*

"Give me the data."

A low chirp sounded as terabytes flowed through the comm link. "Commander, those don't fit any pattern of fusion plant we have on file. And this planet *does* spit 'em out. Anything on microray or deepscan?"

"Negative on that," Sarah answered. *You expect me to find anything in that mass of junk? Not bloody likely.* She turned her eyes back to her instruments, occasionally passing a comment to augment the information they were sending to the *Invincible*.

Suddenly . . .

"I'm getting a steep increase in neutrino output, asymptomatic curve," she said, her voice calm. *Jesus!* she thought, as fingers danced automatically over unseen controls, milking information out of the datastream.

"I'm *definitely* reading ship power plants. Powered down but activating. Coming online fast. High-yield drives." Sarah's forehead began to bead with sweat. "These are warship power plants," she told them. "Are you getting this, *Invincible?*" she asked as their silence grated on her nerves.

"Aye aye, Lieutenant Commander," the *Invincible* comtech stuttered. His voice was as stressed as hers, and much younger-sounding. "I was relaying your message."

"Hull signatures follow. They've gone to active sensors," Sarah said urgently, then frowned. "These are weirdly masked thermal signatures," she muttered.

Suddenly, almost beneath her bow, one of the enemy ships shook itself free of the ice that had cloaked it. It was close by astronomical standards; the detectors went foggy as ice fragments exploded outward and hydrogen slush sublimed into gas.

"Oh, my God," she murmured through stiff lips.

"Lieutenant Commander?"

"Shut up! I'm busy!"

The WACCI wrenched aside, then drifted in zero g as the pilot took evasive action and killed their emissions. A sidebar in Sarah's holohelmet blinked red; Yee was running a firing solution.

"Belay that, Yee," Sarah snapped.

Everyone in the reconnaissance craft was frightened, and they were reacting the way brave, well-trained, frightened people did—concentrating on their assigned tasks. Hers was to coordinate them. But their armament was popguns compared to what she was tracking.

"I don't think they can see us." *At least not yet.*

Three pairs of eyes went wide. The WACCI's artificial intelligence put together the hints from the ship's sensors and presented them with a visual of what was happening. Energies flared, and a ship moved across their sight. Parts of it strobed green—the computer showing uncertainty—but the general outline was clear. It wasn't shaped at all like the double hammerhead of a Space Command vessel, and Mollie naval architecture followed the Commonwealth's closely. Instead it was a flattened swelling disk, like a Mechanist version of a tortoise shell, with two spiky structures curving forward as if it were an insect with mandibles. Eight heavy pods on farings ringed its stern, and the surface bristled with sensor arrays, launch tubes, focusing mirrors and beam guides for plasma weapons. Heavy missiles nestled against it.

"Destroyer class, from the power plant," she muttered. "Two thousand tons. Estimated weapons classifications follow."

"Shall we call it a day, sir?" the pilot asked anxiously.

"We shall not," she answered. *Not yet, anyway.* "But I want you to signal the rest of the squad to head back to base."

She switched her attention back to her sensor array, blinking back dismay. "*Invincible,* we have three, four . . . six corvette to destroyer class warships. All of them were hiding in the ice. Emphasize, *in it.* So far only one has freed itself. Unknown configuration."

Sarah sucked in her breath in shock. Something else was hammering at an ice-asteroid further along the ring, hammering from the inside. Something in a very *big* iceball. She risked a burst of active scan; they were kicking up a lot of particles themselves, firing short controlled bursts from their own weapons to break free of their disguise–prison without reflecting damaging energies back on themselves.

"They are accompanying a very large ship, estimate fifty K-tons, data indicates . . ." She made a quick guesstimate. Neutrino signature gave her the power output; assuming roughly equivalent drive efficiencies, and that power-to-mass ratio would make it . . . "Battlecruiser. Repeat, they are accompanied by a battlecruiser. Unknown configuration. Computer has no match."

"Copy that, Lieutenant Commander. Have your people return to base."

"Copy that," she said. *"Now* we can call it a day," she said to the pilot. "Home, James."

"On our way, sir."

"Thank God!" the gunner murmured fervently.

The command bridge of the *Invincible* had a faint smell of old coffee. The liquid in the cup Knott clutched was as bitter and oily as exhaust-vent cleaning residue, but he sipped it anyway.

"How's it going, Major?" he asked the Marine down on the planet below, in the corridors of the Mollie base.

Hadji's voice came fast and hard, though his helmet camera showed no action in the corridor he was rapidly traversing. "It seems to be going as planned, sir. There's been some fierce resistance, but we've put most of it down. We've secured the Mollies' Speeds and," there was a sudden smile in his voice, "a small delegation of Fibians."

"Fibians!" Knott exclaimed.

"Yes, sir." Hadji turned and his camera trained on four gigantic . . . well, not really insects. They just looked that way to human eyes.

They were dull red, sparsely hairy, with a scaly, rough textured chitinous armor over their segmentations. The eight eyes situated in a diamond pattern on each of their faces, glimmered dully in the corridor's harsh lightlike scum-covered ponds. Their whiplike, acid-stinger tails had been secured to their narrow waists. The ends of the flexible tubes they used for speech were sphinctered shut.

I may be anthropomorphizing, Knott thought, *but*

I don't think they look too happy. They also didn't look possible. It was one thing to know they existed, but quite another to actually see them. The flowing movement of their eight legs fascinated him. The back of his mind told him that they couldn't be real, that this was some very good special effect.

They would be a priceless Intelligence asset. Worth this entire raid in themselves.

"Get those prisoners to the *Indefatigable* at any cost, Major."

Sudden fire erupted from a side corridor and the Major's helmet camera was bobbing and weaving so rapidly that the images it transmitted were twisting blurs to the nervous watchers on the *Invincible's* bridge. Things calmed as they returned to the corridor they'd just left.

"We're almost at the mopping up stage, Captain," the major said, a slight gasp in his voice as he jogged along. "But there are some pockets of stiff resistance."

Or there's a suicide bomb somewhere under that base, Knott thought morbidly. *Which one of those fanatics would be only too happy to set off.* Or Major Hadji was being herded into an ambush. Though whether the Mollies were crazy enough to cut down a delegation of their allies remained to be seen.

Sensors worn by the Marines allowed the *Invincible* to trace their movements, mapping the corridors of the Mollie facility as the troops moved through it. At the moment, Hadji and his people were all alone and moving back and forth in a small, unmapped white space.

"Can you get back the way you came?" Knott asked urgently.

"It doesn't look good, sir. A fair number of Mollies

have circled around behind us and any that are free on the station are in front of us."

"Lieutenant Slater," Knott barked. By speaking the lieutenant's name he automatically directed the computer to put him in touch with her.

"Sir!" she snapped out.

"Major Hadji and his group are sixteen degrees north of your position. He's surrounded. I want you to take your people and relieve him. Major Hadji, you got that?"

"Yes, sir."

"If you need more help, call for it. Your prisoners have just become a priority. Understood?"

"Yes, sir."

Knott turned to his XO as she came to stand beside him. "Anything more from our WACCIs?" he asked. The absence of any raiders or blockade runners made him nervous.

"Lieutenant Commander James is reporting neutrino flux," Ju answered him, one slender finger touching her earpiece.

"Hrrrmp," Knott growled. "Could be that planet. It's almost a sun, and those storms—"

"Captain," Ju interrupted, "the lieutenant commander is reporting . . ." her face stiffened and so did her posture. "Six corvette to destroyer class escorts . . . and a battlecruiser," she rapped out. "Unknown designation, the computer doesn't have a match for them."

"They have to be Fibian," Knott said tensely. "Unless the Mollies have found themselves another alien ally."

The sour acid of the ancient coffee twisted in his stomach. A fast carrier and two destroyers was plenty to assure space supremacy around a minor base with light defenses . . . but now he had an enemy battle group moving in on him.

With all of the Speeds and WACCIs out, Raeder and his people had nothing to do but to prepare for their return, and in Raeder's case, to observe what they were doing. He'd been paying particular attention to the adventures of Sarah James as she searched the tumbled rocks and ice of the gas giants ring. He heard her smooth alto voice reporting the enemy ships.

Peter could feel the blood draining from his face.

My God, he thought, *I can't even do anything.* He ought to be in a Speed, accomplishing something. "God *damn* it," he whispered. He was tied to a chair in an office.

He was only slightly relieved when Sarah reported that the strangers' ships apparently couldn't see them.

Yet, his traitor mind supplied. *This is bad*, he thought, imagining the larger situation. *There are only two choices: cut and run, or fight.* They had only two destroyers to the enemy's six. *And they have a battlecruiser.* Which meant they were facing a ship twice the size, more heavily armed, and almost as fast as the *Invincible*. *Not good, not good at all.*

"I think they may have found us," Sarah's voice said calmly. "Vector . . ." she snapped. After a moment she said, "Yep. They've found us."

Run, Sarah! Raeder urged her mentally. *Run! Don't let them get you.* He was dimly surprised by the sense of outraged protectiveness that came over him. He wished, still more urgently, that he could strap on a Speed and go racing to her rescue.

"Have your people return to base," Knott was saying.

"Copy that," Sarah said crisply.

Her voice was suddenly cut off and a red light blinked on Raeder's console, accompanied by an urgent tone that indicated the captain was calling a meeting via comm.

Knott sat in his command chair, the screen before him divided into squares, one by one each of them was filled by the face of one of his senior officers.

"The choice is simple," he said. "We can abandon the troops and run for the Transit point, or we can fight." Knott's eyes were hooded, like those of a sleepy hawk. "The Marine command estimates it will take approximately two hours to get their people back on the *Indefatigable*. Suggestions," he said quietly.

"The *Invincible* is much smaller than a battlecruiser, sir," Truon Le, the tactical officer, said. "But we are considerably faster in both normal space and Transit, *and* we have Speed support. The Fibians have none, since the Marines have taken the Mollie craft."

"We're also more lightly armed," the quartermaster pointed out.

"The Speeds would mitigate that factor," the XO mused. Then she shook her head. "If it weren't for those six corvettes."

"Could any of the Marines fly the Mollie Speeds?" the astrogator, Ashly Lurhman asked.

"They have yet to secure the base," Knott said. "I'd be reluctant to thin their ranks."

"But if we don't, sir, we may be forced to leave them behind," Truon Le said, his dark eyes pleading.

Peter's mind was still half on the fleeing WACCIs and Sarah. But there was something else niggling at

the back of his mind. Something Sarah had said.
Something . . .

"Captain," John Larkin said. "With all respect, sir,
for our people's abilities. We have two corvettes, a
virtually unarmed troop carrier and ourselves. Despite
the Speeds," he said, rushing over the protesting
sounds made by the others, "we must be realistic. We
are no match for a battlecruiser and six corvettes or
destroyers, even though they lack Speed support. I
think we should withdraw."

"And what about our Marines?" the captain asked,
his voice betraying nothing, neither agreement nor
disapproval.

"Sir, the Marines and their transport are effectively
lost already," Larkin said solemnly. "How can we possibly mount a rescue when we can't even defend ourselves?"

Knott's face sharpened somehow, eyes hooded like
an eagle's. "If we run, the light carrier concept will
be discredited. Those who say that we're too light to
do anything useful and that our speed is only good
for bugging out will be vindicated. Not to mention
an unforgivable number of casualties. Come on, people,
you can do better than this!"

Peter loathed the idea of leaving anyone behind to
test the Mollie concept of mercy. Judging by the faces
looking back at him from the screen, so did the others, including Larkin, who had suggested it.

"We must not be intimidated into ignoring the tactical advantages that we *do* have," Truon Le was saying.

"Sir!" Raeder interrupted. "Our main difficulty is
the battlecruiser, and according to Lieutenant Commander James it's embedded in ice from the planet's
rings. Correct?"

"What's your point, Commander?" Knott said coolly, but his eyes were interested.

"That ice is mostly deuterium, sir. Let the Speeds attack while the Fibians are still trapped in it. If they use their particle beam weapons in coordinated strikes against the ice, they may be able to compress the deuterium enough to start a fusion reaction."

"For God's sake, Raeder. Do you think the Fibs are just going to sit there and let our Speeds do that? You're out of your mind," Larkin exclaimed. "Sir," he said to the captain. "I appeal to you. I know it's a very hard thing to leave twenty-two hundred people behind. But you have over sixty-six hundred lives that you *can* save. Don't throw those lives away on an insane gamble like this. There are too many ifs and maybes in this plan."

"They'll be able to get closer than usual," Peter insisted, "because the Fibians' weapons will be masked by the ice. Their captain will probably figure that the ice will protect them from any damage the Speeds can do. But we'll be striking at the *ice!*" He stopped speaking, but his eyes spoke for him as he looked at the captain from out of the screen. *Please,* they said, *let us try.*

"It's doable," Augie Skinner said in his inimitably matter-of-fact manner.

Knott considered the chief engineer's solemn face. "You think so?" he asked.

"Yes, sir," Augie said firmly.

"And what are those six corvettes going to be doing while all this is going on?" Larkin demanded.

"They're going to be struggling out of the ice," Ju, the XO, snapped. Her delicate face wore a severe expression, as though, at the moment, she didn't very much like the quartermaster.

"If Raeder's plan takes out the battlecruiser," Knott said slowly, "then the corvettes won't be as much of a problem." The captain sat for a moment, pulling on his upper lip. "We'll do it. Thank you for your input, people. Squadron Leader . . ."

The faces vanished from Raeder's screen, and he called up the schematic that would show the movements of the Speeds as they flowed toward the enemy battlecruiser. Sutton's voice discussed possible strike points with his second as they made their approach.

Raeder suggested one or two, and Sutton said, "Ah, so you're in on this, too, are you, Commander?"

"Absolutely, Squadron Leader. It was my idea."

"I rather like it," Sutton said cheerfully. "Wish you could be with us."

"So do I," Raeder said wistfully. "Don't get too close," he cautioned. "That's liable to be one hell of an explosion."

"Teach your granny to tat," Sutton snarled.

Raeder laughed. *What the hell does tat mean?* he wondered.

Now he'd have something to do. The squadrons were going to be *very* busy, and they'd need all the backup he could provide.

Then another time of waiting, once they were launched. He kept to the flight deck this time, behind one of the larger consoles—one large enough to support a full thirty-eight splitscreens, a monitor for every one of the carrier's craft. He licked his lips, not just seeing through Sutton's monitor but somehow *feeling* what he was doing. . . .

"They weren't expecting us to react this quickly," Sutton said. "Execute Alpha."

Acceleration slammed at him, wrenching. The Fibian destroyers were breaking free of their sheaths, two of them coming up from the gas giant's ring in a blazing flare of drive energies. Spectacular, but then a destroyer always was. A wing peeled off toward them, vector cones overlapping in the displays of his holohelmet. Behind him the squadrons spread out in a blunt convex shape, and behind that the two Space Command destroyers bore in.

"Let's eat them head-first, the way a boar hog does a snake," Sutton clipped.

Spots of light crawled among the displays. Heavy missiles leaving the Fibian destroyers, little automated ships in their own right. The markers for his Speeds blinked in his holohelmet as they fired, lasers and light rapid-fire plasma cannon. Then white light shone through the holohelmet, dimmed to merely eye-hurting brightness. He read off the emission signature from the status bars and whistled silently. The missile the Speeds had destroyed had used an antihydrogen warhead—that light came from the total annihilation of matter, not from a conventional fusion explosion. *These bugs take things* seriously, *by damn,* he thought.

Ranges closed with frightening speed. From a convex plate the Speeds turned into a cup reaching to enfold the Fibian destroyers. Plasma bursts sparkled and flared against shielding fields. The AI drew missile vectors across the stars, and lights blinked silently where warheads detonated.

"Too aggressive by half," he said, grimly satisfied. Bad tactics; they should have refused engagement until all their comrades were free to join them. *"Get 'em!"*

The cup became a globe. It shrank inward. Speeds

peeled out of it, jinking and twisting in complex high-speed vectors that brought them within firing range.

"Eat your heart out, Raeder," Sutton muttered to himself as his turn came.

His fingers moved in the cups, the only part of him that *could* move in these circumstances. Acceleration kicked him, pressing down like the soft hugely strong hand of an impalpable giant. Random vector changes tugged, switching the directions his inner ear translated as up, down, sideways—all at random intervals. He ignored it, watching instead the swelling schematic of the alien destroyer growing in the holohelmet's display. Closing in, now; he could probably have seen it as a bright dot trailing drive plasma if he'd had time to look with the naked eye, which he didn't.

"Launch!" he rasped.

A spray of parasite bombs kicked loose from the Speed's upper deck, spreading out and hurtling toward the destroyer as they followed his vehicle's trajectory. Sutton flipped the Speed end-over-end and opened the drive past redline as plasma bolts and flickering lasers probed for him, looping out and away. The parasite bombs were too close for the Fibian's defensive systems to stop. They exploded, each one slamming a spike of bomb-pumped X-ray laser fire into the guts of the alien warship.

On *Invincible* hard plastic crumbled under Raeder's hand. He could see the results in his mind's eye: unstoppable bolts of energy burning through ablative panels and into the hull frame, searing through conduits and corridors and crew, into the sensitive electronic heart of the destroyer.

"Bingo," he whispered. "Containment field failure."

The Fibian destroyer's fusion drive fields had

ruptured, faster than the fail-safes could shut down the reaction. The Speed's AIs let him see the consequences: the flattened disk of the Fibian ship flipping as it tumbled dead through space, bits and pieces glittering as they spun away.

The other Fibian warship had broken away, turning toward the gas giant in hopes of disappearing against the background clutter until the other ships of its flotilla could join it. The Commonwealth destroyers *Aubry* and *Maturin* had been waiting for that. They weren't nearly as agile as the Speeds, but they were *extremely* fast. They closed in, bracketing the Fibian ship, lashing out with their heavy antiship missiles. The Fibian killed more velocity, skimming closer to the gas giant . . .

"Too close," Raeder muttered.

The alien struck the outer fringes of the planet's atmosphere at a speed that made it a glowing meteor, plunging down into storms so vast and wild that the flare of its destruction was barely noticeable.

Sutton's voice crackled through the comnet, overriding the cries of *"Hoo-ah!"* and *"Gotcha, bug!"*

"Vectors, following," he snapped. "Let's get the job done."

"Slater!" Hadji snapped. "Where the hell are you?"

"On our way, sir, but running into heavy resistance. These people seem determined to stop us at any cost." Her blue eyes flinched away from the piled bodies in the corridor before her. The Mollies were using them as a barrier, crouching behind them and then popping up to fire on the Marines.

She'd ordered her people to stop firing with lasers because she disliked seeing the damage they did to the helpless dead. Not that she was all that fond of what the projectile weapons were doing, either, but at least they didn't set the bodies on fire.

Slater shook her head in exasperation. "This is useless," she muttered. "Get a coil-gun up here," she said to her second. "That ought to simplify things."

Major Hadji knew his options were growing more limited by the second. His group had been harried into an untenable position. They were exposed in a corridor with the enemy closing in from both ends. There were doors everywhere, but no means of opening them. They resisted laser fire, remaining cool to the touch even after a sustained blast. Projectiles ricocheted off and kicks just hurt your foot. Obviously alien technology.

Hadji turned to the Fibians. "Open this," he said to one of them.

The alien lifted the trunk that dangled between its sets of eyes and Marines raised their weapons in automatic response to a potential threat. It hesitated, then said: "Why should we help you, human?" Its voice was completely understandable, though high and flat and it vibrated weirdly. "Our allies will come shortly and kill you. Then we shall be free."

The major drew his sidearm and aimed it between its eyes, almost, but not quite touching its dull red head. "When they come, I guarantee you that you will be dead. Now open that door."

"You will not kill me," the Fibian insisted. "I heard your commander tell you to preserve us at all costs."

"Unfortunately for you, he's not here," Hadji told it. "But I am." He pressed the weapon right up against the creature's chitinous head. "And if you won't open that door, maybe one of your buddies will after I've shot you. Three's almost as good as four, and two is almost as good as three, and if worst comes to worst, we only really need one of you."

"This is pointless," the Fibian argued. "You will be conquered. Surrender and we will speak for you. Our word is important to them."

"You don't know your allies very well if you believe that, buddy. Understand one thing: if we go down, you go down with us. I kinda like the idea of us all dying together." Hadji cocked his head with a fleeting smile. "It's kind of romantic. So the better we can defend ourselves, the longer you get to live. Do you understand me?" the major asked.

"Yes," it said, and turned to the door. Four times it pressed its strange three-fingered hand against the door's inner edge. When it finished the door slid aside.

The Marines and their prisoners hustled inside.

"Close it," Hadji ordered, and the Fibian did.

The major looked around the room. There were no other doors. It was obviously a lab of some sort. There was even a ventilator for sucking up fumes. He went over to it and looked up under the hood. There was a good-sized pipe leading up from it. Too small for him, of course.

"Where does this pipe go?" he asked one of the Fibians. The major couldn't tell if this was the one he'd threatened in the corridor.

"To the air-conditioning plant, I would assume," it answered. "It is not something we contributed to."

Hadji could have sworn he heard a touch of pique in the trembling voice. "Benger," he barked. "Front and center."

"Yes, sir!" a light young voice snapped.

"Think you can fit up there?" Hadji asked.

"Yes, sir," she said, her answer freighted with unasked questions.

"We're going to boost you up there. If the air duct is big enough, I want you to crawl through it, find Slater and her people, and lead them to us."

"Sir," Benger objected, "I can't just leave like this!"

"No," Hadji said, "you can stay here and die. Go out there and get me some help, Sergeant. Bear in mind that our lives and our pride are far less important than getting these prisoners to Intelligence. Do you copy, Benger?"

"Yes, sir!" she said sharply, and put her booted foot into Corporal Davies' cupped hands.

The corporal slung her upwards as if she were weightless, and she pulled herself into the air duct with a muffled grunt.

"I can do it, sir," she said, her voice both muffled and echoed. "It's tight, but I can move."

"Then move," Hadji barked. A quiet slithering sound answered him.

He looked at the aliens. *What is it that they know that I don't?* he wondered. *Or maybe I'm imagining things.* How could you read something that looked like a spider's idea of the DTs? Still, he could have sworn that the Fibians thought they had some ace in the hole. The way they held their mandibles looked . . . smug, somehow.

"Marcy's hit!" someone shouted.

"Eject, eject!"

Raeder winced as the green beacon strobed red. Another Speed gone—blown to ionized gas, or tumbling with systems dead through the wreckage. *Aubrey* and a Fibian destroyer were spiraling off toward the northern pole of the gas giant, orbiting each other in a vicious corkscrew path and hammering with energy weapons, missiles long gone. *Maturin* hovered closer to the still-trapped Fibian battlewagon, fighting off the three surviving Fibian escorts; she was leaking air and the status bars showed a third of her compartments sealed. From the readings the Fibian ships were in even worse shape, one of them barely maneuverable, but they kept boring in and trying to bring their weapons to bear against the Speeds.

And the Speeds were easier targets, their trajectories regular and precise, keeping their energy cannons firing at the same spots, building up heat and compression faster than it could radiate back into space. The schematic of the Fibian capital ship showed it surrounded by plasma that was literally sun-hot.

Just a little longer, just a little—

Marine Sergeant Rubin Cohen hoisted the slender coil-gun to his shoulder and waited for the computer to pick its optimum target. There was a high-toned *cheep* as it proclaimed its readiness, and Cohen pressed the firing stud.

"Eat this, you zealots," he muttered.

With a soft *phoot!* the tiny missile burst from the muzzle and the end of the corridor exploded in fire and blood and smoke.

They waited a moment to see what the enemy would do. Then as the air-scrubbers absorbed the smoke and still there'd been no response, Slater said, "Let's move." She stepped out cautiously. With a gesture she sent her second, Sergeant Baird, up on point.

Baird adjusted her helmet camera to full magnification and set it to scan the corridor ahead. The computer in her helmet began interpreting the camera's input, looking for anomalies, or specific objects, such as a wire camera peeking out from one of the side corridors. The legend "passage is clear" came up in orange letters in the upper left quadrant of her visor. The sergeant unreeled her own wire camera, coiled in a retractable spool just under her main camera and slaved to its receiver, and carefully fed the thin wire out into the corridor's end. Its special lens showed views of the passageway to the right and left.

"Nothing but bodies," Baird said into her comm.

Lieutenant Slater moved up to stand beside her. Looking over the bodies she saw that there were no living wounded among them.

"Mollies," she muttered bitterly. There were times when words like "stupid" were superfluous, and even "dumber than doggie-doo" wouldn't quite cut it. But "Mollies" said it all.

She looked to the right, down the corridor they would have to travel, and saw a body lying before a closed door. Slater went to it and stood looking down at him for a moment. From what could be seen of his shredded clothing, this was no Mollie. There was thinfilm body armor under the clothes, also shredded—the sort of thing policemen wore, useless in a combat situation where real weapons were being used. She nudged the body over with her foot.

The front of the suit was unmarred, sleek and expensively tailored. A heavy gold chain encircled one wrist and there was a solid, jeweled ring on the middle finger of each hand. A tiny needler was still clutched in one well-manicured hand.

Slater's people moved past her down the corridor. Baird stopped beside the lieutenant.

"What's an overdressed bully boy like that doing on a Mollie base?" the sergeant asked.

"I don't know," Slater answered slowly, looking at the closed door the dead man had apparently been guarding. "But whatever is in there, I think I want a piece of it."

Reaching out, Slater snagged the arm of one of her men. She whispered something that could only be heard by him. The man stepped forward and pounded on the closed door.

"Sir," he said respectfully. "We have to move out of here."

The door opened and Slater stuffed her weapon up under the chin of the man who stood behind it. *Man, or perhaps bear,* she thought. He was dressed much like the man on the floor, and he was *huge*. Not soft, either. She increased the pressure on the pistol grip of her barker.

"Hands up," she commanded, "no sudden moves."

Baird patted him down and began removing deadly weapons, tossing them to the Marine who'd rapped on the door, and then fastened his hands behind his back with a coil of memory wire.

"I'm sorry, sir," their prisoner said over his shoulder. "They got the drop on me."

"They got the drop on you 'cause you're stupid!" a furious male voice answered him. "I ain't goin' nowhere with these people."

"That's your prerogative, sir," Slater said politely. "But you should know that we plan to blow this base up once we've raped the computers. It's your choice, but I'd recommend that you come with us."

"Who is that?" the voice demanded. He swept his huge bodyguard aside like a curtain and glared up at Slater. The man was short and paunchy, with a small neat nose that didn't go with the rest of his bone structure. "Let me tell you something, girlie," he shouted pointing at her aggressively, "I've got influence! I've got friends! Don't you mess wit me!"

Slater blinked, somewhat taken aback—this one was so completely un-Mollie.

"Uh . . . just who are you, sir?" she asked.

"I'm Mike Fleet, you dumb jarhead!"

A slow smile spread over the lieutenant's features as she remembered where she'd heard that name before. He was very big in organized crime. Very big. And his relationship with the raiders was said to be both close and warm.

"Oh," she said, her voice sweet, "we have a room all prepared for you, sir. I'm sure you'll feel right at home. Would you come with us, please?" And she took his arm and started down the corridor.

"Lieutenant!" a voice said from overhead, and they flattened themselves against the walls with their weapons directed upward. Slater shoved the prisoner behind her, putting her body and cermet armor between him and the voice. This was a *very* valuable prisoner.

Fleet pushed feebly against her. "You're crushing me, you butch bitch," he whined.

"Shut up, sir," the lieutenant ordered.

Through the grid in the air duct they could dimly see a face. "Major Hadji sent me," the voice said quickly. "He told me to guide you to him. The squad's trapped in a room not far from here. Stand back and I'll burn my way out of here."

Slater turned her prisoner over to Baird and

motioned her to follow the others. Then she and the other Marine moved back, still watching the duct carefully.

Their faceplates darkened as they watched the laser cut through the thin metal of the duct, then a pair of small, gloved hands gripped the edge and swung down.

"Private Benger, sir," the miniature Marine said, and saluted. "Major Hadji asked me to lead you to him," she repeated.

"Why did he shut down his beacon?" Slater asked, motioning Benger to lead the way.

"He thought the Mollies were using it to trace us, sir. We have four Fibian prisoners and the Mollies seem determined to stop us from getting away with them." Benger picked up to a trot. "This way," she said, directing them down a side corridor.

Slater had to call her people back to follow the young Marine. They made another unexpected jig and suddenly began to come across bodies, both Mollie and Marine. Benger held up her hand and the whole column came to an abrupt halt.

"This is the corridor," Benger said. She frowned. "But it's so quiet."

As if on cue there was a blast from down the hallway, followed by the unmistakable flash of laser weapons, the explosive hiss of subliming metal exploding into vapor . . .

Slater keyed her communicator. "*Semper fi,* and *duck.*" She looked over her shoulder. "Do it."

A short, stubby weapon coughed. *Ctaaang.* It was quite safe at this distance; the crystal-fragment shrapnel lost velocity quickly . . . although at close range it was like ten thousand miniature buzzsaws. Slater and her Marines poured into the corridor, their hand weapons chuddering, catching the Mollie attackers in a devastating cross fire as the Marines trapped in the breached room fired, too.

"Throw down your weapons," Hadji's voice bellowed. "Surrender!"

Nobody really expected them to give up. The last one raised his hands as if to yield . . .

"Watch it!" Slater barked, hitting the deck.

Her squad followed with drilled reflex. Fragments and pieces of the Mollie spattered over the corridor walls. Something went *ting* off the backplate of her cermet armor, driving a hard grunt from her lungs.

CHAPTER TWELVE

The cheering started on the bridge. It spread throughout *Invincible* as the image of a miniature sun blossoming in orbit around the gas giant flashed from screen to screen. The sound ran down the corridors, a wolfish howl of triumph and relief.

Peter Raeder joined in for an instant, his exultation seasoned with a pardonable pride. *It was my idea, after all*, he thought, slightly smug.

Then he realized what that blossoming sun must mean for the Speeds who'd pushed the plasma around the Fibian battlecruiser past critical. "Like being next door to a Solar Phoenix bomb!" he said.

His feet hit the deck seconds before the alarm klaxons began to howl. He reached the flight deck and latched the helmet of his vacuum-and-decontamination suit; once through the airlock the giant chamber already had the bright, hard-edged look that meant the atmosphere had been pumped out. When the great doors swung open to space, only enough remained to feebly twitch at a few stray scraps of paper or foil, starting them on a very slow journey to nowhere among the stars. The nameless gas giant swung by outside, beautiful and terrible in swirling reds and blues and greens, its ring an arch across heaven. The expanding ball of superheated gas that was the Fibian ship—had been the Fibian ship—was just barely visible to the naked eye.

Raeder and all of his people waited in their decontamination suits. He licked lips salty with sweat; a lot of energetic particles were fogging around out there, from weapons, drives, and what was left of warships after they went to Einstein's Heaven. As the last of the Speeds limped home and the great outer doors closed, he overrode the safety lock that would have kept them waiting outside Main Deck until the air pressure equalized. A crackle ran through his suit systems as the grapple fields shut down. More energetic particles.

But we're all in suits, so it doesn't apply, Raeder thought grimly.

What applied was getting those pilots out of their craft and down to sick bay ASAP. The Speeds could wait, though their tattered look wrenched at his heart. Paths were melted through their ablative coating, showing shiny and slick where metal and ceramic had fused under the pulsing impact of plasma bursts or the sharper laser swords. Frames were distorted, sometimes visibly *bent* where near-misses had tumbled them. The mathematically neat puncture wounds of high-velocity kinetic rounds disguised the melted chaos beneath. And overriding everything was the droning warning of radiation detectors. That enormous, dirty fusion explosion had pumped out a *lot* of energetic quanta. They'd sleeted through the Speeds, unstoppable by shield fields at that point-blank range, ripping through tissue and producing a storm of secondary radiation whenever they struck metal.

Anyone with even minimal first-aid training, Raeder included, had been drafted to help. This was a medical emergency greater than even the most pessimistic had planned for and there was some doubt that there would be enough regeneration tanks.

Well, it won't be hard to identify the ones that need them most, Peter told himself. Severe radiation burns sort of spoke up for themselves. He drew his lips back from his teeth in a parody of a grin when he saw Givens' Speed. Half the right lobe was missing, and components showed naked through sheered plating; the port thruster cone looked like something had taken a *bite* out of it. *How the hell did he even get it to fly?* he wondered. *That man is an amazing pilot,* Peter thought with deep respect, and started his team forward.

Givens hadn't lowered his ramp, so Raeder tapped in the override code on his remote, then leapt aboard as soon as there was room for him to enter.

Givens lolled in his chair, his helmeted head dropped forward onto his breast. Peter gently raised the pilot's head until he could see through the faceplate. And wished he hadn't. Givens opened his eyes slowly and after a second registered who stood above him.

The lieutenant gasped. "Are you trying to kill me?" he demanded suspiciously.

"No." Raeder said. "I'm going to take you to sick bay. Hang on. Moving you is going to hurt, but we'll do this as quickly as we can." *Thank God for regeneration tanks,* he thought fervently. Less than thirty years ago a man in Givens' condition would have been dead in two harrowing days.

Givens fainted before they got him down the ramp. *Which is just as well,* Peter thought. It was necessary to strip him of his suit and helmet before he was sealed into the special gurney they would be using to transport him. *And I'd hate to think of what he'd be going through if he was awake.* Screaming, for starters. Patches of skin were coming away with the suit, and there was no time to be gentle.

The burns were extensive. Raeder glanced around quickly. It looked like every Speed had borne a casualty home, though most were at least able to walk with aid. They'd finished with Givens and closed up the life-support bubble that would maintain him until he could be slipped into the regeneration tank.

"Good luck, Lieutenant," Raeder murmured as one of the techs guided the floater off to sick bay. Then he turned to the next Speed and the next casualty.

"All in all," Lieutenant Commander (Medical Corps) Goldberg concluded, "things weren't as bad as they seemed at first. We've been able to utilize two of our units to aid the less wounded without having to stint those in need of more intensive care. Everyone is progressing normally. And despite the understandable grief over lost colleagues, morale is better than anticipated. I expect to be able to discharge the first two by week's end." The doctor folded his hands before him and beamed at the captain like a bright schoolboy who knows he deserves a pat on the back.

"Excellent, Dr. Goldberg. Thank you—and your staff—for doing an amazing job," Knott said with a warm smile, offering the man the support he deserved. He didn't know exactly what logistic and technical miracles the doctor had pulled off to be able to make that bland, positive report, but the captain was aware that they'd happened. The specs allowed for *almost* the number of the serious casualties they'd actually had to treat. A less capable physician would have been overwhelmed.

Certainly Goldberg had lifted the spirits of Knott's other heads of staff. They looked far less tired already. Even Raeder, whom the captain expected to make a most unwelcome report.

It was extremely regrettable that Goldberg had been unable to save the last surviving Fibian. "Have you anything to report on the alien?" Knott asked.

Dr. Goldberg was shaking his head. "I'm sorry, sir," he said, and meant it. "But there's been no time to perform an autopsy. The most obvious cause of death was the wound in its thorax." The doctor gestured to a corresponding part of his chest. "We were unable to seal it, and as yet we don't know what internal damage had been done."

"And it never said anything except for . . ." Knott consulted his noteboard, "'You have killed me, there will be vengeance, you will pay'?" he asked.

"Not that we could understand," Goldberg said. "It seemed to be speaking in its own language for a time. Whatever it was saying seemed too organized to be sounds of pain. We have a recording of all the sounds it made. Shall I forward a copy to you, sir?"

"Yes, please," the captain said.

"They were genuinely expecting to be rescued," Major Hadji said slowly.

Knott glanced over at him. The man should still be in the hospital, but he'd insisted that he be allowed to attend the debriefing.

"What made you think so, Major?" Raeder asked.

"When the Mollies blew the door, the prisoners struggled to get away. Finally they overwhelmed their guards and rushed for their allies. But the Mollies just cut them down. In fact, I would go so far as to say that was the reason they stood for so long. They wanted to be sure they'd killed the Fibians." Hadji shook his head. "They concentrated their fire on them. It's the only reason I'm alive, in my opinion."

The captain nodded thoughtfully. "And the Fibians were aware of this?"

"The one we tried to save was," the major said positively. He shifted in his chair, but allowed himself no other sign of discomfort.

"I sort of thought that those reports of the Interpreters giving 'traitors to the Ecclesia' to the Fibians to consume as food were just propaganda," Raeder said. "But if it *is* true, it certainly fits the Mollie profile to have them turn on the Fibians instead of their leaders."

It was obvious that everyone around the table agreed, and from the thoughtful expressions they wore, they wondered how this incident would affect Mollie–Fibian relations.

Knott turned the corners of his mouth down.

"If the Fibians did have some way of knowing what happened to their people," he observed, "it's very likely they'd approve. I doubt they'd want us to get ahold of any prisoners."

"Though it would, indeed, fit the—Mollie profile—as Commander Raeder terms it, to fear and despise these aliens," the doctor said. "I've always been astonished that they were able to bring themselves to form an alliance with the Fibians in the first place."

"I didn't much warm to them myself," Major Hadji murmured.

"Commander Raeder," the captain said, "your report, please."

"Our decontamination procedures are now completed," Peter announced. "And I'm pleased to report that everything went very smoothly. None of my people suffered any accidents, all of the contaminated materials were safely sealed up and await disposal. Lieutenant Robbins and I have worked out a plan whereby we can salvage seven of our most severely damaged Speeds by cannibalizing four that were too damaged to repair, leaving us with a total of twenty-six more or less operable, although our supply of spares is dangerously low." Raeder pursed his lips. "It was an expensive victory, sir."

"Still, I am certain," Knott said, looking around the table, "that our superiors will be pleased by this action." He smiled at the major. "Especially Lieutenant Slater's little coup. Mike Fleet is of even more immediate value to us than the Fibians would have been."

Yeah, Raeder thought, *because he's a "businessman." And you can always bargain with "businessmen."*

"Sir," Peter said, "the Mollie Speeds that the Marines brought to us have several unfamiliar components. I'd like your permission for either myself or Lieutenant Robbins to interview the engineers that we took prisoner."

"Permission granted," the Captain said. "Mr. Booth, you will allow the commander and the lieutenant reasonable access to the prisoners."

"Yes, sir," Booth said. His eyes glittered as he looked Raeder over.

"If there's no other business?" Knott said. Heads were shaken all around the table. "Then this meeting is adjourned."

Wayfarer of the Spirit Compton's knees were trembling, and he thanked the Spirit of Destiny that his rich gray robes hid their humiliating betrayal. Though for all he knew the wretched Fibian abomination could see right through the fabric to his naked body. He shuddered. The last execution he'd attended was all too vivid in his mind, and there was always *something* in the Fibians' digestive sacs. He carefully refrained from looking too closely.

But to the Mollie guards posted at the Fibian ambassador's doorway, the Interpreter's face wore an expression of lofty calm, and his demeanor was one of utter confidence. They swept the doors open for him, not bothering to knock. All doors must open to the Interpreters of the Perfect Way.

"Ah," Zoo'dec said to his aide in Fibian, "I wondered when they would send someone."

The two Fibians watched the Interpreter's approach, observing with their ultraviolet-capable eyes the effect his fear was having on his body temperature.

"It does not appear that he is bringing us good news, Ambassador," Leksk, his aide observed.

"No, indeed. I imagine he expects us to tear him to pieces and eat him," Zoo'dec said in tones of amusement. "You know, Leksk, some of our clan brothers actually dislike humans. But I do not! I quite love them. They are absolutely delicious."

Leksk snapped his stinger whip with delight at the ambassador's witticism, and the human stopped dead, several meters from them, his weirdly colored flesh turning still more pale.

Wayfarer barely controlled his bladder as the alien threatened him with its cruel lash. *Yet,* he told himself, *if it is the will of the Spirit of Destiny that I should suffer . . .* the Interpreter swallowed with difficulty, *then I must endure.* He bowed to the monsters, a gesture of terror rather than respect.

"Welcome Interpreter," Zoo'dec said to the Mollie. He had no idea which of them the messenger was. Doubtless someone of low importance, or perhaps someone deserving of punishment. These Mollies seemed to enjoy nothing so much as abusing one another. He could not imagine how a species so obsessed with contrasurvival trivia had survived, never mind prospered sufficiently to make it into space. Fibians fought each other, of course. For territory, power, booty, and the opportunity of their clans to grow. Not for . . . *nonsense,* he decided. It was as close as his language could come to the concept he was groping for.

He decided to wait until the messenger spoke.

"I . . . bear grave news, Ambassador," Wayfarer managed to choke out.

"How unfortunate for you," Zoo'dec observed.

Wayfarer closed his eyes and ran a quick prayer through his mind.

"Ambassador, the four representatives that you sent to our advanced listening post . . ." The Interpreter stopped, quite unable to go on.

"Yes, Interpreter," Zoo'dec said encouragingly.

"They have been killed, and the base overrun by our enemies," Wayfarer finished. He swayed on his feet, feeling a desperate lack of oxygen.

"Yes, I know," the Ambassador said. "Come closer," he said. "I would show you something."

Somehow Wayfarer managed to force himself to approach the two . . . beasts that watched him so avidly. *Spare me,* he prayed desperately, *O Spirit of Destiny. That I may serve you and atone for my miserable sins.*

The ambassador turned a reader toward the trembling human and started it running.

"This was taken by one of our representatives," Zoo'dec said.

Wayfarer stared at the screen. It was difficult to make anything of it at first. The colors were all wrong and the camera was moving rapidly. He saw what looked like human limbs flashing and Fibian arms and legs. Then the view turned suddenly and rushed with amazing speed toward a doorway. Through the smoke he discerned Mollie soldiers. *No!* he shouted in his mind, too paralyzed to speak it. The soldiers fired and the recording ended.

Zoo'dec watched the petrified human, enjoying his terror. Then he decided to break its tension before the creature stained itself. That was the one thing he did dislike about them. They stank. Once he had known a female who would have enjoyed that. But then, she was as debauched as she was beautiful.

"They were pouchlings, nothing more," the ambassador said dismissively. "Your people did right to kill them. We would not want our people to be taken prisoner." Though Zoo'dec doubted that the Mollies on site had notions of Fibian expediency in mind when they opened fire.

"Everyone was supposed to die," Wayfarer stammered. "But somehow, the explosives were never set off. Those of our people who were taken will be damned, their names stricken from the roles of the blessed."

Zoo'dec found this offering pathetic. He could not

help but think that these creatures were *meant* to be prey. And soon would be.

"They are insanely superstitious," Leksk said in Fibian.

"But very tasty," Zoo'dec answered him.

Leksk's stinger whip quivered, but he kept it from snapping.

"We are gratified," Zoo'dec said politely to the Interpreter. "Nothing more need be said of this incident. Though, of course," he continued smoothly, "it can never be forgotten."

"No," Wayfarer husked, his terror not lessened one whit.

"We have kept you from your duties too long, Interpreter. Please do not allow us to detain you any longer." Doubtless there were subordinates somewhere waiting to be beaten and humiliated. Which seemed the primary pastime of this very odd people.

"Thank you, Ambassador," Wayfarer said, bowing and backing hastily away. "And . . . thank you."

"You are most welcome, Interpreter," Zoo'dec said to the closing door and the white, terrified face disappearing behind it.

"Perhaps," Leksk said, "we should have offered it some refreshment."

"Perhaps," Zoo'dec responded, "we should have made it *our* refreshment."

They snapped their stingers in mirth. Leksk opened a cupboard. Yowls and squeals sounded from within. The humans and their kindred life-forms had a biochemistry full of pleasant surprises. These minor predators were almost as tasty as the dominant species, and much more agile.

"Dessert!" Leksk said, opening the cage door. "Let's catch it!"

✧   ✧   ✧

It's a small thing, the Mollie infiltrator thought. *No one's going to get seriously hurt.* Which was some cause for regret. But even the smallest step on the path of service to the Ecclesia was another step toward transcendence. And so, even this little thing brought a warm glow of accomplishment. *But there is greater work to come.* It was to be a busy day. *And this makes a fine beginning.*

The Mollie was wearing a decontamination suit, and a better disguise could not be had. Not only did it protect the agent from the toxic materials stored here, but the suits were everywhere in this area, making everyone equally anonymous. The bulky folds and opaque faceplate hid the gender, build, and features of the wearer; all that was revealed was one's height. And even that was deceptive.

The infiltrator held a small heat-gun, hidden by the suit's bulky glove. The heat-gun would be used to loosen the seals put on the contaminated waste brought in from Main Deck and held here awaiting disposal. There were an amazing number of dangerous substances stored here. Ideas and daydreams floated through the agent's mind, bursting like soap bubbles as the Mollie weighed risk against gain.

This will have to do, the agent thought with a sigh. *Small things are often best. Ah, here they are.* The barrels were well sealed, neatly stacked. *A very creditable job. Pity.*

Working quickly, the infiltrator reached through the stacked barrels as far as possible and ran the heat gun around the small part of the seal that could be reached. Then the agent moved on, using the gun on two others.

No more, the Mollie thought reluctantly. *I mustn't be self-indulgent. That would lead to suspicion.* Which was to be expected, of course, at least in some quarters. But the goal here was to make the common spacer doubt him or herself and their colleagues. *If they will not turn their thoughts to paradise, let the unbelievers think on their sorrows.*

Second Lieutenant Cynthia Robbins strode down the corridor toward the room where she would be interviewing the Mollie engineer prisoners. The fixed scowl on her face matched the acid churning in her stomach, where today's lunch—ham, scrambled eggs, hash-browns and what Hydroponics laughingly claimed were green beans—sat like a lump of reactor-core titanium wave guide.

She was very unhappy about being required to do these interviews. Commander Raeder knew very well that she could barely get the people under her command to speak to her. How in the scattered worlds of the Commonwealth was she supposed to get the enemy—Mollies, at that—to open up? Supposedly only an engineer could interrogate engineers.

They should get that idiot Security chief to do this. Let him be useful for once. At least it would distract him while people with real jobs got on with them.

But most of all, Cynthia was unhappy about the hulking guard who shadowed her footsteps. He was there for "her protection," she'd been told by the officious Security officer she'd signed in with. And maybe he was. But his presence *felt* like an insult. Though under Booth's tutelage half the security force could make "Good morning," sound like something you ought to fight a duel over.

They reached the interrogation room and she stood before it waiting. Nothing happened. The corridor remained neutral gray in either direction, broken only by the black outlines of doors and the slight convex shape of the control pad set into each. She turned to look at Kansy, her guard. He looked at her. They were almost eye to eye. *Probably because he has no neck,* she thought.

"Would you open this, please?" she said quietly.

"I don't have a key, sir."

And no forehead, either. But it wasn't his fault; it was hers for not requesting a key, and it was the desk sergeant's for not issuing one. *Just a little oversight, I'm sure.*

"Then you had better go get one from the sergeant," she said evenly.

"I'm supposed to watch you, sir. Those are my orders."

"If you're implying that I should walk back to the front desk with you, MP, you're wasting your time. *You* will go and get the key, and *I* will wait here for you." She paused. He didn't move. "I will give you five minutes." His face was as expressionless as stone. *And probably about as thoughtful.*

"I have orders, sir," Kansy explained, a hint of desperation creeping into his bright blue eyes.

And I thought Givens was a Neanderthal. "I am a lieutenant, MP. I outrank the sergeant. Therefore *my* orders take prec-" she'd been about to say precedence "—priority," she finished, going for a smaller word. "So you have to do what I say." She thought he looked like he might cry. "The clock is ticking, MP."

"But . . . I . . ."

"I'm locked out," she said as gently as she could.

"There's nothing I can do but wait for you." He opened his mouth as if to speak and then shut it again. "So get moving, Kansy, or I'll have you on report!" she shouted.

A look almost of relief passed over his thick features and he snapped off a "Yes, sir!" saluted, and marched off.

Where did they get him? she wondered. *Obviously he passed the breathe in, breathe out, congratulations you're an MP test.* She was glad she'd stumbled onto the right method of motivating him. With some people gentleness just confused the issue.

He came back over eight minutes later. *Which, since it's a two-minute walk, means there was probably a lot of fuss and bother going on.* Certainly Kansy's honest face was quite flushed.

He opened the door without speaking and stood aside to let her enter.

"You're coming in?" she asked.

"No, sir. I'm to watch the door."

"Watch it from the inside," she snarled, her brown eyes daring him to argue.

She sat in the chair provided and he took up a parade rest stance in front of the door.

The room was gray, small, which was to be expected, and divided in half by a thick plastic wall. It smelled very faintly of ozone, like any spacecraft, and even more faintly of fresh sealant and coating; this *was* a new ship, although it was rapidly getting a disproportionate share of experience. There was a table with three chairs on the far side of it and a table and one chair on her side. No one was seated in the other side of the room.

Cynthia waited. After five minutes she said, "Where are the prisoners?"

"I don't know, sir." But from the tone of his voice, Kansy had been wondering, too.

"Go and tell them to bring in the prisoners," Cynthia said firmly. She looked over her shoulder at him. He blinked. "There's no point in your watching me sit here staring into an empty room, you know." He blinked again. "The captain ordered Mr. Booth to allow us to speak to the prisoners."

That did it: mention of the captain juxtaposed with the word "orders" was irresistible.

"I'll go see what the problem is, sir," Kansy said, and saluted.

She briskly returned it. He left and she turned around to stare sourly into the empty half of the room.

The flesh-foam and wig felt odd to the Mollie, a bit smothering, and a little hot as well. The agent worried about sweating; there was a limit to what the foam could absorb. It might be noticed, and this would only work if no one took notice. The infiltrator was disguised as a singularly stupid MP named Kansy.

I must remember to lumber as I walk, the Mollie thought sarcastically. A vision of the neckless MP answering questions about what was going to happen amused the agent almost to the point of laughter. *Lapse not into frivolity,* the agent quoted severely.

Getting into the brig area had been surprisingly easy once the front desk area was passed. The sergeant on duty actually ignored "Kansy" when he walked by. And the thumb scanner had been compromised weeks ago with the agent's own capillary pattern included under the name Kansy. Later, when this was over, it would be a simple matter to remove the extra name and pattern.

These Welters are weak, undisciplined, and fool-ish. We shall drive them out; we shall break them and fling them mewling back to their own planets. Perhaps in isolation they would find their way to the true path. The agent doubted it, but certainly as things were the Welters had no hope whatsoever of salvation.

Ah. Here we are. The door was numbered thirteen. *According to superstition, a most unlucky number,* the agent thought, running key cards through the door's key slot. The final one worked and the door clicked open. *And I see that it is true.* The false Kansy stepped into the room, almost closing the door behind.

"Who the hell are you?" Mike Fleet demanded. He'd been lying on his bunk, but he sat up and swung his feet to the floor at the intrusion.

"I'm your contact, Mr. Fleet. Do you mind if I sit down?" The agent pulled a chair out from under the small table that extruded from the wall and sat, not waiting for permission.

"This is bullshit. I don't know who you are," Fleet said in contempt. "You send some no-neck in here to mouth some mumbo jumbo and I'm supposed to spill my guts. Whaddayou people think I am, some fool?"

The agent had drawn out a pack of cigarettes and a lighter. He put them down on the small table and made a complicated gesture.

Fleet's eyebrows went up. He responded, with a more subtle movement, and received the correct countersign.

"I'll be damned," Fleet said.

Without the slightest doubt, the agent thought.

"How did you get in here?" the criminal asked in

wonder. "And what the hell do you want?" he demanded in a flatter tone.

"I want you to know that we are still watching over your welfare," the agent said. "Obviously there's nothing we can do to help you now, but rest assured we won't let you languish in Welter hands for long. We find your services much too valuable to jeopardize our relationship."

Fleet leaned back against the wall, looking very gratified.

"So, you're gonna bust me out?" he asked.

"We would hardly let one of our allies rot in a Welter jail," the agent assured him. The Mollie glanced at the time. "I must go. You may not see me again. But remember, I'm watching over you."

"Don't watch me," Fleet said in exasperation. "Get me outta here." His small eyes narrowed. "Or my people will make your Interpreters sorry they was ever born."

"We are all sorry that we are born," the Mollie said gently. "To descend from spirit to the flesh is a great punishment." *One never knows, perhaps in extremity he will hear and understand.*

"Can the bullshit," Fleet said contemptuously. "Just get my ass outta here!"

I tried. "Your people will have no cause for complaint. I must go." The agent suited actions to words, pulling the door closed behind him gently.

Fleet fairly leapt on the highly illegal cigarettes the Mollie had left on the table. He hadn't had one in days and his craving was almost uncontrollable. He lit one and took a deep drag, feeling the heated smoke fill his lungs. *Ahhh, that's gooood,* he thought rapturously. *The goddamn Welters took my last pack and those rotten Mollies wouldn't let me smoke on their*

precious base. Not even in my own goddamn room.
He froze and looked at the cigarette pack in his hand.
They don't smoke, he thought.

Fleet tried to let out his pent breath and couldn't.
He clawed at his throat and beat on his chest to no avail.
Numbness began to spread in a tingling wave throughout his body and he dropped to his knees. He couldn't
raise his hands anymore. He was smothering and his
face felt tight and his eyes wanted to bulge out.

Help me! he thought, but couldn't say. *Help . . .
me . . .*

One of the most dangerous crime lords in the
Commonwealth crashed onto his face, twitched helplessly for several minutes, and then lay still, his eyes
wide open, lips purple, and just a tiny amount of blood
flowing from his open mouth.

The door clicked open and the Mollie agent entered,
tested for a pulse. Finding none, the infiltrator picked
up the cigarettes and lighter and left. Leaving the door
wide open.

"You are a harlot."

Hardly, Cynthia thought. *I couldn't get laid on this
tub if I were paying.* This was useless. She'd been
here for nearly an hour, not including the waiting time,
and all they wanted to do was criticize her sex life.
As if I had one.

"This is a complete waste of time," she said at last.
"I have no idea why they wanted me to talk to you
people. We might have known you wouldn't have
anything useful to say."

"We have much that is useful to say, whore," the
biggest of the Mollie engineers said. "But you have
not the ears to hear it."

"That's right," she said crisply. "I'm not obsessed with sex."

Their jaws dropped open simultaneously and their eyes bugged out. They looked like a cluster of baby owls. It was all she could do to keep from laughing.

"Good day, gentlemen," Cynthia said. Without another word, she rose and left the room with Kansy in tow.

There was an open door along the corridor and she glanced in as she passed. She'd always found it impossible to resist looking through an open door. There was a body.

Cynthia acted without thought, rushing to the fallen man's side, even though she could tell to look at the horrible expression on his face that there was nothing to be done.

"He's dead," she announced, looking up at her guard.

Kansy was already talking to someone on his wrist comm. She heard someone say, *"Stay there, don't touch anything."*

Oh great, she thought. *I am never going to get back to Main Deck.*

Booth came charging through the door, thrusting the hapless Kansy aside ruthlessly.

"No!" he said in horror as he looked down at Fleet. "Get Goldberg down here!" Booth barked.

"There's no pulse," Robbins said.

"You!" Booth roared. "You did this!"

Cynthia's jaw dropped. "I did not! *Why* would I kill this man? I don't even know who he is."

"Oh, you know all right," he sneered, narrowing his eyes. "You're a Mollie spy, lady. I knew it the moment I saw you."

She spluttered for a moment at the sheer idiocy

of it, particularly after this morning. "But there was someone with me almost the whole time," Cynthia protested, pointing at Kansy.

"*Almost* the whole time," Booth said significantly. "What does she mean by that?" he asked.

"Well, sir, I had to go get the key to the interrogation room and I was gone for about eight minutes. And then the prisoners didn't show up, so the lieutenant sent me to find out why. That took about maybe ten, twelve minutes." Poor Kansy looked miserable.

The strain of remembering something that took place over an hour ago must be awful for him, Cynthia thought, not without a trace of sympathy.

"So!" Booth said dramatically. "You had motive and opportunity."

"I had no motive whatsoever." *You blockhead*, she thought. "And I'm only in this area because I was ordered to be here. You might as well accuse Kansy."

The MP looked heart-struck. "No, sir," he protested. "I didn't do it."

"Of course you didn't, son," Booth reassured him. "It was Mata Hari, here. Rushing in to contaminate the crime scene like that. That was a dead giveaway."

"Are you out of your mind?" Robbins asked, honestly wondering if he was. "I saw a man on the floor and the natural impulse is to rush in and help."

"You could see that he's dead a mile off," Booth snarled.

"Well . . . yeah. When you get a good look at him, but I acted on impulse. You don't see that many dead bodies in my line of work."

"Oh, yeah?" Booth said quietly, moving in to loom over the slender flight engineer. "Well, we seem to be accumulating a lot of bodies, Lieutenant. And they all have strings that tie them to you."

"*He* doesn't" Cynthia insisted, pointing down at Fleet. "I never saw him before in my life."

"And still you killed him. That's pretty cold-blooded," Booth said. "The lieutenant is under arrest," he said to Kansy. "Process her and put her in the cell next door. We don't want her anywhere near the other Mollie prisoners."

"I demand that you inform Commander Raeder," Cynthia said.

"Oh, I will," Booth said. "Personally.

CHAPTER THIRTEEN

"You *what?*" Raeder demanded.

"I have arrested Second Lieutenant Cynthia Robbins," Booth said smugly.

Peter stared at the Security chief in complete befuddlement. It took a wrenching effort to refocus his mind, which was slightly overfull with the manifold tasks of trying to get the *Invincible's* Speeds back up to scratch. Granted, they weren't going anywhere but straight back to Antares Base, but it still needed doing. His eyes were gritty and red with lack of sleep and too many stims; there was a limit to how long you could go on doing that.

"What did she do," he asked, "attack one of the prisoners?"

"You might say that," Booth drawled.

In his mind's eye, Raeder visualized Robbins leaping over a table with a soprano bellow and doing the Valkyrie thing all over the cowering Mollie engineers. *Yo ho toh ho, Cindy. Getting medieval on them.*

"She murdered Mike Fleet."

"She *what?*" Peter couldn't believe his ears. He

looked around the clutter of the cubby, trying to relate what he was hearing to reality.

Talking to Booth is always so surreal. I mean, Cindy murdered the crime lord? That's insane! Then he remembered who he was talking to.

"There were witnesses, of course," he said matter-of-factly.

"Darn right," Booth said with a firm nod. "The MP we had watching her had to leave her twice and that gave her ample time to act."

Raeder pursed his lips. "Let me get this straight. The lieutenant and this MP were the only ones there?"

Booth narrowed his eyes suspiciously. "Well, yes. For a while, anyway. Then there was another MP who brought the prisoners to the interrogation room and stood watch outside until she was finished."

"Uh-huh. How long were the lieutenant and this MP separated?" Peter asked.

"Eight minutes the first time, about twelve the second," Booth answered. "Like I said, plenty of time to act. If you're ruthless enough."

"But doesn't the fact that the MP was absent, and therefore couldn't tell you what the lieutenant was doing, mean that he isn't a witness at all?"

Booth's face stiffened and he took a deep, audible breath. "He's a witness that she had the opportunity to act," he said through his teeth.

"What I'm wondering, Mr. Booth, is why you don't also suspect the MP."

"I don't suspect him, because my gut says *she's* guilty," Booth snapped.

Oh, yeah? Well, my gut says your gut is full of it. "Who discovered the body?" Raeder asked. *That seems like the kind of question I ought to ask,* he thought.

"She did, actually. She and the MP were finished with the interrogation and were leaving the cell area when they looked through an open door and spotted Fleet. Your lieutenant rushed right in and contaminated the crime scene. Do you wonder that I was suspicious of her?" Booth favored the commander with a condescending leer.

"Uh, had the MP noticed this open door on his way to rejoin the lieutenant?" Raeder asked.

The smile had vanished, but the Security chief didn't look surprised. He looked like he hadn't heard the question.

"Mr. Booth?" Raeder leaned forward. "Did he notice?" No answer. "If there was—"

"He didn't say," Booth said quickly and somewhat defensively.

"Ah. Well, I ask because if the door wasn't open when he passed it to rejoin the lieutenant and they were together from then until the time they left the interrogation room and noticed the open door, well," Peter shrugged ingenuously, "I'd say that indicated a third person at work."

"An accomplice," Booth mused. He nodded. "You might have something there, Commander."

Raeder looked at him in disbelief. *Wow*, he thought. *In Booth's script it says* Cindy is guilty, *therefore nothing can indicate her innocence. I think we'd better get the ship's script doctor involved before this goes too far.*

"What did the captain say about all this?" Raeder asked.

"I wanted to bring the Old Man some results," Booth sneered. "Not bad news and a lot of questions."

"You haven't told him?" Raeder asked in disbelief.

"You told *me* before you informed the *captain?*" *Are you crazy?* he wondered.

"I said, I want to bring him results." Booth looked the commander dead in the eye.

Oh, Lord, Raeder thought. *Now he thinks I'm a Mollie infiltrator. He was hoping that I'd give myself away when he revealed that my "tool" had been captured—practically in the act of assassination. Or at least in the neighborhood of an assassination. Which, to him, is exactly the same thing.*

"Mr. Booth," he said firmly, "we *must* inform the captain. That is procedure." Before the Security chief could say or do anything, Peter had hit a red key that put him in instantaneous communication with the captain.

"Yes, Commander?" Knott said from the screen.

"Sir, Mr. Booth has something of great importance to tell you."

Raeder stood and motioned Booth over to his vacated seat. The Security chief rose slowly, moved around the desk, and carefully seated himself. His mouth had formed a tiny "o" and his sallow face looked almost green.

And so would mine if I had to tell the Old Man something like this, Raeder thought. But he found it hard to sympathize with the bloated bully. *Poor Cynthia. This is all her reputation needed.*

The captain glared at the screen and the image of Booth within it, alternately wishing Booth were within arm's length and grateful that he wasn't. Knott wondered how he could have been so unlucky as to have had William Booth thrust upon him. There wasn't all that much mystery about it. For years, Counterintelligence had been the place where barely functional Academy graduates with influential connections got parked. It was where they could do the least harm and save the Space Command General Staff the political heat of dumping them out of the service. Now . . .

"Who was the MP?" the captain asked, rubbing a hand over his face. He was exhausted, like every other officer on the carrier with a real job to do. Booth . . . now, Booth looked very spruce.

"Kansy, sir," Booth answered. "A very honest man."

"Kansy? Ah, yes."

Someone from Booth's former command. Knott had always suspected that the reason Booth insisted on bringing this particular MP along was that he made the Security chief look brilliant by comparison. But he *was* honest. The man was too damned stupid to be anything else.

"I think, Mr. Booth, that you are certainly justified in questioning the lieutenant. However, given the total lack of evidence you have to connect her with this murder, you are unjustified in arresting her. I want her released immediately."

"Sir!" Booth protested. "I am convinced that this woman is dangerous."

"You and the quartermaster," Knott said darkly.

You would have thought that after the last fiasco Booth would have been a lot more careful about casting aspersions on the lieutenant's character. She probably had enough cause for a whopping false-arrest-and-defamation suit, and Knott might be tempted to be a witness on her behalf. Not in wartime, of course.

"I suspect that she's been more sinned against than sinning," the captain told him.

An emergency light flickered on Knott's comm.

"Send her back to work," he told Booth. "And don't arrest the lieutenant again without my express permission."

Knott broke the connection and another face immediately replaced Booth's. This face was about fifty standard years old, black hair and eyes, copper-colored skin.

"Sir, this is Chief Petty Officer Mankiller."

"From Toxic Materials Containment. Yes, I know you, Chief. What's up?"

If Mankiller was surprised that the captain knew his name, he didn't show it; he merely launched into his report.

"We've had a containment breach in storage room eight," the chief said. "No harm done, we caught it before it got too bad and cleaned it up right away. The detection system on this ship is amazing," he said enthusiastically. "But the regs say that I have to inform you on an emergency basis."

"Emergency basis, means immediately," Knott said with a scowl.

"And so I am, sir. The leaks were small and precisely located by our warning system. So while I've been talking to you, my people were able to repair the seals and are checking around for more. As I said, sir, I've never worked with any system so perfectly calibrated." The chief's face showed his keen admiration.

"Very good, Chief," the captain said. "Which containers leaked?"

"The ones from Main Deck, Captain. Which is odd, because my people double-checked them before they put them into storage, and there wasn't a sign of a leak then."

Why am I not surprised? Knott thought with resignation. "Thank you for informing me, Chief. I commend you and your people for your quick action. I'm also going to order both you and your people not to discuss this with anyone. Nor are they to discuss it with each other outside of the confines of your department. Do you understand?"

"Yes, sir," Mankiller said, though he didn't really. But, then all he really needed to understand was that this was a gag order and it was his duty to enforce it.

The captain nodded and said, "Carry on." As soon as he disconnected he called Raeder. "Are you alone, Commander?" he asked when the commander's face appeared.

"Yes, sir. Mr. Booth left as soon as you disconnected."

"Come to my ready-room, Commander. We need to talk."

Raeder felt so tired he could almost cry. "Sir," he said slowly, "those containers were fine when they left Main Deck. I checked each one myself. Personally. If they leaked it had nothing to do with my people."

"I never thought it did," Knott said.

I've seen eyes that reddish boiled egg color lately, in the mirror. But then it's been an up and down week. Raeder thought. *We beat the Mollies, but lost the Fibians. We captured a major player in the crime world, but he was murdered in our brig. And now this. Kinda makes me glad I'm only a commander.*

"When you first came aboard, Commander," Knott said, his face unreadable, "I assigned you a task. I'm asking you for a report."

"Sir, what I've done, mostly, is to eliminate suspects. At least to my own satisfaction."

The captain made a face. "Well, that's progress at least. Of a sort." His gray eyes bored into Raeder's. "Do you have a suspect?"

Raeder considered for a moment. *Well, do I?* "Ye-ss, sir, I do. But it is merely suspicion. I have absolutely nothing to hang that suspicion on. Therefore, I'd rather not say anything further at this time."

Knott raised his eyebrows. "Not even to me?"

"Sir, I wouldn't want to prejudice you against someone who may be totally innocent. I don't think I could bring myself to say that name in a completely empty room. It's that tenuous."

The captain leaned back in his chair with a sigh. "All right, Commander. I'll respect your integrity. For now." He leaned forward again, crossing his arms on his desk. "Can you at least tell me who you've eliminated as suspects?"

"Sir, I don't believe our problem is on Main Deck."

Knott raised his brows. "Well, since that eliminates about five hundred suspects, I guess I'll have to compliment you on your fast work," he said. "How did you come to this conclusion?"

"I've changed the way parts are distributed. Whoever requests a part, signs for it, and it's inspected when it's handed over. If the part fails after that we know who to talk to. Also, I've mixed the crews around. I haven't kept the same crews together for more than a week, so that if someone wasn't doing their job right it would be more likely to attract attention. But my people *do* their jobs right, sir. They watch each other and double-check things. They're aware of the importance of what they do and they're proud of their work." Raeder shrugged. "I just can't imagine a spy surviving in a climate like that."

The captain was nodding. "No, I can see your point. All right. I'll let you have your head . . . for awhile. See what you can do to hurry things along, though, would you? Thank you for coming, Commander."

Raeder stood and saluted. The captain returned it and Peter turned to leave.

"Oh, Raeder," Knott called as the commander was about to close the door.

"Yes, sir?"

"Try not to drop the ball."

"Yes, sir."

The Mollie knelt upon the rod, arms outstretched and weeping piteously. Though the pain was great, the agent couldn't help but feel it was insufficient.

O Spirit of Destiny, Mighty One, please hear my prayer. I beg your forgiveness for the foolish risk I took that had so little result. For all that could be told, no one had even noticed the broken seals on the barrels of contaminated waste. Or else they'd been found so soon that no harm had been done. In fact, this whole mission seemed to be doing very little harm, considering the effort that was going into it. The Mollie gulped. That was a very unpleasant thought.

O Spirit guide my stumbling steps. Aid me that I may serve you better. Do not let me waver in my resolve, do not let me fail in my task. It was impossible to use the whip, though the agent longed to do so. It was, unfortunately, all too likely to leave damning traces.

Still, in the Ecclesia, the agent had been renowned for stringent discipline. Many acolytes wore their whip marks as badges of honor. But none could compare to the agent, neither for depth of cut nor number. *Those* had been good days.

But the agent's task seemed so overwhelming, to destroy the Commonwealth's light carrier program single-handedly. The Interpreters, in their wisdom, feared these craft, sensing that they would tip the balance in the loathsome Commonwealth's favor.

Let it not be so, Spirit. They have so much on their side. The ship-building facilities, the munitions plants, the manufacturing. Almost all that we have is truth.

Truth and all the fuel. The agent was startled. This was such an uncharacteristic thought that the Mollie recognized it as direct contact with the Spirit itself.

"Oh, I am unworthy," the enraptured agent whispered. The Mollie fell facedown and groveled, weeping in joy this time. "We shall succeed. O Mighty One, with your aid we shall overcome!"

Two days later as Raeder and Lieutenant Robbins were finishing up one of their "leadership" sessions, Cynthia broke her usual pattern of taking whatever reading material he'd assigned her, thanking him shyly, and bolting like a deer in a forest fire. She simply sat there.

Her face and body language were so blank that Raeder knew that she must be extremely nervous or upset.

"How's everything going?" he asked. "Is Mr. Booth leaving you alone?"

His question seemed to surprise her, because her eyebrows went up a fraction.

"Yes, sir. He's left me completely alone."

Then she fell silent again, looking, more or less, expectantly at Peter.

Speak! he thought. "Lieutenant," he said aloud, "it is perfectly permissible for you to ask a question or make a statement without forcing me to drag it out of you." He thought for a moment. "Unless, of course, you plan to ask something really personal or to say something extremely cruel. You don't, do you?"

"Oh, no, sir," she said. Then she leaned forward confidentially. "I, ah, think I may have found a way to solve your problem, sir."

"My problem?" he asked. *What problem? BO, bad breath, bad hair? Whatever it is, I'm in deep trouble if I need Cindy's help.*

"I was referring to your piloting problem, sir." The lieutenant seemed much more at ease.

Raeder, on the other hand, felt a sharp twist in his gut. *Remember what I said about saying something extremely cruel?* he thought. *No, I guess not,* he thought as she continued, oblivious to Peter's discomfort.

"I don't fly anymore, Lieutenant," he said curtly.

"Only because the current equipment doesn't match your needs," she said eagerly. "But it could, and it wouldn't be all that difficult."

"Lieutenant," he said, through his teeth, "I was told that there was no way—"

"That's because, frankly, sir, you're probably a minority of one, at the moment. So they don't want to spend R and D time or money on the problem. But sir, this war is just really warming up, and there'll be plenty of people suffering from wounds like yours." She looked positively animated by this time. "And this is such an easy fix!"

Jeez, he thought. *Don't you know what a sensitive subject this is? Sand would know that I don't want to talk about this. Rocks would.* Booth *would!* He threw up his hands. "What do you want from me?" he asked, a little too loudly.

"It's a feedback problem," Cynthia continued as though she hadn't heard him.

I'll say it is, Raeder thought sourly.

"The prosthesis can't interact with the Speed's computer," she was saying. "*But* it's not that far to your wrist! The tendons in your wrist are almost as sensitive to the motions you need to make as your fingers would be, and the chemical component is obviously right there." She looked at the commander hopefully, her eyes shining with enthusiasm. "All that's really needed is an extension," she said.

Raeder could feel his jaw dropping and he just let it go. *She's right, by God. It could be an easy fix.*

"So," he said again, "what do you want from me?"

She wrung her hands together in her lap. "I need four hundred dollars," she confessed. "For development costs."

Raeder ran his finger below his lower lip. "If I authorize the expense," he said, "then the Commonwealth will own your invention."

"Actually, I would be entitled to one-third of the gross profits, if any. Which is fine by me," she said dismissively. "I'm an engineer, not a businesswoman."

Raeder could hardly believe his ears. His unworldly little Cindy sounded a lot like a businesswoman to him. *And as for me, I'm an engineer, not a sugar-daddy. I want this so bad I can taste it. But can I justify this?*

Unconsciously, he tapped the fingers of his right hand in a rhythm his physical therapist had taught him. After a moment he became aware of what he was doing and he stopped it.

"All right," he said. "I'll authorize the expense."

✧   ✧   ✧

Raeder sat at the bar in Patton's feeling very surly and just a little sorry for himself. He ignored the cheerful holos that covered most of the walls of beaches and palm trees and laughing people with tans and implausibly little on. He even ignored the sound of combers hissing on the beach, and the expensively realistic smell of ocean and seaweed. It had been a hard day. He ground his teeth, remembering the first part of it . . .

"*Seven* Speeds?" the man asked.

He had a sing-song accent much like Captain Bethari's, but that and his complexion were about all he had in common with the captain of the *Africa*. This man was short, very plump, and looked like exactly what he was: a military bureaucrat. His office looked like the sort of thing you'd expect the overlord of a supply dump to have, too. Subtly luxurious, and with plenty of souvenirs. The rug on the carpet looked like a genuine Kashmir, worth three years of Raeder's pay.

"Yes," Raeder said, grinding patience out of his soul by a boulderlike effort of will. "There's this thing called *combat*, lieutenant, and in it things get *used up*. We just fought a major battle against enemy capital ships. In case you hadn't heard."

"Seven Speeds," the man went on. "Oh, I am thinking that that is *most* excessive."

Raeder sighed and settled down to dicker.

Forward Supply behaved as though no one had ever used anything they'd seen fit to issue. And as for losing Speeds! It seemed the *Invincible* held the all-time record for Speed squandering. And munitions, parts, and fuel, thrown about with a prodigal hand all regardless of the cost, or the fact that others were waiting for the very same things.

He knew that the *Invincible's* requisitions had priority, and they knew he knew it. Even so the game required him to approach them, hat in hand, metaphorically speaking, and humbly beg for what they had no choice but to give him. And they had to act as if every wave guide and field generator came out of their own personal retirement funds.

"Well, I got what we needed," he mumbled into his drink, trying to banish the session with the logistics officer like the nightmare it was.

Raeder allowed himself a brief daydream in which he once again led a squadron and dealing with the gringing misers in Forward Supply wasn't even a cloud on his horizon. He smiled fondly.

Maybe it will be possible, he thought. *Maybe Cindy will pull it off.* He believed that it was possible, at least. Her idea had merit, and the schematics she'd sketched out for him looked promising. *Oh, but that would be a wonderful thing,* he thought wistfully.

He glanced up at the mirror over the bar and peeked at the other reason this had been a bad day. He'd asked Lieutenant Commander Sarah James to dinner and she'd turned him down. "Other plans," she'd said. She was seated at a table behind him with several other officers from the *Invincible.*

She might have invited me to go along, he thought. But he'd noticed that there weren't any Speed pilots among her group. He frowned slightly. *I wonder just how widespread this anti-Speed pilot prejudice is.*

He'd also noticed that their eyes met in the mirror rather frequently. He took a sip of his drink. *So at least she's aware that I exist.* He really couldn't quite figure this out. He'd never been rejected before solely on the basis that he'd once flown Speeds. Back when he had flown Speeds, he'd found it a social asset, if anything. Glamour, glory, wild black yonder, rah rah.

While being an outcast is an interesting experience, he thought, *I can't say that I recommend it.* He caught Sarah's eye in the mirror and winked. She ducked her head and pretended she hadn't noticed. *Hmm,* he thought.

But she didn't look back and his attention began to wander. The other reason it had been a bad day was that John Larkin had told him that the joke going around the station was that the *Invincible* had been renamed the *CSS Butterfingers*, call sign "Oops!" Raeder had given the quartermaster a severe tongue-lashing and now he was regretting it.

Still, Peter thought, *an officer should know better than to spread a joke about his own ship like that.* It was like insulting your own mother. Raeder wasn't looking forward to seeing Larkin at breakfast tomorrow morning. *But I'm damned if I know which of us should apologize. Ah, well.* He sighed. *Sufficient unto the day are the evils thereof, as my father used to say.*

He got up from his stool, nodded to Sarah, and made his way to the dining room. *Till then, at least I can eat.*

They actually had crottled greeps on the menu here. Fresh.

CHAPTER FOURTEEN

"I have a message torpedo coming in," Louise Hypher said, her voice cool and professional. "Broadcasting Space Command Alarm code, A-Seven. Preparing to take datadump. Receiving."

Communications and Traffic Central for Antares Base was a large circular room deep in the core of the installation, with consoles all around the walls except for the entrance doors at the rear. More semicircular consoles covered the floor, converging on the officer of the watch at his desk near the center. The chamber was dimly lit, mostly by the blue glow of the holoscreens hovering above the consoles, and full of a murmur of voices.

The watch commander's head came up. Message torpedoes usually were sent by ships in distress for one cause or another. He moved over to stand by the petty officer's shoulder.

"Military codes, sir," Louise said.

Lieutenant Commander Bashki stood beside her and tapped his earplug until her station came up.

"zzzzt . . . CSS Dau . . . zzz . . . pursued by Mo . . . zzzt . . ."

"Can't you refine it any better than that?" the lieutenant commander snapped.

"No, sir," she said crisply. "It's too far out." *And I can't change the laws of physics, sir, even when I want to.*

"Where is it coming from?" he asked. His eyes searched her station for the answers he wanted.

"Transit point two, sir." Louise turned to look at the officer of the watch. "The one that leads to Mollie space."

Sector Commander Montgomery listened to the lieutenant commander's report gravely, going over in his mind who they had to send out.

"Captain Knott," he said nodding gravely to the man standing at parade rest before him. "The *Dauntless* is coming in from a raid on the Mollie processing plants, and she's got a full load of antihydrogen. They were being pursued by three Mollie destroyers and a Fibian light carrier. *Dauntless* lost all of her Speeds and has taken heavy battle damage. As things stand, they were so closely pursued at the time the message torpedo was sent that they didn't think they would shake off the enemy even in Transit. Though it wouldn't take a genius to figure out where they were headed. Ontario Base was practically the only place they could go.

"You see my dilemma, Captain Knott," he said.

"I'd suggest sending the *Diefenbaker* and the *MacKenzie*, Sector Commander," Knott said positively. "We are not up to strength as yet."

Montgomery lapsed into thought. They would need something heavier. Unfortunately, all the capital ships of the Antares Squadron were out responding to a possible Mollie attack—probably a feint, all things considered—and the *Invincible* was the obvious choice. But her Speeds had been somewhat battered in the last engagement and she was still taking on supplies . . .

"The obvious ship for this, sir, would be the *Butterfingers*," the lieutenant commander said without thinking. Then he froze as the color rose in the sector commander's face and his eyes began to blaze. Knott's face on the screen might have been carved steel.

"I will not tolerate that kind of levity in my command, Lieutenant Commander!" Montgomery bellowed, rising from his chair and moving swiftly around his desk. "I do not like name-calling or mockery, and if you insist on indulging in it, *I* will give you cause to change your ways. Am I clear, Lieutenant Commander?"

"Yes, sir." The lieutenant commander sought safety by snapping to attention, the military's behavioral equivalent of protective camouflage. *I can't believe I said that!* he thought.

"Captain Knott is one of the finest officers in the service, Lieutenant Commander. We are lucky to have him. And I will *not* tolerate some arrogant, junior *officer* who's never even been on the deck of a battleship, let alone in combat, making fun of him or his command. Is *that* clear, Lieutenant Commander?"

"Yes, sir!" came out louder than before.

"As it happens you are right. The *Invincible*," Montgomery paused to glare at the now totally humiliated lieutenant commander, "is the only ship to send. With apologies, Captain," he said to Knott. "There is no one else. See what you can do to expedite things for them," he barked at the unfortunate lieutenant commander. "Contact the *Diefenbaker* and the

MacKenzie and brief them. Leave the *Invincible*," again the poisonous glare, "to me. You are dismissed."

"Thank you, sir." And never did a subordinate welcome dismissal more. The lieutenant commander saluted, pivoted, and marched out of the station commander's office with perfect military precision, glad to have survived rousing Montgomery's legendary temper.

"My apologies, Captain Knott," Montgomery said. "It's really not a job for a fast carrier. If I had a couple of cruisers, or better still a battlewagon . . ."

"But you don't, sir. And the *Invincible* will be glad to take on the job."

Knott had decided to save time by calling a comm conference. He'd briefed his officers on the situation and now he needed information back from them.

"Commander Raeder," he said, "what's our status on Main Deck?"

"We can fly twenty-five Speeds, sir. Four were destroyed fighting the Fibians, four we cannibalized because they were too damaged to repair, two are waiting for parts, and we have two pilots still in sick bay." He looked thoughtful. "We have enough fuel for this, sir. But we're short on parts. If something vital gets shot off, that could put another pilot out of action."

"Noted, Commander." Knott turned to Larkin. "Any way to expedite the parts situation?" he asked. "We only have three hours, but the station commander assured me that we would find Forward Supply unusually cooperative."

"I'll get right on it, sir, with your permission?" Larkin hovered expectantly.

"Do you know Commander Raeder's needs, Quartermaster?" the captain asked.

"There's a copy of my list on your computer, John," Raeder said. "And of course, Forward Supply should have a copy. My advice would be not to speak to them without that list in your hand."

"Don't worry, Commander, I know their tricks," Larkin said, a little stiffly.

Raeder concealed the wry twist of his lips with his hand. The quartermaster had been like this for two days now. *This is so high school,* he thought.

"Needless to say, people," Knott said after dismissing Larkin, "we're really going to have to scramble to get the *Invincible* ready for departure in the short time we have. So, I think we should get to it."

"Captain," Raeder said, raising a restraining hand. "Perhaps, since we're so short of our full complement of Speeds, there might be a small squadron going begging that would like to accompany us?"

"Excellent suggestion, Commander. How small are you looking for?"

"Main Deck has room for eight Speeds, Captain," Raeder said.

"However," the squadron leader put in, "we're down *six* pilots, so we're going to have to borrow two to fill out the squadron."

If you can find two pilots willing to fly an unfamiliar Speed on a combat mission under a leader they've never seen before, Peter thought. Then again, the *Invincible* was going to permanently need four pilots. Raeder cringed at the knowledge that his idea had brought about their deaths. *Anyway, this could be considered a practical demonstration of their abilities prior to an interview.* Ghoulish, but probably true.

Pilots were a competitive bunch, and *Invincible* was a desirable assignment.

"I'll look into it," Knott said.

Raeder was relieved. It would be difficult; there would be turf fights between the pilots and even the squadron leaders. *Right up to the time they go into combat,* he thought. And then they'd unexpectedly turn into the smoothest war machine you ever saw. He'd seen it happen before.

Everybody would squabble so much you'd figure that *this* time the miracle wouldn't happen. *But, so far,* Raeder thought, tapping lightly on his block of wood, *it always has.*

"I see no reason why my people have to move their Speeds," Sutton complained, watching one of the big machines roll forward.

"They don't," Raeder said watching the signaler guide the Speed into its new berth. "The techs are moving them." *Rather awkwardly,* he thought, frowning.

Since they were squeezing the craft in as close together as they could, the computerized guides built into the floor of Main Deck were useless. Everyone learned the basics of doing things the old-fashioned way when they began their training, but since no one had ever expected to have to do this procedure manually things were going painfully slow.

Sutton made an impatient sound. "Don't be obtuse, Commander. Obviously what I mean is, why can't *they* take the empty berths?"

There are two things going on here, Sutton, Raeder thought. *One, this is a turf thing. You're afraid of losing face before they even get here. But two is pure superstition. None of your squadron, you included, wants to take any of the "dead men's berths" because you're afraid of being jinxed. Well, I'm not going to pander to that crap.* Though, to be fair, if he'd still been flying he might have felt very differently.

"Well, first of all, Squadron Leader, it's a matter of respect. I didn't think you would want strangers occupying those spaces." Raeder watched Sutton blink. The thought had obviously never occurred to him. *One for me,* Peter thought with satisfaction. "Second, we don't know what all we'll be getting. And some of the older models were somewhat larger. I figured we should be prepared for the worst. Also, we don't know how much experience these pilots will have at landing on a carrier." He shrugged. "We can sort it out on the way, if necessary, but we've got to be sure we've got the room *now.*"

"Yes, of course," Sutton said thoughtfully. "I hadn't thought of it quite like that."

And Raeder knew he was talking about those four berths, rather than the relative size of different generations of Speeds or inexperienced pilots. *I don't have time for this,* he thought.

"Where are you going to put these people?" Raeder asked. The placement of the Speeds was his problem, but the pilots were all Sutton's.

"My God! I hadn't thought of that," Sutton exclaimed.

Raeder spared him a look that said, "You'd better." Looking back to the bustling deck, he snapped into his headset, "Watch your head, Sousa!"

The man guiding a Speed to its new berth ducked, narrowly missing the sidetip of the parked Speed beside him.

Raeder tuned his set to general broadcast. "Heads

up out there, people. Nothing's where it used to be, so don't get complacent on me." He saw arap Moi physically direct two bewildered techs toward their lost Speed.

"Well," Sutton said, "I'd better go. I've a great deal to do."

You do? Raeder thought in mock astonishment. "Then you'd better not let me hold you," he said aloud. "Thank you for taking the time to talk to me, Squadron Leader."

"Not at all, Commander. Glad to. Carry on." And Sutton turned and trotted off to finish up his own tasks.

Raeder watched him go with a genuine grin. A conceit so thick that it hadn't even heard the irony in his remark only made the squadron leader more human. *And therefore more likable.* Peter turned and dove into the maelstrom on Main Deck, hoping he'd have it all sorted out before the new people showed up.

Peter, Cynthia, and arap Moi stood together at the window in Raeder's office wall, looking out over Main Deck. The outer doors were open and the voice of traffic control guided in the visiting squadron.

Raeder had insisted on deploying the magnetic grapples, knowing full well that the borrowed pilots would resent the implication. *But better safe than sorry,* he told himself.

The grapples were primarily used in training. They had the ability to fend off or grasp a Speed, bringing it in safely in spite of the pilot.

The first Speed to come in clearly had no need of such aid. It landed with a panache that even Raeder could envy. Particularly considering the antique he or she was flying.

"My God," arap Moi, said softly. "That's a Mark II."

"I didn't think they existed anymore outside of museums," Robbins breathed.

Raeder glanced at her and smiled at her expression. The young lieutenant positively glowed. It was obvious she couldn't wait to get her hands on one of them. They weren't actually out of service, but they *were* generally restricted to operating out of fixed bases and planetary-defense orbital forts these days.

"Remember," he said quietly, "they're just visiting."

"Yes, sir," she said. But it was clear she wasn't paying attention to what either of them had said.

The second, third, and fourth came in without the grace of the first but competently enough. Raeder turned away started to go through parts reports. *I insisted on getting them, I might as well review them.*

"That's seven," arap Moi said. "Good thing we tightened up out there."

Cynthia grunted acknowledgment.

"Oh, my God!" the chief said.

Raeder was on his feet and looking out the window before he could draw breath to ask what was wrong.

The final borrowed Speed was approaching at an angle that was sure to crash it into the *Invincible's* side. Traffic control was aware of it and was trying to get the pilot to either lower the angle or to make a new approach.

"Your instruments are wrong," said traffic control. "Pull your nose down two points." There was a pause.

Raeder could see no difference in the pilot's approach.

"Abort your approach and come around again," traffic said.

But the pilot came stubbornly on. Either stubbornly, or frozen with terror and operating on autopilot.

"Good thing you had them activate the grapples," arap Moi said. His voice was quiet, but his posture was stiff.

"I ordered the crew to extend it to maximum reach," Robbins said.

"Good," Raeder told her. "I ordered them to act at the first sign of trouble."

"Abort your approach!" traffic said sternly, though by now it would take a miracle of piloting to do so.

Where any normal human being would be gibbering with panic, Peter thought, *traffic controllers merely harden their voices.* "We did tell traffic that we'd deployed the magnetic grapple, didn't we?" he asked.

Cynthia and the chief looked at one another, then at Raeder. They shook their heads.

Oops. The Speed was closer now. "I'm beginning to wonder if we told the grapple crew," Peter murmured.

Robbins and arap Moi slowly turned their heads to look at him, their eyes wide and horrified.

"I . . . thought *you* told them, sir," the chief said.

"So did I," Robbins managed to say in a choked voice.

"Well, I did," Raeder said gesturing at the oncoming Speed. "But look at—ah, that's got it."

The Speed had been coming in at its dangerous angle when suddenly it slowed, as if it had run into a soft wall. The pilot tried to turn, and slewed sideways, still trying to power its way out of the grapple's hold.

"What does he think he's doing?" Cynthia demanded, puzzled.

"I don't believe he's fighting it," arap Moi said, shaking his head.

I wonder if we can send him back and keep his Speed, Raeder thought, frowning. The Speed was still fighting to get loose, while the grapple drew it and turned sideways, toward Main Deck.

From the comm behind him Raeder heard something he'd never imagined hearing. "Turn your engines *off!*" bellowed traffic control.

All three of them turned to stare in wonder at the panel. When they turned back to Main Deck they saw that the pilot had complied and the grapple crew manipulated it neatly through the outer door and onto the deck. The door began to close. Without a word, all three of them turned, with identical looks of frozen fury on their faces, and marched toward Main Deck.

Peter was ready to chew his way through the doors by the time the air pressure equalized and they began to rise. They scooted under the rising door and made a beeline for the last ship in.

The pilot had powered open the cockpit's hood and was climbing down the side.

Lieutenant Robbins stopped dead in her tracks, her jaw on her chest.

Raeder kept going with the chief at his shoulder. By the time they reached the Speed, the pilot was on the deck, pulling off his helmet.

"Haven't you ever landed on a carrier before?" Raeder demanded furiously.

"Plenty of times," the small, slender man said, "Commander. In the simulator."

"That is one lousy simulator," arap Moi growled.

"Are you aware, Pilot Officer, that you almost crashed your craft into this ship?" Raeder asked levelly.

"No," the pilot said, "not until the very end there.

I had no idea what had happened to my Speed when you grappled me and my instruments told me I was doing just fine."

"And you believed them? Even when traffic control told you to pull up and try your approach again?" Raeder asked in astonishment.

"Actually," the pilot said, looking embarrassed and a little harassed, "the closer I got to the *Invincible* the harder it got to understand them."

"But you cut your engines when they told you to," Raeder said.

"That's because they shouted. I had to ask them to repeat themselves about four times." The pilot frowned at Raeder. "This whole mess is actually the *Invincible's* fault," he said.

"*Our fault?*" Peter asked in disbelief. "Your lousy piloting is our fault?" He held back his rage with a great effort. "Would you care to explain that, Pilot Officer?" he asked with alarming calm.

"No one mentioned that you'd have your magnetic grapple deployed, Commander," the pilot said. "If they had I would have told them to turn it off. It screwed up all my instruments and the comm, too."

Raeder just looked at him, too astonished, for a moment, to speak. He adjusted his stance and finally managed to say, "Magnetic grapples can't effect instruments. The EMP shielding protects them.

"They could on the Mark I," Cynthia said.

Peter and arap Moi looked up slowly. Then they turned and looked at the Speed. It was about twenty percent larger than the Mark IVs the *Invincible* was flying. Experienced eyes darted to the placing of sensor arrays and weapons bays.

"I should have known that," the chief said. "They

were the last ones where the pilot had to climb in and out like that."

"What is this thing doing outside of a museum?" Raeder asked in awe.

"Well, they keep promising us new ones," the pilot said cheerfully. "But you folks keep gobbling them up."

Peter blinked. *Well, I suppose we do at that.* He looked around to see Sutton bearing down on them, and a small group of the station's pilots gathered around them.

"This is Squadron Leader Sutton," Peter said loudly when he arrived. "He and his people will take care of you. Once you're settled I'll be glad to introduce you to your flight crews." He smiled broadly and generally, hoping they'd all troop off for a nice debriefing and give him and Robbins and arap Moi a chance to crawl around in these classics.

He'd always wanted to fly a Mark I.

CHAPTER FIFTEEN

The *Dauntless* emerged from Transit thirty AUs from Antares and Ontario Base. The bridge was lit red and blue by the emergency lights and the sparking flicker of ruined components; they still had pressure, but the command deck crew were working in their vacuum suits, with the faceplates open and the gauntlets off their hands. So were the emergency repair crews from Damage Control, cursing and praying as they yanked components and shoved in replacements, splicing and soldering and improvising in a frenzy of organized chaos. The air was thin and heavy with the stink of ozone, also with less pleasant odors from the dark stains across several of the consoles.

And the normal-space velocity indicator stayed stubbornly fixed at .02 *C*, exactly what it had been when they made that last desperate jump into Transit.

"Paddy," Captain Montoya snapped into her comm. "We need those engines now!"

"I can't do it, Captain," the engineering chief answered.

His thick New Hibernian accent sounded worried

and sincere. Behind him in the holo display she could see the same sort of chaos as the bridge, only worse in the cavernous spaces of Engineering. When shield fields overloaded they backlashed through the support systems; there were supposed to be stops and fail-safes, but sometimes they were overloaded, too. This was one of the sometimes. Massive superconducting busbars had shattered like fragmentation bombs as power surges went beyond redline, spreading havoc through the core of the ship. A row of bodies lay under some matting in one corner, with a chaplain whose face was half plast-bandage giving the last rites—and they included every commissioned officer in Drive Systems. The remaining crew were in white insulated hardsuits, and the arcing lightning of discharges flashing across the spaces between the cores showed why.

"I had to shut reactors three and four down. The coils took a terrible beatin' in that last surge where the plasma bursts hit us, sir. With only one and two up, we just can't get as much delta-v out of the reaction mass. And I've no likin' for the way the containment fields on one are fluctuatin'. She'll not take it if I try to get more power."

"Give me a miracle, Paddy. I won't accept anything less. Montoya, out."

The captain broke the connection and leaned back in her chair, watching her people as they worked. The damage was *bad*. It was a wonder they'd made it through Transit, and she knew the Mollies and their alien allies were right behind her.

Suddenly her comm came alive. "Sir, I've intercepted a message," a young petty officer exclaimed. There was hope under the hoarse exhaustion in her voice.

"Let me hear it, please," Montoya said calmly.

" . . . Lieutenant Commander Sarah James of the CSS *Invincible* to the CSS *Dauntless*. Do you copy?"

"Yes, we do, Commander. This is Captain Catherine Montoya speaking."

"Captain, I'm an advance scout for the *Invincible*. She is two hours behind us. What is your status, sir?"

Montoya pursed her lips for a second before she answered, as though tasting something unpleasant.

"As you can see by the speed we're making, our status is very bad, Commander. Two engines are down, our flight deck is inoperable . . ." She swallowed hard. "Our Speeds are entirely gone. We've lost nine of our laser emplacements. We have a significant hull breach, a third of our compartments are open to space, and we've had heavy casualties."

That was one way of saying a third of your crew was dead and nearly as many again wounded.

"We took direct hits from heavy plasma weapons in the last few minutes before we jumped. Field backlash put half the electronics on the ship out of action. In addition, Commander, there are far too many enemy ships *less* than two hours behind us." Montoya took a deep breath, holding back her fear for her people, for her ship. "We're also carrying a six-month supply of antihydrogen. So we make a great target."

"Understood, Captain," Sarah said crisply. "We've brought along two destroyers and thirty-six Speeds. So we can whack their hands if they get too grabby. And I'm sure you scratched them up pretty well yourselves," she speculated.

"We certainly did our best," Montoya said dryly.

"I've requested that Captain Knott send out the

squadron to escort you, sir," Sarah said. "They'll meet us well before we rendezvous with the *Invincible*."

"Good," Montoya said, "because the people behind us have no brakes. They obviously intend to destroy what we're carrying."

She didn't need to point out that the enemy would be destroyed, too, if they got close enough to fight a serious engagement and then the antihydrogen went. That would be like a small but very active star. Everyone knew that the Mollies were fanatics. And for all they knew, the Fibian ship could weather the explosion.

"You might like to warn your colleagues that those Fibians are crack shots. And they have a much longer reach than you might expect."

"Will do, Captain. Thank you. James out."

"The prey bleeds, Hunt Master," the Fibian tech told his commander. "It limps and staggers." There was malicious glee in the harsh trembling voice.

"And yet it flees," the Hunt Master said grimly. Fek-tk was very unhappy with the way things were going. He had no wish to die and their human allies were most definitely going to get them all killed.

"We should offer the enemy terms," his second suggested.

Fek-tk clicked his mandibles in agreement. Short of a miracle it was the only hope of survival that any of them had.

"I will speak to the Mollie commander," he said.

Instantly the comm light on his console lit, showing that his call had been received by the Mollie ship. He had to wait several, increasingly anxious, minutes before the Mollie captain answered.

"What is it Fecktet?" the captain demanded. His

expression, which he knew to be virtually unreadable to the Fibian, was one of great disdain. "We're busy."

Fek-tk knew he was being insulted, the deliberate mispronunciation of his name told him that, let alone the captain's curt manner. *Two can play this game, human* he thought. The Hunt Master placed his pedipalps in the position of the fourth degree of respect; well below what the captain's status demanded.

"Your people will be greatly hurt by the loss of three ships," he suggested. "The destruction of the vessel we pursue will guarantee them great sadness. I respectfully suggest that we offer the enemy terms of surrender."

"*Terms*? To that scum!"

"We need not honor terms made with such loathsome creatures," Fek-tk soothed. "But surely it would be better to bring ourselves and the antihydrogen back than to die here and lose all."

"I would not lie to save my very soul," the Mollie shouted, clearly incensed, even to Fibian eyes, "let alone to save your whole soulless crew! Your orders are to pursue that ship and kill it. Don't bother me again with your cowardly suggestions. Out!"

There was silence on the Fibian bridge for a moment.

"Why must we die because they are fools?" the second asked.

"We must die because our Lady gave us to the Ambassador to use as he saw fit. And because I would rather die in battle than on a bureaucrat's table."

The second clicked mandibles in agreement. Clearly, it was a better death. "We are born to die," he said.

"So we are," Fek-tk agreed. "And so we shall."

✧   ✧   ✧

"Burn. Give it everything you've got, Paddy."

The *Dauntless'* damaged internal compensators flickered. Montoya waited stolidly; if they failed, everyone on board would be crushed to strawberry jam. *Odd*, she thought. *We're decelerating to get away.* They had to match vectors with the *Invincible*, which was boosting at maximum in their direction; at some point they had to be going at the same velocity and in the same direction, otherwise, they'd just flash past each other uselessly.

The *Dauntless* passed quietly through the cloud of Speeds—separated at last from their light carrier—and they greeted her with a flurry of IFF beacons, then were gone. She flowed between the *Diefenbaker* and the *Mackenzie*, moving on toward the *Invincible* and aid.

"Transit signatures," the sensor desk said. It was one junior technician, doing the job of ten dead comrades. "Multiples. Four. Heavy footprint, Captain. It's the enemy task force. Boosting after us, point-oh-seven cee and rising, from the particle plume."

The enemy were through Transit and closing fast, but that was a problem for the task force that had come to meet them. Captain Montoya and her crew had more immediate problems.

"Engineerin' here."

"Give me the bad news, Chief."

"It's the antihydrogen containment vessels, Captain. Their guide coils picked up surge overload when we got hit. One of them's goin' to go, the creature," Engineering Chief Patrick "Paddy" Casey said. His accent tended to get thicker under stress, and this was about as stressful as things got.

"Vent it!"

That meant reversing the procedure that pumped it through specially fitted magnetic "pipes" into the containment vessels. A desperation measure, the stuff was so bloody *dangerous*. Having a containment vessel fail, though . . . well, at least it would be quick. And sentient beings all over this spiral arm would see the light of destruction as it traveled through the centuries and millennia between the stars.

"Not possible, Captain. The same flux overload sheered the ventin' system on that one, sure."

"How long do we have, Chief?" Captain Montoya asked. Her eyes met those of her XO and she signaled him to get on her comm.

"Unless I find a way of stoppin' it, Captain, I don't think we can hold her for more than an hour and a half." Casey's voice sounded distracted and impatient, as though he'd much rather be working than talking. His eyes flickered offscreen to some readout, and the freckles stood out like brown beacons against skin even more milk-pale than usual.

Montoya bit her lip. "Give us that time if you can, Paddy. I'm evacuating the ship and we've got more wounded than well, so it's going to take time. And let the engines run, kill her insystem vector. No need to preserve them now."

"Aye, Captain. I'll give ye my best. Casey out."

She turned, heart leaden, looking around the pie-shaped bridge at the ship she'd fought to ten-tenths of its capacity, and the crew who'd given more. Her lips seemed to freeze, and she forced them to shape the words by a wrenching effort of will.

"Prepare to abandon ship."

Klaxons began to howl through the shattered corridors

of *Dauntless*. Damage control teams abandoned their efforts to restore function and turned aching muscles and fatigue-deadened brains to the task of punching through safe passage to the lifeboats spaced along the shaft that joined the twin hammerheads of the ship's frame. Officers and noncoms chivvied the hale and the walking wounded into work parties to carry the wounded. The medics moved among them, patching and administering painkillers and stimboosts, anything to keep the burned, crushed, irradiated bodies going until they could reach real help.

Captain Montoya waited until the last of the crew had left the bridge, then ceremoniously stepped to the main comstation and pulled out the data package that would be presented at the Court of Inquiry. There was a long moment's silence, then she slapped the faceplate of her suit shut and walked away.

"Ooooh, somebody didn't *like* them," the Speed pilot said as the AI gave him its interpretation of the enemy's condition.

Bleeding atmosphere; that meant hastily patched hull breaches. Drive trail well below optimum temperature; that meant power losses. Visual showed several of the fin-mounted pods around the stern of the Fibian ship were missing or glowing, melted ruins. Empty weapons bays on the surface of the double-hammerhead Mollie ships showed that the long-range armament was depleted.

God knew what conditions were like inside, how many systems were down, what gaps there were in the sensor arrays and close-in defensive systems.

"Let's find out, children," he said to the squadron. "*Get 'em!*"

✧ ✧ ✧

Peter raised his head from behind the launch-crew barrier. The flight deck of the *Invincible* looked huge and somehow lonely, now that the full complement of Speeds was gone. Crews waited tensely, ready to refuel and rearm if the constraints of the engagement allowed.

"Commander Raeder." Captain Knott's voice was steady with tightly controlled tension. "Prepare to receive lifeboats. Working details are heading your way with lifters to get the wounded out." A swift, concise summary of details followed, seeming to flow into Raeder's appalled mind like a datadump into a computer.

"Yes, sir," Raeder said crisply. *Lifeboats?* he thought. *Wounded?*

It was the first indication he'd had that the *Dauntless* was in that kind of trouble. Correction; the *crew* were in that sort of trouble. The ship was dying.

He grabbed Chief arap Moi and Lieutenant Robbins. "Lifeboats from the *Dauntless*," he said. "They're abandoning ship. Lots of wounded."

Arap Moi's eyes went wide. "*All* of them, sir?" His deep voice wobbled up toward a squeak. "Sir, that's three thousand people."

"Not anymore," Raeder said grimly. "And half the survivors are wounded." Then the three of them spread out and briefed the flight crews. Once again, Raeder ordered a crew to the magnetic grapple, then they cleared the deck in preparation for the new arrivals.

"All right, people," he said over the command push. "They're going to be coming in hot with nothing but amateurs and AIs at the controls. And they're going to be coming in fast. We need the flight deck back as quickly as we can for operations. Let's cycle things through *quickly*. Let's do it, people."

There was a lot of storage in the locker compartments along the flight deck's walls. Much of it was medical: lifter-stretchers, first-aid equipment. Raeder walked along the side thumbing them open, while the Speed flight crews handed things out and set them to wait.

"Good!" Chief Medical Officer Goldberg suddenly said from behind Reader's shoulder. "We're going to need those. According to the captain a solid proportion of them will be badly hurt." He looked at Raeder, his eyes worried. "This is going to make our last emergency seem like a tea party."

"Fewer radiation burns," Raeder said encouragingly.

"There is that," Goldberg said like a man who has lost everything, except his watch. "Just wound trauma and explosive decompression."

There were forty-one lifeboats expected . . .

"Flight Control, patch me through," he said. "General push to the lifeboats."

"Yessir . . . through."

"Now hear this," he said. "We've got enough room, but only just. Don't try to stick your ships in."

Lifeboats were clumsy at best, just a very basic drive and guidance system in a blister that spent most of its time as a structural element in the ship's hull. Some of them would be damaged, at that.

"Just follow the vector the *Invincible* gives you, and let the grapple fields do the rest. We can't disembark you until *everyone's* in, remember."

Lifeboats didn't run to luxuries like airlocks.

"We'll get you all in. Now do it."

No need for the pumps; they'd kept the flight deck open. Now the great doors slid silently out of the way, into their recesses in the hull. The hard brilliance of the stars shone through. And against that velvet blackness were moving dots of pale blue flame, the lifeboat drives trying to reduce the relative velocities to the point where the *Invincible* could grapple and bring them aboard.

"This is going to be chancy," Raeder said, licking sweat off his lips.

Robbins nodded somberly. "Calculate it wrong and they could rip the field generators right out of the hull," she said, exaggerating only slightly.

They all felt it, a slight surge and lurch under the boots of their hardsuits. The first four of the pale blue lights turned and headed for them, looking like a fixed constellation growing brighter against the blackness. The blue-white drive flares expanded, from points of light to oblong halos—then all at once they flickered and died.

"Limited fuel capacity on those lifeboats," Raeder said. A glance at the status bars running along either side of his helmet made him whistle in relief. "Grapple field's got them."

The lifeboats grew, swelling, until suddenly the tiny points of light were big—bigger than Speeds, featureless oblongs curved above and below like pumpkin seeds, with only a few small vents at the stern to show they were spacecraft at all. Glowing patterns of light flashed into existence on the plates of flight deck, not the normal flow patterns but new ones tailored to the dimensions of the boats. He grunted with surprise.

"I ran it up, sir," Robbins said. "Seemed like it would save time."

"Good work," Raeder said.

The lifeboats touched down . . . or rather, nearly down, kept above the surface by the grapple fields. Effectively they were weightless, but that didn't remove their multitonne inertia. Starting them moving required work, and so did stopping them.

"Let's do it, people, let's *go!*" Raeder shouted.

Men and women dashed forward, with lifter and dragger units, some sitting in pull carts. Some forethoughtful soul had brought along spare coupling hooks and bonding epoxy. Raeder clumped forward in his hardsuit, grabbed the can, and began slapping a gob of the bonding agent on the hooks under the "chins" of the lifeboats. That way the pull carts could snap on and drag them off, assisted by anyone who could reach.

"No, no, remember it's got to *stop*."

Raeder's voice through the command channel brought the foot of the pull cart's driver down on the brake. That turned it into a pushcart, as the mulitonne momentum of the lifeboat drove it inexorably toward the far bulkhead of Flight Deck. He winced as it butted sideways into the plating, bulging it slightly . . . and then halted, canted over.

"Move, move!"

More lifeboats, and more—some so close that they jarred together as they landed, and one went cartwheeling off like a juggernaut top, a frictionless bludgeon pinwheeling through the vast cavern.

"Dog on," he snapped, grabbing at the bonding dispenser.

He leapt, as high as he could with a cable in one hand, the dispenser in the other and a hardsuit weighting him down. *Gerglop* and a hand-sized bead of the stuff was holding a cable to the lifeboat's hull. Fifty hands grabbed the cable; one unusually intelligent pair dogged the other end around a stanchion on the deck used to tie down Speeds. It held, although he could feel the composite groan through his feet; the sound would have been ear-splitting if the Flight Deck had held air. As it was all he could hear was the babble of voices through the suit comm, the whistle of the life support blowing cool dry air on the back of his sweating neck, and his own panting breath.

At last he staggered, turning to watch the entry doors and feeling horror creeping up his spine at the massed lifeboats right on the approach ramp . . . then sagging with relief as he realized that they were crowded there because they were all in. All forty-one of them.

"Go, go!" He wasn't sure whose voice he heard as the great doors slid shut and a hurricane of air vented into the flight deck. *Maybe my own.*

Thank God, lifeboats were built to disembark rapidly. The curves of the upper decks opened like flowers, and the lower split in the middle and sagged down on either side. That threw wounded crew from the *Dauntless* to the decks. The *Invincible's* people were dashing forward, loading lifters and stretchers and heading for the now-open airlocks. Medics ran beside them, fitting blood dispensers and stabbing injectors. Occasionally one would halt, swear, or just shake his head, go on to the next. Peter opened the faceplate of his helmet and wished he hadn't. The smell of the burns and eviscerating wounds filled even the great open space of flight deck with a charnel-house odor.

Peter was directing a group of stretcher bearers who

looked like they could use a stretcher themselves when Mai Ling Ju, the XO, touched his sleeve.

"Have you seen Captain Montoya?" she asked.

"She was on number forty-one, sir," one of the stretcher bearers said. "The last boat off."

"That would be over here, then," Raeder said, gesturing and starting off in the direction of the space door. "What's happening, sir?" he asked her as she hurried along by his side.

"One of the *Dauntless*'s six containment vessels for the antihydrogen is starting to weaken," Ju said. "Losing its field."

"No!" Raeder said.

He felt like he'd been hit in the stomach. *Dauntless* was supposed to have a complement of three thousand. If he'd thought about it at all, which he hadn't had time to do, he'd have realized what this many wounded meant. *And their captain's with them.* He felt stupid. *A thousand dead.*

It was wrong. It was just damned *wrong* to lose everything those people had died for. *There has got to be a way to rescue that antihydrogen.*

Captain Montoya was directing some of her crew when they reached her. She had managed to bring several regeneration units with them. All of them occupied, Raeder noticed. And the things were heavy and awkward to move.

"We'll get them out first," Montoya was saying. "Then we'll worry about where the ships surgeon wants them."

"Captain Montoya? I am Mai Ling Ju, the executive officer. Captain Knott sends his compliments and invites you to join him on the bridge when your people are settled."

"My compliments to Captain Knott," Montoya said, sounding a little out of breath. "I would be honored to join him on the bridge." She looked around and shook her head. "But I'm afraid it won't be anytime soon."

"Understood, Captain. This is Commander Raeder, our flight engineer. When you're ready he'll find someone to escort you."

"My pleasure," Raeder assured her.

"Until later then, Captain, Commander," Mai Ling said, she saluted briefly, then briskly marched away.

"My own chief engineer seems to be missing," Montoya said. "He's probably trying to fix that containment vessel." She bit her lip. "I know there are still lifeboats over there, but he's so damn stubborn, I'm afraid he won't get to them in time."

"What exactly happened, Captain?" Raeder asked.

"What exactly?" The captain gave a short laugh. "I'd have to be Chief Casey to tell you. All I know is that the containment field in bottle six began to fluctuate." She shook her head. "We'd taken a lot of damage. Probably something shorted out, or something got dented—you know what it's like with multiple plasma strikes. I don't know." She gave him a weary look.

"We should just get these units out into the corridor," Raeder said quickly. "We've got to clear the deck in case a wounded Speed comes our way." He called over one of his people. "Show these people to corridor five," he said. "Excuse me, sir," he said to Captain Montoya, who nodded. He turned away and moved on.

It was incredible, but there weren't any traffic jams at the exits from flight deck. *They're doing this as smoothly as if it were a drill,* he thought, with a surge of fierce pride for his ship. *CSS* Butterfingers, *my hairy butt.*

In less time than he would have believed possible the lifeboats were empty.

"Check on them!" he said, overriding half a dozen subordinates giving the same order. "Don't rely on indent beacons, do a visual—every damned lifeboat!"

Good thing we did, he thought, as several unconscious bodies—or possibly just bodies—were carried past to the airlocks. He did a final visual himself, to make sure that nobody was here but the flight deck crews in their suits.

"Prepare for vacuum," the sweet feminine voice of the AI said. Some theorist had decided long ago that people paid more attention if computers sounded like a sixteen-year-old boy's daydream. "Prepare for vacuum. Emergency entry override."

"Secure yourselves!" Raeder barked into the command push, shoving a foot under a bracket and hanging on.

The pumps were running, but the entry doors didn't wait for them. They began to open as soon as the computer stopped talking, and while they didn't snap open, it was still a fairly close approximation to explosive decompression through a hull breach. Light tools and *hundreds* of cushions from the lifeboats cataracted out through the growing slit, and one crewman started to go the same way, torn from an inadequate handhold. Three of his comrades slapped hands on the harness fixtures of his suit and held him, feet outstretched to where the air was going. The suit fell silently to the deck as the pressure dropped to zero.

"Get them on the launch paths," Raeder said. "Work

your way out from the center, and don't bother about alignments."

That needed to be said. A Speed launched off center would result in an extremely bad-tempered pilot at the very least, but they just wanted to get this junk out of the way as fast as possible. The first two lifeboats were catapulted out into the blackness less than two minutes after the doors opened. They shrank more slowly than usual—most launches were of powered vehicles, not redundant deadweight—but by the time the second four were on the slides and being gripped by the fields, they were featureless dots.

"Leave the last two," Raeder said. "Action stations. We've got Speeds in combat and they'll be coming in hurt or hungry. Pay attention! Get the readouts on the weapons mix they'll be asking for. Positions, positions, let's *go*."

Activity died down slowly. Every crew was up to strength, waiting by monitors and fueling stations, with fresh missile clusters waiting and their deadly color-coded heads peeping out of the canisters. At last he took a deep breath.

All right. Containment bottle failure. Just one of the bottles, though. That would be more than enough. *Dauntless* was carrying enough antihydrogen to power the whole bloody *fleet* for six months—more than they'd been able to squeeze out of the Mollies in the whole war so far. One bottle of six would be more than enough, and when it went, the rest would, too. Every gram of antihydrogen would meet a gram of normal matter and convert to energy at one hundred percent efficiency. The explosion would go on until every last atom of antihydrogen had met its counterpart. It took energies on that scale to drive ships through Transit.

"Ee equals em cee squared," he muttered to himself. "And truer words were never spoke."

The Commonwealth *needed* that antihydrogen. Badly. He ducked out through the airlock, into corridors where the lightly wounded from *Dauntless* were lying on pallets; the others were being commandeered to help, or shown how to get out of the way. Raeder put his shoulder to the wall and scooped his way through the crowds to his cubby.

"Captain Knott, this is Flight Engineering calling. Priority override."

You're doing something stupid again, Raeder, his mind said, with a voice remarkably like his mother's. Well, he hadn't paid much attention to warnings of that sort back then, either. *I'll check it out.* The plan in his mind was still vague. It might not be possible. He half hoped it wasn't.

"Yes, Commander." Knott looked very harassed and quite busy. The XO leaned over to say a word in his ear and he turned away from the screen.

"Sir," Raeder said, speaking over the XO, "I have an idea for a new procedure that might help to alleviate our current problems. If I have your permission to proceed, sir."

Impatiently the captain signaled Ju to wait a moment. "Yes, yes, Commander. Use your initiative. Knott out." The screen blanked.

"Yes!" Raeder said and rushed from his office. He'd have to find Montoya to get the details.

Wait a minute, Knott thought two seconds after disconnecting. *That was* Raeder *I just gave carte blanche.*

"Sir," Mai Ling said, gently but insistently.

"Yes," Knott said, and the subject of Raeder slid from his mind.

"If the captain asks for me," Peter told Robbins and the chief, "tell him you don't know where I am."

They just blinked and nodded, mumbling, "Yes, sir." The commander had been missing for about twenty minutes and had reappeared carrying a sealed bag and what seemed to be a guilty attitude.

"Good," Raeder said. "You're in command, Lieutenant, until I get back. Now get everybody out of here so the grapple crew can do their work."

"Until he gets back?" Cynthia murmured to arap Moi as they walked away.

"Don't ask," the chief said, looking straight ahead, "don't tell."

Cynthia frowned darkly, but said nothing as she returned to work.

Getting the lifeboat to one of the launch ramps was easy enough; the crews were experienced at it now. Raeder could feel the queasy dip and turn as he studied the console before him. *These things are obviously meant to be foolproof,* he thought. It was extremely simple, just a few controls on a flat keypad. *And I'm sure this lifeboat is about as maneuverable as a hippo in a desert.*

He felt the grapple seize the boat, shaking it slightly with a greasy, quivering pulse. It seemed *wrong* inside this absurd spacegoing bus, without the protective second-skin shell of a Speed around him. Instants later savage acceleration rammed him back into the elementary and ill-fitting acceleration couch. Blood trickled into his mouth and his vision grayed at the edges, no special suit squeezing his limbs, no molded half-liquid gel cushioning him. *And maybe I'm out of practice.*

His hands danced on the simple controls. The crowd of abandoned lifeboats was well ahead, showing as minute flickers on the equally rudimentary sensor system; the *Invincible* was decelerating, her stern and the huge glowing plasma cloud pointed outsystem. The *Dauntless* was still decelerating, too, its AI trying to match velocities with the *Invincible*. It wouldn't, but with luck the lifeboat could one more time.

CHAPTER SIXTEEN

Raeder whistled when the *Dauntless* came close enough for visual observation. It was one thing to hear "heavy damage"; it was another to see a capital ship that looked like a Speed back in from a close encounter of the hostile kind. Whole sections of hull were showing bare down into the frames with the plating peeled off . . . and the plating was an important structural member itself. It was a wonder the whole thing hadn't folded like an accordion when they tried to use the main engines. He could look inside and see crew quarters and machinery spaces, as if it were a model or computer simulation. Other sections showed the characteristic star-shaped craters and blast patterns of directed-charge nuclear warheads, or the blobby melted look of plasma bursts, or the long sword-slash mark of heavy lasers. The engines cut out as he was on approach, and he could see the ragged look of the exhaust cones, and the way bits and pieces were still breaking away and slowly spinning off into space, glittering and tumbling.

He whistled again, or tried to. His mouth was uncomfortably dry; the ship could blow at any minute. *Which would be a huge disappointment. Not to mention ruining my day.* His whole life, actually. There was no rational reason to be frightened, no more than in any dangerous situation—if the antimatter went, he wouldn't even have time to know he was going to die. His subconscious still tried to retract certain vital organs at the thought of being near an explosion of that size.

He stared at the nearing ship, amazed not so much by the extent of the damage but by the sheer, astounding luck that had kept her moving. If any of five major hits that she'd taken had landed a meter one way or another she wouldn't be here. *And if we don't take care of that little containment problem, she sure won't be here long.*

He steered the lifeboat toward the open flight deck doors and realized that landing here wasn't going to be easy. The door itself had been blasted in, the thick metal bent and torn like a cheap toy or vaporized and refrozen in lacy patterns like giant alloy snowflakes. *Close-range hit with a plasma cannon burst.* From what he could see the deck itself had been breached. *Great, that's going to make landing a joy.* Fortunately he'd brought an emergency with him, so he'd be able to move around out there.

Raeder cut power to the engines, more or less parking the boat, and went to put on his suit. It was violent orange and very basic. Even so, when fully activated it'd keep him alive for a week or more in hard vacuum. *May I never need to rely on it for that,* Peter prayed fervently. He changed quickly, catheter and all, and sealed the helmet carefully before returning to the pilot's seat. *Another of the many occasions I thank God I was born male.*

Both the *Dauntless* and his little craft had drifted,

and Peter found himself closer and a little further down the ship from where he'd been. He looked speculatively at the enormous hole before him. *Nah,* he told himself. *My best bet is to go for Main Deck. Everything around any of these breaches will be sealed off. But if the inner doors are all right, then I should be able to get to where I want from Main Deck.* The containment area was one deck below and easily accessible by elevator. If they weren't running, then he'd be able to use one of the emergency ladders.

He twiddled his fingers in the air over the control keypad like a pianist about to play. Suddenly there was a high, whining sound. The lifeboat began to tumble . . . very, very slowly, with a wobble, around its long axis. Raeder looked incredulously down at the main screen. A small gyro-shaped icon was flashing red in the upper left corner.

He felt his mind go blank. *How do you steer a ship without gyros?* he thought. The answer was appallingly plain; you used the attitude thrusters to balance the main drive as well as pointing the nose on the vector you wanted . . . and the two were contradictory.

He swallowed dryly. "Oh, well. Virtuosos R Us."

His fingers tapped delicately at the keys. Attitude jets made their shrill yips. One eye kept skipping across their fuel supply, which was low and going down. Lifeboats didn't have anything elaborate, like plasma conduits from the main drive; they just used compressed gas. A very limited supply of compressed gas, which he was using extravagantly as the little craft bucked and yawed and threatened to tumble as it drifted in surges toward the Main Deck doors. Coriolis force surged at his inner ear, convincing his stomach that it was on a small sailboat on a very stormy sea. And using the thrusters like this made it very difficult to keep directional control. . . . Which he discovered when he tried to maneuver his boat out of the path of a jagged piece of metal and nothing happened.

Nothing happened except that the huge mitten-shaped protrusion clawed a chunk of the boat's roof aside before it sent the boat plunging toward an upraised spear of the torn deck below him.

Oh, great! Raeder thought, annoyed and feeling foolish. It was the last thought to cross his mind as skill took over. He cut power to the two starboard thrusters and gunned the portside. The boat plunged forward, turning as it went. He cut power, knowing he was going too fast and that a crash was inevitable. Teeth gritted in unconscious reflex.

But with luck I won't break through the inner doors. Because if he did, the ship would automatically react to such a breach by sealing off the Main Deck area, leaving him trapped in the wreckage. *And pretty much wasting my time.* Not to mention his life.

He impacted one of the side walls and bounced off, spinning away from it like some Frisbee in a giant game of catch. The crash netting that bound him to the pilot's chair strained but held when the boat struck the far wall, smashing it down onto a fairly level part of the deck, where it slid helplessly back toward the breach. *Well, that answers that question. Ship's gravity is still on.* Then the pinwheeling lurch turned to a floating tumble. The ship appeared to spin dizzily around him. *On in some places.*

Peter watched as the boat rode back toward the stars, cursing in his mind at the wasted time and wondering how he'd manage to turn the bloody boat around to get back in. Blood was leaking from his nose and mouth, as well, and the suit's life support hummed as it sucked the fluids up.

A small, serrated lip around the blast site snagged the nose of the lifeboat and brought him to a jarring halt, sliding sideways into unidentifiable rubble.

Raeder waited a moment to see if the little craft was secure. Then he released the safety harness. *I'm buying stock in this company, too,* he thought as he thrust it aside.

Then he snatched up his bag and opened the hatch. The soles of the suit he was wearing stuck to the deck, meaning that the gravity function in this area had been destroyed. *Well, and no wonder,* Raeder thought looking around. The scene before him was surreal. It seemed impossible that humans had built such a massive construct. *And then destroyed it.* The chaos around him was beautiful in its way, like a stage set. If people had died here, there was no sign of it. But the *Dauntless* herself was in imminent danger of dying. He tore himself from the magnificent view and headed away from the breach.

It annoyed him that people would be willing to destroy on this scale for some esoteric belief. *How is it,* he wondered, *that if we're the bad guys, like the Mollies claim, we don't go to Paradise and bomb the crap out of them?* Which, frankly, was the sort of behavior you'd expect from soulless scum, as the Mollies liked to refer to Space Command. *Ah, well, as my mother used to say, "There's people for you."* He trudged toward the emergency door; the green safety lights were still on over that particular airlock. Presumably there was air behind it. . . .

✧   ✧   ✧

Once through the airlock Raeder divested himself of the spacesuit. It was awkward in gravity. *And I can't take the color anymore.*

After the destruction on Main Deck the untouched corridor was almost eerie; there was no sound but the low humming of life support. *Correction.* There was a broad streak of drying blood around one corner, where someone had been dragged toward the lifeboats. The elevators were out of commission, flashing PLEASE TAKE EMERGENCY STAIRS messages from their control plates. Which were actually a ladder in a man-sized tube. Slinging his bag onto his shoulder, Peter began to descend.

"And here I thought I was in good shape," he muttered to himself. His knees twinged, the calves of his legs burned, and his good hand hurt by the time he got to the bottom of the ladder and wobbled upright with a groan of relief. *Maybe I should add something like this to my regimen,* he thought, looking up . . . *then again* . . . and up . . . *maybe not.*

Beside the emergency stair exit there was a general map of the area served by this shaft; a large blank area was designated CONTAINMENT TOP SECRET AUTHORIZED PERSONNEL ONLY. Raeder slung the bag from his shoulder to his hand and headed that way.

He found the area without trouble, but a sign warned that anyone not wearing a clean suit would not be admitted. Even a particle of dust in the wrong place could be deadly in dealing with this stuff. He looked up. There were sensors located in the ceiling that could easily determine who was and who wasn't clean.

Raeder chafed at the delay. *But it is a good idea.* If so much as a flake of dandruff met a particle of antihydrogen, the results would be . . . exciting.

He ran down the row of lockers, plucking out white coveralls and dropping them in disgust. *God!* he thought in exasperation. *The* Dauntless *has a runty bunch of containment techs.* Finally he found a suit that fit and struggled into it. It was less bulky than the spacesuit, no catheter, and so on, but it covered him completely, from the top of his dark head to the tips of his fingers and the soles of his feet.

The slippery white material and clear face mask were made of materials to which nothing would cling. By the time he walked back to the door anything he'd left on the fabric had dropped off. There would be four succeeding doors beyond this one, each leading to a cleaner environment.

Finally he was released into the containment sector. It was a single long deck, a uniform off-white except for color-coded pipes. Massive power conduits ran along the overheads, and the vessels themselves ran down one wall like giant two-story thermos bottles. Peter began to jog, looking for bottle six. *I wonder,* he thought as he made his way down the passage, *if Captain Montoya's engineer is still in here.*

He was there. In front of a containment bottle a very big man was seated cross-legged on the decking. In his hands he held a power coupling, joined to another. Raeder followed the cords with his eyes. One led to bottle number six, the other was borrowing power from the bottle beside him.

"You're in a hell of a mess," Peter observed.

The man on the floor looked up with a start. "Who the hell are you?" he demanded in rich New Hibernian accent, unlike anything spoken on Earth for centuries. The place had been founded by nationalist antiquarians, and the planetary anthem was *The Rising of the Moon.*

Peter put down his bag and knelt to unzip it. "Raeder's my name, and engineering's my game," he said flippantly. "I command the flight deck on the *Invincible,*" he continued. "You are?"

"Paddy Casey," the man said, "the engineering chief." He looked Raeder over with a clear blue eye. "I'd salute, sir, but as ye can see that might create a problem. So I hope ye'll accept my informality when I say yer a damned fine sight for bloody sore eyes."

"Pleased to meet you, too," Peter said. "I take it you can't let go?"

"No, sir. D'ye see this little coupling link here?" He tapped a piece of metal with his forefinger. "It broke. D'ye know that's the first time in years one of these has broken on me. I never thought of such a thing and sent the last of me techs off, thinkin' I'd be right on their heels. I locked it in place and it snapped like an old bone." He clicked his tongue in disgust. "Nothing is made the way it used to be. Nobody cares for quality anymore."

Raeder grinned. "You sound just like my mother," he said.

"And it's right she is, God bless her," Paddy asserted.

"Why didn't you just push in another clip?" Peter asked.

"Because, sir, I've only got two hands, d'ye see, and they're holding this mess together. If I was to let go to reach for another coupling, sir, then they'd fall apart and number six here would blow and I'd get to find out if there really is a heaven. And whether ye get golden crowns there for eating yer vegetables, like me mother used to tell me."

"I see your point," Raeder agreed. He reached in and yanked a roll of tape out of his pack.

"Now, what are ye goin' to be doing with that?" Paddy asked, his eyebrows rising.

"Duct tape," Peter said, coming toward him. "It's the force that holds the universe together. Didn't you know that?"

"I've heard the philosophy," Paddy said weakly. "But I don't see it working in conjunction with antihydrogen. Call me crazy."

"Ye crazy great mick," Raeder said obligingly. He carefully wrapped the tape around the loose coupling, winding it around in the big loops as if he was bracing a sprain. "That ought to do it."

"God bless ye, sir!" Paddy exclaimed. Then with a grunt he stood, and stood, and stood until Raeder was looking up.

Wow, Raeder thought. *That's one tall mick.* He was at least six five, maybe more. And New Hibernia was a heavy-gravity planet, 1.12 Standard; he was almost as broad as he was tall, with arms like trees and huge spatulate hands. They quivered slightly as he worked the fingers loose; Raeder imagined sitting there, holding the cable connectors and waiting for the weakening field to blow. . . .

"We'd best be going," Paddy said, and started off.

"Nope." Raeder bent and reached into the bag again, yanking out the jury-rigged magnetic bleed he'd cobbled together from a Speed's acceleration system. *Let's hope our saboteur hasn't had his way with this.*

"What in the hell is that?" Paddy asked. His snub nose wrinkling at the sight of the mechanical abortion in Raeder's hand.

"It's what I'm going to use to blow the contents of that bottle," Raeder indicated number six, "into space."

"Now *that* is a fine idea," Paddy said. "But whatever did ye make it from?"

"A Speed's acceleration system."

"Ah! Yes, I see it now. Brilliant! It's all we need to do is get this one empty," Paddy said, jerking his head at the bottle. "But we'll need to work fast. Bleeding power from number five isn't doing its containment field any good at all."

"Then we'd better get to it," Raeder said. Suiting action to words, he climbed around the bottle to the spaceward side of the container.

"Oh, I see your problem."

"And the problem of the world it is, I'm sure," Casey said.

You couldn't touch antihydrogen with any normal matter. Luckily, in its refined form—ionized, stripped of its electron shells—you *could* manipulate it, after a fashion. With laser cooling systems to keep it dense, and with magnetic fields to move it until you bled carefully controlled amounts into annihilating encounter with ordinary matter. Tanks like this also had an emergency shunt, to blow the stuff out into vacuum. He could see exactly what had happened to this one; it was about the way he'd thought, an elbow-shaped section blackened and twisted, its internal field-guides destroyed by the power surge that had weakened the containment bottle itself. "Right, let's get this section out," he said, pulling out a handheld laser cutter. "This should fit." *I can't believe it'll be this easy,* he thought, as he fitted the improvised section.

Or tried to fit it. And failed.

"It's too big!" Raeder said in astonishment. "But

according to the specs it should fit perfectly." And it most definitely did not, though only by a minute fraction. Forcing it was unthinkable. It might leave a scraping of metal inside where it could react with a particle of antihydrogen, or the field-guide simply wouldn't work.

"Those specs yer talkin' about," Paddy said lazily, "they'd be for a number four, am I right?"

"Yeah," Raeder said slowly.

"Tsk, tsk. New ship, the *Invincible*. Everything of the best. These are threes," Paddy said, reaching for the part in Peter's hands. "There's a machine shop just a step away. C'mon." And he headed out of the containment area.

Raeder had to jog to keep up with him. "How will you know how much to take off?" he asked.

"It's just a hair or two difference," Paddy said. "None at all, really. Just enough to make sure that parts aren't interchangeable. D'ye ever think the fellows who design these things might be in league with the quartermasters? It makes them feel needed, y'know, to have a dozen different parts on hand that all do the same thing, but the attachments are different sizes."

They'd entered the little machine shop and Paddy had inserted one end of the accelerator into the clamp of a large cutter. He calibrated the machine with seemingly careless haste. Then he started it and with a basso hum its laser began to slice away the offending molecules of metal. In seconds it was finished and he turned the part and inserted the other end.

"That's got it, the creature," Paddy said. "Let's get it done, then."

✧   ✧   ✧

When they returned to the containment area an alarm klaxon was sounding. Number five containment vessel was loudly protesting the drain on its power source. Container six, as it destabilized, was pulling more and more of it, and five was on the verge of redlining.

"Great," Raeder said, and snatched his jury-rigged part out of the New Hibernian's big hands. He slid back behind the containment vessel and inserted it into the empty couplings. "It fits!" he said as he activated the magnetic field. "Good job, Chief!"

"Thanks," Paddy said, looking like he wanted to send Raeder to the bleachers so that he, the *Dauntless*'s chief engineer, after all, could finish the job.

Raeder started the antihydrogen flowing. "What a glorious feeling of waste," he said, plugging in his portable readout unit. At least *those* were fully compatible throughout the surface. He watched the figures scroll. "I'm throwing away a whole planet's GNP every minute." It made him feel rich and wicked.

"Come over here," Paddy said. He led Raeder to a screen and activated it.

They watched the antihydrogen flow out in a great burning plume. It created a huge tail of plasma as it reacted with normal matter, air leakage, and debris from the *Dauntless*, on its way out into space. Its momentum carried it away from the hull, and the great ravaged mass of the hull creaked and groaned under the sideways stress.

The Speeds, the *Diefenbaker*, and the *Mackenzie* would be traveling the long way around on their way back to the *Invincible*, so they would be in no danger from the escaping antihydrogen.

I hope they can see it, though, Peter thought. *It looks like victory.*

He tilted his head. *Or a comet's tail, without the comet.*

"I suppose the Christmas star may have looked something like that," Paddy murmured.

If it did, then it meant big trouble for somebody. Raeder knew better than to say it aloud. Paddy was *big*. More, he was the sort of man who'd joke sitting next to a containment vessel full of antihydrogen, holding a coupling together with his hands.

Raeder sighed, feeling the iron-tense muscles of his neck begin to relax. "We did it. With six empty, the others should be—"

Klaxons began sounding, loud and insistent. One after the other the big containment vessels showed red danger lights.

Peter turned to Paddy, who looked as though he'd lost his best friend.

"She's dying," the New Hibernian said. "The last of the fusion engines is shutting down."

"Why?" Raeder asked. "Battle damage?"

Paddy shook his head. "Overheated," he said. "Crystalization in the focus coils. Two have been doing the work of six for several hours now. They can't take it anymore."

"We'll bleed power from the Transit engines," Raeder said.

"They're out of fuel. We used the last of it coming through Transit to get here—expectin' to refuel at Ontario Base, d'ye see."

"We are not out of fuel," Raeder said, sweeping his arm to indicate the bottles of antihydrogen around them. "Yet," he amended, diving for the shunt on number six.

He quickly turned off the flow and shouted to Paddy, "Have you got a baffle?"

"That I have," the chief answered, and dashed off.

He'd vanished by the time Raeder got out from behind the bottle, so Peter had to kick his heels and wait while the klaxons screamed. *The wonderful one-hoss shay,* he thought, remembering a story he'd read in his childhood. Beautifully put together, like a Space Command capital ship. Nothing stinted. So when it was stressed past the point of failure, everything tended to go at once.

Paddy returned in moments, dragging what looked like an old-fashioned steamer trunk. Peter grabbed the handle on the other end and helped him maneuver it into the tight space at the bottle's rear. It was awkward, but not impossible; after all, it was designed for moments like this when you had to bleed an emergency ration of antihydrogen from the containment vessels. Of course, it might have been damaged along with so many other systems. . . .

He unfastened his painfully improvised shunt. Paddy heaved the baffle up one-handed to give him room to work, and he guided it home with infinite care. A panel lit up on the side, the readouts confirming that the system was running and properly meshed with the venting fields.

"Let her go," he said.

The klaxons kept up their deliberately saw-edged scream. Out of the corner of his eye he could see one light after another on the containment bottle displays going from red to amber. The light panels overhead flickered; fairly soon they'd be on emergency power, stored in superconducting coils. Fine for keeping the lights on, but these bottles took a *lot* of power.

He made an unaccustomed try at prayer. Casey was running through a list of saints.

When they'd transferred the last of it they rushed toward the elevators, moving as if they'd trained together on emergency transfers for years.

"Wait a minute," Raeder said. "Wait a *minute!*" he snapped as Paddy kept moving. "It's not on this level?"

"No, it is not. It's the next one down," Paddy said tugging on the big box.

"The elevators aren't working."

Paddy looked at Raeder blankly for a moment. Then he put down his end and, turning, walked a few steps away. "Well, can't be helped," he said and turning back picked up his end again. "Let's do it."

Peter visualized carrying the not heavy but very awkward baffle down that steep ladder and shuddered.

"Have you got any rope?" he asked.

"Rope, is it?" Paddy said. "Now what would I be doing with a bit of rope? D'ye see any mountains I'd be climbing?"

"Cord, then. String?"

"Commander Raeder," Paddy said gently, "there's no time to go rummaging through stores. We've an emergency upon us, don't ye know."

Raeder snapped his fingers and ran back. He returned smiling, the roll of duct tape in his hand.

Paddy grinned. "Y'know, I might become a believer in duct tape theory after all," he said.

The New Hibernian held the roll at the top of the ladder, while Peter pulled the baffle that dangled from it down after him. It was slower than he liked, but he was moving faster than was safe. *So I guess it evens out,* he thought. The baffle was supposedly safe under far higher stress than dropping it down a shaft. He didn't intend to test the theory. The smell of his own sweat was rank in his nostrils. *At least it's only sweat,* he thought. *I'm passing the diaper test, so far.*

When Raeder had dragged the baffle out of the shaft, Paddy slid most of the way down, only catching himself every tenth rung or so.

His palms must be like leather, Peter thought, watching him, knowing that his own hand would be rubbed raw by such treatment.

When they reached the Transit engines time became a flurry of connections, shunts, and cross connections that would have had the safety inspectors screaming. But it worked.

"Pity about having to shut down life support," Paddy said wistfully. "I rather liked having the old girl to meself."

"Well, it was peaceful," Peter agreed, grinning. "But we sure could have used some helping hands the last few minutes there."

Paddy grunted agreement. "We'd better find some suits before the air runs out and it gets too cold," he suggested.

"If there's a lifeboat handy, we won't need them," Raeder pointed out.

"Ah, but there are no lifeboats handy," Paddy said. "Any that could be reached are no doubt gone. There'd be some left in the sealed areas because there was no one to take them. But then," he shrugged his big shoulders, "we can't get to them, either." Paddy frowned. "How did you get here? And why don't we leave the same way?"

"Um. I came in one of the lifeboats, but . . . it crashed," Raeder said.

"Ye crashed a lifeboat?" Paddy said in disbelief. "Sure, I thought those things were supposed to be foolproof."

"The stabilizers went, okay? It was not my fault," Raeder snarled. Paddy raised his brows and his hands and smiled placatingly.

"But it does have a radio," Peter said. "Let's find some suits."

The WACCI slid neatly into position beside the rent in the Main Deck space door and Raeder winced at the sight. *Oh, no*, he thought. *Not her.*

There were small magnetic grapple discs located at their waists, once again designed to be foolproof. You aimed your whole body at your target and fired. The discs flew out, impacted with your target and automatically began reeling you in like a hooked fish.

He and Paddy fired, waited to be sure the discs were solidly planted, then pushed themselves off rather than wait for the reels to do all the work. They were spacers, after all. And on the opposite side of the ship from what remained of the giant plume of reacting antihydrogen.

"Commander Raeder," Sarah's voice said in his ear. "Is that you I hear thumping around out there?"

"Yes, Lieutenant Commander," he said wearily. *And I've just saved the Commonwealth a five-month supply of antihydrogen, a capital ship, and one very big engineer. Not that I expect you to be impressed, Lieutenant Commander.*

"We don't usually pick up hitchhikers, gentlemen, but in your case we'll make an exception. You just hang on tight, Commander," she said, her voice full of laughter. "We'll get you home all right."

"Thank you, Lieutenant Commander, I expected no less of you." *Than to humiliate me as much as you could.* And it was humiliating to be clinging like a barnacle to the side of her sleek ship, his arms and legs floating uselessly. *I wonder if Captain Knott will be as impressed with me as Sarah James is,* Peter thought ruefully. He also wondered who had given Sarah her apparently unrelenting dislike of Speed pilots.

He felt even more foolish when they returned to the *Invincible* and its gravity. As soon as the space doors began to close he cut the power to his disc and slid to the floor like a stone. Paddy let his reel out and descended more gracefully. The air pressure lights signaled green and he opened his helmet.

"Don't want to be seen dangling by yon sharp-tongued harpy?" he asked, indicating the WACCI behind them with a jerk of his head.

"Not hardly," Peter answered.

"Now, who would that little angel be?" Paddy asked, indicating Robbins as she rushed toward them.

She looks mad, Raeder thought. *And happy.* "That's my second," he said to Paddy. "Second Lieutenant Cynthia Robbins."

"A lieutenant," Paddy sighed. "What a pity."

"Sir," she said, stopping before Raeder and saluting. "You didn't tell us."

"No, Lieutenant," Raeder answered, returning her salute. "I didn't want to get you," arap Moi had arrived and was standing at her shoulder, "either of you into trouble."

"The captain wants to see you, sir," arap Moi told him, looking grim.

Well, I didn't actually expect to be carried shoulder high, Peter thought. *But I sure wish everybody would stop acting like I just mugged the prom queen.*

"This is Paddy Casey," he said to them, "Engineering CPO from the *Dauntless*. Could you see that he gets settled, Lieutenant Robbins?"

Cynthia blinked, and looked up at the huge, smiling, red-headed chief. "Yes, sir," she said. "Welcome aboard," she said to Paddy.

He gave her a brisk salute, his smile growing brighter still. "Thank you, Lieutenant."

Her lips twitched as though to answer his smile, but then she frowned. "Follow me, please," she said stiffly, and turned away.

"I think the little darlin' likes me," Paddy whispered to Raeder. "Sir," he added with a wink, and sped off after Robbins.

Peter and arap Moi looked at them as they departed. Then at each other, then at the Paddy and Cynthia. Paddy said something to her and she answered him, looking up into his face.

"I think he may be right, Commander," arap Moi murmured thoughtfully.

"Good." Raeder said. "She needs a friend."

"You'd better get along to the captain, sir," arap Moi said. "We can handle Main Deck a little longer."

Without me, Raeder finished for him. "Okay," he said. Sarah's ramp came down. *Anything to get away from Sarah's sharp tongue.* Though he knew Knott's would be sharper still. "Time to face the music."

Knott kept him waiting. Which was not surprising and probably not intended to make him stew. They'd just come out of battle and the captain was phenomenally busy.

I suppose I should be glad he's making time to see me, Raeder thought, tapping his fingers on his armrest. Though he'd like to get back to work. Cindy and the chief could handle things between them perfectly, he knew. *But that's not the point.* The point was it was his job and he wasn't doing it at a time when every hand was needed.

"Commander Raeder, the captain will see you now," the captain's secretary announced quietly.

Raeder marched in, saluted, and stood at attention.

The captain returned his salute, then glared at the commander.

He's got a great glare, Raeder thought. *I ought to practice until I get a glare like that.*

"Commander Raeder," Knott began softly, like the rumbling of distant thunder. "Would you mind telling me just what the *hell* you thought you were doing?"

"Sir, I saw an opportunity to act and by doing so to save the *Dauntless.*"

"Your post is here, Commander, and your duty is to the *Invincible.* You had no right to leave this ship while she was in combat." Knott was warming up and his voice was growing louder.

"Sir, you said to use my initiative," Raeder reminded him.

Knott shot to his feet and leaned over his desk. "*Don't* you try to twist my orders to fit your needs, Commander! If I'd had the slightest notion that you intended to leave the ship, you know damned well that I never would have said that. We don't have enough troubles on this ship, now I can't expect one of my officers to behave rationally, let alone responsibly?" The captain rounded the desk and stood close to Raeder, glaring into his face. "I need to trust my officers, Commander. I need to know that when I call on them to do their duty they won't have gone off to perform one of the most hair-brained pieces of showboating I have ever witnessed in my entire *career!*"

The captain was breathing heavily in his fury and Raeder could feel the color rising his neck. *Jeez,* Peter thought, somewhat sadly, *what does it take to get some appreciation around here?*

"Do you have anything to say for yourself, Commander?" Knott asked in a quiet voice sizzling with fury.

"Sir, I saved a five-month supply of antihydrogen, the *Dauntless,* and her acting engineering chief."

"That's the *only* reason I haven't put you on report!" Knott bellowed. "Why didn't you tell me what you had planned?" he demanded.

"I thought you might say no, sir."

"Damned right I would have," Knott agreed. "To *your* going. But not necessarily to sending someone more expendable."

Raeder blinked.

"Didn't think of that, did you, Commander?" Knott said. "It's one of the disadvantages of rank. Sometimes you have to send someone else to do what you're sure you could do better. If you can't handle that reality, Commander Raeder, you've risen as far as you're going to and farther than you should have. You are dismissed."

Raeder swallowed, then saluted.

Knott stepped back around his desk, saluted, and sat, picking up a notepad.

Raeder spun on his heel and marched to the door.

"Commander!" Knott snarled.

"Yes, sir," Raeder said, turning.

"Good job. Now, get out of here."

Raeder left, smiling.

CHAPTER SEVENTEEN

Sighing with pleasure, Peter Raeder raised the stein toward his lips. The beer was cold, drops dewing the sides of the frosted glass. He smiled in anticipation. And then he was going to get in touch with a certain WACCI pilot. . . .

The mirror behind the bar was far more subtle than it looked—for one thing, the AI governing what showed in it made everyone look younger, better looking, and happier than they were. Not that it wasn't a happy crowd; there was a babble of cheerful noise behind him, and some ill-advised contralto was trying to sing something classical, in the Key of Off. As his lips touched the rim of the stein, the mirror flashed once and then started showing the Space Command logo.

A chorus of groans and curses rose from every corner of the bar, stool, table, booth, the corridor leading to the restroom and the nook where darts and billiards were being played. That logo could mean only one thing, an emergency, and an emergency meant canceled shore leave. The only people who weren't looking worried were unassigned survivors from the *Dauntless*. Their ship was in the graving dock and would be for months.

"*All personnel from CSS* Invincible *to report on board immediately. Repeat, immediately. All person-nel from—*"

More groans, heartfelt from the carrier's crewpeople, mock-sympathetic from station personnel and the crews of other ships. One bystander muttered "What ho, the *Butterfingers*," as they moved toward the exit, gulping down their drinks and calling farewells. Two of his comrades grabbed a short, choleric-looking drive tech and walked him out before he could dive for the mocker. Raeder exercised an officer's privilege and scooped up the first sled to float by.

"Why *us*?" he muttered. This just wasn't fair.

"Life isn't fair," Captain Knott said with cheerful lack of sympathy as he looked down the table at his division heads. "And neither is the Service, not in wartime. The reward for doing good work is more work."

There were mutters of agreement. He called up a stellar map on the holowall, a schematic that showed the Transit points and routes. "The *Dauntless* picked up more than that antihydrogen."

He looked slightly smug. So did a number of oth-ers around the briefing table; it had been quite a feather in the *Invincible*'s cap. Raeder let himself bask slightly in the approving looks. And he'd picked up CPO Paddy Casey, who was too—slightly irregular, but you could always use someone that good. The *Dauntless* could do without him for a while, certainly.

"She also brought back some intelligence data,"

Knott went on. "The Mollies are evidently getting sick of our, ah, requisitioning their antihydrogen from the scattered processing plants in their cluster."

A few chuckles. So far, and particularly with what the *Dauntless* had brought in and the *Invincible* saved, Space Command was getting nearly as much as it had *bought* from the energy companies before the war . . . and the Mollies weren't getting anything from the transaction but busted heads and boot-printed backsides.

"So they're consolidating their operations into a series of better-defended sites. As you know, moving *raw* antihydrogen is a job for specialists." And horribly dangerous at that; one in ten of the automated ships didn't complete their missions. "It'll be more expensive for them to ship it all to a limited number of refineries, but they think that they can make it more expensive still for us."

"The high command," he went on, "thinks we should disabuse them . . . and that if we retaliate immediately after the *Dauntless* incursion, we can catch them on the hop. Their own tactics tend to be somewhat conservative, so they won't be expecting anything."

There was a moment of silence. One important reason for that was that the Mollies had fewer capital ships and couldn't afford to risk losing them on anything but high-return or unavoidable engagements. Commonwealth Space Command could afford to take more risks because it had more ships . . . but any loss to the ships concerned was unpleasantly final and total to their crews.

"So we're going after one of their new defended central plants, to show them it isn't a good idea. We'll be working with the *Aubrey* and the *Maturin,* as before. I'm downloading the initial ops plan to you all, but that's just a framework. We boost from Ontario Base at oh-nine-hundred tomorrow, and we Transit thirty-six hours later. Gentlemen, ladies, let's get going. There's a great deal to do."

"Prepare for Transit. Prepare for Transit."

Peter Raeder slumped back into the seat in his cubby, rubbing at red-veined eyes. His mouth tasted as if a coffee tree had died there long ago, with several rats entangled in the roots. "We're ready," he muttered. "We're actually ready. In from a major action, *another* bloody major action, then out on a raid—all in a week. But Flight Deck is ready."

"Sir."

Raeder looked up. *Well, there's the long and short of it,* he thought. There was Lieutenant Robbins and Chief Casey, with something on a gurney.

"Sir, here it is," Robbins said. "Pa—er, Chief Casey gave me some real help with it. He's an artist with a micromanipulator."

Raeder blinked, looking at Casey's huge paws; they looked more suitable for bending horseshoes. Then the fatigue drained away as he saw the synthetic hand resting on the gurney's surface beside a tangle of electronic equipment. It looked less sophisticated than the one he was wearing; the ship didn't have the facilities for plastics that duplicated the appearance and texture of human skin and hair and nails. But what was underneath the plain beige surface . . .

Paddy coughed. "Lieutenant, sir, why don't we let himself try it out? We'll come back in a bit and run the tests," he said with elephantine tact.

Robbins looked at him blankly. Another cough, a

wink, a nudge with a foot. "Oh, sure, Chief. Sir, we'll be back in a bit."

The door hissed shut behind them. Raeder forgot it, forgot even the rasp of fierce embarrassment at the thought of taking off his prosthesis with somebody else watching. Slowly he reached out for it, then drew back his left hand. Instead he *thought* the command that weeks of biofeedback had taught him. Sensation in his right hand ceased at once, except for a phantom itch at the base of his right thumb. The techs and doctors had never been able to eliminate that one, no matter how they adjusted things. He willed again—it was like telling a muscle to move— and a hairline gap appeared all around his right wrist, just above where the joint would have been if he still had it. There was a muted click.

He took the right hand in his left, closing his eyes to lessen the weird sensation of gripping one hand with the other and only feeling it with the first. A quick tug, and the artificial hand was off. The stump was a smooth convex surface with four evenly spaced conduits for datajacks and two stout prongs that supported the hand while it bore weight. He put the first hand down on the surface of the gurney and picked up the one that Robbins had developed and built with Casey. It was slightly heavier than the first—probably they didn't have access to all the fanciest material—but the couplings on its inner surface were identical. He slid it home with another faint click.

All right so far, he thought, and gave the same mental command. There was a flash of bright heat, and sensation returned with a tingle. He wiggled the fingers, touched each in turn to the thumb, and stroked them down the surface of his keyboard. The sensations . . .

"Hard to say," he muttered.

Raeder brought the fingertips up to his lips. "Yes, *definitely* a bit more sensitive," he said. "But there's always the acid test."

The top of the gurney held a duplicate of the control pad of a Speed, a testing unit used to calibrate AIs. Raeder pulled the gurney in front of him and slid both hands into the pads. And waited . . .

Seconds later, Robbins and Casey looked up as a grinning Peter Raeder pushed the gurney out into the corridor. "It works! It works!"

"Transit signatures. Recent. Data follows—"

Raeder swore under his breath at the relayed voice from the bridge. A similar chorus of groans spread across the flight deck, where the pilots were already sealed into their Speeds.

"How many ships do the eight-legged spalpeens *have*?" Casey swore as he pulled his head out of an access panel of a Speed. "'Tis the secondary wave guide on this plasma gun, aschula, sir."

"It's not the ships, it's the fuel," Lieutenant Robbins said, climbing the access ladder. "They can run more standing patrols than we can through areas that just *might* need it."

"Ah, and isn't that the clever thing to see?" Paddy said.

"Right, it *is* the wave guide. These things are always giving out."

"Sure, and it's the plasma flux they're guidin'," the engineering tech said philosophically. "Spillover."

"Okay, let's pull the unit and slap in a spare—easier to work on the wave guide on the bench."

They guided down an overhead waldo and fastened it to the massive bulk of the Speed's port plasma gun. An amplified voice rang through the cavernous depths of flight deck:

"Prepare for Transit. All hands prepare for Transit."

"Much more of this and Himself will be gettin' plump," Paddy grinned. "Right back the way we came, a two-day Transit, and then we're trying a new route. It's out of fuel *we'll* be, soon."

A motor whined and the complex shape of the gun rose. He prepared for the difficult task of worming an arm in to disconnect the fuel feed line that ran from the weapon to the Speed's plasma bottle.

"Let me handle that," Robbins said.

He nodded, then blinked in astonishment as she chinned herself and wormed her whole torso in. There was an interesting wiggle as she worked on the connection.

"Clear!"

He keyed the control on the lift and the gun swung free; with casual strength he guided it down to the surface of a trolley. The machine trundled off, heading for a workbench in one of the bays off the flight deck. Another came with a replacement gun fresh in from a rebuild, and helpfully raised it to the level of the working platform that surrounded the fighting vehicle. Humming under his breath, Casey swung it down.

"I'll get the connector," Robbins said.

"Sir," Paddy replied, watching her work, "yer the first livin' soul I've ever seen who can do that without gropin' around blind. A sad frustration to the designers, I'm sure."

"They do always put the vital parts on the bottom

or back," Robbins answered. "For this you either have to be small, or have arms like an ape."

They slid the access panel closed and looked down at Raeder.

"Sir, would you run the verification check? Quicker than getting a member of the squadron."

Raeder nodded briskly. *Unusually tactful,* he thought. *She didn't say* real pilot *at all. Maybe she's learning to be a human being.*

He flexed his new hand and went up the ramp; it sealed behind him with a sough of hydraulics and a *tung-chink* as the seals went into place. The Speed closed around him, infinitely familiar. Alone in the blue-lit gloom as he settled into the control couch, he grinned to himself at the bittersweet pleasure. He didn't bother with the restraints as he slid his hands into the control gloves and the holohelmet sank to cover his face and shoulders.

"Main power off," he said. "Shipside power feed on."

The status bars came up green on either side of his vision, and the deck sprang into being around him. "Three-sixty."

That gave him a compressed view of the outside, an all-around view squeezed down into a hundred-twenty degree arc ahead of him. Weirdly distorted to a lay eye, but second nature to a pilot.

"Sim run, plasma cannon, port," he said. The AI brought up the icon, circled with a red bar through it to show that the weapon wouldn't actually be firing. It *couldn't,* not without a feed from the main fusion bottle, which was powered down at the moment . . . but better safe than sorry. Even a partial wasn't a nice thought, not in a pressured-up flight bay.

"Lieutenant Robbins, Casey, give me a direct confirm on the cannon, please."

He could see the squeezed-looking figures jacking in to the plasma gun, datalinking directly, then Casey making a physical check . . . and sticking a marker between two components that had to touch for the weapon to function.

That guy is thorough, Raeder thought. Just as thorough as Robbins, which was saying something. He just did it without *looking,* as if he was an obsessive-compulsive. It was a wonder a ten-year man with his abilities wasn't higher in rank, until you looked at his record. Wonderful on shipboard, even better in action, but his idea of recreation appeared to be to walk into a bar frequented by Marines and drag his uniform jacket along the floor, daring anyone to step on it. He'd gone up and down the pole several times, reaching CPO twice. And how on Earth had he managed to get a kangaroo out of the Lunaport Zoo and halfway back to his ship before Shore Patrol caught him? Both of them drunk as lords, to boot.

"Casey. How do you get a kangaroo drunk?"

There was an injured silence for a moment. "Why, to be sure, with whiskey, sir. In beer; they're partial to it, I find."

Maybe Robbins will give him an incentive to try for Officer Candidate School. God knew Space Command needed all the leaders it could get, with casualties and the expansion program.

"Confirm stimulation status on port plasma cannon, sir," Robbins said, sneaking a sideways look at Casey. Raeder saw her lips move: *a kangaroo?*

The holohelmet showed the weapons board. Raeder's hands moved instinctively in the glove, and he felt a surge of triumph as the cannon came out of its slot and tracked smoothly on its swivel pivot. The aiming pip slid over the arched interior of the flight deck, a complete three-sixty turn and then up to vertical.

"Excellent," Raeder whispered. An instructor's voice came back to him from flight school, a martinet with a tongue like a rasp and cold gray eyes, named Oleg Katchaturoff. It had been a triumph ever to get a word of praise from him, until that day when Raeder outflew him in a practice dogfight. He'd come up to Raeder afterwards, and said two words: *ochen korrosho.* They fit here. "Most excellent."

"Nominal on the plasma cannon," Robbins said. "Thank you, sir."

"Thank *you*," Raeder replied. "Both of you."

"This is the decision point," Captain Knott said, looking down the table. "We've finally found a Transit route the enemy isn't checking or patrolling. Unfortunately, our antihydrogen reserves are now at critical levels. If our mission succeeds, we'll be sitting pretty. If we fail, we may be trapped outside Commonwealth-controlled space and unable to Transit back to base. Comments, please, ladies and gentlemen."

"It's an important target, but not worth the ship," Larkin said promptly, absently knocking his academy ring on the table. Knott had one just like it. "Sir, I recommend that we return, refuel, and try the route we've found."

Sutton scowled. "With all due respect to the quartermaster, sir," he said, his voice making a liar of him, "We've got a narrow window here. The enemy are patrolling the Transit routes to our target zone vigorously and may step them up. We'd lose two weeks that way with no guarantee that there wouldn't be a task force or at least a scouting corvette waiting right here when we got back. *And* there's the waste of fuel to consider."

Knott gave him the same polite nod he'd accorded Larkin. Council of war or no, the *Invincible* wasn't a democracy; the captain could ask for advice, but the responsibility was his.

He looked to the destroyer captains. One of them spread his hands. "We're better set for fuel, of course, sir."

Raeder cleared his throat. "Sir, even if we drop below the level needed and can't pick up any at our target, we can always Transit out to somewhere intermediate and wait for a supply ship. That would still allow us our mission priority."

Sutton nodded to Raeder. He'd been much more friendly since the *Dauntless* incident. *Grapefruit and peas,* Raeder thought wryly. You could take a pilot out of the Speed, but you couldn't take the attitude out of the pilot.

Larkin frowned. "Our priority is to commandeer—" he preferred the euphemism "—the antihydrogen."

"No, it isn't, quartermaster," the captain said. "It's to capture *or destroy* the antihydrogen, or in any event to destroy the new fortified processing facility before the enemy start building more of them. And that is a very high-priority mission. Denying the fuel and facilities to the enemy is as important as capturing them for us."

They all knew what that meant. Mission first, comrades second, yourself third—the unwritten motto of Commonwealth Space Command.

"We will Transit to the target system at—" he looked

at the watch woven into his uniform cuff "—eleven hundred hours. Ms. Ju, please begin."

The XO stood and went over to the wall; it flashed into display mode. "Our initial tactical formation will be . . ." she began.

Raeder felt his pulse leap. Soon the task force would be moving into the unknown, probably into another deadly surprise. He felt a grin fighting to grow and suppressed it. You shouldn't look like a kid at Christmas, not when life and death was at stake.

You can take the pilot out of the Speed, he thought, focusing on the briefing.

"Now, isn't it a fine thing that they've gone t'all that trouble to welcome us," Paddy said.

Raeder grunted, looking at the same tactical display in his hand unit. There weren't any real planets in this system; just one hell of a lot of junk, and junk rich in antihydrogen. It was often that way. Whatever had enriched this sector with antimatter had been rather profligate with it, and the results must have been spectacular while they lasted. What remained was thoroughly mixed up, mostly asteroid belts in orbits where planets would have been otherwise. The sun was an F5, running slightly hot, and variable—plenty of solar-particle fog in this one, too. A pilot's nightmare and a guerrilla fighter's dream.

"Pièce de la résistance," Raeder muttered, calling up the refining station specs the WACCIs had gotten on their stealth approach.

The refinery itself was the usual tangle of scattered modules, with the living quarters and control facilities roughly in the center. They were armored, though, with thousands of meters depth of nickel-iron from the plentiful asteroids and a layer of silica regolith on top of that. You could burrow through that sort of thing with nukes, but it took time—and it was virtually invulnerable to beam weapons, which liberated all their energy on the surface layers. The mass also provided a heat sink for really *big* defensive beam weapons, bigger than anything a ship could mount. The whole area around the refinery was also sown with parasite mines, disguised as floating bits of rock and ice. They'd stay that way until you came within range, and then explode, driving an X-ray laser burst like the Ice Pick of the Gods at you.

That was bad enough. Orbiting with the refinery to the solar north and south were two forts, with the same sort of armament, only much more of it—and swarms of shipkiller missiles, kinetic-energy railgun mounts, you name it. And being located right next to an antihydrogen processing facility, he very much doubted there would be any power shortages here.

"Well, there aren't any enemy capital ships here," Robbins said stoutly.

No, they don't need them, Raeder thought. "We'll see," he said.

Wing Commander Sutton was visibly restraining himself; he looked as if he'd like to thrown his helmet on the deck and kick it. Raeder listened to him debriefing to the XO with half an ear, the other nine-tenths of his attention on the crews working frantically on the returned Speeds. Two wouldn't be coming back, but they'd picked up one pilot. The other was ionized gas, along with her craft.

"Sir, it's like sticking your . . . arm into a laser cutter," Sutton said. "Here—"

He touched the monitor helmet he was wearing. Casey had gotten Raeder a very nice little pirate feed. It gave an excellent view of the Speeds' first run at the targets, with Sutton commenting on the recorded view from his own holohelmet:

"This part went fine—"

The picket ship was a converted merchantman; the weapons and sensor arrays looked tacked on. A second later it looked like an expanding globe of white light. Raeder interpreted the complex weaving of vector cones and data-displays effortlessly; half the Speeds peeling off to keep the orbital forts busy, the others boring in on jinking, weaving courses to take care of the refinery, and the destroyers in a sun-and-planet defensive formation, giving long-range backup with their more powerful beam weapons and long-range missiles.

"This is where it all went to hell," Sutton said disgustedly.

A Speed exploded, flashed into molecular powder by a multigigawatt particle beam. Parasite mines were exploding all across the quadrant the Space Command forces were traversing. Then the holohelmet picture began to degrade, status bars going to the amber of uncertainty, the recorded positions of Sutton's Speeds turning vague.

"Captain, we handled the picket ships; we handled their fortress-based Speeds. But for those forts, you need a battle group—a dozen dreadnoughts, five fleet carriers, and supply ships to keep them topped up with Solar Phoenix bombs and whatnot. The ECM in there alone is a killer; their jammers are pumping out too many watts and turning on a marker laser is a death sentence if those parasite mines pick it up. We can't land a precision strike and just throwing stuff at them is hopeless, the way those things are hardened."

Captain Knott frowned. "Could they have been softened up enough for a second run to work?" he asked.

"Captain, now they're *ready* for us. If I take another run in there and we futz around trying to hit something vital, they'll kill every last one of us, and we *still* won't hit anything vital. We might be able to do *one* pass through the target zone, at really high speeds, because their sensors aren't as good as their firepower. But that's it—and our chances would go from near zero to goddamned *zip*. Sir."

Raeder looked at the wing commander's face. *There is the original* Can Do *guy,* he thought. *If he thinks it isn't worth trying, then it isn't.*

Or . . . *Wait a minute.* Sutton was as brave as lions were supposed to be but weren't. On the other hand, he was a bit of a linear thinker. He did what he did extremely well, but always in the same old way.

Let's put together two things he said, Raeder thought. *Put them together in a way he didn't.*

"Do you think this will work?" Robbins asked.

"If I didn't, would I be doing it?" Raeder asked. "Pass the number seven."

It was a heavy power cable. He crawled inside the missile's housing, where the warhead and guidance systems would be normally, and tried hooking it to the broadcast sequencer. It was an awkward, difficult task, in a cramped space with equipment never designed for it. And . . .

"Doesn't *fit*," Raeder cursed. "Paddy! You useless bogtrotter! This coupling's incompatible!"

"Sure, and aren't they all sassenach dear, sir?" Paddy said. A hand like a mechanical grabber came in and took the coupler out. "We're not doin' with them what the Great Gods of Supply wished we should, and they're havin' their revenge. You just get me a reading on the dimensions of the securin' ring, and I'll have it right as rain. And then Lieutenant Robbins here will do the hookup. And yourself will get back to brain work, which is what you're suited for."

Reluctantly, wiping the sweat off on the arm of his coverall, he obeyed. The missile was sitting on a floater cradle, adjustable for height . . . but there was only one way into the guts of a Dagger Mark IV. From the outside it looked like a funhouse mirror version of an egg, one that had been stretched out to four or five times its proper length and slightly grooved. The exterior looked like a mirror that was perfectly reflective and absolutely black at the same moment— something impossible, but the Commonwealth had put a lot of R&D money into things like this against the day of need.

"It's going to *work*, goddamn it!" Raeder said.

Captain Knott was standing nearby, looking perfectly relaxed. Then Raeder saw a slight tick in the skin under one eyelid. *All I have to do is my song and dance number,* he thought, suddenly humbled. *But Knott's in charge. It's his responsibility. Thousands of people, the ships, the mission—who knows, this engagement could turn the course of the war.*

If it all went wrong, nobody would blame Commander Peter Raeder, ex-Speed pilot, not-quite-first-Ace of the Mollie War, obscure and insubordinate chief engineer of the *Invincible's* flight deck.

They'd blame Knott. The worst of it was that Knott

didn't give a damn what people thought about him; his anxiety was entirely for his ship, his people, and his mission.

"Sir, we're doing our damnedest, and it *will* work. I'm not grandstanding."

Knott smiled wryly, the fine wrinkles beside his eyes crinkling almost to the cropped white hair. "Mr. Raeder, the hell you aren't grandstanding. But in our brief, exciting acquaintance I've come to have some confidence that somehow you'll pull off these outrageous stunts." Then, less formally: "How's it going?"

"Well, sir, at first I thought someone in a suit would have to ride these in," Raeder said enthusiastically. "But then Paddy . . . Chief Casey, that is . . . remembered an *old* technique. We've got the equipment. That's the good news."

Knott sighed. "Don't keep me in suspense."

"Well, the bad news is that with an improvised setup like this . . ."

Sarah James eased the WACCI closer. The long slow trajectory in from the outer reaches of this not-quite-solar system had left the coverall inside her suit smelling badly. The whole little triangular cabin did; the scout craft weren't meant for journeys this long. They *could* have zipped in much more quickly . . . but even the most heavily stealthed craft in the world couldn't do that without shedding energetic quanta. And even Mollie sensors would have found them.

Inside the holohelmet the brush of microrays across the hull was almost like the wing of some questing bird brushing her face with featherlight deadliness. This was too delicate even for the finest pilot. Instead the WACCI's engines burned in precise synchronization with the swarming sunspots of the hot F5 sun, covered by bursts of radiation and the detritus of the antihydrogen processing plant. Raeder was quiet behind her. He'd been quiet all the way in, running through simulations except for a few brief naps.

Well, maybe he isn't entirely *a Speed pilot,* she thought.

"Coming up on it," she said—quietly. That made no unearthly difference, of course, but she couldn't help herself. "So far, nothing to indicate their active sensors have caught us."

He gave her a smile—not a pilot's reckless grin, just a smile—and put his fingers into a set of improvised control gloves mounted on the arms of the couch where her gunner would normally have sat.

If she'd been wrong, or if the Mollies had made them on passive scanners, the first thing they'd know was when the plasma burst or laser beam hit them. They might just have time to realize what had happened, if they were unlucky.

"Now," Raeder said tonelessly. Sweat matted a lock of black hair to his high forehead as he pulled his helmet down. That turned his face to a nonreflective globe. "Mark. Three. Two. One."

There was a very faint *tung* sound through the hull. Sarah keyed her own holohelmet, and the ship disappeared from around her. The modified Hawk missile was drifting away from the WACCI like any other piece of the space debris that filled this star's neighborhood instead of planets. She killed the scout craft's engines, taking it down to minimum emissions, drifting cool and signatureless among the manifold specks of light that crawled across the motionless stars. One of them was the orbital fort that was their target. . . .

There. A brief tenth-second burn, and the Hawk's drive filled the field of view with a moment of luminous fog—the AI translating emissions into visible light. It curved away from Sarah, trailing an invisible length of fiberoptic cable. That gave it a link to the cabin of the WACCI, unjammable, undetectable; the technique hadn't been used in war in generations. Velocities were too high in modern conflict, engagements over too quickly, for something so cumbersome to work. Except in this one, special, unique application.

So it's a good idea, she grumbled mentally. Through the helmet she could see the missile's feed. Hour after hour passed, with only an occasional sip from the water tube to mark its passing. Raeder burned the missile's engines for absolute minimum signature and at random intervals. At last it matched velocities with the target. An artificial moonlet of nickel-iron and silica rock, still jagged and foamed from the construction process that had used fusion to melt and shape it. The surface of slag and stone might have been natural, if it hadn't been so raw . . . and if it hadn't been for the installations that pocked it. Railguns poked out, plasma cannon loomed on turntables, and the black caves hid shipkiller missiles. And . . . *there.*

Sarah admired the delicacy that nudged the Hawk within kilometers of the crucial spots. *Did the other one do as well?* she asked herself. Impossible to know. There hadn't been any detectable fuss, and that was all she could say.

"Done," Raeder said. His voice was croaking and hoarse with fatigue and tension. "Disengaging line. Over to automatic."

"Signaling," she said, sending a tightbeam coded burst. Risky, but one they had to take. "Gone."

"Now get us out of here!" Raeder was virtually twitching against the restraints that held him in the gunner's couch. *And here he was so patient for so long, the dear.*

She grinned, half-sympathetically. "Sorry, Commander Raeder. That isn't how we do it, in the WACCIs. We wait for a diversion and sneak out."

"But—" He forced silence on himself and sank back. "It's your bird, Lieutenant."

"La jou commence," her navigator murmured.

Drifting in zero g, the cone paths traced across the holohelmet's schematic looked deceptively peaceful. They represented the entire squadron of Speeds boosting at maximum toward the enemy installations, at maximum evasion—maneuvers that would stress pilots and machines at ten-tenths of capacity. Behind them the *Aubrey* and *Maturin* were boosting inward, as well. Heavier than the Speeds, and slower off the mark, but their massive engines and inertial compensators meant they could reach much higher velocities. None of them could outrun a beam weapon, though.

All at once the helmet's view dissolved into chaos, fog, static. Sarah's hands tightened. Every Speed was launching countermeasures: screamers, false IFF signalers, nanochaff, beacons, fake ships. The field swam with ghost vessels and voices calling commands with Mollie codes, and databursts carrying viruses that would sow havoc in command-and-control systems if they punched through the Mollie defenses.

"Lieutenant, it's your bird, but I suggest you get us out of here. We won't know if it worked until it worked, and I can't think of better cover."

"Roger Wilco," Sarah said.

She wasn't a Speed pilot, to risk her skin for no good reason. The good reason was over; she brought the WACCI's engines live and began a fast but prudent burn away from the Mollie orbital fort. The fort was stabbing out almost at random, lighting up her detectors like a Christmas tree, but the fire was wild. Once everything on the ship flickered as a heavy plasma burst went roaring by and an X-ray laser spike from a parasite mine came cringingly close. Behind them the modified Hawk would be doing the same thing as the mines—firing a one-megaton thermonuclear warhead to generate a spike of laser energy of enormous power. That spike would be at a different wavelength, though, and designed to carry something other than pure destruction at the other end. And in this flurry of high-energy disruption and energetic jamming, it would probably go unnoticed.

The Speeds were not carrying anything but their loads of jamming and deception apparatus. The destroyers were loaded for bear, but they were approaching far too rapidly for precision aiming . . . except maybe for the Solar Phoenix missiles; they could with luck—

The holohelmet shut down after an instant of pure white light, brighter than a thousand suns. She tore it off; the fixed displays on the consoles were showing shields burning out under the impact of a cloud of particles and gamma radiation that did not diminish like that of an ordinary warhead. It went on and on, like the radiation from the surface of a newborn star.

"The gas shell," Raeder said tautly.

In anything like normal circumstances, they'd be worried about the radiation that was sleeting through the WACCI and their bodies. Right now they had more immediate concerns. The Bethe bomb was converting millions of tons of mass to a very rapidly expanding shell of gas. Explosions in space had no blast effect beyond close range, because there was no atmosphere to carry the shockwave. A self-sustaining fusion reaction with that much mass to push made its own tenuous atmosphere, and if they were within range . . .

Blackness.

CHAPTER EIGHTEEN

Cynthia Robbins was running down a checklist with one of the pilot officers prior to his flying his repaired Speed. The pilot officer wasn't happy to have her so involved in the process and was freely showing it. Actually it wasn't something that she should have been doing. This was a tech's job.

But she reasoned that if she didn't force them to interact with her, they could very easily get into the habit of ignoring and working around her, which would cut into her efficiency. *And nothing cuts into my efficiency.* Besides, she got a lot of satisfaction out of making them do it. Petty revenge for their nasty suspicions, now mostly laid aside except for some diehards like this. The tasty little triumph at the Mollie base had ensured that.

This task was also done by computer, but Commander Raeder thought that going through it with the pilot avoided complacency. *And,* Cynthia thought, *it means they can't avoid me.*

"Main sensor array data bus?" she said.

"Check," the pilot said in a bored, annoyed voice. Then he coughed.

"Weapons readiness," Cynthia was saying over the pilot's coughing, which was now continuous. "Monitoring." He was hacking now, loud enough to drown her out, which is what she supposed he was trying to do. "Subsystems?"

"Che-ck," he squeezed out between spasms.

"Are you all right?" she asked.

"Help," the pilot said, choking. Then there was silence.

His ramp was up, so Cynthia used her remote, but nothing happened. She dashed over to the emergency release and pressed in the code. The ramp descended reluctantly. Cynthia looked up into the Speed; nothing moved, so she went in.

The pilot was slumped over in his chair, the faceplate of his helmet frosted with moisture. Cynthia broke the seal and took it off.

"Oh," she gasped and took an involuntary step backwards. Whatever gas his life-support system had been feeding him, it definitely wasn't pure air. Her eyes were watering, so she cut the feed. Then she reached for his pulse. It seemed a bit fast, but it was there, and his face hadn't turned any of the off colors you'd expect in a situation like this.

The ramp began to go up.

"Hey!" Cynthia yelled. She rushed forward, but it was too late. "Hey!" she yelled again through the closing door. *I hope someone heard me,* she thought as it fitted home.

Her ears popped.

That could only mean that the Speed was pumping the air out preparatory to takeoff. *Oh, great,* she thought, rushing to the control board. *Nothing in the life-support system but knockout gas, and no air in the*

cockpit. Cynthia tried to get the Speed to stop draining the air, but it wouldn't obey her commands. She
tried shutting it down, her fingers blurring over the
console. It ignored her. *Only one thing left,* she thought.
Remembering the last time things went so badly wrong,
she didn't even try to get to the Speed's innards. She
had no doubt that they would be protected from her
interference. Pulling the pilot's helmet over her head,
she blew on the microphone to start the radio set.

"Mayday, Mayday," she said. It was getting hard to
breathe.

"*Robbins?*" It was Raeder's voice.

"Sir, I'm trapped in Friedreich's Speed. The air is
being pumped out and the ramp won't open."

"On my way," Raeder said. He grabbed the comm.
"All personnel on flight deck, whoever is closest to
Friedreich's Speed, this is an emergency. Get his ramp
down." Then he bolted for the door.

Cynthia grabbed the pilot under his arms and
dragged him toward the ramp. All well and good for
the commander to be on his way, but it wouldn't hurt
to help herself. Robbins was a fit young woman, but
Friedreich's dead weight was more difficult to move
than she'd expected. She clenched her teeth and
dragged, bracing her heels against bits of equipment.
Blood hammered in her ears, and she was panting
far faster than she should even under the circumstances. She hadn't made it halfway before she dropped
to her knees, straining at the thinning air like something in a bad dream, like running at top speed and
getting nowhere. Her lungs strained, but found almost
nothing to breath. *This isn't going to work,* she
thought. Her chest hurt and she began to see speckles
of white in her vision.

Then she thought of something. Something dangerous, but it might work. Doing nothing was death.

There was a switch at the lower edge of the ramp
door; it was hard to reach without taking the covering completely off, but her hand should be small
enough to reach in and press . . . Cynthia twisted
her body around on the floor until she could get her
hand into position. It was incredibly awkward. She
pressed a small catch home and the ramp began to
descend. Robbins rolled down with it, trying to keep
her hand in place.

Easiest to roll off the ramp, she thought. That way
she'd be out of the way of Friedreich's rescuers, and
in a slightly more comfortable position as well.

People rushed past her and gathered the pilot up,
carrying him down the ramp and laying him on the
deck.

"Get some oxygen," Raeder shouted. "Are you all
right, Lieutenant?"

"Yes, sir, perfectly fine."

"Good job, Robbins," he said. "Lister, bring that
stretcher over here."

Cynthia released the pressure of her hand on the
catch and the ramp snapped up. She tried to pull her
hand out, but it was caught. "Hey!" she shouted, and
tried to push her hand back onto the catch. She
couldn't find it. The ramp closed over her wrist. It
had the finality of memory; she was watching it, disbelieving it, and knowing it was absolutely inevitable
all at the same time.

"Nooooo!" she screamed, even before she felt the
pain. With horrible finality the ramp crushed the tiny
bones of her wrist and she screamed with the shock,
falling to her knees. And the worst of it was that it

didn't even *hurt*, not at first. She could feel bone snap, *hear* it, feel the stretching and rending of tendon and muscle. The ramp clicked home, slicing the flesh that held her upright and Cynthia sprawled on the deck unconscious, the stump of her wrist spouting blood like a severed hydraulic hose.

It had happened too quickly for anyone to react. The ramps weren't supposed to be able to raise that fast.

Raeder rushed to her, one glance at the blood running down the Speed's side told him the story and he pulled out his belt as he ran. He whipped it around her arm, using it as a tourniquet.

"Get Goldberg!" he shouted. "Now!"

Cynthia woke to the darkness and the quiet and the medical scent of a sick bay room. She opened her eyes, which felt so very heavy, and sighed.

"Ah, ye're awake," said a deep voice beside her.

Robbins blinked in surprise and turned her head. Paddy Casey smiled at her.

"How are ye then, darlin'?"

"Mm," she said, licked her lips and tried again. "You should call me lieutenant," Robbins told him trying to look aloof.

"How are ye then, Lieutenant darlin'?" he obliged.

She fought it, but Cynthia couldn't help the smile. Then she remembered. Her arm seemed too heavy to lift, so she turned her head and looked down. The wrist was bandaged, but she could see the contours of a presurgical nerve regeneration unit. It would keep the nerves in her wrist functional and receptive while blocking pain impulses. Without it a synthetic hand like Commander Reader's would be impossible.

Her eyes filled with tears. She closed her eyes, trying to regain her composure, but a sob welled up in her chest and broke through her reserve. Paddy was beside her in an instant. He took her in his big arms and gently stroked her hair.

"It's good to cry," he said. "The very best thing for ye. Cry it all out now, dearling." He dropped a kiss on top of her head. "There, there."

She was so surprised that she stopped weeping with a little hiccup. She sniffed and said plaintively, "You shouldn't . . ."

"Lieutenant dearling," he amended. He loosened his hold and smiled down at her. "That was a brief storm," Paddy observed.

She choked up for a moment, then got herself under control. "Not the last, though," Cynthia said. She pulled away from him and he left the bed and sat down on the chair beside it. "What are you doing here, Chief?"

"Paddy," he said.

"Chief Paddy," she said with a small curve to her lips.

He grinned. "Ye're a maddening woman, Lieutenant. I'm here because I thought ye might like a friend beside ye for awhile."

She looked at him for a moment. Hopeful blue eyes, curling red hair, snub nose, infectious grin, and big, very big.

"Yes," she said. "I do like it."

"I could almost believe that our saboteur wants us to catch him," Raeder told the captain. "Lieutenant Robbins was one of his best defenses. While everyone thought she was the one, he could go about his business undetected."

Knott pursed his lips, his hands steepled before him.

"There are those who would remind you that the Mollies are fanatics who are capable of almost anything." He looked Raeder over carefully; a week in the regeneration tanks had taken care of most of the radiation damage. He just looked ten years older than he had, and that would fade.

"Maiming themselves unnecessarily, and thereby removing themselves from their assigned duties wouldn't be just fanatical, sir, it would be very stupid," Raeder said grimly. "I honestly believe that if our spy had known of that method of opening the ramp door, then it wouldn't have worked. Our man has grown increasingly bloodthirsty."

Knott leaned forward. "You think you know who it is," he said slowly.

Raeder nodded. "With Cynthia removed from suspicion I became convinced it could only be one person. Catching him will be the problem."

"Do you have a plan at all?" the captain asked.

"Yes, sir. The problem has to be in the quartermaster's area. My people are watching each other too closely; no one is alone with any part at any time. If they are, the part is removed and inspected. Ergo, my people were not breaking these parts."

"So the defective parts problem is solved?" Knott asked, his brows rising.

"Sir, we haven't had a one in quite some time."

"Then why do you think the problem is in Larkin's area? Maybe one of your people is guilty, but doesn't see the sense of getting caught just to be annoying. As you said, our spy is getting more bloodthirsty."

"True. But our serious problems have always been in sabotaged software. Which can only be accessed by plugging into the Speed's computer directly."

"Well, the security cameras—" Knott began.

"Can be fooled, sir. A really clever spy, like this one, would be prepared for them."

The captain nodded. An alert security chief might have set up something a little more tamperproof. But William Booth was far from on the ball; or he'd chased the one he was following right off Planet Consensus Reality some time ago.

"What's on your mind, Commander?" the captain asked finally. "You wouldn't be here unless you wanted me to do something."

"Yes, sir. I need for you to call a meeting of the quartermaster's staff, himself included."

"And?" Knott asked, spreading his hands.

"The meeting room should be rigged with a black light. It will illuminate the powder I've sprinkled all over the Speed's computer interface replacement parts. Those are the core of our problem. When those lights go on, we'll have our spy."

"What about your people?" Knott asked reasonably. "They must be touching those surfaces all the time. And what if he or she has washed their hands?"

"The surfaces that need to be accessed to change a program are inside the console," Raeder said. "There's a special keyboard for it and those are locked. It's a lock that can be picked, I grant you. But it's not all that easily accessible. And the only people who can legitimately access it are me, Lieutenant Robbins, Chief arap Moi, and Larry Taugh our computer specialist. None of us had any of it on our hands."

"Not even you?" Knott asked.

"No, sir. I wore gloves. Nor did I confide this plan to anyone."

Knott sipped his coffee. "Where did you get this powder?" he asked. "I don't imagine it's commonly stocked by the quartermaster."

Peter smiled. "No, sir. I bought it at the Spy Shoppe on Ontario Base."

Knott spluttered into his coffee. "You're kidding! There's a spy shop on Ontario Base?"

"Shop-pe, sir," Raeder corrected. "It's for people who are paranoid abut their spouses and coworkers who want to get the goods on them without being caught. Kind of an upscale outfit, actually."

Knott shook his head, his expression sour. "I don't imagine we carry black light in our stores, either," he said.

"Not that I'm aware of, Captain." Raeder placed a small bag on the captain's desk. "This will fit any standard fixture. But I only got one." Peter stopped speaking before he could put his foot in his mouth.

"So be careful with it or be prepared to waste time rigging a replacement." Knott smiled. "Will do." He opened the bag and took it out, looked at it, then put it back. "What if he's washed his hands?"

"The powder is so fine it's absorbed by the skin. It won't show up in any but black light, and it won't wash off. It has to wear off."

Knott shook his head, smiling. "It seems too easy," he said. "All right." He rose. "I'll take care of it, Commander. Do you want to be there?"

"If you wouldn't mind, sir."

"Not at all. I'll have my secretary call you with the time and place."

"Thank you, sir." Raeder saluted, the captain returned it, then Peter turned and left.

✧   ✧   ✧

"D'ye know, Commander," Paddy said, "I do believe you people have been seriously misjudgin' the darlin' little lieutenant."

Raeder nearly jumped out of his shoes. For a big man Paddy moved like a cat.

"Which darlin' little lieutenant are you referring to?" Raeder asked.

"Tsk! Sure, you know who I mean, sir. It's Lieutenant Robbins I'm talkin' about."

"And how have we misjudged her, Chief?" The expression on Paddy's face was serious and concerned, so Peter stopped teasing him.

"Sure, she's from Clive's Home. D'ye know it?"

Peter thought a moment, then shook his head.

"It's a perfect horror of a place, sir. It was a real mistake to colonize it, if ye ask me. The people live in crowded habitats and the only way to get a little privacy is to keep yer thoughts to yerself. Y'know what I mean," he insisted, though Raeder hadn't said anything. "The masklike face, the carefully controlled voice and gestures. Not everyone can do it. They have a high suicide rate there."

"So when the lieutenant seems so cold . . ." Raeder began thoughtfully.

"She's merely bein' polite. And I'll tell ye something else, sir. She thinks the world of you."

"She does?" That was disconcerting. And how had this big, bluff aggressive New Hibernian found all this out? *I've been beating my head against her reserve for months without getting a reaction. He's here two days and she's spilling her guts.* On the other hand, you wouldn't think Paddy was an artist with a micromanipulator just by looking at the hands with the callus scar across the enlarged knuckles.

"Oh, aye. No one's ever tried to help her get along before this. She's never had many friends, but since she joined the service she's had none. It's lonely she's been. But you helped her and she's that grateful."

"Really?" *Well, that's nice to know,* Peter thought.

"That's a fine girl, sir," Paddy said, a speculative light in his eye. "She's enough of a catalyst to make me want to go for officer's training."

An image of Paddy as an officer loomed in Raeder's mind. *Actually, he might be pretty good,* he thought. *They'd be good for each other, actually. He could roughen her edges; she could smooth his.*

"I'll be along to see her later," Peter said.

"Good, good," Paddy said.

He stood there, looking at the deck until Peter asked him, "Was there something else, Chief?"

"Yes, sir, there is, thank ye for asking. I was wondering, whereas the *Dauntless* is goin' to be laid up for a while and so's the little lieutenant . . ." He bit his lip and took a deep breath. "Would ye be willing to consider keepin' me on to do her work?" He looked at Raeder hopefully. "I'm experienced," he said. "And I wouldn't try to throw me weight around. Better the divil ye know than whatever Personnel yanks out of their files."

Like Booth, Raeder thought. "I'll see what I can do, Paddy. No promises, though."

"Understood, sir," the chief said, beaming. "Ye won't be sorry."

Jeez, I hope not, Raeder thought, watching the big man walk away. *He could be a real handful.*

Stewart Semple dropped the bag on his desk, listening to the distressing tinkle of broken glass. The captain had told his secretary to guard it with his life. *Nothing has ever fallen off my desk and broken,* Stewart thought miserably. *Why this?*

There was only one thing to do. He pressed a key on his comm.

"Larkin, here. Oh, hello, Petty Officer. What can I do for you?"

"Would you have such a thing as a black light?" Semple asked. "I just broke the captain's and I'd rather he didn't know it."

"Gee, I don't know," Larkin said slowly. "What's the captain doing with one of those?"

"He didn't say, sir. He just told me to guard it with my life."

Larkin grinned. "I'll see what I can do," he promised. "I wouldn't want you to have to pay the forfeit."

"Thank you, sir," Semple said gratefully.

The quartermaster broke the contact and sat thinking for a moment. What would the captain want with a black light? Some people used them during kinky sex, but that didn't fit Knott's profile.

What else does black light do? he wondered. Then it dawned on him. *It makes some substances glow.* He rose from his desk and left his office.

As it happened, he did have a black light. It was in his quarters and he headed there now. Entering his room he pulled the black light unit out of a cupboard and set it up, then he turned off the overhead light and turned on the lamp. His hands glowed green.

Damnation upon them! He'd washed his hands several times since he'd rigged Friedreich's computer. *The mark of iniquity,* he thought in dull horror. *Their iniquity!* It could not end this way. He could not allow himself to be taken like a lamb when he was a true warrior of his faith. *The shame of it would kill me.* And the failure would damn him forever.

Larkin sagged onto his knees and knelt with his head in his hands. *O Spirit of Destiny, this test is so hard.* It was up to him to craft his own salvation, even at the cost of his life. He took a deep breath and straightened. *What is mortal life against the life of the soul?* he asked himself. *It is nothing, a moment, a passing dream beside eternity.* He could not bear the price of failure.

Therefore I must not fail.

Capture was failure.

They were still on their way back to Ontario Base, so avoiding the Welters was impossible. Larkin knew that as a spy and saboteur his life was forfeit. *Therefore, victory lies in choosing the method and the moment of my death.* And if possible bringing these evil ones with him into judgment.

"Where is the quartermaster?" Knott asked.

"I don't know, sir," Larkin's second answered. "No one has seen him for the last hour."

Knott frowned. There was no use in waiting, they might as well proceed. Though he suspected that none of these people would bear the mark of Reader's trap.

"Mr. Semple, where is the black light?" he asked.

Semple swallowed audibly. "I don't have it, sir. I . . . broke it."

Knott looked at the man steadily. Semple was a good secretary, but Knott suspected that he'd just made a fatal mistake.

"You didn't by chance try to obtain a new one from Mr. Larkin, did you?" Raeder asked.

"Yes, sir," Semple said.

Semple's error had pointed the finger of guilt at the quartermaster as surely as if they'd all witnessed the stains on his hands. The only problem was that it left him free.

"Shut down the elevators, sir," Raeder said, "and lock the emergency stair doors."

Larkin heard the alarms go off. *Too late,* he thought. *I shall achieve my goal. I shall take this ship of evil with me into the night.*

He ducked into the emergency stair well. They would seek him here, but by then it would be too late. He would have carried the bomb to the containment area and set it off, bringing five thousand of the enemy the death they deserved.

That they know it is good, he told himself. *They will suffer more.*

The bomb was not large, but then all it needed to do was breach one containment vessel. *Then the antihydrogen that they have stolen will do its work,* he thought gleefully. His glee glimmered as suddenly as it arose. He had hoped and planned to accomplish the release of the antihydrogen while the ship was in the vicinity of major facilities. *Ah well . . . Surely this would be enough to spare him Hell.* Stuffing the infernal device into his shirt he began the long climb down.

When Larkin reached the bottom of the ladder, he thought, *I should set the timer now. I dare not take the time later; I would not want them to take it from me and disarm it.* He knelt on the floor, praying as he set the timer for the shortest time possible. *It will take me two minutes, no more, to reach the containment area.* He was a good runner, and he hadn't had to kneel on the rod of punishment for several days.

He imagined the explosion. It would be beautiful and pleasing to the Spirit of Destiny. Larkin chanted a song softly as he worked. Words like "flog" and "extirpate" abounded. When he was finished, the timer was running.

He rose and reached for the dogging lever. There was a click from without, and when he tried to turn it, it wouldn't move.

Larkin rattled the lever, but it wouldn't budge. *They've locked me in,* he thought in disbelief, frantically keying the pad beside the hatch. It rejected his codes. *The sons of bitches locked me in!* Should he pound on the door, cry out for help? Everyone knew by now that he was the spy, so that would be the same as turning himself in. He looked at his bomb. One minute and thirty seconds left.

The least I can do is try to take some of them with me, he thought, disappointed. He sighed. Then he knocked on the door.

"Hello," he shouted. "Anybody out there? I'm locked in, could you please let me out?"

All he heard was the emergency klaxon. No one seemed to be out there. He yanked on the knob and kicked the door, bellowing to be heard over the klaxon. "Hey! Open up! Hey!"

There were only fifty seconds left and sweat beaded his upper lip. "Shit!" he said passionately. He knelt down and studied the bomb. He would have to change the timer. *I refuse to die alone,* he thought.

He pressed the stud that would stop the clock. The timer kept ticking down the seconds. Only thirty-nine left now.

"Hey!" Larkin shouted, on the off chance that someone was passing. "Let me out of here!" He tried to pry it open to get at the timer's power source, but it was a well-made bomb, all of a piece. And he'd brought no tools with him, never thinking they'd be needed.

Spirit of Destiny, he prayed, *help me. Don't let me die like a fool.*

He pried at a seam until his nail bent back below the quick and he dropped it with a startled cry of pain. Picking it up again he saw that he had only five seconds left. Larkin jumped to his feet and began to climb. He was less than seven feet from the bomb when it went off.

"And so it's over," Knott said sadly.

"Yes, sir," Raeder agreed.

The damage to the ship hadn't been too bad. The emergency stairwells were heavily constructed, especially on the containment level, and all the blast had done was to blow out the door and rupture the metal at the scene of the blast.

Larkin, however, had all but disappeared.

"Damn," Knott said.

"He failed, sir," Raeder said.

"I wouldn't say that," the captain said sourly. "I'd say he was pretty damned successful. He came very close to ruining the light carrier program."

"But he failed," Raeder reminded him. "That's the thing with the Mollies. It doesn't matter how many times you succeed. They only count the failures."

"The lunatic killed a lot of good people, Commander. I hate to say it, but I hope the bastard suffered."

"He did, sir. He died knowing he was going to hell."

✧   ✧   ✧

"Clever," Sarah said, after hearing Raeder's plan for trapping the quartermaster.

"Thank you," Peter said. He paused to admire the candlelight on her face. *It softens her,* he decided.

Sarah grabbed the candle and held it close. The dark shadows it made at this new angle made her look like a ghoul. He laughed and she put it down with an answering grin.

"So what made you change your mind about accepting my invitation?" Raeder asked.

She looked around. "I really like Patton's," she said.

"Oh. I thought maybe you'd decided to give an ex-Speed pilot a second chance." He raised an eyebrow at her.

"Who says you're an *ex*-Speed pilot?" Sarah asked.

Peter blinked, then grinned. *She likes me!* he thought. *She really likes me.*

It was enough to make you forget that the war was a long way from over. Forget, for a while.